Sarah Alderson is a London-born, LA-based writer whose previous books include *Friends Like These* (Mulholland) and most recent release *In Her Eyes* (Mulholland). She also writes women's fiction under the pen name Mila Gray. Sarah is currently writing on the CBS show *SWAT*. This is her first thriller with HarperCollins.

You can follow @sarahalderson on Twitter.

THE
WEEKEND
AWAY

SARAH ALDERSON

avon.

Published by AVON
A division of HarperCollins*Publishers* Ltd
1 London Bridge Street
London SE1 9GF

www.harpercollins.co.uk

HarperCollins*Publishers*
Macken House
39/40 Mayor Street Upper
Dublin 1 D01 C9W8, Ireland

This paperback edition 2021

First published in Great Britain by HarperCollins*Publishers* 2020

A catalogue copy of this book is
available from the British Library.

ISBN: 978-0-00-841186-2

This novel is entirely a work of fiction.
The names, characters and incidents portrayed in it are
the work of the author's imagination. Any resemblance to
actual persons, living or dead, events or localities is
entirely coincidental.

Typeset in Bembo by Palimpsest Book Production Limited,
Falkirk, Stirlingshire

Printed and bound in the U.S.A.
by Lake Book Manufacturing, LLC

For Nichola

Prologue

There's no disguising the absolute terror on Rob's face.

'Will you be OK?' I ask anxiously.

'Yeah, totally,' Rob says. 'We'll be fine. Go and enjoy yourself.'

Marlow frets in his arms, reaching out her pudgy hands towards me and I have a sudden urge to change my plans. I'm not sure Rob's got this, despite his protestations that I should go and enjoy myself. It's the first time I've left him with the baby all by himself, and while a weekend in Lisbon with my best friend seemed like a good idea at the time, now I'm regretting it.

But it's too late to back out now. Kate's already texted me that she's on the way to the airport.

Marlow lets out a hiccup and I reach for her, letting her sticky hands grab for my hair. 'Make sure you remember to feed her,' I say to Rob. 'And put her down at the right time.'

'I think I can manage,' Rob says.

I kiss Marlow, squeezing her gorgeous bao bun cheeks, and then peck Rob on the lips.

'Don't worry,' Rob says, seeing that I blatantly am.

I nod and pick up my suitcase. He's right. It's only a weekend away. A few days, that's all. It's not going to kill me.

I might even have some fun.

Chapter One

'Bloody hell, Kate, this is gorgeous,' I say, abandoning my suitcase by the front door and taking a few flabbergasted steps inside the apartment, drawn like a newly hatched moth to the flaming view ahead of me. The sun spills through huge French windows. I take in the jumble of pastel-coloured buildings and, through the gaps in the roofs, a sparkle of blue not too far in the distance. It must be the river, which I think is called the Tagus. Whatever it's called, it's way more inviting-looking than the mud-coloured Thames.

Kate joins me over by the windows, which are floor to ceiling and run the length of the living room. She squeezes my shoulder then turns to me, grinning. 'Not bad.' She laughs before turning around and making a beeline towards the suitcases. 'Right, where's that duty-free bag? Let's get this party started.'

As Kate locates the bottle of Dom Pérignon she bought at the airport, I find the latch on the window and slide it open, stumbling outside onto the balcony. A thrill of excitement courses through me like an electric current. It takes me a moment to realise the buzz I'm feeling isn't a result of the coffee I had on the plane, but the illicit thrill of freedom. I feel like a prisoner who's tunnelled out of jail, poked her head above ground and realised she's successfully pulled off her escape. I'm giddily triumphant.

As soon as I recognise the feeling for what it is though, I experience a twinge of anxiety that cancels it out completely. How is Marlow doing? Will Rob have remembered to put her down to sleep at the right time? Fifteen minutes late and she's a monster the entire next day. Will he hear her in the night if she wakes? He sleeps like the dead normally. And what if he doesn't change her nappy and she gets a rash? Oh God, what if he gives her grapes that haven't been cut in half and she chokes to death?

My hand twitches, automatically reaching for my phone, before I remember it's in my handbag, which I dumped somewhere by the front door. I resist the urge to find it and text him. I don't want to be that kind of a mother or wife. Rob's fine with Marlow. He's a hands-on dad and has looked after her before on his own. But he did seem nervous about having to take care of her for the whole weekend by himself. No, I tell myself forcefully, I need to shake it off and enjoy myself. No point worrying.

I close my eyes and take a deep breath, inhaling the scent of a new city, and enjoying the balmy warm air against my skin. The lovely electric buzz of excitement returns again. For three entire days I have no one to worry about but myself. I can eat what I want, drink what I want, lie in as long as I want and basically go back to living the way I lived before I had a baby, when I totally underestimated how glorious it is to be able to pee in peace or how lovely it is to wear clothes that aren't stained with baby vomit.

'Here!'

I turn around to find Kate thrusting a glass of champagne at me. I take it. 'Cheers!' she says.

'Cheers!' I answer, chinking my glass against hers.

'This is amazing,' I say, gesturing at the view and the apartment. 'I can't believe this place.' I glance around the balcony with its elegant outdoor seating arrangement, sun-loungers and . . . I cock my head at the square object in the corner – 'Wait, is that a hot tub?'

'Yes,' says Kate. 'Didn't I tell you?'

'No,' I say. 'Or I'd have brought my swimsuit.'

'We don't need swimsuits.' Kate laughs, heading back inside to grab the bottle of champagne. I trail after her, thinking that once upon a time I might not have batted an eye about being naked in front of her or anyone, but now even being naked in front of Rob is something I'd only do under imminent threat of death.

There's just so much wobble that wasn't there before. My boobs are like two helium balloons that once floated proudly but are now wrinkling at the seams and drooping back down to earth. My belly too is yet to return to its previous flat form, my abs covered with a soft roll of fat that no amount of exercise seems to erase, though to be fair, managing the odd five sit-ups once a week is probably not going to do much, and neither is the pain au chocolat that I buy most mornings when I take Marlow to the park or to a mum and baby group. I've tried giving up sugar but I find that cake is the only thing that makes those groups bearable, and sometimes the only thing fuelling me through twelve gruelling hours of solo babysitting.

No one tells you how hard parenting is, or how hard it is to get your figure back, certainly not those bloody celebrities posing in their leggings and crop tops a day after giving birth. I suppose that's not completely true; plenty of people say parenting is hard, but the notion is totally abstract before you have a child. It's like being told that serving a life sentence in solitary confinement has its challenges. You can sort of imagine it but it's not until you're actually sitting alone in your cell, staring at the walls, knowing this is it for the rest of your life, that you start to fully appreciate exactly *how* challenging.

As Kate tops up my champagne glass, I sneak a look at her and can't help but feel a wave of self-consciousness. She's so chic and put together, in skinny jeans tucked into Louis Vuitton boots, and a low-cut top that shows off her unfairly perky breasts and toned arms. Her make-up looks freshly applied too, even though we've been travelling for about six hours. I can't remember the last time I wore lipstick, let alone shaved my legs, and my upper arms have lost all the tone I once had from weekly Pilates classes, and are in danger of becoming fully fledged bingo wings.

Kate and I used to be roughly the same size and shape, five feet four and slim – enough that we could share clothes – but now we're very different. I've never before been jealous of Kate's figure and I try not to fall into the trap of comparing myself to her. I've had a baby for Chrissake! It'll take time to get back into my skinny jeans.

'I made a reservation at a restaurant my friend told me about,' Kate says, oblivious to my unhappy comparisons between our figures. 'Table's booked for ten.'

I glance at my watch. It's almost seven. 'Blimey,' I say, stifling a yawn. 'I'm normally asleep by ten.'

'You can sleep when you're dead, Orla,' Kate says, setting her glass down and winking at me.

I groan. That used to be our thing when we were young twenty-somethings, living together in a tiny flat in Stoke Newington and clubbing every Friday and Saturday night. We'd stay out until dawn before heading home via the bagel shop on Brick Lane or the kebab shop on the corner of Old Street, and stuff ourselves stupid before falling into bed and sleeping well into the next afternoon.

Kate must see my expression as I contemplate my exhaustion and wonder where those youthful stores of energy disappeared to. 'Fine,' she says, 'take a nap and I'll wake you up at nine.' She grins at me. 'Come on, let's check out the bedrooms.'

I hurry after her, both of us acting like excited toddlers as we throw open doors and explore the apartment. The kitchen is shiny and full of brand-new high-end appliances and there's a dining table big enough to host a dinner party for twelve.

'How on earth did you find this place?' I marvel, opening the cupboard doors and admiring the fine china and delicate wine glasses on display.

'Airbnb,' Kate answers, pulling open the refrigerator to reveal bottles of sparkling water, milk, eggs and coffee. 'I think the owner lives in the apartment downstairs. He owns this one too and rents it out.'

'How much was it?' I ask, slightly tentatively.

'Don't worry about that.' Kate smirks. 'Toby's paying.'

I glance sideways at her.

She shrugs. 'He forgot to take me off one of his credit cards. Don't worry, he won't notice.'

I shake my head but can't help laughing.

'Bastard owes me,' she mutters and I silently agree. I never liked Kate's ex, Toby, much to begin with but after he cheated on Kate I gave up pretending I ever had. He isn't even good-looking, which isn't to say that if he had been I could have forgiven him, but it is hard to see how a man of his very mediocre looks could cheat on a woman like Kate, who is ten million miles out of his league.

I never understood what Kate saw in Toby, with his dome-like bald head and contradictory masses of thick black body hair, though I suppose he has got charisma, and as Kate liked to joke, short, bald men work harder to please in the bedroom. Not that I want to imagine that.

There are two enormous bedrooms in the apartment: a master bedroom with a marble en-suite bathroom and another smaller bedroom that is still far nicer than any hotel room I've ever stayed in. Everything is white – the cloud-like duvet cover, the pillows, the walls, the Eames armchair in the corner, the linen curtains – but whoever decorated the place has also added bold splashes of colour to stop it from looking too clinical. Blue and yellow patterned pillows are perfectly aligned on the bed, as though arranged using a protractor, while one wall is tiled with beautiful blue-patterned ceramic tiles. It's like something you'd see in *Condé Nast* magazine.

'You take the big room,' Kate says to me.

'Oh no,' I say, 'I'm fine in this one. It's great.'

'I insist,' Kate argues. 'You deserve it.' And before I can say another word she wheels her suitcase into the smaller room. Kate's suitcase is huge enough that she needed to put it in the plane's hold, while I only brought a carry-on. She said she had too many shoes and too many toiletries to fit in a carry-on-sized suitcase, which is typical Kate, who used the second bedroom in the flat she lived in with Toby just to house her clothes and the third bedroom to store her shoes and handbags.

I wheel my own scruffy bag with a broken wheel into the master room, which is done in much the same colour palette as the smaller bedroom, and I collapse down on the bed. Through the window I can see puffy white clouds wafting across the bruise-coloured sky. It feels glorious just to lie here, feeling the stress of the last couple of years already starting to melt away. It's amazing how a comfortable bed and the prospect of a weekend of lie-ins and laughter can do that.

Kate wanders into my room a minute later and flops down

beside me on the bed, her arm brushing mine. We lie there in silence, staring at the clouds, which are starting to turn the colour of candyfloss.

'I'm so happy we did this,' I say after a minute of contented silence.

'Me too,' Kate answers.

I turn my head in her direction and am taken aback by the sadness etched on her face as she stares out the window. For a moment I wonder if she's been crying but then I figure it's just the pink evening light filtering into the room. Kate doesn't do sad. Whenever she's upset about something she turns to dark humour to survive. She never mopes. Back before she met Toby, if a boy dumped her she'd never cry about it, she'd just laugh and whip out a Kate-ism: 'Onwards and upwards, plenty more dick in the sea.'

If she ever lost a client she'd pick up her phone and go about finding an even bigger fish to net. Even when she found out that Toby had been sleeping with escorts on his frequent business trips to Seoul and Shanghai, she didn't cry or stay in bed for days eating ice cream like I would have. No, she took his credit card and booked a first-class flight to Mauritius where she spent a week at The Four Seasons, lying on a beach drinking cocktails and having wild sex with the pool boy, telling me afterwards that she was following the sage advice that the best way of getting over someone was by getting under someone else. No one in the world does depression better than Kate. In fact, I should probably learn from her, but my credit card has a much lower limit.

As I stare at her now in the golden glow of the sunset though, I wonder whether Kate is hiding the truth from me, and if all this time when I've thought she's been doing fine, she's actually been struggling. It would hardly be surprising given all she's been through and, now I think about it, I realise

9

I'm stupid not to have considered it before. The thing with Kate is that she's one of those people who always seems so put together that you sometimes don't spot the cracks hiding beneath the wallpaper.

Now I look closer, she does seem on edge. Beneath the make-up I notice there are shadows under her eyes as though she hasn't been sleeping, and she was unusually quiet on the flight here. She's bitten the skin around her thumbnails too – something she only does when she's anxious.

It hits me then that I've been a totally shit friend. Once upon a time, Kate and I would tell each other everything. We were closer than sisters, definitely closer than I am to my own sister who lives in Ireland and who I rarely see. When I moved to London from Cork as an eager twenty-two-year-old, desperate to get the hell out of my small hometown, I moved into a flat-share in West Hampstead. That's where I met Kate. She rented the other bedroom.

From the minute we met it was as if we'd known each other forever. We were both Sagittarians, we both had a dad who'd died when we were eight, we both loved Richard and Judy books and reading gossip magazines, and we both loved going out clubbing. On Wednesdays we'd celebrate making it halfway through the week in our crappy temping jobs by buying a four-quid bottle of Black Tower wine, which we'd fully decant into two enormous glasses in order to avoid having to get up from the sofa to refill them, and then we'd settle in for *Buffy the Vampire Slayer* marathons. We're the kind of friends who interrupt each other constantly, talk faster than a bullet train to Busan, and can also communicate an entire conversation if we need to, purely with facial expressions.

We lived together for eight years until I finally moved in with Rob. And even after that we'd still see each other at least once or twice a week and speak on the phone all the days in between. But now I realise we go whole weeks without talking, and when we do speak I'm always distracted or having to hang up mid-sentence in order to deal with one baby-related crisis or another.

If I'm honest with myself though, I wasn't a good friend before I had Marlow either. Three years of failed IVF turned me into a *grumpy-sore-arse*, as my brother liked to tell me. I was depressed, and probably more than a little self-absorbed. Kate tried to be sympathetic but I could tell she didn't really understand, not wanting kids herself and therefore unable to fully get why I was so down about not being able to have any.

After Kate broke up with Toby six months ago, I did call her more often to check in, but Marlow was only a few months old and I was in the throes of breast-feeding and dealing with so many sleepless nights I felt like I was living at the bottom of a well. And besides, Kate acted so upbeat about the break-up that I honestly thought she was OK. She was doing a Kate – moving on, not looking back. But perhaps I failed to miss the fact it was all bluster – and maybe she isn't doing as well as I had thought.

'I've missed our girlie weekends,' I say, linking my arm through hers.

She turns to me and smiles, the sadness vanishing in an instant, making me wonder if I imagined it. Maybe I'm just projecting some of my own secret unhappiness onto her. 'Yeah,' she says. 'How long's it been?'

I have to cast my mind back. 'At least two years,' I say, doing the sum in my head, 'because I was pregnant last year.'

'It's longer than that,' Kate says. 'You were doing all the IVF. I think the last time we got away was maybe four years ago.'

'It can't be that long,' I say, frowning, though I think she might be right. 'Where did we go?'

'Valencia,' she says, not missing a beat.

11

'Oh, yes, that was so lovely,' I say, remembering the boutique hotel we stayed in with the four-poster beds and fireplaces.

'Remember Paris?' Kate muses. 'We stayed in that crummy little hotel in the Marais.'

I laugh. 'God, I remember the chocolate mousse we ate in that little restaurant by the Place des Vosges – I'll remember that for the rest of my life. It was the best thing I've ever put in my mouth.'

'Don't tell Rob that,' she giggles.

'You told that American at the table next to us that you spoke French—'

'So he went ahead and ordered what you told him was duck and really it was pig face.'

We burst into a fit of laughter at the memory.

'You know that was a long time ago,' I say, 'because it was before smartphones and translation apps.'

We lie there counting off all the places we've been together, starting with the Paris trip. We took the Eurostar. It was my first time and I thought myself oh so sophisticated. I even bought a beret from Accessorize so I could fit in with all the Parisian women. Then I saw how French women actually dressed and hid it in my bag. I bought a scarf instead but could never figure out how to tie it as elegantly as French women did.

After that trip to Paris, Kate and I decided we'd go away for a weekend together every year for the rest of our lives, to a different city each time. We laughed that by the time we were in our nineties we'd have travelled the globe and would settle for two deck chairs on the Margate seafront. We made a promise and kept to it for years, each year seeing a slight bump up in the level of hotel we stayed at and the quality of the restaurants we ate at and the booze we bought at duty-free. But ultimately, it's a promise I've failed to keep.

'I'm sorry we haven't managed to get away for a while,' I say to Kate, a wave of guilt washing over me.

'No matter,' she says, squeezing my hand. 'We're here now. Let's make the most of it.' She rolls off the bed, grabbing her empty glass from the bedside table. 'You take a nap and I'll wake you up in a couple of hours so we can go out for dinner.'

Chapter Two

'Wakey, wakey,' Kate says, shaking me by the arm.

I blink blurrily and struggle to sit up, feeling groggy and disorientated. The room is dark and when Kate switches on the bedside lamp, it takes me a second or two to get my bearings.

'It's nine-fifteen,' Kate says. 'Time to get up.'

I yawn and swing my legs out of bed, ignoring my desire to roll over, pull the covers over my head and go back to sleep. As my vision clears I see Kate's ready to hit the town. She looks stunning, in a black mini-dress with ruffle sleeves and gold high heels that show off her tanned, toned legs. My stomach sinks a little as I contemplate the clothes in my own suitcase. I kept it sensible thinking we'd be walking a lot and sightseeing, knowing that Lisbon was a city built on hills. I didn't bring any heels, only trainers and a pair of flat sandals, and I know I didn't pack anything as fancy as the dress Kate's wearing. I don't own anything that nice for starters. Kate owns tons of gorgeous dresses, partly as she loves clothes and shopping and has the money to afford new things, but also because as a movie publicist she often has to go to premieres and after-parties and, like the Queen, she'd never be seen dead in the same thing twice.

As Kate pours the last of the champagne into my empty glass, I unzip my bag and root through the contents: jeans, a sundress, a pair of shorts, a shirt, a hooded sweatshirt, a couple of T-shirts and last of all, my plaid, flannel pyjamas. There's one semi-glitzy top with sequins from H&M, that I had thought I'd pair with my jeans if we went out to dinner, but I wasn't expecting Michelin stars. I had figured we'd eat at small local places without a dress code.

'I don't know what to wear,' I say to Kate, feeling frustrated and shoving my H&M top back in my bag. I wish she'd warned me she'd booked a posh restaurant.

'Do you want to borrow something?' she asks and before I can respond she's out the door, shouting over her shoulder for me to follow her.

Her room is no longer an oasis of white but looks like it's been ransacked by a particularly desperate thief. Clothes and shoes are strewn everywhere. It was the same when we lived together. It used to drive me crazy how she'd leave shoes, coats, bags, dirty plates and mugs lying about the place, as though she had grown up in a stately home and was used to servants clearing up after her, when in fact she had grown up on a North London housing estate.

When we clashed over it, Kate would explain that life was too short to spend time worrying about a bit of mess and would convince me it would be a better idea to go to the pub or out shopping. Eventually my own OCD would win out and I'd have to set about cleaning the place, and Kate, seeing me on my hands and knees scrubbing at the tiles in the bathroom, would grudgingly always join me, albeit grumbling. When she got a promotion and started to earn more, the first thing she did was pay for a cleaner once a week.

Now I watch Kate hastily shove a few things back in her suitcase and slam the lid down, before picking up a dress from the floor and offering it to me. It's a jacquard blue silk mini-dress and though I love it, I have zero doubt if I tried to get it on over my hips it would get stuck and a comedy skit would unfold of me trying to wriggle out of it like a grub forcing its way out of a cocoon. Kate sees my expression and tosses the dress back on the ground before picking up a maxi-length embroidered dress with a low-cut neckline.

'Here,' she says, holding it against my body, 'try this.'

I take it into the bathroom and shut the door, not wanting to strip in front of her. The dress, by a designer I actually recognise, slides on and much to my surprise looks quite good, though because of the spaghetti straps I have to take off my bra. I assume that will do me no favours, but luckily the empire line of the dress pushes my boobs upwards as effectively as an underwired bra. I have never worn a maxi dress but contemplating my reflection, I start to wonder if I need to rethink my style now I've hit forty.

The counter top is littered with serums, bottles, make-up and hair products, and I pick up a hair wand and think about the last time I bothered to do anything to my hair besides wash it and shove it in a ponytail or messy topknot.

Kate pokes her head around the door. 'Ah!' she exclaims, walking in. 'That looks great on you! You have to keep it.'

I start to protest but she cuts me off. 'No, I insist. It's much better on you than me. Look at those boobs! They're like watermelons! I'm so jealous. Maybe I should have a baby.' She takes the wand from my hand. 'Do you want me to do your hair?'

'OK,' I say. She moves my discarded things aside to plug the wand in. 'Nice,' she says, holding up my bra and tossing it to me.

'Rob bought it for me for Valentine's Day,' I say, catching it. It's a silk padded bra and though it's a nude colour, which isn't the sexiest, it is Agent Provocateur. Rob's never been the best at buying gifts so I had to give him marks at least for that. Normally he gets me socks from M&S or an Amazon voucher or perfume that he's obviously chosen because it comes in a fancy box, but which smells like something Joan Collins would wear.

As we wait for the wand to heat up, Kate grabs an eyeshadow palette and a brush and starts doing my make-up. This is how we used to get ready before one of our big nights out, with me gamely letting Kate treat me as a canvas as she acted out her Picasso dreams. As she strokes the soft brush over my eyelids I realise how much I've missed getting glammed up. When I had a life, before Marlow, I used to spend fifteen minutes each morning following a skin-care and make-up routine; now I'm lucky if I remember to put on deodorant.

After she's done, Kate turns me towards the mirror and I startle, almost unable to recognise myself. She's put a burnt orange colour along the edges of my eyes – not a colour I'd ever go for normally, but surprisingly it makes the blue in my eyes stand out. They look almost cobalt and whatever she's dusted me with has given me a glow that has lifted my ghost-like pallor.

'Yummy mummy,' Kate declares with triumph.

I flush a little at the praise. I haven't thought of myself as sexy or beautiful for a long time – it's hard to when your breasts are leaking milk and you have stitches in your vagina, but now I'm wondering if all is not lost and I might actually still have it, or if not 'it' then something. Standing next to Kate, I might not feel like Cinderella but I no longer feel quite like the ugly sister either.

'I'll get us an Uber,' Kate says, reaching for her phone.

A few minutes later, we leave the apartment and head down the three flights of stairs to the street, Kate clattering in her heels and me following behind in my sandals, checking the door is locked and that I have the address programmed into my phone in case we get drunk later and can't remember where we're going.

My sensible mum gene was activated long before I had Marlow. I'm always thinking ahead and worrying about things, whereas Kate refuses to worry about anything that might not happen. Perhaps it's down in part to personality but it's also to do with my job. I manage HR for a big housing development company with hundreds of employees, or at least I did before I went on maternity leave, so I have to constantly make sure we're following rules, that all the i's are dotted and t's crossed. Risk assessment is part of my job description and being organised is essential. Whereas Kate spends her life wheeling and dealing, massaging actors' egos and wooing big-name studio heads. She has to constantly deal with crises and think on her feet.

Thinking about work elicits a rush of excitement, though the excitement is immediately snuffed out by guilt. It feels wrong to admit, even to myself, that I can't wait to get back to work. I thought I'd love maternity leave and though Rob and I planned for me to take a full year off after Marlow was born, I'm rather wondering if nine months would have been enough. It's not something you can generally admit to though, that you'd rather be at work than taking your baby to monkey music or baby gym.

I find refuge online sometimes among chat rooms of mums venting about the monotony of being a stay-at-home parent, and it makes me feel less alone, but I'm still not confident enough to share my frustrations with anyone in the real world. I'm afraid they'll think I'm selfish and horrible, especially after the battle I went through to have Marlow.

As Kate and I pass the door to the apartment below ours, it opens and a man steps out in front of us, blocking our way.

'Hi,' Kate and I say.

The man, around thirty-five with thinning hair and wearing round artist-like glasses, looks us both over, unblinking as an owl.

'Hi,' he says. He holds out a slender hand to Kate. 'I'm Sebastian, nice to meet you. I own the apartment you're staying in.' He speaks good English with only the faintest trace of an accent.

'Right,' says Kate, shaking his hand. 'I'm Kate, this is Orla,' she says, indicating me.

'Nice to meet you,' I say, shaking his hand.

His gaze dips briefly to my exposed cleavage. It makes me flush a little, both self-consciously and also with a little pride. I can't remember the last time a man looked at me in that way, not even Rob.

'It's just the two of you staying?' Sebastian asks.

I nod. 'Yes, just us.'

'You're going out?' he asks, though that much is pretty obvious.

'Yes, for dinner,' I say.

'We better get going,' Kate adds, impatiently, 'our Uber's waiting.'

Sebastian doesn't move. 'Well, I just wanted to say hi. If you need anything, anything at all, let me know. I'll be happy to help. I work from home and I am here all weekend so just come and find me if you need anything.'

'Great,' I say. 'Thanks. We'll let you know if so.' I try to get past him but he doesn't move.

'If you want me to show you how to use the hot tub . . .' he says in his slightly high, reedish voice.

19

'I'm sure we'll manage,' Kate says with a tight smile, pushing past him.

I smile politely as I squeeze by. 'Thank you.'

'Have a nice dinner,' he calls after us.

In the Uber Kate reapplies her lipstick using her phone camera as a mirror and I stare out the window, taking in the city by night, the illuminated castle on a hill and a dazzling bridge over the river, which looks exactly like the Golden Gate Bridge. There's no mistaking Lisbon for San Francisco though. Lisbon is distinctly European. The buildings are a mix of baroque and roman and even gothic architecture. I know all this because I read it in the guidebook. The area we're staying in, Alfama, is the old Moorish part of the city and it's a maze of cobbled lanes that wind up and down several hills. It's quite beautiful and I'm rapt by the magical feel of it, with its steep staircases, waterfalls of flowering pink bougainvillea and colourful brick-work. It's like stepping back in time or into the pages of a fantasy novel.

When she's done with her lipstick Kate puts her arm around me and pulls me in close for a selfie. She turns to me and kisses me on the cheek, leaving behind a red mark she then has to rub off. After, she takes my face in her hands. 'You know I love you, don't you?' she says, her tone and expression turning uncharacteristically solemn.

'Of course,' I say, bemused.

'Good,' she answers.

I wonder at the sudden declaration of love and friendship. We do tell each other we love each other all the time, though I suppose not too often recently. She must be drunk. She holds her booze well but I do remember that once she's two sheets to the wind she can get very emotional. It's one of the giveaways.

'You're my best friend,' she says. She says it forcefully, as though I might contest it.

'You're mine too,' I say, laughing.

'Never forget that,' she says, looking into my eyes in such a strange way that my laughter dies.

Chapter Three

We arrive at the restaurant, a candlelit place with a glass roof and so much greenery it looks like a hothouse at Kew Gardens. Our waiter leads us to a white-linen-clad table in the back but Kate insists on a table in the centre of the room. She always likes to see and be seen, and I roll with it because I've decided that tonight I want to make the most of my freedom and have fun.

'That's better,' says Kate, shaking out her napkin with a flourish and ordering a bottle of champagne.

I bite my lip as I scan the menu and notice the prices. The champagne alone is eye-wateringly expensive at almost two hundred euro a bottle. Does it come in a gold-plated bottle? I'd be happy with Prosecco, which is only a quarter of the price and tastes, at least to my unrefined palate, exactly the same.

'Dinner's on me,' Kate says, as though she's read my mind.

I start to argue with her. She's already paid for the apartment and she upgraded our seats to business on the flight over. 'Honestly,' she says, reaching her hand over and squeezing mine. 'We deserve it, and besides, Toby's paying, remember.' She winks at me and laughs.

'Are you sure?' I ask. 'Won't he be mad?'

'Yes, but he doesn't have a right to be after what he's done.' She straightens her shoulders and lifts her chin, scanning the room. 'And anyway, the lawyer says we're going to screw him in the divorce so whether he pays now or later doesn't really matter.'

Toby owns his own events marketing company that stages big launches for brands as well as music events. I'm guessing he earns a very good salary, given the amazing penthouse flat that the two of them used to live in and the five-star luxury holidays he and Kate used to take every year to the Seychelles and the Caribbean.

'He's sold his company you know,' Kate says, as the waiter comes over with the champagne in an ice bucket. 'To an American agency. He's going to make millions from it. My lawyer says he'll have to give me at least half. Half of everything.'

My jaw drops open. 'Oh my God,' I whisper. What are you going to do with all that money?'

She shrugs. 'I don't know yet. Buy a house I think.'

'Where?' I ask.

'Maybe Richmond,' she says.

I look at her, astonished. She's always looked down her nose at any place outside of Zone one and definitely at neighbourhoods she considers rich and *rah*. Kate's a city person and likes to be in the bustling heart of things; she jokes that, like a black cabbie driver, she won't go south of the river. For all her money and lifestyle, Kate grew up working class and scoffs at toffs and posh people, and Richmond's bursting at the seams with them. I can hardly see her hanging out in her Barbour jacket and Hunter wellies walking her Labradoodle in the park.

'Seriously?' I ask her. 'You'd give up living in Zone one and move to the sticks?'

She frowns at me. 'Yes,' she answers. 'I think it's time for a change. You can't live the same way all your life. It'll be nice to have a house and a garden. I might start growing my own veg.'

'Next you'll be saying you want two point four children.' I giggle into my champagne, noticing I'm getting a little light-headed from drinking on an empty stomach.

Kate summons the waiter with a nod of her chin then turns back to me. 'I'm starting to think I might,' she says.

I almost choke on my champagne and have to set the glass down. 'What? Want kids? Really?' I ask, shocked to my core. She honestly couldn't have said anything more surprising to me, not even that she was quitting the rat race and the male race to enter a nunnery.

Kate looks wounded. 'Why's that so shocking?' she asks.

I shake my head, not wanting to upset her. 'It's not. It's just . . . I didn't think you wanted kids.'

'I didn't,' she says, carefully folding the napkin on her lap. 'Not until now. And thank God I didn't have any with Toby. Can you imagine? He'd have been an awful father. What are you going to order?' she asks, changing the subject and opening up her menu. 'The octopus sounds good, doesn't it? But I've heard the pork belly's great too.'

We order, with Kate choosing the most expensive thing on the menu, oysters, followed by octopus – and me the cheapest, sardines, which I have heard are a local delicacy.

When the waiter has gone Kate smiles at me and raises her champagne glass once again, to chink against mine. 'Here's to being a mum.'

'To being a mum,' I agree, trying to wrap my head around Kate wanting children. I had always assumed she didn't want kids. She's said so multiple times over the years, talking about how she loves her job too much, as well as her freedom, and making it clear how boring she finds those friends who drone on and on about their kids. After hearing her mocking them I made sure to keep my own gushing talk about Marlow to a minimum around her. And though I did make Kate godmother and she did lavish expensive designer clothes and expensive handmade wooden toys on Marlow, I've never asked her to babysit or to change a nappy. I know what Kate's limitations are but I also know – and argued to Rob, who had his reservations about choosing her to be a godparent – that when Marlow grows up Kate will come into her own as a godmother, or *oddmother*, as she likes to call herself.

Admittedly I have felt a little pique of envy at the thought that Kate will be the glamorous aunt figure in Marlow's life, with her glittering career and enviable wardrobe and global travel to film festivals and the like, but until now I have never thought that Kate might be the one envying me. Does she? It feels strange to even imagine it.

I wonder at her age, forty-one, if it would be likely she'd even get pregnant. I certainly struggled to, though not just because of my age; I also have a duff uterus. But some women conceive at the drop of a hat, and who's to say Kate wouldn't be one of them? It would be typical of her. Everything comes so easily her way: men, success, attention. Why not a baby too?

'I froze my eggs,' she says, out of nowhere.

'What?' I ask, almost spitting out my champagne.

'A few years ago,' she answers with a shrug. 'I decided I might as well. I knew Toby didn't want kids and I wasn't sure I did either, but then seeing what you went through I thought I should, just in case I changed my mind later.'

I stare at her, completely flabbergasted. 'Why didn't you tell me?'

She gives an apologetic smile. 'It was when you were going through IVF and having a hard time and I didn't want to mention it I guess. I didn't want to upset you.'

'Why would it have upset me?' I ask, put out that she kept such a big secret from me. Was I that self-absorbed? Would it have upset me? Annoyingly I have to admit perhaps it would have. Any reminder of another woman's fertility upset me back then, even the sight of prenatal vitamins with a picture of a pregnant woman on the label would send me scurrying in tears from the chemist.

Kate bites her lip. 'I don't know. I'm sorry. I didn't think it was a big deal. It wasn't like I was deciding to have a baby. I just put my eggs on ice. Everyone's doing it these days. It's the new Botox. People have egg-freezing parties.'

My eyebrows shoot up. Not in my world they don't.

'I'm not shitting you,' she says. 'It's all the rage in Hollywood.'

Hollywood. Of course. Kate lives and operates in a different world to me altogether and sometimes I forget that. I take a sip of water, trying to regain some composure. 'Do you think you'll use them?' I ask. 'The eggs?' I don't know why but for some reason the thought of Kate becoming a mother bothers me.

'Haven't decided,' she answers as the waiter lays down a plate of oysters.

'You'd have to give up eating stuff like that,' I joke. 'And drinking too.'

She cocks her head to one side. 'Are you saying I couldn't give it up?'

I shake my head. 'No of course not, I mean, if I managed . . .' I trail off. I hadn't intended to suggest she wouldn't be capable of hacking a nine-month pregnancy but maybe subconsciously I actually had. Maybe that's what's annoying me about all this. Her decision seems so sudden and so unthought-through, so typically Kate. Does she have any idea how much work is involved in raising a child? How hard it is? It isn't like deciding to buy a new pair of shoes. You can't take them back

26

if you decide you don't like them and you can't toss them to the back of your wardrobe and forget about them. It isn't like when she decided to get married on a whim and ran off to Vegas with Toby.

You can't just throw kids away when you get tired of them. And how would she do it on her own, without help? I know she has money but even with all the nannies money could buy it's difficult being a single mother. I have two friends who are and they deserve medals. I couldn't do it I don't think, and I can't see how Kate would ever have the patience for it.

'Have an oyster,' she says, pushing the plate towards me.

I shake my head. It would be just my luck to eat one that was off and get food poisoning.

'Go on,' she says. 'They're great.'

Oh, what the hell. It's been years since I've eaten any shellfish. I was too worried when I was trying to get pregnant of eating anything that might make me sick. I take one, squeeze some lemon on it, and let it slide down my throat, leaving behind the taste of seawater. 'That was good,' I say. 'Thanks.'

I'm being judgemental. Kate's my best friend and I should support her whatever her choice is. 'You'll be an amazing mum,' I tell her.

She smiles. 'Thanks.'

'Do you think you'll get a sperm donor?' I ask.

She slides another oyster into her mouth. 'Maybe,' she says. 'It's an option. Though I don't want to be a single parent. Maybe I'll find a new man. A decent one this time. One who doesn't sleep with prostitutes and treat me like shit.'

She puts her fork down and reaches for her champagne glass, which the waiter has been kept busy filling up.

'Here's to that,' I say, picking my own glass up to cheers her.

She smiles as our glasses chink together. 'Do you really think

27

I'll be a good mother?' she asks and I hear the note of anxiety in her voice.

I force a nod. 'Of course. Look how much Marlow loves you.'

She smiles wider at that. 'Well, Marlow and I have a lot in common. We both love to guzzle from a bottle and we both like to have someone do everything for us!'

I laugh along with her, happy to think about Marlow for a moment. I wonder how she and Rob are getting on.

'Anyway,' Kate says, interrupting my thoughts and sitting back to let the waiter remove our plates. 'How are things with you and Rob? Are they better?'

I pause as the waiter replaces the plates with our main course and a bottle of Sauvignon Blanc.

'OK,' I say. I've told Kate something of the ups and downs our marriage has suffered over the last few years but must admit to having put a better spin on it than is perhaps the truth. 'Improving slowly.'

I dig into my sardines, which are more delicious than they look, lying grilled on the plate staring up at me.

Kate saws through an octopus tentacle covered in tiny suckers. 'Have you got back on the horse?' she asks. 'Are you having sex?'

Straight to the point as always. 'Yes,' I say. 'I mean, not like we used to . . .'

'What do you mean? How often are you having it? Once a week? Once a month?'

'Probably a couple of times a month.'

Her eyes go wide. 'God,' she says, 'I'm amazed your hymen hasn't regrown. How on earth do you manage without regular orgasms?'

I blush and check over my shoulder that no one around us can hear, but luckily no one seems to be listening.

'I'm so tired,' I say by way of explanation. 'What with

28

housework and Marlow the last thing I want to do in the evening is have sex. Besides, you should try it after you've had fifteen stitches in your vagina.'

She winces. 'No thanks.'

'Well, if you want a baby . . .' I say, laughing at her. 'You better be prepared. They don't just pop out like the cork from a champagne bottle.'

'Maybe I'll opt for a C-section,' she shoots back, laughing.

'That's not any better,' I tell her.

'You can have a tummy tuck at the same time.' She grins. 'All the celebs do it. That or they hire a surrogate and skip the whole getting fat part altogether.'

I glance down at my plate; the sardine, sitting beside its nest of potato, looks back accusingly.

'Not that you got fat,' Kate adds quickly. 'Besides, I'm only joking,' she says. 'I'm not too posh to push.'

'You might become too posh if you move to Richmond.'

She laughs even louder and pours us more wine, without waiting for the waiter to do it. I hold up a hand to stop her filling my glass because I can feel myself getting quite drunk already, but she bats my hand away. 'Come on, we're going to have fun tonight.'

Reluctantly I let her refill my glass. 'I just don't want to end up with my head in a toilet bowl later.'

Kate has always handled her drink much better than me and now, after giving up alcohol when I was pregnant and breast-feeding, I'm more than a lightweight. I take a small sip and then sigh. 'Honestly, I just don't feel like it.'

'Like what?' Kate asks. 'Champagne? What's wrong with you?'

'No, I meant having sex with Rob.'

'Why not?' she asks. 'Did you stop fancying him?'

I shake my head. 'No. It's not that.' Rob's still good-looking, still in shape from his daily cycling, and we still get on as friends and as partners. We still love each other and I know he wants to have sex with me because he keeps trying to. 'I just don't feel in the mood ever,' I explain. 'I don't feel attractive. I think that's the problem. I don't want him to see me naked. And he's a visual guy. He likes the lights on.'

She smirks. 'You've still got it, what are you talking about? You're a hot MILF. There's a guy over there by the bar who checked you out when we came in.'

I glance over towards the bar but it's rammed with people and I can't figure out who she means. 'Thanks,' I say turning back to look at her. 'Most days I feel like a fat, frumpy, middle-aged hag.'

'Well you're not,' she tells me. 'You're gorgeous. How's Rob taking the lack of sex?' she asks.

'Fine,' I say, though truthfully, I'm not sure. He acts fine and understanding but of course he would because he's a nice guy.

'Be careful,' Kate warns. 'Look at Toby. We had a great sex life and he still played away.'

My knife and fork hover in mid-air. 'What do you mean? Rob would never have an affair.'

'I know,' she says, 'that's not what I'm saying. I'm just warning you that if a man doesn't get sex he'll start to look elsewhere. Even the nice ones.' She must see the look on my face as she hurries on. 'But not Rob. I can't imagine Rob ever having an affair. He adores you. And Marlow. I'm sorry. I'm just projecting.'

I put my cutlery down. 'No, you're right. It did cross my mind,' I say. 'But only because he seemed distant for a time when Marlow was a couple of months old. But we talked it out. He said he was feeling left out, you know, because I was breast-feeding and I got to be at home with the baby while he had to go to work. I think it's quite common for men to feel like a spare part in the early days – that's what the books say anyway. But everything's been good since we talked. I mean,

30

he tells me he loves me all the time and buys me flowers and when we do have sex it's good. Well, good considering I don't have much of a pelvic floor anymore.'

'Well then—' she laughs '—ignore me. What do I know about marriage or relationships? I'm a disaster at them. So long as you're happy, that's all that matters.'

I nod and look down at my plate, trying to blink away a sudden welling up of tears.

'You are happy, aren't you?' Kate asks.

I look up, swallowing hard. She's staring at me, her eyes narrowed. She knows me better than anyone and has seen through my stiff upper lip.

'I don't know,' I blurt out. The wine has made my tongue loose and I think to myself I should probably not say anything but the words tumble out of me before I can stop them. 'I know I should be happy. I've got an amazing husband and an amazing child and I've got so much to be grateful for but somehow I don't feel happy. I feel quite down actually, quite a lot of the time.'

Much to my horror tears slip from my eyes. Why am I admitting all this? Kate stares at me, her blue eyes widening with surprise at this out-of-nowhere admission. Her cutlery clatters to her plate and she reaches across and grabs my hand. 'Oh my God, why didn't you tell me?'

I bite my lip to stop from crying any more. 'I don't know. I haven't told anyone. I just keep pretending everything's OK, hoping that if I fake it I'll make it. But I feel so tired and I know I should be happy, so then I feel even worse.'

Kate looks stunned. 'I can't believe you didn't tell me you've been feeling this way! I would have been there for you. Does Rob know?'

I shake my head. 'No. He's seen me cry a few times but he doesn't understand it. He thinks it's just hormones. Maybe it is.'

31

'Do you think it's postnatal depression?' Kate asks.

My lip wobbles. It's the first time someone has asked me directly whether or not I'm depressed other than the health visitor who I lied to because I was scared of being judged. 'Maybe,' I say, feeling like there's a stone lodged in my throat.

'Have you spoken to the doctor?' she presses.

I shake my head. I keep thinking about going but then changing my mind. I'm not that sad, just a bit down. And I don't want to take any drugs. I want to figure it out on my own. Like Rob says, I'm sure it will pass.

'There's no shame in it you know,' Kate says, reading my mind. 'Drugs can help.'

I nod. If anyone knows it's Kate. She's been on and off antidepressants for years.

'Why don't you make an appointment to see the doctor when you get back? Speak to someone. Get some help.' She frowns at me in consternation. 'I really wish you'd told me before now.'

I nod and with a shaky hand take a big gulp of wine. Having admitted it to Kate it already feels like a weight has lifted off my shoulders. She's right. I should have admitted it to her before now. I guess I felt ashamed that I was sad after having spent so long striving for a baby and being upset about it not happening. It felt churlish and ungrateful to feel depressed after I got what I wanted and had a healthy, beautiful baby in my arms.

'Talking of drugs,' Kate says, fishing a little silver pillbox out of her bag with a flourish.

'What is that?' I ask, my eyes darting to the tables around us because I already know what the little pillbox contains. Or at least, I can make an educated guess.

'Fancy a line?' she asks.

'Coke?' I whisper in astonishment.

She nods. 'It'll lift your mood.'

32

'How on earth did you get that on the plane?'

'Oh, it's easy if you know how,' she replies with a wink and a secretive smile. 'You just pack it in with your tampons. Do you want some?'

I glance around again, nervously. 'What? Here?! Now?'

'Yes,' she says deadpan. 'I'm going to snort a line of coke off the table in front of everyone.' She shakes her head. 'No. I'm going to the bathroom. Are you coming?'

'I'm good,' I say.

She narrows her eyes and looks at me with that same sly smile, the tempting devil on my shoulder. 'Come on,' she pouts.

Once upon a time I would have said yes to that and to whatever pills Kate offered up. We never used to go clubbing without first dropping ecstasy or doing coke, usually both. But those days are long gone. 'I can't,' I tell her. 'I'd be off my head.'

'Exactly,' she says, her eyes lighting up. 'Let's have some fun. Go clubbing. My friend told me about a place—'

'Clubbing?' I interrupt, trying not to splutter. 'I thought we were just having dinner.'

She pulls a face at me. 'Lisbon's known for its nightlife. I thought we could head to this bar I heard about and then to a club . . .'

My expression must show my surprise because her smile fades.

'Oh,' she says, a little downcast. 'I thought you'd be up for it.'

I don't know what to say. I don't want to upset her but I'm definitely not up for clubbing. Honestly, I just want to go to bed. It's my first night away from Marlow in nine months – my first night of freedom since she was born – and all I can think about is catching up on sleep.

'I really wanted to let my hair down and have some fun,' she says. 'It's been such a hard few months with the divorce.'

I nod, sympathetic. 'I know. I'm sorry.'

She gives me a little half-smile. 'And it sounds like you could use a reminder of what it's like to be footloose and fancy free.'

I sigh, letting her twist my arm. 'Sure, we can go to a bar.' I don't say anything about the club though. I'm definitely not going out clubbing. Besides we'd surely be the oldest people in a club, like parents overseeing the school disco. Isn't it a bit sad at forty to still be acting like one of the kids?

Grinning, Kate gets up from the table. 'Great,' she says. 'I'm just going to the bathroom. Back in a sec.'

I watch her weave between the tables, wondering if Kate will still be a wild partier in ten years' time or if she'll be a frumpy mum like me who just wants to stay home, read a book and get an early night. It's hard to picture the latter. I imagine if she does have a baby she'll be the most glamorous mum at school pick-up. Everyone else will be there in sweats and PJ bottoms stuffed into Uggs and Kate would be there with a full blow-out and wearing her Manolos. The thought makes me smile.

As soon as Kate is out of sight I pull my phone out to check my messages. There's a sweet one from Rob telling me to have lots of fun. He's sent a photo of him and Marlow. She's sitting in her high chair, covered head to toe in orange sauce and looks like an Oompa-Loompa. Even her hair is standing on end, just like Rob's does in the morning. The sight of them gives me an instant pang of longing. 'I miss you,' I text back.

'We miss you too,' he replies, with a heart emoji.

'Remember to cut grapes in half,' I type before deleting it.

When Kate returns from the bathroom it's with a noticeable pep in her step. Her face is more animated, her gestures more jerky, and her voice louder. 'Shall we get dessert?' she asks, sitting down and grabbing for the menu.

I'm torn. My thighs don't need the calories but, as Kate reminds me, 'Toby's paying,' and I could use the extra carbs in my belly to soak up all the alcohol, especially if we're heading to a bar next.

We order chocolate mousse and a Portuguese custard tart, which are both deliciously decadent, though Kate barely touches either. She's become all fidgety and keeps pulling out her phone to check it. It buzzes in her hand and she frowns at whatever message pops up, then mutters under her breath.

'Everything OK?' I ask.

'Fine,' she says, furiously tapping a reply. 'Just an angry client. Wants the impossible.' She signals the waiter for the bill and then stands abruptly as the phone starts to buzz once more in her hand.

'I have to take this,' she says, already striding for the door.

I watch her through the window as she starts pacing up and down the pavement outside the restaurant, angrily gesticulating as she talks on the phone, and I wonder what the call's about. A part of me secretly hopes that whatever it is will curtail the bar and clubbing adventure she has planned.

As I watch Kate a waiter comes and places the bill in front of me and I glance down at it, shocked at the amount – almost five hundred euro, mostly for the wine and champagne, but still, that is the most expensive sardine in history – before sliding it over to Kate's side of the table. I feel awkward but she did say she'd pay. Or rather, that Toby would.

Kate returns a minute later and sits down, shoving her phone into her bag. Her face is red and her mascara has run a little.

'Who was it? What happened?' I ask in alarm. It's not like Kate to cry. In fact I think maybe in the whole time I've known her I've only seen it happen a couple of times and once was while watching *The Little Mermaid* when we were hungover in our twenties, and she only cried then because she was upset Ariel gave her voice away for a man.

'It was Toby,' she admits, dabbing at her eyes. 'The credit card company called him. They'd flagged unusually high spending.'

'Oh,' I say, trying not to glance in the direction of the bill.

'Damn,' she mutters, chewing on the skin by her thumbnail. 'Bastard's gone and put a stop on the card.'

I glance at the bill in front of her. She notices it too then bursts out laughing. 'Shit! If only he'd waited five minutes.' She rustles around in her bag for her wallet and fishes out another card. 'Let's hope this one works,' she says, laying it down.

'Why don't I help?' I say. 'We can go halves.'

'No,' she says firmly, shaking her head. 'I've got it. I'm the one who wanted to come here. Besides, once the divorce is finalised I'll be laughing all the way to the bank.'

'How long will that take?' I ask as the waiter brings the card reader over.

'Who knows? My lawyer says it could take up to a year, maybe longer if he contests, which he will because he's a shithead and doesn't think I'm owed a penny. After putting up with him, though, I should say I'm owed the lot. I had to get tested for herpes and gonorrhoea thanks to his dirty little escapades. My lawyer's putting it all in the papers. The judge will totally rule in my favour.'

'But until then?' I ask.

'I'm earning enough,' she says, waving a hand. 'Don't worry.' She taps her number into the machine the waiter is holding and luckily the card is accepted. I breathe a sigh of relief. It's not that Rob and I are broke – we both earn good salaries, though I've not been earning while I've been on maternity leave – but our mortgage is large and we're saving up for an extension on the house. He'd go mad if he saw I'd spent five hundred quid on one dinner.

'OK then,' Kate says, with a dangerous sparkle in her eyes, 'shall we go?'

36

Chapter Four

As we get in the Uber Kate's phone buzzes again. She glances at it quickly. 'It's Toby,' she says, huffing. She shoves the phone back in her bag. 'He's paranoid. Wants to know who I'm here with. As if it's any of his business anymore who I'm with or what I do. For God's sake,' she says, as the phone keeps ringing. 'I'm going to have to get a new number at this rate.'

The Uber driver looks over his shoulder at us. 'Do you have the address?' he asks gruffly. He's in his forties, with salt and pepper hair and a darkly stubbled jaw that looks like it could sand rust off a ship's hull.

'It's a bar called the Blue Speakeasy,' Kate tells him. 'Do you know it?'

He nods and starts driving.

'Are you sure you don't want some?' Kate asks me and I look down to see she's holding the little pillbox in the palm of her hand. I glance at the driver then back at Kate, shaking my head and widening my eyes in warning.

Completely unabashed, she sprinkles some of the white powder onto the back of her hand and then snorts it, throwing back her head to sniff loudly, before wiping a hand under her nose. I shoot a look again at the driver and find him watching in his rear-view mirror.

'Are you from here?' I blurt out, trying to distract him, though it's rather too late for that. He's obviously seen.

'No. Kosovo,' he answers before his gaze shifts back to the road. 'But,' he goes on, 'I've been here a long time.'

'Your English is good,' I comment.

'Thank you.' He glances at me again in the mirror. 'Are you from the UK?'

'Ireland,' I tell him. 'But I live in London.'

'The Irish are good people,' he says. 'They are good at talking.'

I laugh. 'Yes, I can't argue with that. We do like a good conversation. And a drink!' I'm blathering, aware that Kate is still messing around with her pillbox. Is she doing another line of coke? Dear God, how does she stay standing?

'How long have you been driving an Uber?' I ask, over-eagerly.

'A few years,' he says. 'It pays the bills.' His gaze shifts to Kate, who has pulled out her phone again and is busy texting, stabbing at the buttons in a frenzy while muttering to herself.

The Uber driver drops us a few minutes later in what appears to be a red-light district. 'The bar is just up that alleyway,' he says pointing to a narrow, cobbled lane to our right that is inaccessible to cars. 'Have a good night,' he says as we get out.

'You too,' I start to say but Kate slams the door shut.

'He's not getting a tip,' Kate remarks, linking her arm through mine as he drives away.

'Why not?' I ask.

'I saw the way he was looking at me in the mirror.'

'You were snorting coke in the back of his car, Kate.'

'Oh please,' Kate scoffs. 'It's not like I vomited all over the seats.'

At the mention of the word vomit I notice how queasy my

stomach is. The alcohol is sloshing around with the Michelin-starred sardines, but gamely I swallow down the acid taste of bile in my mouth and follow Kate down the alley.

It's past midnight and the main streets all around are packed with people, mostly buzzed tourists, wandering between bars and open-air cafés and clustering in the middle of the road, oblivious to the fact it's not a pedestrianised zone and that cars are trying to squeeze past them.

The alley with the Blue Speakeasy is quiet though, skipped over by the tourists. We spot several people standing outside a door beneath an electric blue light, smoking and vaping. I notice even from a distance of a hundred yards that this crowd seems sophisticated and better dressed, as though they're all models posing for a photoshoot, or artists hanging outside a hip new gallery opening.

One glance as we get closer tells me they're locals, not tourists. It's not just the olive skin and dark hair on display, or the fact they're way better looking and a lot more glamorous than the people you see gathered outside pubs in London's Soho or stumbling drunk and rowdy through Leicester Square. They seem to exude exoticism in a way that makes me, frankly, very jealous. I might have inherited the Irish gift of the gab but I'd definitely swap it for whatever magic gene these people are obviously gifted at birth.

As we approach – Kate leading the way with her head held high and her gold heels striking the cobbles like flint – I notice a red velvet rope in front of the door and a boy standing in front of it holding a clipboard as though it's a ceremonial shield. My gut clenches tightly as we reach him. It reminds me of being twenty-five and trying to slip the line at Cargo by flirting with the bouncer, except that was then and this is now and I'm not sure I've got the balls or the blag or the confidence of youth to pull it off. But Kate says something to him, something I don't hear, then hands him something I don't see, and suddenly the red rope is lifted and we gain entry.

The bar is lit like the inside of a crypt, flickering candles on the tables look like votives and in dark alcoves ghost-like shadows stir. Kate pushes her way through the crowd, ushering me ahead of her as I imagine she does with her famous clients at premieres when she's trying to get them past the paparazzi and to the best spot on the red carpet to have their photo taken. The place is busy and a heavy beat thrums in the spaces between all the packed bodies, making my head pound and sweat break out on my brow.

Kate elbows her way to the front, gets the attention of the barman and then shouts over her shoulder at me. 'What do you fancy?'

I glance at the multitude of bottles behind the bar and my stomach responds with a gurgle. 'Water,' I shout back, trying to be heard over the percussive thump of the music and roar of conversation.

Kate rolls her eyes at me. 'Water?'

'Yes, tap's fine,' I say, glancing around. It doesn't look like there's a table free. Are we going to have to stand among the shouting, overheated bodies to drink our drinks? I hope not. It crosses my mind once again that I'm getting far too old for this. I'd rather be in bed, in my pyjamas, reading a book, or scratch that, sleeping. Kate hands me a glass of water and then, with her own cocktail in hand, pushes her way across the bar area, towing me behind her, like an old rowing boat attached to a fancy pants yacht.

She makes a beeline straight towards the booths in the shadowy recesses along one side of the room and stops beside one. Two men are sitting there.

'Mind if we join you?' Kate asks them.

I start to open my mouth to protest the intrusion and pull

Kate away – the booth is small after all and we'd have to squeeze in next to them on the leather banquettes – but one of the men smiles and gestures to the seat beside him.

'Of course, please be our guest.'

Kate sits down right beside him, forcing him to squeeze over to make room. Embarrassed at Kate's forwardness, I perch on the very edge of the banquette opposite. 'Hi. Sorry,' I say, smiling apologetically at the man next to me.

He smiles back at me. 'No problem.'

'I hope we're not . . . intruding.' I say, stumbling over the last word as my brain processes just how ridiculously, insanely good-looking he is – almost unreally so. He's about thirty, I'd guess, with thick dark hair, tanned skin and luminous green eyes framed with lashes so long and so thick they look false. I wonder if he's a model or an actor. He is, without a doubt, the best-looking person I've ever seen in real life. His skin is smoother than cream, so flawless it's like he's wearing a magic foundation.

'Not intruding at all,' he says, smiling at me in a way that suggests our interruption is the best thing that's happened to him all night.

I glance over at Kate who is chatting to the other man. He's just as gorgeous; darker-skinned, with almond-shaped eyes and cheekbones you could slice Parmesan on. Are all Portuguese people this beautiful? Kate says something to make the man next to her laugh and his teeth flash white in the darkness.

'I'm Joaquim,' the man next to me says.

I turn back to face him and find him holding out his hand to me. I shake it. 'Orla,' I say, noting the fluster in my voice. 'Nice to meet you.'

He nods at his companion. 'This is Emanuel.'

I shake hands with Emanuel too, who grins back at me. They're both dressed in expensive-looking clothes: dark trousers and crisp shirts, the top buttons undone. My gaze starts to track downwards before I stop myself.

Even more flustered I turn back to Joaquim. 'Are you from here?' I ask, aware as soon as I say it that it sounds like a pick-up line. I cringe inwardly.

'Yes,' he answers, his voice mellow and husky. 'You?'

'No, can you tell? I'm actually from a little town in Ireland. More a village really. You won't have heard of it. People have only ever heard of Dublin. But I live in London now. I have done for almost twenty years. I suppose it's home. Though I haven't lost my accent.' I'm prattling on, my face heating up like an electric hotplate. I can't take my eyes off him but I'm also too overwhelmed by his beauty to hold his gaze for longer than a second. I feel almost star-struck and internally berate myself for acting like a teenage girl stuck in an elevator with her boy-band crush. I'm a grown woman.

'I love London,' Joaquim says.

'Yes, it's a great city,' I say, nodding enthusiastically and glancing over at Kate. She's locked in conversation with Emanuel, leaning her head close in to his as though she's struggling to hear him, though in this corner the music isn't as loud.

'How long are you here in Lisbon?' Joaquim asks.

I look back at him. He's moved his arm so it's now resting along the top of the banquette behind my head.

'The weekend only,' I say, reaching for my drink. 'I've got to get back.' I stop myself abruptly. I'd been about to say 'to my baby' but I wrenched on the brakes for some reason.

'Do you have plans?' Joaquim asks.

'What?'

'Do you have plans while you're here?'

'Er, yes,' I say feeling massively self-conscious under his gaze. 'We're doing an e-bike tour tomorrow morning, taking in all the sights. I've heard that you need an e-bike. I don't much

42

fancy pedalling up all those hills! And then we're doing a food tour in the afternoon.'

'There's great food in Lisbon. Maybe I can show you some places.'

'Oh,' I say, 'we just ate actually.'

'I meant tomorrow.'

I'm too startled to respond at first. Is he asking me out? Surely not? But it did sound like he was. I'm so out of the flirting and dating game I have no idea whether I'm reading into things. Probably. Why on earth would he want to go out with me? Not withstanding the fact we met less than a minute ago, I'm old enough to be his mother – almost, and he's so beautiful he could have anyone.

'Tomorrow?' I echo, trying to gauge his intent a little more.

He nods enthusiastically. 'There's a little place I know. Only locals go there. It would be my pleasure to take you.'

'Um . . .' I flounder. Now is probably the time to mention I have a husband. But what if I'm reading into things wrong and he's just being friendly? He might think it odd if I lob the fact that I'm married into the conversation like a hand grenade.

I look to Kate, but she's fully turned to Emanuel – I watch her hand brush his arm as she throws back her head and laughs uproariously. A penny drops. This is why we're here, why she made a beeline for this table – Kate's on a mission to pull! And it looks like she's succeeding. Emanuel's hand is on her thigh, inching north. Damn it that was fast, I think, then remember Kate's pre-Toby days. Within minutes of entering a club Kate would have located the hottest man on the dance floor and would be gyrating up against him. She's like a homing pigeon for hot men. And nine times out of ten they respond like . . . horny pigeons I suppose.

I turn back to Joaquim. He's staring at me expectantly, a

half-smile playing on his lips. Is he flirting with me or am I imagining it? With all these women in the room – most of them looking like they stepped straight off a catwalk – why would he flirt with me? Or is it because Kate is so clearly making moves on Emanuel he thinks that's what I'm after too? Or maybe I'm reading it wrong and Portuguese people are always this friendly.

'You want to come with me?' Joaquim asks, smirking a little as he says it, and I wonder if the double entendre is innocent.

'Maybe,' I hedge, then immediately feel a flush of shame. What is wrong with me?! I shouldn't even be hesitating to say no. I have a husband at home right now looking after our nine-month-old baby. 'Actually, now I think about it, we're busy all weekend,' I tell him, smiling politely. 'We've got all these plans to do stuff. Like cycling and things. But thanks.'

I gulp my drink nervously and almost spit it out, right into Joaquim's lap. 'Oh my God, what is this?!' I splutter.

'Gin and tonic,' Kate says, shouting across the table.

'I asked for water.'

'I must have misheard.' Kate laughs before turning back Emanuel.

Joaquim offers me a napkin. 'Here.'

I take it and he indicates my dress where I've spilled or spat some drink. I dab at it.

'Excuse me,' Joaquim is standing up, trying to get past me. I move to let him out and he disappears hurriedly into the crowd. I wonder what I said to make him bolt. I check the time. It's one-thirty in the morning. 'Do you think we should go?' I ask Kate but she doesn't hear me – she's flirting too hard with Emanuel, touching his thigh as she emphasises a point.

'Kate?' I say louder, trying to get her attention.

She turns to look at me. 'Yes?'

'Shall we go?'

'What?' she asks, frowning. 'We just got here.'

'I'm tired,' I tell her, frustrated and suddenly angry at her for dragging us here, for foisting more alcohol on me and now for ignoring me as she works to get in some random stranger's pants.

She frowns. Emanuel's hand is brushing her arm, his fingers tracing a circle on her shoulder. Goodness, that moved fast, even for Kate.

'Get a rum and Coke or something,' Kate tells me. 'Come on, let's stay, I'm having fun.'

You might be, I want to grumble, but I'm not. I'm not single. I'm not trying to pick up a stranger for a one-night stand. I make to stand – deciding to head back alone – but before I can leave Joaquim returns, drink in hand.

'Here,' he says, offering it to me. 'It's water.'

'Thanks,' I say, grateful and not a little surprised.

'You're welcome,' he says with a smile that immediately defuses some of my anger. I move aside to let him get by into the booth, his aftershave filling my nostrils and making me dizzy. My headache starts up again and I realise how drunk I feel, the world blurring at the edges. I down the water in one go.

'Better?' Joaquim asks.

I nod, noting he's sat down closer than he was before, his thigh almost brushing mine and his arm resting again behind my head. Normally I'm the first to get annoyed by manspreading but there's something about the languid ease of his body and his confidence that's sexy.

'Cheers,' he says, tipping his glass to mine. 'Here's to new friends.'

I knock my empty glass to his. I'll give it five more minutes, I decide. I don't want to appear rude to Joaquim.

'What do you do, Joaquim?' I ask, setting the water glass down.

'I run a business,' he says. He points at his friend. 'Emanuel and I are business partners.'

'What kind of a business?'

'Design,' he answers. 'What about you? What do you do?'

I'm about to answer that I'm on maternity leave but the split second before I blurt it out I change my mind. 'I work for a housing association,' I say.

He looks at me blankly.

'A charity,' I explain. 'Sort of. It helps people on low incomes.'

He leans in closer, head cocked to one side, as though it's the most interesting thing he's ever heard. 'You help the poor. That's nice.'

I study him. Is he being sarcastic? I don't think so. He looks genuinely curious. I'm so used to English people and their sarcasm that when I meet someone genuinely earnest I'm always suspicious.

'I mean, it's not that exciting,' I add, my cheeks warming again under his incessant gaze. Does he have any idea of his effect on women?

When Joaquim reaches for his own drink his hand brushes my knee, and my pulse leaps and skitters like I've been whipped by a stinging nettle. He must have noticed and I feel mortified. I don't know how to flirt anymore, and definitely not with someone who isn't my husband.

'You're married?' Joaquim suddenly says, pointing at my wedding ring.

'Oh,' I say. Rumbled, I hold up my ring finger as though I've only just noticed it myself and am wondering how on earth it got there. 'Yes.'

He cocks his head, a smile playing loosely on his lips. 'But your husband is not here.'

I shake my head and my vision swims from the sudden movement. I was hoping the water would help me sober up but instead I feel even drunker. That sip of gin has pushed me over the precipice between mildly drunk and completely wasted. I need to drink more water. Joaquim inches closer to me so our thighs are pressed together and his hand rests against the nape of my neck. Oh God.

'My husband's at home,' I blurt out. 'We've got a baby.'

Kate suddenly interrupts. 'What say we all go back to ours?'

I stare at her, my head thick. 'What?' I slur.

'We can all jump in the hot tub,' she says, clapping her hands with glee.

I shake my head. 'I don't think so. I'm tired and I'm not feeling great.' I widen my eyes at her to indicate that I'm not into the idea but she ignores me completely and turns to Emanuel whose arm has snaked around her waist.

'Sounds wonderful,' he murmurs.

'Kate,' I say quietly through clenched teeth. 'I don't think it's a good idea. We have to be up early tomorrow for that e-bike tour.' I'm already worried at how hungover I'm going to feel. Even with an e-bike I'm not sure I'll manage to get up those hills.

'It'll be fine,' Kate says, dismissing me. She stands up, dragging Emanuel with her by the hand. 'Let's go.' And with that she moves for the exit.

I rush after her, wobbly on my feet and my head heavy as a bowling ball, my neck a toothpick holding it up. I don't want these two men to come back to our apartment. It isn't a good idea. We don't even know them. But how can I stop Kate? She's paying for the apartment after all. I can't really ban them from entering, not without looking like a total bitch.

By the time I make it outside Kate's already on her phone, ordering a taxi. Emanuel walks over to Joaquim to confer about something and I rush over to Kate, stumbling and grabbing her by the arm to steady myself. 'Kate,' I say in a whisper.

She shrugs me off, busy with her phone. I pull her arm, tug on it. 'Did you have to invite them back?'

'What's the problem?' Kate asks, looking at me bewildered.

'The problem is I don't want them to come back,' I hiss. 'I just want to go to bed. I'm wasted.' My words are slurred, I notice, as though my tongue has doubled in size and I'm feeling very woozy all of a sudden.

'Come on. It'll be fun,' Kate says with a mischievous look in her eye. It takes me back to so many times in our twenties. We'd be at the petrol station on the corner, buying beer for a party and Kate would get chatting to the person ahead of us in the line. They'd invite her to something else and suddenly we'd be changing our plans and going to a house party or an art opening or one time a wedding. If ever I raised objections to following a random stranger who might turn out to be a serial killer, Kate would always shrug it off and say, 'Come on, it'll be fun!' And the thing is, she was usually right.

We ended up having the maddest adventures, all because Kate was a beacon for fun and would talk to anyone. We partied once in a white stuccoed mansion in Hyde Park, which was owned by a Russian oligarch, discovering by snooping around that there were three floors below ground, including one that housed a shooting range and a subterranean swimming pool that Kate insisted we skinny-dip in.

We also ended up one time at an event at the Colombian embassy where we got drunk on the free wine being served and ended up stealing a flag, which we only recalled when Kate woke up the next morning and found herself wrapped in it. Another time we ended up joining a protest outside the Shell building because Kate fancied the man on the bullhorn who was riling everyone up. We followed him and his eco-warrior mates back to their squat in Elephant and Castle for a house party that lasted all weekend. Looking back, I barely recognise the person I was back then, before I met Rob.

'We don't even know them,' I argue, my voice coming out a lot louder than I intended.

'I don't need to know them.' Kate smirks. 'I'm not planning on having a deep and meaningful conversation with them. I just want to have no-strings sex.' She nods in Joaquim's direction. 'Why don't you sleep with Joaquim? God, look at him. He's bloody gorgeous.'

'I'm married!' I hiss.

Kate shrugs at me. 'Rob will never find out. And it's just sex. It's not a big deal.'

'Yes, it is,' I answer but my powers of reasoning seem dulled and confused, as though my brain is encased in lead.

'What happens in Lisbon stays in Lisbon,' Kate says, grinning wickedly. 'One night of sin. I won't breathe a word. God, it might even help you get your mojo back with Rob. Fire up the old furnace. Get you back on the horse.' She glances at Joaquim. 'Though he's more a stallion.'

I look at Joaquim and my brain, despite the fog surrounding it, manages to conjure up images of us having sex. Maybe it isn't a big deal, maybe I could sleep with him like Kate's suggesting and it could all stay in Lisbon, but then cold reality kicks in. 'No,' I say, shaking my head. I realise with a start I'm shouting and people are turning to stare. 'It is a big deal. I can't . . . I love Rob.'

'All right, calm down!' she says. 'You don't have to do anything but let me have some fun, won't you? I deserve it.'

I can't argue with that, and even if I could I don't have a chance to as the taxi arrives. Kate piles in the back with Emanuel jumping quickly in behind her. Joaquim opens the passenger door for me and I get in, slumping unhappily against the door.

For the whole journey back as I listen to Kate laughing and kissing Emanuel I can feel my irritation building. She's acting like a teenager. This isn't the trip I signed up for. I want to go home. I want to see Rob and Marlow.

'We're here,' I hear Kate say.

I stumble from the car, the ground shifting beneath my feet like a rocking deck, and fall against Joaquim who puts an arm around me to steady me.

'Let's get you to bed,' he murmurs.

Chapter Five

Bleached white light scours my eyeballs. I wince. My head throbs as though an axe is embedded in my skull. I roll over, noting the fact I'm lying under the covers. How did I get here? Memories jostle through the blur, fragments from last night, no whole picture. We went out for dinner, then to a bar. There were two men. I vaguely remember the one I was talking to but I can't recall his name. He had green eyes, dark hair. Kate brought them back with us. God, I was so drunk. How on earth did I get so drunk? Maybe it was the jet lag? But there isn't a time difference so that doesn't make sense.

I press a hand to my aching, fuzzy head. Oh my God, I feel sick; my stomach is bubbling. A jagged piece of memory rises suddenly to the surface. I threw up last night. I remember leaning over the toilet bowl, gagging, and I can still feel a chemical-like burn at the back of my throat. Was it the oysters? Is that what made me feel so wretchedly awful? Was it food poisoning as well as too much booze? Or maybe a combination? It felt like I'd been anaesthetised and I still feel sluggish, as though my head and my limbs are buried in thick tar.

The man was there though. I remember that. He held my

hair as I heaved over the toilet. I remember feeling desperately humiliated that a stranger was watching. Where was Kate? I have a vague recollection of her shouting – or was she screaming? Or laughing? Why can't I remember? I must have blacked out.

As I look around the bedroom I wonder again how I got there. Then it comes to me. Another fragment piercing through the fog. The man carried me to bed. I suddenly see his face, hovering over me as he laid me down. Asking me if I wanted him to take my clothes off.

Aghast, I throw back the covers. I'm wearing my dress. Feeling sick, I lurch upright and check I'm still wearing my underwear. I am. The movement makes me dizzy. Or perhaps it's relief. I take stock. My throat is dry as sandpaper, my skull as fragile as a paper lantern. Any sudden move and I think it will tear. For a few moments I sit on the edge of the bed trying to dredge through my memories of the previous night, desperate to find some clues. Did I have sex with that man? The last thing I remember is him leaning over me. But then what happened? Why can't I remember?

Are they still here? My bedroom door is closed. I crane my head to listen but it's quiet. What time is it? I reach for my phone, sitting on the bedside table, and am shocked to see it's almost ten-thirty in the morning. I've slept through an alarm and three messages as well as a call from Rob. How drunk was I?

No. It hits me then, stupidly late, that I wasn't blackout drunk and I didn't have food poisoning. I was drugged. It's the only thing that makes sense because there's no way that amount of alcohol would make me pass out like that. I can only recall one other time I blacked out, back when I was eighteen, at university when someone gave me a glass of straight gin and I thought it would be a laugh to drink it without adding tonic.

But when could I have been drugged last night? And by who? It must have been the men we were talking to. I remember the one I was talking to gave me a glass of water when we were at the bar. Did he slip something into it? How could I have been so stupid as to accept a drink from a stranger?

Feeling a surge of bile shoot up my throat I drag myself into the bathroom and lean over the sink, breathing deeply, fighting nausea. When I glance up at the mirror I see my face is wan and pale and my mascara has streaked, giving me raccoon eyes.

Did I have sex with him?

It wouldn't have been sex. It would be rape, wouldn't it? Shit. Suppressing a mounting panic, I pull off my knickers. They're dry. I don't feel any soreness either. Maybe nothing happened. Maybe he just let me sleep. I would know – surely I would know – if something had happened.

I splash cold water on my face and take a glass from the side and fill it from the tap, drinking it down like a camel. My body demands more and I fill the glass a second time and a third time until my stomach sloshes with water. I ease open the bedroom door and walk into the hallway, on shaky, fever-dream legs.

The kitchen and living area are empty. There are several water and wine glasses scattered about and an empty wine bottle on the table. I notice Kate's jacket flung on the back of the sofa and her shoes, kicked off by the sliding door to the balcony. There's a wet towel lying in the middle of the living room floor and I pick it up. They must have gone in the hot tub.

I wander outside onto the balcony, squinting against the bright morning sunshine. The hot tub is bubbling away like an unwatched saucepan, and I find Kate's dress abandoned on one of the sun-loungers.

I head back inside. Is she in the bedroom? Nervously, I

approach the door to her room. What if she's in bed, passed out with the other guy? Or even with *both* of them? I wouldn't put it past Kate. What if they're having sex right now after an all-night bender? I press my ear to the door but can't hear anything so I crack it open and peek in. The shutters are drawn but a sliver of morning light streams through a gap and illuminates the rumpled bed. The contents of her suitcase are still strewn about the room as though they've erupted out of her bag, but there's no sign of the men or of Kate.

I push open the door more fully and turn on the light.

'Kate?' I call, crossing to the bathroom.

There's no answer and she isn't in the bathroom either, though I pull back the shower curtain to double-check in case she's passed out in the bathtub as happened one time in Ibiza.

'Kate?' I shout, heading back into the living room, feeling a little worm of worry burrowing into my gut.

Silence greets me. Where on earth is she?

Chapter Six

'She's gone,' I tell Rob over FaceTime. 'I don't know where she is.'

'Have you tried calling her?' he asks.

'Yes, of course, but her phone's switched off.' I've tried calling at least a dozen times already and each time it goes straight to voicemail.

Rob frowns. He's balancing Marlow on his arm. I've caught him heading out with her to the park. 'Did she leave a note?'

'No,' I say, frustrated at the lack of concern he's showing. He doesn't seem to appreciate how worried I am, but perhaps that's because I haven't admitted to him that we brought two men back to the apartment last night. How would I explain that?

'She's probably gone out to get a coffee or to get some food,' Rob says, batting Marlow's hands away from his mouth. 'You said you had a lie-in. She probably didn't want to wake you.'

I press my lips together and nod. I told him I'd slept in late and that's why I missed his calls. I couldn't bring myself to tell him that I thought I might have been drugged and possibly sexually assaulted. I've ruled that last part out anyway – it seems

55

impossible and I don't want to think about it. And besides, I was worried Rob would be angry and blame me if I told him. And he'd have a right to be. I did flirt with the guy. I didn't put my foot down strongly enough when Kate insisted they come back to our place. Though, actually, now I come to think about it, I do remember an argument. I recall Kate shouting angrily. But I can't remember clearly what it was about.

It's eleven o'clock in the morning. Maybe Rob's right and she has nipped out to get coffee or milk or some groceries. But then I remember the stocked fridge. What if she went out with the men for breakfast or brunch? What if they decided after the hot tub to go out clubbing somewhere else? There are lots of reasons she might not be here.

But she knew about the e-bike tour this morning, which we've now missed. Would she abandon me like that? I don't think she would. We had plans to get lunch too, at a famous seafood place by the dock after we finished the bike ride, and then we planned to do some shopping. She was excited about it. We spent the plane ride chatting about all the things we were going to do when we got here. But maybe she tried to wake me up and couldn't so went off on her own?

'Look,' Rob says, 'I need to get Marlow in the car.'

Marlow is getting fretful in his arms so I nod, forcing a smile. 'Bye, darling.' I wave at my daughter. She doesn't seem to recognise me or to hear – she's struggling wildly to get out of Rob's arms. Since she started crawling a couple of months ago she's not stopped wriggling and trying to pull a Houdini out of any place we put her.

'I'll call you later,' Rob says. 'Try not to worry. She'll show up. Call or text me as soon as she does.'

I hang up, feeling a distinct lack of reassurance. I wish I could have told Rob more about the circumstances but, aside from the fact I feel ashamed as much as alarmed and he seemed distracted, I also know he'd be less than sympathetic if he heard about Kate's drug taking and her sleeping with random strangers. Rob and Kate have known each other since university. I actually met Rob through Kate, at a party hosted by one of their mutual friends. Rob's always found Kate a little much, a little too into herself, and way too loud for his liking. He's also not a fan of her wild partying. Rob's a round of golf, pint down the pub kind of guy, who cycles to work and works as the financial director of an environmental charity. Kate prefers swanky bars, private limos and wouldn't date anyone who didn't earn at least seven figures.

She's never said it but I think Kate thinks Rob is boring with his accounting job and his love of DIY, though even she has to concede he's one of the good ones. He's hard-working, thoughtful, kind, funny and smart. He does the dishes and the laundry and even came with me on the Women's March in London earlier this year, carrying Marlow in the sling and wearing a T-shirt that said 'Raising a Feminist'. He might not be Kate's cup of tea, but he's definitely mine. I feel a sudden wave of hot shame wash over me as I remember briefly contemplating having sex with Joaquim. How could I have done that when I'm married to someone as lovely as Rob?

I try Kate's phone again though it still goes straight through to voicemail. Something doesn't feel right, a buzzing feeling in my gut. If those men drugged me last night then who's to say they didn't drug Kate as well? What if something has happened to her – something bad? It occurs to me then that maybe she's had an accident. She could be in hospital. I remember the drugs she was taking last night – all that coke, probably pills too. What if she overdosed?

I rush into her bedroom, scouring it for clues. There's an empty wine glass on the side and on the floor beside the bed I find a pair of black lace knickers and a foil condom packet.

I check the bin and find a used condom. I back away from it, feeling a little grossed out, my queasy stomach flip-flopping. It confirms she had sex last night.

OK, I think to myself, scanning the bedroom for more clues. There are two wet towels on the floor. Kate and the men must have been in the hot tub and then come in here and had sex. Did she sleep with one of them or both? One by the looks of things, there being only one condom. But then what happened afterwards? I go into the bathroom and glance in the bin beside the toilet and find another used condom. I stare at it, wondering if it's proof that Kate slept with both men. It seems a little extra, even for her.

When I walk out into the bedroom a glint of something shiny catches my eye. The thin filament of light coming through the shutters is refracting against something shiny. I walk around the bed and bend down to examine several fine splinters of glass on the carpet, half hidden beneath one of the decorative pillows that has been flung off the bed.

I pick up the pillow and stare down at the remains of a broken wine glass beneath, lying among several splashes of what looks like dried blood.

Chapter Seven

After spending thirty minutes trying to assess the stain I give up. I'm no CSI expert. Gnawing hunger pains alert me to the fact it's past lunchtime and I haven't eaten since last night. My head throbs dully and the thought of eating makes my queasiness return full force, but I make myself eat some of the bread and butter the landlord left in the fridge for us, and while I make coffee I consider my options.

I try to soothe the anxiety knotting my stomach by telling myself that Kate's fine. She's off shopping or getting groceries or she's gone out to lunch with those two men, or she's avoiding me for some reason I don't fully understand. It isn't blood spilled on the bedroom carpet; it's red wine. I comfort myself with thoughts of the telling-off I'll give her when she eventually turns up. I won't hold back. She's ruining our trip away. If she has abandoned me for a drug-fuelled weekend of partying and sex, I will be so mad I'm not sure I'll ever forgive her.

My anger doesn't last though. As I walk outside onto the balcony with my coffee and take in the still boiling hot tub and Kate's discarded dress, an ominous wet cloud settles on me and douses my rage. I set the coffee down and locate the switches for the hot tub to turn it off. In the silence that fills the air after I've switched it off, I pick up Kate's dress and shake off a sudden shiver that runs the length of my body. The worm in my gut has burrowed in deep. If she's just out shopping why is her phone off and why hasn't she called me?

In an effort to cast off my fear I head back inside and in a flurry of activity start to clear the empty wine glasses and bottle of wine, dumping the glasses in the sink. What happened last night? All these gaping black holes have me freaking out. Maybe I should go to the hospital and do a drug test, find out definitively if I was drugged. But what a waste of time. Even if it proved I had been drugged, I still wouldn't be able to prove who by, so there's no point and how would I even be able to explain myself when I don't speak the language?

As I'm doing a rudimentary tidy-up I have an epiphany. Her handbag! It strikes me then that I haven't seen it anywhere in the apartment. It's a Hermès Birkin bag. I'd know it a mile off as I'd enviously admired it when Kate showed it off to me at the airport. I'd assumed it was a fake, given they cost the same as a down payment on a house, but she'd reassured me that it wasn't, had bragged that it was a divorce gift to herself.

How could I have forgotten to look for it? I rush back into her room and search, then when I don't find it, I do another more frantic search of the whole apartment, turning over cushions and opening up cupboards. It's not here. She must have it with her. That's a good thing I suppose. It means she has her wallet and her ID with her.

I jump in the shower – keeping the door to the bathroom and bedroom ajar, so I can hear if Kate returns. As I dry off and throw on some clothes, I decide on a plan of action. I grab my bag and slip on my sandals to run downstairs to the landlord's apartment. I should have thought of it sooner. Maybe he's seen her or heard something.

But there's no answer when I knock and, thwarted, I head back upstairs. OK, I think to myself, trying to be methodical and practical rather than giving in to the mounting panic I'm feeling, I'll call the hospital and see if anyone matching Kate's description has been admitted.

It takes me a few minutes of searching online to find the number but when I ring I get put through to an automated system that's in Portuguese. I wait until the very end and, as I'd hoped, the recorded voice tells me to *press two for English*. It takes me another five minutes to navigate the system and reach an actual human being.

'Hello, do you speak English?' I say, feeling embarrassed that every English speaker in the world expects the rest of the world to speak their language while making no effort to speak theirs.

'Yes,' the woman on the end of the phone says.

'Great,' I say, relieved. 'I'm looking for my friend. I don't know what's happened to her.'

There's a pause on the end of the line. 'She has an accident?'

'No,' I explain, wishing I'd rehearsed this. 'I don't know. I wondered if I could check if anyone had been brought in last night or early this morning. Her name is Kate.'

'I'm sorry,' the woman says, clearly confused. 'You think your friend is here in the hospital?'

'I don't know,' I say. Am I being ridiculous? Kate will probably burst in the door any second, her arms full of shopping bags, laughing at how much of Toby's money she's just spent.

'What is her name?' the operator asks.

'Kate – I mean Katherine – Hayes.'

I spell it out and can hear some tapping going on in the background. 'I cannot find in the system,' the woman tells me.

'OK, thank you. And no one came in without identification?'

'No,' she says. 'Is there anything else I can help with?'

'No,' I say, and the woman hangs up.

I check my phone again, wondering if maybe Kate's sent an email – though God knows how she could if her phone is dead – but she hasn't. I send her one, just in case somehow she has access to a computer. I tell her to call me or email and give her my phone number in case she doesn't have it memorised. Finally, I scribble a note to her and leave it on the hallway table.

When I step out onto the street I have to pull on my sunglasses. The sunshine burns my eyes and exacerbates the dull throb at my temples. It's a gorgeous day and the city looks ripe for exploring. With a pang I think about our now-shelved plans. I should be sitting at a little restaurant on a cobbled side street with Kate right now, eating tapas and drinking chilled white wine, gossiping and laughing, faces turned to the sun, hoping to catch a smattering of rays. Resentment knocks shoulders with anxiety. The ongoing refrain marching through my head gets louder; *where the hell is she?*

On a mission now, I start to walk in a grid pattern around the apartment, stopping in any shop, café or bar that looks like somewhere Kate might visit, but the streets are winding and labyrinthine and very soon I'm lost. Still, I keep pounding up narrow lanes and down stairs, the cobbles glossed with age and slick as ice beneath my feet, the sun blistering the sky above my head.

I know her well enough to know what Kate's drawn to – anywhere selling handbags and shoes for one, any bar that looks sophisticated for two – definitely no tourist traps, and no restaurants with photographs of food on the menu, and doubt-fully any museums or art galleries, though those would be on my list. There are lots of tacky souvenir shops and not much in the way of boutiques but I make sure to check every dark cave-like bar I pass, in case she's decided on hair of the dog after waking up with a hangover like mine.

I wonder for a second if the e-bike tour she claimed to be enthusiastic about was actually not something she wanted to do and if she's therefore run off for a few hours to ensure missing it. Maybe she didn't hear the part about the bikes being electric and thought it involved actual pedalling. But that seems childish, and why would she lie to me? Kate's blunt and to the point. She would tell me if she didn't want to do something. She put the kibosh on us going to the monastery, laughing that it was valuable time when we could be eating or drinking or shopping; why waste it on monks?

On the corner of a small square beside a church I discover a little café selling coffee and pastries. Kate isn't inside and I stop myself from going in and asking people if they've seen her and showing them a photo on my phone – taken at the airport yesterday of us grinning and drinking champagne. It feels over the top and hysterical to start asking strangers if they've seen my friend – the equivalent of putting up missing posters on lamp-posts. Because she isn't missing. She's just not in touch.

I've been trying her phone every five minutes or so and I try it again, though without much hope. It rings through to voicemail and I leave another message, perhaps my third or fourth, begging her to please call me back.

An hour into my search and I still haven't found her, though what were the chances, really? We could have missed each other in passing easily enough. It's like trying to find a needle in a haystack, and in a foreign city that I don't know, it's also like wearing a blindfold. I start to wish I had unspooled a red string as I walked, so it could help me find my way back to the Airbnb. Even using Google maps is difficult as the roads bend in the most frustrating ways.

Tired, I stop in a little bar with pavement tables, to have a coffee and a custard tart. The waiter takes forever to bring my order – something I realise might be the standard for Lisbon – and I eat the tart without even tasting it. I can't focus on enjoying anything, even though I tell myself to. I may as well because otherwise when I get back to the apartment and find Kate sitting there among a pile of shopping bags, I'll be annoyed that I spent the afternoon worrying and not making the most of it. But when I spill the coffee on the white linen tablecloth all I can think about is that red stain on the carpet in Kate's room. Was it blood? Or was it wine? All sorts of images try to push through the meniscus of my mind, furnished by far too many true crime podcasts and documentaries, but I force them away, mentally refusing to go there.

My phone rings just then and, hope bursting, I dig it frantically out of my bag. Disappointment hits me when I see it's Rob, video-calling. I answer.

'Hi, wow, that looks nice,' he comments, obviously meaning the blue sky and pavement café culture in view behind me, though possibly the remains of the custard tart I'm holding. 'Did you find Kate?'

I shake my head. 'No. I've been looking for her. I just stopped for a coffee.' I pause. 'I'm worried, Rob. She still hasn't been in touch.' I don't tell him I already called the hospital – he'll accuse me of over-reacting.

'Did you get in a fight with her or something?' Rob asks.

'No, of course not,' I tell him, though as soon as I say it, I pause. Could that be it? Is she annoyed with me for putting up a fight last night about those two guys coming back to the apartment for a hot tub soak? I rack my sinkhole of a mind, trying to dredge up some memories of last night. I do vaguely recall arguing with Kate outside that bar I can't remember the name of – she ignored me, or at least ignored what I had to say, but we didn't fight exactly. I was too drunk – or drugged – to offer much resistance. I just wanted to go home to bed.

Did I say something else to her that I don't remember? Perhaps when we got back we argued and I don't remember it. I was so out of it, all I remember is feeling like I was going to be sick, my stomach squirming and bubbling like a cauldron on the boil and my vision blurring. The man – goddamn, what was his name? – helped me to the bathroom. I can still feel his arm locked around my waist. He almost had to haul me upright. But there's nothing after he put me to bed except blankness, with the occasional shards of memory embedded like slivers of broken mirror that I don't want to look at too hard in case they reveal glimpses of something I don't want to see.

There was shouting. I can hear Kate yelling or screaming. Or am I imagining it?

I realise that Rob's been talking this whole time I've been searching my memory. 'What was that?' I say.

'I was asking where you went last night. Maybe Kate went back there. What if she lost her phone, left it there?'

'Maybe,' I muse, wondering why I hadn't thought of it sooner. 'But I think she had her phone,' I tell Rob, remembering she used her phone to call a cab when we were outside the bar.

He's planted the seed now though, and I wonder if I should head back to the bar to find out if Kate did go back for some other reason, maybe she left something else – not her phone, perhaps her wallet – or maybe after her marathon sex session she wanted to go out for more drinks. Maybe she hit up a club like she wanted to.

'When did you see her last?' Rob asks. 'What time?'

'Last night. I went to bed around two I guess.' Should I tell him the truth now about the men we met – how Kate invited them back? 'I was pretty drunk. I don't remember much.' As soon as I say the words I know it's now too late to admit the full story. He'll wonder why I held back from telling him to begin with and he'll be suspicious.

'Blimey,' Rob says, 'how much did you have to drink?'

I swallow and force a smile. 'Oh, you know Kate, quite a bit. We had dinner then went to a bar.'

Rob raises his eyebrows, smiling. He knows what Kate's antics can look like. But all I can see is the man with green eyes. What was his name? I wish I could remember. A bolt of nausea shoots through me as I remember that I thought about sleeping with him. I imagined what it would be like. I can hear Kate telling me to do it, encouraging me. *What happens in Lisbon stays in Lisbon.*

In the cold light of day as I look at Rob's open, honest face and worried smile, I feel a huge wave of self-loathing. How could I have even considered it? And now it's too late to tell him. He'll think the worst of me and I don't need to get into a fight with him. I've got enough on my plate worrying about Kate without having to deal with that too.

'Do you think I should go to the police?' I ask.

Rob pulls a surprised face. 'What? No. It's only been a few hours. She'll turn up. You know Kate. She's not exactly reliable. She's probably lost track of time. That girl can party like the end of the world is coming.'

He's right about that – but it's not entirely fair to call her unreliable. She's always on time for things and she does stick to her word.

She's my best friend and has been for almost two decades, the first person I turn to when I need a shoulder to cry on or to have a bitch and moan, whether about work or relationship stuff. She always picks up the phone whenever I call and she sends me cheer-up texts when I'm down, silly things designed to make me laugh – videos of fruit porn or cats falling down stairs or *Game of Thrones* memes that posit that the age of men is over and heralding the end of the patriarchy.

'Try to enjoy yourself,' Rob says, jarring me back into the

moment. I nod and try to smile but I can't. How can I smile or enjoy myself when I don't know where Kate is or what's happened to her?

'Is Marlow OK?' I ask, realising I've been so concerned with Kate I've not asked a single question about her.

'She's fine,' Rob says. 'I put her down for a nap.'

'Don't let her sleep too long,' I tell him. 'Or she'll be up in the night.'

'I know,' he says, his tone edgy. He hates me telling him what to do when it comes to Marlow; he says it implies he doesn't know how to parent. 'I've got it. Everything's fine. I better go. Call me when Kate shows up.'

'OK,' I say and hang up, sipping the rest of my now cold coffee.

Chapter Eight

Another thirty minutes walking the neighbourhood yields nothing except sore feet, though several times I could have sworn I'd spotted Kate in the distance, only to be disappointed when I'd drawn level and seen it wasn't her at all but a stranger who looked like her. I'm tired and grumpy by the time I decide to call it quits. I haven't been able to enjoy the sights or been able to browse the shops I've entered looking for her, and I'm annoyed about what a waste today has turned into. I think about hailing one of the many taxis that prowl the neighbourhood, obviously trying to pick up silly tourists like me who've walked too far and can't handle another hill, but decide to stick it out in case I spot her en route.

When I finally make it back, the apartment feels quiet as a tomb. I call out Kate's name anyway and even after getting no response I still check her room, hoping against hope I might find her napping on the bed. *Damn you, Kate*, I think to myself, when I find it empty.

Annoyed, I walk into the kitchen and drink three glasses of water, glugging them down. My body seems unable to sate my unquenchable thirst, as if whatever I drank or was drugged with last night has turned my body into a dried-out husk. Will drinking so much water affect any drug test, I wonder? But I know deep down I have already dismissed the idea of going to the hospital to get tested. It's probably too late anyway and I can't imagine having to explain last night to a nurse or a doctor. And the thought of a sexual assault exam is too much to bear.

I had to go with Kate one time after she was sexually assaulted by a guy on the street. He grabbed her from behind when she was walking home alone at night from the bus stop and forced her down an alley. It wasn't full penetrative sex but he did assault her and beat her before she managed to get away and run into a petrol station for help. They never found the man and Kate, after a few shaky days and once her bruises had faded, put her own spin on it, casting herself as the plucky heroine who kicked butt and fought off her attacker, leaving out the cruder details for anyone curious. She said her attacker 'copped a feel' when it had been much more aggressive and terrifying than that. I knew as I'd been with her, holding her hand, when she gave her statement to the woman detective. I never saw her cry though. She was stoic throughout the interview and the exam, as well as afterwards.

I can't claim anything as horrible as that happened to me last night. In fact, probably nothing happened at all. The man put me to bed. End of story. It seems silly to make a thing of it when lots of worse things happen to women every day.

After standing in the middle of the living room for several minutes, thoughts drifting, I decide that I need to distract myself. I do a quick bustle through the apartment and balcony picking up towels, finding a pair of boxer shorts underneath one of the sun-loungers and a pair of red lace knickers beneath the coffee table in the living room.

I start to rinse out the glasses I dumped in the sink earlier, hesitating as I dunk them in the soapy water. There's a fine powder in the bottom of one of the glasses. I examine it closer. It might just be dishwasher powder. Or it might be something else. There's a faint lipstick mark on the rim – a coral pink colour that I recognise as my coloured lip balm. Kate wears actual lipstick – she's never seen without it – the brighter and more attention-grabbing red the better.

I set the glass down on the side, my hand trembling. Is this evidence I was drugged last night? But I remember being woozy before we returned home. If I was drugged it was by the man at the bar. They probably thought when we sat down with them at their table that we were easy prey. They might have gone to the bar hoping to pick up some women and we stumbled, almost literally, into their laps.

Was it their intention to rape both of us last night? Did Kate being up for sex stop that plan in its tracks? They didn't need to force her. But did something go wrong perhaps? Did she find out they drugged me? Or did they try to drug her? All these questions flit through my mind like poison arrows. The not knowing is the difficult thing. Am I being hysterical and leaping to outlandish conclusions based on nothing? I wish I knew. I wish Kate were here so we could talk and piece it all together.

I stand up. I need to do something. I need to go to the police. I can't just stay in the apartment waiting for her to turn up because what if she *is* missing? What if something truly awful has happened to her, what if she's somewhere needing my help right at this moment? In fact, now I've decided I can't believe I've waited so long. What kind of a friend am I?

After quickly gathering my things I head out once more, stopping at the landlord's apartment below ours and rapping loudly on the door. There's a beat and I think I hear footsteps approaching the door but then there's silence and the door doesn't open. I stare at the spy hole directly ahead of me and feel suddenly creeped out that he might be watching me through it.

The door opens immediately. 'Hello,' Sebastian says. He isn't smiling and I notice his arms are crossed over his chest and he's blocking his doorway as though afraid I'm about to barge right past him.

'Hi,' I say, words suddenly deserting me. 'Um, this is going to sound strange but have you seen my friend?'

'Your friend?' He shakes his head. 'No.'

'I don't know where she is,' I say. 'I haven't seen her since last night. And I can't get hold of her. Her phone's switched off.'

'Well, I haven't seen her,' he says.

'Right,' I sigh. 'It was a long shot. You didn't hear anyone leaving this morning?'

He arches his eyebrows at me and purses his lips. 'If you mean last night, yes. I heard plenty of leaving and coming.'

There's an acid archness to his voice and a slight flare to his nostrils that puts me on the back foot, but I work in HR; I interview people all day and so I'm good at adjusting my technique depending on who I'm speaking to. 'I'm so sorry,' I say, understanding that he's annoyed about the noise we made coming in last night and deciding to play the role of contrite and apologetic supplicant. 'Did we wake you up last night? We tried to be quiet.'

He draws in a loud, self-righteous breath. 'I think you woke the whole street.'

'I'm sorry,' I repeat, giving him an obsequious smile, while wondering how loud we actually were.

'You only made the booking for two people,' he says sniffily. 'You even told me last night that only two of you were staying. Any extra guests incur a charge. You should have informed me.'

'There weren't extra guests,' I say.

'Yes, there were,' he argues back, irritated. 'I heard you. It sounded like you were having a party. Parties are forbidden. It's in the rules.'

'We didn't have a party,' I protest. 'We just had two friends back for a drink.'

He rolls his eyes at me. 'I heard the music and all the shouting and doors slamming. It was a party. And extra guests, which you'll need to pay for.'

I ignore his last comment and latch on to the other information. Shouting? Doors slamming? What's he talking about?

'What time did you hear people leave?' I ask.

'Around three a.m. That still counts as an overnight guest.'

I couldn't care less about his petty rules or extra costs or whatever punishment he wants to lay at our door. 'What did you hear exactly?' I press, suddenly excited that he might know something that could lead me to Kate.

'Music, shouting, people running down the stairs, doors slamming,' he says with a loud sigh.

'Did you see who?'

'No,' he says, but his eyes slide sideways and I wonder if he's telling the truth. 'I was in bed,' he sniffs.

'You don't know if it was Kate then who left at three? Or someone else?'

'It sounded like men.' He gives me a very pointed look and I feel my cheeks flush. It's as if he's implying I'm some kind of prostitute for bringing men back to our apartment. I refuse to be shamed though.

'They were definitely running?' I ask. 'Like they were in a hurry to get somewhere?'

Sebastian nods. 'Yes. It woke me up. Like elephants on the stairs.'

'Did you hear anyone come back after that?'

'No,' he says. 'I put my ear plugs in.'

What could all this mean? I'm more confused now than ever.

'I hope you don't plan on having any more parties,' Sebastian remarks.

I shake my head. 'No,' I say, stunned. It's almost like he didn't hear me when I told him Kate was missing.

'Well then, I need to get on,' Sebastian tells me, turning back into his apartment. 'Goodbye.' And he shuts the door firmly in my face.

Chapter Nine

The policeman taps his pencil against his notepad and looks at me with a barely suppressed sneer. 'You brought two men you didn't know back to your apartment?'

He makes it sound like there's something illegal about that, and I'm reminded of being called before the nuns at school to explain why my skirt was rolled up at the waist and flashing a centimetre of unholy knee, or why I was wearing lipstick that made me look like Mary Magdalene. The nuns wondered if I wanted to be mistaken for a whore and, though he isn't saying it, the policeman is undoubtedly thinking the same thing. After Sebastian's pointed snark an hour ago I'm not feeling very patient. It's the twenty-first century, I want to argue, and my morals aren't the mystery here.

The policeman, whose name is Nunes, is younger than me, maybe early thirties, and good-looking, which is what I've come to expect from anyone Portuguese, but he has an oiliness to him that I don't much like. Maybe it's the gelled hair, or it could be the pouty mouth. I'm surprised that someone of his age has such outdated views on sex but, then again, Portugal is a Catholic country like Ireland, so maybe that has something to do with it. I'm sure that it would be the same back home where there are also completely double standards when it comes to women and men.

'Yes, we brought two men back,' I say, refusing to be embarrassed about it, though the truth is my cheeks are hot and I do feel a squirm in my stomach, especially when I notice his gaze slipping to my wedding ring.

'Whose names you don't remember.'

I nod, sheepish. I've been scouring my memories all day but they're filled with Swiss-cheese gaps.

'And your friend had sex with one or both of these men—'

'No, I didn't say that,' I interrupt. 'I mean, I think she had sex with one of them. I don't know for sure.' I try not to think of the condoms in the bin. The police don't need to know those details – and this guy is already being judgemental enough. I check but he isn't wearing a wedding ring. He's in his early thirties; is he telling me that he's never had a one-night stand?!

'You don't know because you were . . .' He looks down at his notes and reads off from the statement I just gave: '"Blackout drunk", yes?'

I nod, my face flaming hotter than the sun. 'Yes, but I didn't mean to get that drunk. I think I was drugged.'

At this he looks up sharply, but is unable to hide the scepticism on his face or in his voice. 'Drugged?' He raises his eyebrows laconically.

I nod, irritation rising up. He's treating me like I'm a madwoman or like I'm lying. 'Yes, maybe. I don't know but I was completely out of it, wasted. It's not like me. I mean, I can hold my booze.' I stop myself. That makes me sound like an alcoholic. 'Not that I have an issue with alcohol,' I hasten to add, realising I'm only putting my foot in it further. 'I rarely drink. I've got a baby.' Shit. Even worse. His scornful look grows deeper, his eyebrows rising even higher as he scribbles a note on the pad. What is he writing?

'Were you taking any drugs? Besides alcohol?'

I cock my head not understanding and then the sudden memory of Kate snorting coke in the back of the cab and taking out her little pillbox dances into my head. 'No,' I say. 'Definitely not.'

'And your friend, did she take any drugs?'

I open my mouth. 'I . . . um . . . I don't know. Maybe,' I hedge. I don't want to get into trouble or get Kate into trouble and I'm not sure what the laws are here, though I know cocaine obviously isn't legal. I don't want the police thinking any worse of Kate than they are already and I don't want to admit something that could get her arrested when she shows up.

Nunes looks at me sternly, his brown eyes drilling a hole right through my skull. 'Did you buy drugs from these two men?'

'What? No!' I say, shocked. 'Absolutely not.' I shake my head and a flurry of nerves hits me. I twist my hands into knots in my lap. 'That isn't what happened. We met them in a bar. And invited them back – that's all.'

But now he's planted the idea I wonder if it's possible that's where Kate went at four in the morning. Was she buying more drugs? Maybe I should admit that Kate was doing coke. I don't know what to do. I feel like I'm being interrogated and that I should ask for a lawyer – which is ridiculous as I'm just trying to report my friend missing.

Nunes sighs loudly and puts his pen down on the notepad. I wait for him to say something. I came here hoping that if I told someone – someone official – they could help somehow, do something, but he doesn't seem to be reacting with any kind of interest, let alone urgency. 'Have you considered that

76

your friend might have gone off with these two men some-where?' he asks me.

I struggle not to roll my eyes. 'Yes, but she wouldn't go without telling me.'

'You were unconscious – you said it yourself – maybe she did tell you but you don't remember.'

'But she hasn't called all day.'

Nunes shrugs again. 'Maybe she wanted to be by herself. Or maybe she wanted to be with these two men.'

I start to shake my head – no, that's not it – I know her. I know she wouldn't just walk off like this and not come back and not tell me where she was. But Nunes cuts me off before I can say anything else. 'I'm sure she'll turn up. People go missing all the time.'

'That's reassuring,' I say, stonily.

'People go out and have fun and forget the time. You said she recently went through a divorce and was looking to have a good time; that's why you came away. If your friend was drinking and doing drugs—'

'I never said she was doing drugs,' I mutter.

He ignores me. 'Maybe she is passed out in a bed somewhere. It happens.' As he says it he gives me a pointed look and I glare back at him as much as I dare. I'm a foreigner and he's a policeman. I definitely don't want to piss him off, but if I wanted judgement I'd go to confession and see a priest, and I had enough of that during the first twenty-two years of my life to last me until I die.

'And what if she's passed out somewhere and in trouble?' I press. 'What if she's hurt?'

'Did you check the hospital?'

I nod. 'Yes.'

He scribbles something else on the pad. 'We'll check too.'

'Thank you,' I say. 'Should I file a report that she's missing?'

I ask, feeling silly. It seems so over the top and I don't know the protocol in Portugal.

'No,' Nunes says, standing up and walking to his door, which I take as my cue that this interview, or whatever you could call it, is over. 'You have to wait twenty-four hours before you can report a person missing.'

'OK,' I say. The thought that I might be back here tomorrow makes me want to burst into tears. Surely Kate will show up before then?

Nunes shrugs, bored, trying to usher me out of the office. 'Don't worry,' he says. 'She'll turn up.'

Chapter Ten

Once again, I find myself standing on a pavement trying to figure out what to do next. I feel desperately alone, with a slightly panicky feeling of being far from home, among strangers. I don't know what to do.

Once, when I was about five, my mum lost me in the supermarket and I remember that mounting feeling of hysterical panic swirling inside me, like I was trapped in a gigantic nightmare maze that I'd never escape from. That's how I'm starting to feel now. The thought of going home to the apartment and waiting for Kate to show up is impossible to wrap my head around. It's getting late, almost eight, and the light is fading fast. I shiver. I should have brought a cardigan or a jacket with me but I was in too much of a hurry when I left.

I start to walk, not sure where I am or where I'm heading, but wanting to feel as if I'm moving towards something – hopefully an answer. I think through what the policeman said. He gave me his card when I left and I pull it out of my pocket, surprised to see he's a detective.

Was Nunes right about Kate going with the men to buy drugs? I didn't get a look at her pillbox but from the amount of white powder Kate tipped on her hand in the back of the Uber I assume she had quite a lot on her. Enough to last all night though? I have no idea. But she does have her handbag with her, which reassures me a little.

The best thing I can do is go back to the bar and see if I can find the men – they could be regulars. Someone might know them at least and I could find out their names. Then I could track them down and find out what happened last night after I passed out. But the problem is I don't remember the name of the bar. I spent ages on my phone earlier, scouring a map online, trying to figure out where we were last night – but all I remember is an alley and a blue light, which isn't very helpful.

It hits me then that the Uber driver who drove us there from the restaurant would know the name of the place. And I was the one who called the service using the app on my phone. Triumphant that I've finally figured something out, I unlock my phone and scroll to the Uber app, pulling up the last trip and the name of the driver. *Konstandin.* His picture fills the little oval in the corner.

I message him via the app – asking him to call me urgently. I follow it up with a promise of cash as I know he might not have any other incentive to contact me, and then I wait.

He calls back within minutes and I quickly explain I need to go back to the bar he took us to the other night. There's a pause on the end of the line.

'Do you remember?' I ask. 'It was me and my friend. You picked us up around eleven forty-five last night.'

'I remember you,' he says, his voice gruff. It sounds like perhaps I woke him up.

'I just need the name of the place you took us to,' I say. 'That's all.'

He clears his throat. 'The Blue Speakeasy,' he says.

That's it! 'Thank you,' I say. At last, something to work on!

'Do you need a ride there?' Konstandin asks.

'Um . . .' I hesitate.

'Where are you?' he presses.

'I'm not far from the police station in the centre of town.'

'I'll be there in five minutes.'

I don't have time to argue before he hangs up. I stare at my phone as I head back towards the police station. Is it weird that he's offered to take me there? But no, he's probably just hanging about town trying to pick up passing tourist trade. And if he doesn't book it via the app he doesn't have to pay commission. I try to remember him from last night but my memory refuses to offer much up other than a fuzzy recollection of talking to him about Ireland. Oh God . . . and Kate doing drugs in the back of his Uber.

Five minutes later Konstandin pulls up in his black Volkswagen Passat and I hesitate again, uncertain whether to get in the back or the front. It feels weird to get in the back but weirder still to get in the front. In the end it feels wiser to sit behind him.

'Hi,' I say, glancing at the door lock. My imagination keeps leaping to dark places involving kidnap and rape and murder. Like most women I'm always on alert but today I'm even more so. Everything is making me nervous and getting into a stranger's car strikes me as possibly a very stupid thing to do. But don't we do that all the time these days? Ride-service apps have become the norm.

Konstandin glances at me in the rear-view mirror. 'Are you OK?' he asks as he starts to drive, his eyes shifting between me and the road. 'Where's your friend?'

'She's missing,' I blurt out.

He double-takes in the mirror. 'What?'

'I can't find her,' I say. 'I woke up this morning and she was gone. I don't know where she is. I've been looking for her all day. I even went to the police.' It feels good to tell someone else, to share it with someone who isn't a sceptical policeman or on the end of a phone.

'The police?' Konstandin asks.

I nod. 'Yes, but they said they couldn't do anything and I should come back tomorrow.'

'You've tried calling her?'

'Yes. Her phone isn't switched on.'

'After I dropped you at the bar, did you go anywhere else?' he asks me.

'Home. Back to our apartment.' I hesitate. 'The thing is . . .' I'm about to admit to him that we brought two men back but stop myself. 'I wondered if maybe she forgot something at the bar or went back for some other reason.'

He nods thoughtfully.

I shrug. 'And I can't stay home waiting for her and not doing anything to find her.'

Konstandin nods and we drive along in silence. I stare out the window, taking in the arched plaza we're passing, with its bright yellow buildings and giant statues of horses and men on plinths. Tourists are milling about, some on Segways, many posing for photographs, and I feel a pang. That's what Kate and I should be doing right now.

A few minutes later Konstandin drops me in the same place he did last night – at the end of the alley on a main street crammed with people, both tourists and locals. I glance up the narrow street and spot the red velvet rope, the sight of it jarring loose another memory from last night, of us walking towards it.

'Thank you,' I say to Konstandin as I get out the car, handing him ten euros.

'I hope you find your friend,' he says as I shut the door.

Heading down the cobbled alley towards the blue light, a few more shards of memory start to catch the light; the argument I had with Kate outside after she invited those men home with us comes back to me. I was angry. I shouted at her. She wrenched her arm from mine. Now she's missing.

There are no model types lounging outside smoking and posing – I guess it's too early for that – but there is a man wearing impossibly tight jeans and a silk kaftan, sitting on a wooden stool to the right of the door. I'm not sure of his exact purpose but I can see him assessing me as I approach with not quite a sneer on his face, but not quite a smile either.

Maybe his job is to only let inside people who meet his strict standards for beauty and fashion. Is it the same man who Kate spoke to last night and who lifted the rope to let us past inside these hallowed doors? He's an androgynous-looking, skinny-as-a-whip twenty-something. I think it might be.

I decide to turn on the Irish charm. It nearly always works, so I smile broadly though it feels fake as anything and ratchet up my accent because I know that people love an Irish accent.

'Hello!' I say with forced jollity. 'I was here last night with my friend. I don't suppose you remember me?'

He looks me up and down again, frowning at my jeans and T-shirt, and I shift uncomfortably. 'My friend chatted to you,' I continue. 'I think it was you. You let us in.'

He narrows his eyes then gives a small nod of recognition. 'I remember her. Gold shoes.'

'Yes, that's right! She was wearing gold shoes. We left with two men.'

He nods again, giving a slight smirk.

'Do you know the people we left with?' I ask, feeling a surge of hope.

He gives a non-committal shrug. 'No.'

Frustrated, I gesture at the door he's guarding. 'Can I come in and maybe speak to the barman?'

He cocks his head towards a poster nailed to the wall

beside him. I read it. It's a dress code, top of which is the edict 'no jeans'.

'Oh, for goodness' sake,' I say, losing patience. 'I won't be staying. My friend's missing. I just want to ask the barman a few questions.'

He shrugs again. Why the hell is he being so obstinate?

'Please. My friend is missing,' I say. 'And I'm trying to find her!'

'Is there a problem?'

I turn around. Konstandin is walking towards us. What's he doing here? He ignores my frown and looks at the doorman. 'Why won't you let her in?' he asks.

'It's because I'm wearing jeans,' I explain.

Konstandin turns to the boy barring the way and I watch the poor kid cower on his stool like a dog that knows it's done something wrong and is about to be punished. When I look back at Konstandin I'm startled to see an expression of such intensity and ferociousness even I shrink away, noting for the first time his height and build. He's at least six feet two, and broad like a boxer, and with those dark hooded eyes, he's definitely not someone you'd want to meet down a dark alley.

Konstandin says something to the doorman in Portuguese and the boy sullenly lifts the rope to allow us entry. Konstandin steps aside to usher me through ahead of him. Startled, I obey.

'What did you say to him?' I whisper as we enter the bar.

'I told him if he didn't let us in I would pull his kidney out through his rectum.'

I turn to look at Konstandin over my shoulder, letting out a shocked laugh, but the laugh dies when I see the stern expression on his face. Did he mean it? Or was he joking? It's very hard to tell.

'Why are you . . . .?' I break off, not knowing how to ask him what he's doing following me. I'm grateful that he helped me but I don't know why he is.

He shrugs. 'I figured maybe you need my help,' he says.

Konstandin takes the lead once we're inside the bar, heading straight towards the barman. I look around, there are only a dozen or so customers sitting at tables and I glance at the table Kate and I sat at, half-hoping to spot the two men from last night sitting there, or even Kate, but it's empty. I hadn't expected to find them here but I'm disappointed nonetheless.

Konstandin rests an elbow on the bar. 'This lady is looking for her friend,' he begins, gesturing at me. 'They were here last night.'

The barman glances at me blankly. 'I don't remember.'

'We were sitting over there,' I say, pointing at the table where Kate and I sat. 'With two men. They were about thirty, dressed in suit trousers and shirts.' I feel Konstandin's gaze and my face warms. 'They were very good-looking. Like models.' Even as I say it I remember the clientele last night. Perhaps that doesn't much narrow it down.

'You know who they are?' Konstandin asks the barman.

The barman turns and grabs a cloth and starts wiping down the counter. 'Maybe,' he grunts.

I latch on to that, my pulse leaping. It's the first real clue I've had so far – a tiny breadcrumb that might signal the beginning of a trail that will lead me to Kate. 'Do they come here often?' I ask.

'Sometimes,' the barman answers. 'I see them here.' He stares at me coldly and I wonder why. I'm starting to feel like I have a scarlet letter stamped on my forehead. Is it not the twenty-first century? Is this not a bar where men and women come with the express desire to get drunk, meet people and hook up? Do people not have sex anymore? I never thought the Portuguese were that puritanical but I suppose it is a Catholic country. I just assumed because it was a Latin country the morals were looser but I could be wrong. Or maybe I'm leaping to conclusions. Maybe I'm not being judged at all by this man, and I'm merely paranoid.

'They come here to meet women?' Konstandin asks.

The barman gives a half-shrug. He doesn't seem to want to answer the questions.

'Do you know their names?' Konstandin asks. 'Or anything else about them? Perhaps they paid with a card. It's important. A woman is missing.'

The barman hesitates then shakes his head.

Konstandin lowers his voice and says something to him in Portuguese. The barman's expression changes minutely, a flicker of fear registering in his eyes. I glance at Konstandin. His expression is mild, non-threatening, and his tone is even and quite friendly. What on earth is he saying? Why is the man looking so afraid? My gaze flits back to the barman who still eyes Konstandin warily, before finally launching into some complicated-sounding explanation, gesturing at the table where we were sitting then at the door.

Konstandin finally nods and walks away from the bar. I smile at the barman who doesn't smile back and then I rush after Konstandin.

'What? What did he say?' I ask, catching up to him as he moves towards the door. 'Did he give you their names? Did he tell you who they are?'

It's not until we're outside on the street, past the gatekeeper, that Konstandin finally stops and turns to me. 'The two men you met, you went home with them?'

'Kate invited them,' I find myself explaining, like a teenager making excuses to an angry parent. 'I didn't want them to come.'

He nods to himself, grimacing a little.

I ignore his grimace. 'Who are they? Did you find out?'

Konstandin weighs his words, as if trying to find the right ones.

'Are they drug dealers?' I ask, because that's what I've guessed, and what I imagine Konstandin was asking the barman. After all, he saw Kate in his Uber snorting coke. Plus, the barman would likely have a good idea of who deals drugs inside the bar, as too would the boy guarding the velvet rope – which could explain their reticence to let me in or to answer my questions, and also would go some way to explaining the looks they were both giving me.

'No,' says Konstandin. 'They aren't drug dealers. They're escorts.'

Chapter Eleven

The first thing that comes into my head when Konstandin says the word escort, is that he means prostitutes, but I dismiss that and move on to the second thing that enters my mind. 'You mean like a Ford Escort? Is that the car they drive?'

Konstandin stares at me blankly, confused, then shakes his head. 'No,' he says, 'I mean they're escorts. Prostitutes,' Konstandin clarifies. 'That's what the barman told me.'

'I don't get it,' I say, still not understanding.

'They are men who are paid for sex,' Konstandin clarifies even further, as though prostitution is something I haven't ever heard of.

He's staring at me, studying me, hands on his hips. It dawns on me then he thinks we hired them!

'But . . .' I splutter, my head spinning, 'we just randomly sat next to them. You can't think . . .' Oh my God . . . judging from Konstandin's expression he actually thinks I might be the kind of woman who pays for sex. 'Do you really think I would pay for sex?!' I hiss at him.

'No,' Konstandin admits, though it takes him a split second too long. 'I don't think that, but that is what the barman told me. The men work for an escort company. High end. Expensive.'

I stagger towards the wall, holding out a hand to steady myself. 'My God, I didn't even know that was a thing, did you?'

Konstandin gives a non-committal shrug. 'Prostitution? It's the oldest job in the world.'

'But men doing it? Sleeping with women?' I ask, shaking my head. 'I mean, it's easy to have sex if you're a woman. Why would you need to pay for it?'

'Same reason I suppose men do. To skip the small talk. To make sure you get what you want. Maybe your friend has a sexual desire she can't get filled normally.'

'Oh, gross, no!' I say, pulling a face. I'm fairly sure Kate would have told me if she was into something kinky. It's not like she's shy and she loves to shock.

But what if Konstandin is right and it's some weird fetish I don't know about? What if Kate wanted to hire escorts to do some weird threesome involving rubber or . . . I remember suddenly how hard she was pushing me last night to sleep with Joaquim and how much she wanted to go out. She kept looking at her watch at dinner.

Is it possible that she planned for us to meet them there, at the bar?

'Also,' says Konstandin, interrupting these disturbing thoughts, 'these men, you said they were good-looking, no?'

I nod. Suddenly it's all starting to make more sense. I mean, I did wonder at the time why they were all over us like rashes.

'Your friend, maybe she booked them,' Konstandin says, pulling out a bashed packet of cigarettes and lighting one up.

'What?' I say.

He inhales deeply. 'Apparently they work for an agency. You call, you make a booking.'

I wave the smoke away from my face, though truthfully the

smell takes me back to my teenage smoking behind the bike shed days and a part of me feels like stealing the cigarette from him and inhaling. I could really use it about now to steady my nerves. 'What are you saying? That Kate arranged to meet them? After she booked them?!'

Konstandin nods and shrugs at the same time. It's a signature gesture of his. 'The barman said he didn't remember their names but he knows the name of the agency. He has a friend who worked for them for a time. Another model. To make cash on the side.'

'How did you get him to tell you all this?' I ask, wondering if maybe he's pulling my leg.

Again with the shrug. 'I told him if he didn't give me the information I would slam his head against the bar like a raw egg, and then scramble his brains for my breakfast.'

My mouth falls open again. 'Are you joking?'

'Yes,' he says, but there's a twinkle in his eye and a tiny shadow of a smirk at the edge of his mouth. He takes another slow inhalation of his cigarette.

'Are you?' I ask, narrowing my eyes. 'Because I don't know.'

'Look,' he sighs. 'I am from Kosovo. I lived through a war. I survived it. I came here as an asylum seeker. I survived that too. You think I could do either if I didn't know how to get by, convince people to help me, and if I hadn't learned a few things about human nature along the way?' He tosses his cigarette butt to the ground, which irritates me. He threatens people *and* he litters.

'What's the name of the escort agency?' I say, deciding to let it go.

'Lotus Models.'

I stand there, reeling. It can't be true. The whole idea is ridiculous.

'I can't believe Kate would hire escorts,' I mutter, starting

90

to walk down the alley at a clip, my arms crossed over my chest. It's more likely that Kate didn't realise they were escorts. Maybe, I think, after they had sex they demanded payment and she got angry.

Konstandin strolls after me, catching me up with no trouble.

'Why is it so hard to believe?' Konstandin asks.

'Because,' I huff. 'She didn't need to pay for sex.'

'Maybe she hired them for you.'

I round on him in disgust. 'I'm married.'

He gives a one-shouldered shrug, seemingly unperturbed by any of this strangeness. 'From what I know of marriage, there's not much sex happening.'

'Well, that's not true for me,' I say, flushing and walking off again down the alley. 'And Kate wouldn't do that,' I argue, albeit weakly because I'm starting to think she very well might have. I can almost see it . . . Kate giggling at the idea, planning it all out, thinking that our girls' weekend could be enhanced with some male models for company.

Maybe she only planned on sleeping with them herself, or maybe she figured she'd see if she could entice me too. She would have known that if she told me I wouldn't have been up for it, so perhaps she did it behind my back, arranged to meet them in the bar – which would explain the hurry to get there and why she walked straight over to their table and sat down so fast; it would also explain why Kate was almost inside Emanuel's pants just seconds after meeting him. Though it pains to admit it, it would go some way to explaining why Joaquim was so flirtatious with me. I was an idiot to think he actually thought I was attractive. My cheeks flame at what a fool I've been.

Honestly, it's a gut punch and one I have to try to ignore. Now is not exactly the time to get my feelings hurt over the fact a good-looking man only talked and flirted to me because he was being paid to do so.

We reach Konstandin's car, parked around a corner, illegally I note. He beeps the doors open and I get in before I realise that I'm starting to treat him like a chauffeur.

He gets in and immediately hops on his phone. If he's from Kosovo does that mean he fought in the war? Is he an ex-soldier? His hands are large and scarred and his face, now I study it, is the face of someone who looks like they've been through a lot. It's craggy, weathered and lined and something in his hooded dark eyes tells me he's seen some bad stuff.

I can't remember much about the Kosovo war – but I do remember watching the news when I was a teenager and hearing the most awful tales of mass killings. What side was Konstandin on and how old must he have been? If he's late forties now and the war was around twenty years ago, then around his late twenties?

'Here,' Konstandin says, handing me his phone.

I take it.

'Call,' he tells me.

I look down and see a number on the screen.

'It's Lotus Models,' he explains. 'I looked them up online. Call them, give them your friend's name. Pretend to be her. Ask if you can meet the same men again tonight.'

'But what if they did something to her?' I ask. 'What if they know what's happened to her? They'll know it's a trap.'

'So, tell them you want their names to give to a friend of yours. All you want is their names and a phone number.'

I nod and press dial, hoping that whoever picks up didn't speak to Kate and won't remember she doesn't have an Irish accent.

'Hello,' a woman's voice purrs when the call connects.

'Hi,' I say. 'How are you?'

'Good, how can I help you?'

I have no idea how this works. What am I meant to say

92

next? I panic and look at Konstandin who urges me on with a look.

'Are you calling to book a model?' the woman asks. She sounds like she might be Australian.

'Um, yes,' I say. I glance at Konstandin again and he nods encouragement. 'Actually,' I say, 'I'm wanting to book two models. I . . . um . . . enjoyed their company last night.' I wince at how hammy I sound.

'OK, do you remember their names?' the woman asks.

Damn. 'Um, actually I was really drunk and it's slipped my mind, but they were about thirty, one had green eyes, dark hair, the other guy was black, maybe North African?'

'Emanuel and Joaquim.'

'Yes! That's them!' I look at Konstandin, grinning, and see he's pulled out a scrap of paper from somewhere and a stubby pencil. He scribbles the names down. 'Is it possible to get a number for them?' I ask the woman on the end of the phone.

'I'm afraid you have to book directly through us. We don't share personal information.'

'Oh,' I say. What do I do? I can't book them. If they think I'm Kate they might get spooked and disappear. I could call back I suppose and pretend to be someone else.

'Would you like to make a booking?' the woman on the end of the phone prompts.

I panic again, and not knowing what else to do, I say, 'No, you're all right, I'll call back.' I hang up and look at Konstandin. 'I couldn't book,' I say. 'If they think I'm Kate they might not show. And she wouldn't give me their numbers.'

'We have their names,' he says. 'Maybe it's enough. Do you remember anything about them?'

I shake my head. 'I don't remember anything, that's the problem. I think they drugged me. Maybe even Kate. I don't know for sure.'

He scowls. 'Did they do anything to you?'

I shake my head, unable to hold his gaze. 'I don't think so.'

'Maybe they drugged you because they didn't want to go through with it. It's easier. They get paid for nothing, and in the morning can claim they had sex with you but you were too drunk to remember.'

'Thanks,' I say, unable to keep the annoyance out of my voice.

'I don't mean to be rude,' he says.

'It's fine. It's a possibility I suppose.'

Someone honks behind us, probably at his bad parking, so Konstandin starts the car and pulls out into traffic.

'Are you OK to drive me back to my apartment?' I ask, fishing around for the address.

'Sure,' he says. 'But have you eaten?'

I shake my head. 'No.' We're just passing a restaurant with candlelit tables on the street and a Fado band, and I stare longingly. I'm so hungry.

'There's a place I know,' Konstandin says. 'Good food.'

I glance over at him. 'OK,' I say, because it feels easier than having to figure it out on my own. As soon as I agree, though, I regret it. Isn't it a bit weird? He's a total stranger and I don't know him from Adam. Can I trust him? And why's he helping me?

The thought crosses my mind that maybe he has something to do with Kate going missing. What if he got mad at her for snorting coke in the back of his cab and hung around outside the bar until we came out? What if he followed us home? What if I'm sitting in a car with the person who abducted my friend? Terror seizes hold of me, gripping me tight so I can't draw breath. I glance at the door. It's not locked. I glance back at Konstandin. *Stop it*, I tell myself, *calm down*. He's helping you, that's all. And you couldn't have got this far without him.

He has his uses. I'm a stranger in a strange city; having someone who speaks the language and knows his way around could be useful.

I watch him switch on the radio to some obscure station and start singing along under his breath to some kind of Turkish or maybe Albanian pop song.

My phone buzzes and I pull it out of my pocket with the same desperate hope springing awake in me as earlier. But it's not Kate. It's Rob FaceTiming.

'Hi,' I say, answering.

'Where are you?' he asks.

'I'm in an . . . Uber,' I say, angling the camera lens away from Konstandin. I can't really explain to Rob why I'm driving around with someone I don't really know and that now I'm going to dinner with him. Rob would call me crazy and he'd probably be right too.

'Where are you going?' Rob asks. 'Are you with Kate? Did she show up? Was she shopping?'

'No,' I say. 'She's not shown up. I'm trying to look for her.'

'Did you go back to the bar?'

'Yes,' I say. 'They haven't seen her. She never went back there.'

There's silence on the end of the phone and silence in the car too – Konstandin must be listening. He's probably wondering why I'm not telling my husband about the clue we just found out, but how can I tell him that I went home with two male prostitutes last night and I can't actually remember what happened after that?

'Can I do anything?' Rob finally asks. 'Is there anyone I can call?'

I shake my head, tears stinging my eyes. I really wish he was here. He's always so good in a crisis, so calm. 'No. I don't think so. I'm going to wait until the morning and report her missing to the police if she still hasn't shown up.'

'God,' Rob whispers under his breath, as the seriousness finally hits him. 'I wonder where she is.'

'Me too.'

There's a beat then: 'Look, I'm sure she's fine,' he says, forcing a lighter tone into his voice. 'Don't worry.'

'Hard not to.'

'I know, but best not to go down that path. She'll be OK. I'm sure.'

I don't reply. The words get stuck in my throat like dry twigs, because *I'm* not sure. I'm not at all sure that she's OK. And it's impossible not to worry.

'Call me later, before you go to bed,' Rob says. 'Or anytime you need me. I'm right here.'

I choke down the lump in my throat. 'Thanks, darling, I will. And give Marlow a kiss for me.'

'I will. Love you,' Rob says.

'Love you too.'

I hang up. Konstandin glances at me. 'Your husband?'

I nod. 'His name's Rob. I've got a baby too. Marlow. She's nine months old and she's just got her first tooth.' Why am I telling him this? I don't know. I just feel enormously sad and depressed right now. I don't know what's happening and I miss my family. I don't want to be in a strange city with a strange man trying to look for my friend and trying, too, to ignore the increasing panic that's crawling through my veins. I want to be with Rob and Marlow, back home, where everything is familiar and everything is fine.

'You will get to see them soon,' Konstandin says.

'Yeah,' I mumble, blinking away a few tears. *Hold it together*, I warn myself.

Chapter Twelve

We're in a neighbourhood away from the hustle and bustle, somewhere I doubt tourists venture. There are several ethnic-looking shops selling fruit and veg and phone credit, I'm guessing from all the signage, and there are women in head-scarves and people of all nationalities going about their business. It reminds me of Hackney a bit.

Konstandin gestures down the street. 'Come,' he says, and strides off.

I follow him, irritated at the way he's giving me orders but also relieved that someone is making decisions for me when I feel incapable of doing so myself. And he is right. I do need to eat. Nothing has passed my lips since that custard tart earlier. Perhaps if I consume some calories my brain will kick into gear and I'll be able to formulate a plan. Right now I'm falling into a melancholic depression caused by tiredness and fuelled by a hangover, a lack of food and a general sense of hopelessness and despair. If I'm going to find Kate I need to pull myself out of this funk and get focused.

I need to find these two men – Joaquim and Emanuel. They must know where Kate is. Maybe she's even with them right now, on a massive drug-fuelled bender having sex. It's possible, I suppose. I try to imagine it, just because that image is a lot better than the other ones lining up for preview. If she is with them, I don't even think I'll be angry. I'll just sob with relief.

The restaurant Konstandin leads me into is Turkish. I surmise it from the pictures of pita bread, hummus and kebabs on the menu. The sight of the kebabs makes me immediately think of Kate and our early morning, giggle-filled walks back from whatever nightclub we'd been to that night, inevitably detouring past the kebab shop on our way home, where we'd wait in a line of other tired, drunk revellers to order our shish kebabs and where Kate would flirt with the guy carving the meat until he gave us extra chips.

I don't order kebabs today, I order falafel and Konstandin orders in what I assume is Turkish, talking to the waiter, who I think is also the owner. He's an older gentleman who seems deferential to Konstandin, taking both his hands in his own when we entered and kissing him on both cheeks. He waits on us with keen interest and lots of smiles in my direction and I wonder what Konstandin is telling him but focus on pulling out the scrap of paper and pencil from my bag so I can start to formulate a plan. I stare at their names – Joaquim and Emanuel. How could I have forgotten? Now I know their names, I remember them introducing themselves. 'How will we find them?' I mutter.

'Eat first, then we think,' Konstandin says.

I set the pencil down. 'Why are you helping me?' I ask.

Konstandin stares at me for a beat. 'Because you need help,' he answers finally.

I frown. He holds my gaze with his even, steady expression. His eyes are dark brown, almost black, and fine lines are etched around them like sunrays.

'Did you really threaten those people at the bar?' I ask seriously. 'Or were you joking? Be honest.'

He pauses again. 'I threatened them.'

I'm shocked even though I half-guessed it. 'Why?' I ask.

He shrugs again. 'I want to solve the mystery.'

'Why? She's not *your* friend.' He's a stranger. Why does he care about Kate going missing?

'She was in my car,' he says.

It seems like an odd reason and I'm about to press him on it further when the waiter appears with hummus and warm pita. Before he's even walked away I'm tearing off the bread and dunking it in the garlicky dip, then shoving it in my mouth. It's so good I swallow it whole and reach for more. Konstandin smiles, pushing the hummus closer. We eat for a few minutes in silence.

I study him as he eats, his gaze fixed on the food, the frown line rigid between his eyebrows. Am I being stupid? His reasoning seems off. It doesn't stack up. Strangers don't just help people like this. Is Konstandin really someone I can trust? What if my previous thought is right and he's involved somehow in Kate's disappearance? I stare at him. What if he's done something to her? He was looking at her funny in the car. I've read about killers – about how they like to return to the scene of the crime, ingratiate themselves with the cops – they get off on it, and they like to have one ear to the ground to find out where suspicions lie.

But what am I thinking? We're not talking about a killing. Kate's alive. She can't be dead. I shouldn't be thinking such thoughts.

But she has *disappeared*, the voice in my head points out. *And you don't know where she is.*

Konstandin looks up just then and catches me staring.

'You said you were from Kosovo,' I say, deciding to see if I can eke out a little more information on his background. 'You left in the war?'

'Yes,' he answers, a little gruffly, possibly suspiciously too.

'Was it . . . bad?' I ask, kicking myself for how stupid I sound. It was a bloody war, not a holiday. 'I mean,' I add hastily. 'Of course it was, otherwise you wouldn't have left.'

He smiles at that, though perhaps it's more a smirk. 'It was bad,' he says before turning his attention back to his plate.

'I'm sorry, you don't have to talk about it,' I say, feeling awkward. I shouldn't have brought it up.

'It's OK,' he says.

'Did you ever want to go home?' I ask.

'This is home now, I suppose,' he says, looking up at me, and I remember something from last night. I said the exact same words to him about London. I'm sure of it. It feels good to get a piece of last night back, even if the fragment isn't very useful; perhaps it signals that there are other memories lying in wait, ready to be retrieved.

'But it never really does feel like home, does it?' I say.

'No,' he agrees. 'The sun is never as warm as it is at home.' He glances at me. 'It's something we say in Albania.'

I smile. 'Do you still have family there?' I ask, trying to be subtle. I'm angling to find out if he's married or has kids. For some reason if he has got a family it will make me feel just a little bit more at ease about him.

'They're all dead,' he answers.

'Oh God,' I stammer. 'I'm sorry.'

'It was a long time ago. You weren't to know.'

'I'm sorry,' I say again. 'Did they die in the war?'

He nods and a small muscle pulses in his jaw.

'No wonder you don't want to go back.'

The rest of the food comes and we eat for the most part in

silence until finally Konstandin pushes aside his plate and pulls out his phone.

'What were their names again?' he asks. 'Joaquim and Emanuel?'

I nod, taking a final bite of my food before pushing my plate aside as well.

'What else do you remember about them?' he asks.

'Nothing,' I say. 'That's the problem.'

'What do you do?'

'Excuse me?' I ask, frowning in confusion.

'What do you do?' Konstandin repeats.

'You mean as a job?' I ask, confused as to what my job has to do with anything.

He nods.

'I work for a housing charity.'

'Did they tell you what they did for work?'

'Design.'

I inhale sharply. The answer came to me so quickly and out of the blue. 'How do I know that?' I whisper.

Konstandin shrugs. 'It's the question that people always ask in conversation. When we first met you asked me about how long I'd been an Uber driver.'

'You're right,' I say, a blurry memory coming back to me, of Joaquim and I sitting next to each other, talking in the bar. He looked so interested in what I had to say about my job. I remember feeling suspicious at the time because no one ever shows that much interest in my job, not even my mum.

'What kind of design?' he asks. 'Do you remember?'

I scour my memory, trying to retrieve another clue. 'I'm not sure. I think he said they were in business together though.'

Konstandin nods and pulls out his phone. He types something and then a few seconds later turns the screen to me. 'Is this them?'

'Oh my God,' I whisper as I stare astonished at the photo on his screen. 'Yes, that's them.'

I grab the phone and pull it closer to my face. It's Joaquim and Emanuel, dressed more casually than they were last night – in jeans and open-necked shirts. Emanuel is leaning against a desk with a computer on it and it looks like they're in an office. I zoom in on their faces. Yes, it's definitely them. I'm so relieved I almost laugh. It's ridiculous to admit it out loud but I was starting to believe that maybe I'd imagined them or dreamed it all. Seeing them makes me feel dizzily triumphant. We've found them.

'I typed in their names and the Portuguese word for design,' Konstandin tells me. 'They do graphics, logo design, branding that sort of thing it looks like.' Konstandin takes back the phone and taps on the page. 'But it doesn't seem like they have many clients. Here, see.' He shows me the screen. 'They mention a couple of small clients, a T-shirt company, a bar, nothing big. And I think maybe they just started the business this year. That's probably why they're also escorts. They need the money.'

He puts his phone to his ear.

'What are you doing?' I ask.

'Calling them.'

My eyes widen in alarm. Don't we need a strategy first? He can't just ask them where Kate is. What if they're the people who've done something to her? But before I can speak up one of them answers and Konstandin rattles off something in Portuguese, then hangs up.

'What just happened?' I ask.

'I left a voicemail for them. Told them I wanted a website designed. Asked them to call me back.'

'Right,' I say.

'When they do we'll arrange a time to meet them and we'll ask them about your friend.'

'What if they don't know what happened to her?' I whisper. We'll be back to square one.

'We have to start somewhere.'

'Maybe I should go back to the police and give them their names,' I say, looking at Konstandin for his thoughts.

Konstandin purses his lips. He doesn't say anything but I can tell just from his expression that he's not a fan of the police, which gives me pause. I ponder my options. The policeman, Nunes, certainly didn't seem too interested before when I mentioned Joaquim and Emanuel to him. And the police won't do anything tonight, no matter what new information I bring them. It makes sense to try and find out what I can before I go back there.

'What are their full names?' I ask, pointing at the website open on Konstandin's phone. 'Does it say?'

Konstandin shows me their names on the contact page. Emanuel Silvas and Joaquim Ruis.

'They must have social media.' I pull out my own phone and type the names into my phone.

I'm not wrong. I find Joaquim's feed first, in a matter of seconds. It's a shrine to narcissism. The entire feed is made up of professional headshots, selfies of him in Aviator sunglasses in various locations and pictures of him in his underwear, showing off his biceps and six-pack.

I glance at his most recent photograph. It's an image of him grinning to camera, wearing sunglasses and holding a glass of champagne. I click on it to see when it was posted. 'This was taken three hours ago,' I say, showing Konstandin.

'They were together.' Konstandin shows me his own phone. He's found Emanuel's Instagram. We set them side by side and compare. Emanuel has posted a picture of him with Joaquim. It's also from around three hours ago. They're on a rooftop somewhere. It looks like a bar and behind them I can make out the castle and the jumbled red rooftops of Alfama with the river in the background. Konstandin scrolls along to the next photo in the series. It's Joaquim with his arm around a woman. They're both smiling at the camera.

'Is that Kate?' Konstandin asks.

I grab the phone, my heart leaping as quickly as it sinks down in my chest. 'No,' I say, shaking my head. But who is she? She looks to be late twenties, dark-haired, tanned, attractive. From the intimacy of the photo I wonder if it's Joaquim's girlfriend? Or is it a client?

'He's tagged the name of the bar,' Konstandin says, pointing out the name. *La Giaconda.*

'Do you think they're still there?' I ask.

Konstandin checks the time. 'Maybe. It's a twenty-minute drive from here. Let's go and find out.'

He's already on his feet, pulling a battered wallet out of his back pocket and throwing money down on the table before I can reach inside my bag and get my purse.

'Please,' I argue, 'let me pay.'

He shoots me a look that teeters on the verge of being a scowl. 'No,' he says simply.

I want to argue some more with him but the owner of the restaurant comes over and offers a deferential goodbye to us. Konstandin is patient at first but then, after the owner doesn't appear to be letting go, extricates his hands from the man's grasp and ushers me quickly to the door.

'Thank you,' I say to the owner over my shoulder.

'See you again.' The owner waves.

As we head out onto the street, I glance at Konstandin out of the corner of my eye. He's lighting a cigarette while scanning the street.

'You're certainly popular,' I say, nodding my head back towards the restaurant.

Konstandin, who is drawing a lungful of smoke, stops to look at me sideways. 'We have a history,' he says, nodding at the restaurant owner, still standing in the door waving at us. He stalks off towards his car and I hurry after him wondering what that means.

'What kind of history?' I ask, curious.

Konstandin opens the car door for me. 'I helped him with something a few years ago. He tries to repay me every time I see him.' Konstandin shuts the door before I can ask any more questions.

As he walks around to the driver's side, I scan the inside of the car for clues as to Konstandin's life, my gaze flying over the interior and the back seats. Am I still suspicious of him? He definitely has a dark past and possibly a shady present. Surely if he meant me harm, though, he wouldn't have taken me out for falafel.

My instinct tells me not to be afraid of him. I've felt a sixth sense before – a worming gut feel, a voice in my head yelling at me to avoid someone or move to the front of the bus, and I don't hear it now – but I'd be lying if I said I wasn't curious about Konstandin and his reasons for helping me. In my experience people aren't that nice to strangers unless they want something from them.

I pull out my wallet and when he gets in the car I clear my throat. 'I really have to give you some money. It doesn't feel right you driving me around and paying for dinner.'

Konstandin starts the car. 'Put that away,' he says, without even looking at me.

'But aren't I stopping you from working? You could be driving right now, earning money, instead you're ferrying me around all over the place.'

He cuts me off. 'Please, let's not talk any more about money.'

Maybe I'm insulting him, being culturally insensitive. But

still, he can't be well off. He drives an Uber for goodness' sake. I decide not to press it for the moment. 'Thank you,' I murmur, shoving my wallet into my bag but only after I've taken fifty euro out of it. I'll leave it in the side of the door when I get out.

When we get to the bar Konstandin comes inside with me. Joaquim and Emanuel aren't there but one of the waitresses confirms that she served them earlier and that they were with the woman in the photograph. I show the waiters a photo of Kate but they shake their heads. She wasn't with them.

Dejected, we leave and start to walk back to the car. I stop in the middle of the street. Konstandin looks back at me.

'Do you think something bad has happened to her?' I ask, hearing the tremble in my voice.

He pauses for a long while. 'I don't know,' he finally says.

Chapter Thirteen

I walk through the empty apartment, unable to call Kate's name because I don't want to hear the silence that will follow it. Hysteria is trapped in my throat, wedged there, and I keep swallowing it down. I'm scared of letting it out because the voice in my head keeps telling me not to panic, ordering me to stay calm. Kate might need me. And if I let the hysteria take over I'll be no good for anything, I'll just curl into a ball and sob like a child. I need to stay focused and practical. What if Kate's in trouble and needs me? Isn't the most critical time after a person goes missing the first seventy-two hours?

Konstandin told me he'd call if he hears back from Joaquim or Emanuel. And he's going to pick me up first thing in the morning to take me back to the police station so I can make a formal missing person's report. Tomorrow morning feels like forever away.

I sit on the sofa in the living room and take out a pen and piece of paper from my bag. I need to make a list. It's something I do when I feel life getting out of my control. I make lists: at work, at home. I make lists of things to do, shopping I need to buy, presents I need to get, wish lists of places I'd like to visit, cities I'd like to go on weekend breaks to, budgets and goals I want to reach.

The blank page taunts me. What should I write that will help me feel less helpless and more in control in this particular situation? I remember one time I saw a doctor, when I was struggling with getting pregnant and feeling depressed and she told me to go and write down the very worst that could happen. The very worst that could happen was that I couldn't have a baby. Once I wrote that down and accepted it as a possibility it didn't seem quite so bad.

My hand moves across the page.

I stare at the words I've written and take a deep, shuddering breath in.

Kate is dead. It's impossible. She can't be dead. I refuse to go there.

Kate is kidnapped. I almost laugh at the idea.

Kate has been sold into sex trafficking. I almost laugh at this one too. It sounds like the plot of a Liam Neeson movie. And anyway, aren't sex trafficking victims always teenage girls? Or at least women who are vulnerable? Kate's as vulnerable as a lioness.

Kate has had an accident, been hit on the head and is in a coma somewhere. I've called the hospital though. No one has reported her injured.

Kate went out to buy more drugs and either a) is passed out somewhere b) overdosed and needs help c) got into some trouble with a drug deal gone wrong. I don't like to dig too deep into what c might look like as I only have movies to go on.

Kate decided she didn't want to be friends with me and has gone home. Did I say something to her that I don't remember? Did I upset her? Maybe in my drugged, drunken state the truth came out and I told her how I really felt about her becoming a mother. Shit. What if that's it? What if she's just gone to

108

another hotel, or gone back to England? But why would she leave her bags and all her things?

Kate went for brunch or went shopping because I was asleep and then met some guy and went home with him. It's a possibility and I choose to focus on that rather than the other possibilities on the list.

<u>What to do next?</u> I underline this and then wait, pen hovering over paper, for inspiration to strike. I already know that I'm going to the police station in the morning to speak to Detective Nunes. There's not much I can do until then. I could contact people Kate knows, people back in England, to see if they've heard from her, I suppose. If I did piss her off without my knowledge, maybe she has left me to it and maybe one of them might have been in touch with her.

I log into Facebook and check my messages in case I've missed something from Kate but I haven't, and I check her Facebook page too to see if she's posted anything. She hasn't posted anything since the picture we took of the two of us just before boarding the plane on Friday. We're smiling, both so unsuspecting of what is just up ahead. I quickly turn back to my own page and spend twenty minutes trying to write a post that walks the line between sounding an alarm and not setting off a panic.

Hi everyone. I'm in Lisbon with Kate but haven't seen or heard from her since last night. I've been trying to get in touch with her to find out where she is but I think she might be out of juice on her phone. If anyone's had any contact with her today could you let me know. Thanks!

I post it on her page and my own. It's probably pointless. How will anyone in London know where she is? But it's something proactive at least. It's only then it occurs to me that I should call Toby. They might be exes but they're not yet divorced. I don't have his number but I do have his email, so I fire off a quick message to him, asking him if he's heard from Kate today and to please call me as soon as he can.

Then, in the spirit of keeping busy, I walk into Kate's room, deciding to go through her things. I didn't want to invade her privacy before but now that seems stupid. What if there's a valuable clue I've missed? For a minute I stand in the doorway of her room and take in the scene, trying to imagine what went on in here, but I'm not a detective and I don't know what on earth I'm looking for.

I start by picking up all her clothes and piling them on the chair, going through pockets and shaking them out. I'm not sure what I'm looking for but it seems like it's something I should be doing. One time I took a team from work to an escape room and it reminds me of that. The clues were hidden in places, sometimes right in front of our faces, but we had to search the room thoroughly to find the clue that would take us to the next clue and then the next. I feel like I'm doing that now, finding one clue that will lead me to the next and to the next and finally, hopefully, to her. But I don't find a thing.

On my knees I study the rust-coloured stain on the floor. Is it blood or wine? I sniff it but it's hard to tell if it's the tang of blood or the bitterness of tannins. There's some comfort to be drawn from the fact that if it *is* blood there's not a great deal of it. It's not great arterial sprays, more like the amount you might get from slicing your finger with broken glass.

After I've piled her clothes on the chair I move to her suitcase. It's only half full as most of her things are scattered around the room, but I find a net bag filled with underwear. I search through it, feeling uneasy. It's all scanty lace bras and thongs. Personally, I stopped wearing dental floss underwear in my twenties, and every year since my knickers seem to get bigger and bigger so now I'm wearing boy shorts a lot and even caught myself perusing the granny pant section of M&S the other day before I hurried over to the three-for-two boy shorts.

Kate doesn't have any garden-variety underwear. It's all proper lingerie, including a couple of items from Agent Provocateur. I think I own one set of lingerie – the one Rob gave me for Valentine's Day – and though I wear the bra I don't ever wear the knickers, as they have a gaping hole in the crotch, which is thoroughly impractical. Rob pointed out the hole made them very practical for the use for which they were intended. I laughed at him in reply and never wore them beyond that one night. I mean, Jesus, what woman alive wants crotchless knickers? As useful as shoes with no soles.

I shove all the lingerie back in the bag and, flustered, search the bathroom, sorting through the bottles and serums and make-up, remembering how we got ready last night, how much we giggled and laughed. Before I can stop it, a tear slides down my cheek. I swipe at it, blinking hard to stop more from falling.

There's a bottle of perfume on the shelf, and a washbag containing tampons and panty liners and a bottle of Ibuprofen. I empty out the tampons and find a small round tin, a bit like the pillbox from last night. This one originally held breath mints but when I open it I find it's full of small white pills and a bag of white powder.

I dip my little finger in the powder and touch my tongue very slightly to it. I think it's coke but I'm not sure – it's been years since I had any. And it's strong too. Maybe it's been cut with something else. My head spins even from that very slight amount. The pills could be anything but I'm fairly sure they're ecstasy. I'm not about to try one to find out though. The sight of all these class As makes me realise that Kate can't have gone out last night to find more drugs. She's got enough to start her own pharmacy right here, and that's not even counting the stuff she had in her other pillbox, the one she had on her.

It makes me feel somewhat better I suppose. At least I can discount the theory about her getting involved in a drug deal gone wrong.

Detective work is all about a process of elimination and so it feels like I'm making some progress. So far I've discovered Kate probably hired escorts, she didn't leave the house to buy drugs, and that she has her handbag with her. It's not a lot, but it's something to go on, something to tell the police tomorrow.

My phone beeps from my bedroom and I run to get it. I've got a missed call and a voicemail from a number I don't recognise. My hopes rise but are quickly dashed when I hear Toby's terse, annoyed voice on my voicemail. 'I haven't heard from Kate but if you're with her can you tell her to call me. I've got a credit card bill I want to discuss with her.'

So much for that, I think to myself.

I check Facebook. There are a few comments responding to my post about Kate being missing – all of the 'Oh no, hope she shows up', or the 'Kate's probably gone shopping!' variety. Rob's texted too, asking what's going on and if I'm OK. I text back to tell him that I'm at the apartment and Kate still hasn't shown up and that I'm going to the police in the morning.

'Call me when you wake up,' he says. 'Love you.'

'I wish you were here,' I reply.

He sends me a heart emoji back. I crawl under the covers in my clothes, clutching my phone. My bare foot brushes something. I throw back the covers and reach to pick up a piece of shiny foil beside my leg. My hand shakes as I bring it close to study it. It's an empty condom wrapper.

I leap out of bed. What in God's name . . .?

Next thing I know I'm leaning over the toilet throwing up what I ate for dinner. When I'm done I lean back on my haunches. Jittery and sweating, I stare at the crumpled condom wrapper on the side by the sink and retch again.

Chapter Fourteen

Sunday

I don't sleep. Or at least I sleep fitfully, barely grazing the surface of dreams. My imagination keeps fetching up hideous images of what's happened to Kate. I see her lying dead in a coffin. I see her trapped in an underground cave. I see her tied up in an attic or a basement. I basically see her in a million different scenarios taken from every movie, book, true crime podcast or news report I've ever read that has made me shudder about the violence and horror and evil in the world. And when I'm not thinking about awful things like that I'm thinking of myself lying unconscious in this bed being raped. I've tried to tell myself that it didn't happen, it can't be true, because I would know, surely? But a seed of worry has been planted and it keeps on growing.

At three in the morning I give up on sleep and get up and make some coffee, stupidly forgetting and washing up the glass with the powdery substance in the bottom. There goes whatever evidence that might have been.

I check the details for the British embassy online and find the number of the British newspaper in Lisbon too. I make a plan to call both once they open. I need to do more than just go to the police, I decide. I worry the police aren't going to do anything – not after the lackadaisical response yesterday – so I need a back-up plan. I also need help. Maybe Rob can ask his mum to look after Marlow and he can come over here to be with me. I need to tell him everything about that night but I can't do it over the phone. I need to do it face to face. And I just need him here. He'd know what to do.

As soon as it's six o'clock and the sun has risen I call him. He's asleep but picks up straightaway.

'Can you come?' I ask, barely holding back tears.

'To Lisbon?' he answers, blearily, his dark hair sticking up all over the place. 'I've got work tomorrow,' he says. 'And you're meant to be coming home tonight.'

Damn. He's right. It's Sunday. 'But I can't come home. Not without Kate,' I say. 'I have to find her.'

'Are you still going to the police?' he asks, yawning.

'Of course,' I snap, tiredly. 'She's been missing for over a day. I'm really worried, Rob.' The sob bursts out of me, everything too much. 'Something's wrong. I can just tell.'

He doesn't answer. I watch him sit up and rub his eyes. 'It's going to be OK,' he says. I wonder if I should tell him now about the escorts, about the drugs, about my fears about what happened to me, but before I can decide I hear Marlow in the background starting to cry. Rob sighs. 'The boss is awake,' he says. 'I need to go.'

'OK,' I say. Shit. I can't keep putting it off.

'Call me when you've been to the police. Let me know what they say.'

I nod. When I hang up there's a message from Konstandin asking me what time I want to go to the police station. I text him back to say as soon as it opens at eight.

There's something comforting about not doing all this alone. It's why I wanted Rob here. 'Konstandin is my stand-in,'

114

I mumble, then half-laugh. It's the kind of joke that Kate would make.

In the thirty minutes before Konstandin arrives I jump in the shower and drink more coffee – trying to wake up my sluggish mind. As I grab my phone from the side I remember to check Joaquim and Emanuel's Instagram to see if they've posted anything since last night, something that might either reveal where they are, or by some miracle show them hanging out with Kate, but neither one has posted since yesterday.

By eight o'clock we're parked outside the police station. Konstandin asks if I want him to come in with me but I say no. It feels weird, like they might wonder or ask questions about our relationship and question who Konstandin is, and I don't know how to explain it so I tell him he doesn't need to wait for me but he shrugs me off and pulls out his cigarette packet. I stare at it longingly for a moment and he offers me one. I shake my head and walk inside.

The detective I spoke to yesterday, Nunes, isn't in so I end up telling the whole story to another person, an older woman, also a detective. The sign on her desk says *Reza*. She's about my age I'm guessing, though possibly younger – it's hard to tell. She isn't wearing any make-up, except for a bright red slash of lipstick that only seems to emphasise how thin her lips are, and her hair is pulled back into a knot at the nape of her neck. Overall the effect is severe. She isn't wearing a uniform but an ill-fitting black suit.

Now I watch, frustrated, as she carefully and slowly fills in the missing person form. When she's done she tells me she'll circulate the information to all the hospitals and every police officer in the city so they know to keep an eye out for her.

'That's it?' I ask her when she puts down her pen.

'Was your friend depressed or having suicidal thoughts?'

'What?' I say, aghast. 'No, of course not. She was totally fine.'

115

Why is she asking me that? 'What about the men who came back with us to the apartment?' I press, frustrated. 'Don't you want to interview them? I gave you their names. You could call them.'

'We'll look into it,' she says, her English fluent.

'What does that mean?' I ask, frustrated. Why isn't she taking this seriously? It's a missing person!

I wonder if I should mention the fact Joaquim and Emanuel are escorts. The thing is I'm not sure prostitution is legal in Portugal and I'm pretty certain that solicitation isn't. It's the same reason I don't mention the drugs either. I know as soon as I do the police will make an assumption about Kate. It looks bad on paper and it might make them less inclined to prioritise her case. I know how these things work. But I'll be lying if I also keep it to myself, as I don't want them to search the apartment and find her stash of coke. I should have flushed it down the toilet. I don't repeat my concerns either about potentially having been drugged and raped. There's no way I can prove any of it and the detective yesterday seemed so dismissive it puts me off telling this woman. I feel like all I am is a nuisance to them.

'I said we will look into it,' she replies calmly.

I'm not sure I believe her.

'Your colleague, Detective Nunes, he told me yesterday he would check the hospitals. Do you know if he did?'

She frowns and taps at the computer. 'You spoke to Detective Nunes?'

I nod. 'Yes.'

Reza scans the computer. 'But you didn't file a report with him?'

'He said I needed to wait twenty-four hours to file a missing person's report.'

She nods.

'But do you know if he called the hospitals?' I press.

'I'll find out,' she says.

Reza stands up and I wonder if she's going to do that right then but no, she ushers me to the door, a sign that she's done with me.

'But . . .' I stammer as I get to my feet. 'Something's happened to her.'

'How do you know?' she asks, staring at me as though I know something that I'm not revealing. I struggle to look innocent. 'Did you have a fight before she disappeared? Is there something you aren't telling me?'

My cheeks flame. I shake my head.

She narrows her eyes at me. My pulse speeds up and a cold sweat breaks out all over my body. At the same time a memory that's as sharp as a blade slices through my mind. Kate screaming 'bitch!'

It hits me with the force of flying shrapnel, almost knocking me backwards. I can't picture it. I can only hear her voice screaming it at me. When though? And why can't I see it?

The detective is still staring at me, suspicious.

'I just know something's happened,' I say, my voice shaking. 'She isn't the kind of person to disappear like this. Not unless something really bad has happened.'

Reza sighs. 'Do you know how many people go missing each year?'

I shake my head.

'Ten thousand people. Just in Europe.'

'Wow,' I mumble. How is that possible? Where do they all go?

'And eight hundred thousand children go missing every year. Total.'

My jaw drops open. That's a truly astonishing number. 'I had no idea,' I mumble.

She points at a board behind me on the wall of the waiting

area. One side is covered in missing posters. I walk over to it. There are dozens and dozens of posters. I scan all the faces – mostly teenagers and young women. Where are they all? Where do they go? Are they dead? Are they runaways? Have they been trafficked? How can this many people just vanish into thin air?

Reza comes up behind me. She reaches past and tacks up another poster. I glance at it. The photo I emailed five minutes ago of Kate fills half the page and her name is printed underneath, along with her height and a description. A lump rises up my throat as I stare at Kate's smiling face. It's so surreal.

'Is that all you're going to do?' I ask.

The woman looks at me, not unkindly, but a little wearily. 'We will circulate her description. It's all we can do. You said she has her phone and bag with her. Probably her passport also. She possibly has left the country by now, rented a car or left by train. She could be anywhere in Europe. If she tries to leave, the country border police will know. They'll tell us. And if we hear anything we will let you know. Likewise, let us know if you find her.'

If. If. 'But she left all her things,' I protest. 'Her suitcase. Her clothes. Why would she leave her stuff?'

'OK,' she says, 'I'll look into those two men.'

'Good,' I say, feeling a rush of relief. 'Please call me if you find anything out.'

She nods but I'm uncertain if she's saying this to get me to go away or if she really is going to take it seriously and look into Kate's disappearance.

Shaken, I head outside to find Konstandin still smoking. 'I need a cigarette,' I say to him.

Wordlessly he hands me one and lights it for me.

'They aren't doing anything,' I tell him, taking a huge inhalation

118

of smoke. Instantly my head spins and I feel like I'm going to throw up.

'What do you mean?' Konstandin asks.

'They just added her picture to a wall,' I say. 'But there are dozens, hundreds of missing people. They treated me like I was making a big drama. As though she's decided to run away from her life, as though her going missing isn't a big deal.' I'm pacing up and down, drawing on the cigarette as though it's feeding me life.

'It isn't a big deal for them,' Konstandin says. 'They won't care unless there's a body.'

'What?' I say, almost dropping my cigarette.

He shrugs, his expression cool. 'She's an adult. There's no evidence she's been hurt. She wasn't depressed or mentally ill. Unless the police have an actual crime to investigate they won't look for her.'

I shake my head, refusing to believe it. 'How?' I splutter. 'How can they not care?'

Konstandin shrugs again. 'Come,' he says. 'We have an appointment.'

'What? Where?' I ask him.

'Emanuel called back. I'm meeting him for coffee in forty minutes' time.'

Chapter Fifteen

Joaquim and Emanuel walk in, dressed casually, both wearing sunglasses, and my breath catches in my chest as though someone is twisting a corkscrew into the gap between my ribs. Seeing them in the flesh brings memories swimming to the surface: Joaquim putting me to bed, sliding off my shoes, his fingers brushing the back of my neck. As though I can feel the ghost of his hand still pressing there, a shiver runs down my spine. I thought I'd managed to convince myself that nothing happened between us but seeing him brings all the doubt and anxiety flooding back.

They don't notice me when they walk in as I'm lurking at a corner table, holding the menu up to obscure my face. I peek over the top of it and watch Konstandin stand and wave them over. They shake hands with him, both of them smiling and chatty, trying to impress someone they assume is a potential new client.

Konstandin told them he wanted a website to promote a wholesale import business selling olives and olive oil. They must be really desperate to get their design business off the ground if they fell for it and are showing up so eager.

Konstandin and I figured that if we waited until they sat down we'd have a better chance of them not bolting. Not that we know what their reaction will be when they see me and realise they've been duped.

As I stand up I notice my legs are wobbly. I walk over and stop behind Joaquim's chair where, unsure how to go about it, I start by clearing my throat. 'Hi,' I hear myself say.

Joaquim turns with a smile on his face that quickly vanishes the moment he recognises me. His eyes widen with alarm and he says something under his breath, maybe a curse word. I glance across the table at Emanuel who takes a slightly longer beat to recognise me but then his mouth falls open too. They glance across the table at each other and then before I can get another word out they're both on their feet and sprinting for the door, shoving a waiter out the way in their haste to reach it.

Konstandin jumps up a split second later and runs after them, but I'm frozen in astonishment, unable to move as all three of them race out the door and onto the street, leaving behind a café full of bewildered, gasping customers. Some start looking my way and their curious looks spur me finally into action. I dash for the door, heart thumping hard. They ran! That means they must know something or they've done something. That's not what innocent people would do.

When I emerge onto the street I catch sight of Konstandin turning the corner up ahead. I run after him. We're in a quiet, leafy neighbourhood, deliberately having chosen a place to meet where if they did see me and run they wouldn't be able to vanish into crowds. Turns out it was a good idea. When I turn the corner Konstandin is darting across the road, jumping the tram lines embedded in the street, and chasing after Joaquim, who has bolted into a park. Emanuel must have taken off in another direction and Konstandin has chosen to

121

stick with Joaquim. I run after them across the road, almost getting taken out by a passing tram, and run into the park behind them.

It's similar to one of the parks in squares in London; a cross-hatch of paved paths, wrought-iron railings and benches sitting among patches and triangles of green. I see Konstandin up ahead closing in on Joaquim, who has disappeared behind a shed-like structure close to a fountain. Most people are too lost in their phones to notice us running by.

Behind the shed I pull up short. Konstandin is on top of Joaquim, pinning him to the ground. Joaquim's face is squashed into the dirt and Konstandin has his knee pressed firmly into the middle of his back while his hand grips Joaquim's collar. Joaquim struggles like a fish out of water, squirming and trying to buck Konstandin off him, but Konstandin isn't letting go. Joaquim only stills when he looks up and sees me.

'You remember her, then?' Konstandin says to him.

Joaquim grunts a response.

'We need you to answer a few questions,' Konstandin says to him, then looks at me.

'I think we should call the police,' I pant, out of breath from running and sweating rivers.

'Don't call the police!' Joaquim shouts hoarsely and I notice there's blood on his chin from where he's struck gravel or something sharp.

'We don't need the police,' Konstandin says to me. 'Ask him about your friend.' He glowers at me and I realise that calling the police could get Konstandin into trouble. Joaquim could accuse him of attacking him and he wouldn't be far off.

Joaquim starts to struggle again, shouting something in Portuguese, and I look around, worried that someone will hear, but behind the shed we're relatively sheltered by bushes.

Still, we don't have much time. Someone could easily come upon us, think we're mugging him, and call the police.

'Where's Kate?' I demand.

'I don't know,' Joaquim says. He looks genuinely confused by the question and it surprises me.

'Why did you run then?' Konstandin asks, shaking him by the scruff of his neck.

Joaquim doesn't answer.

'What did you do to her?' I hear myself ask, thinking of the maybe bloodstain on the floor of her room.

Joaquim struggles to turn his head to look at me, with his cheek still pressed hard to the ground. 'Nothing,' he says through gritted teeth, his indignation shining through.

'Then why is she missing?'

'I told you, I don't know!'

'Why did I find blood in her room then?' I ask. 'And a broken glass?'

'She knocked over a glass of wine!'

Is he telling the truth?

'What happened that night?' I ask. 'I passed out. I don't remember anything. I woke up and Kate was gone. You're the last people who saw her.'

His expression alters, his indignation giving way to puzzlement. He frowns and shakes his head. 'I don't know,' he croaks. 'We left. I swear to God I don't know where she is!'

Konstandin's knuckles are white where he's gripping Joaquim by the collar, almost strangling him. He looks at me and I nod. He eases his grip.

'Don't try to run again,' he warns and then says something in husky Portuguese that makes Joaquim turn pale and stare at him with unchecked fear. I wonder if it's something about kidneys and rectums but this time I'm grateful because we can't have him disappearing on us, not now.

I take a deep breath and turn to Joaquim who is now sitting up, dusting off his trousers with a scowl. Konstandin hovers over him, one hand on his collar still, keeping him in place.

'Did you drug me?' I ask, my voice shaking.

Joaquim is wiping at the blood on his chin but double-takes at me. 'What?' he asks.

'Did you put something in my drink to make me pass out?'

'No,' he says, angrily spitting the words. 'You were drunk,' he tells me, scornfully.

'I was more than drunk,' I shoot back.

'Well, if you were drugged it wasn't by me,' he answers. 'I don't drug women.'

'Did we have sex?' I ask, trying to block Konstandin out. I can feel his eyes snapping to me and the humiliation is almost too much to bear but I need to know the answer.

Joaquim looks at me like I've punched him in the face. 'No,' he says. 'I don't have sex with drunk women.'

'So why was there a condom wrapper in my bed if we didn't have sex?'

Joaquim's mouth purses tightly. Konstandin's fist suddenly connects with Joaquim's temple, knocking him sideways. He lets out a cry of surprise and pain.

'Answer her,' Konstandin demands, bringing up his fist again and threatening him with it.

'She put it there,' Joaquim says, wincing and shooting an angry look at Konstandin.

'Who put it there?' I interrupt, not understanding what he means.

'Your friend,' he hisses, turning on me.

'Why?' I ask, so confused I wonder if he's understood the question correctly. 'Why would Kate do that?'

Joaquim shrugs. 'I don't know. Maybe she wanted you to think you'd had sex with me.'

'Why?' I ask, confusion battling with the almighty relief I feel that nothing actually did happen. I wasn't sexually assaulted without my knowledge.

'I don't know,' Joaquim growls. 'Ask her.'

'I can't!' I shout at him. 'She's missing. I've told you!'

'And I've told *you* I don't know where she is.'

I study him. Is he telling the truth? My gut says he is. His confusion and anger seem too intense to be fake.

'But she hired you?' Konstandin asks. 'You admit that?'

Joaquim scowls at Konstandin, then he nods. 'Yeah, she hired us.'

'To sleep with her?' I ask, still trying to wrap my head around the condom wrapper in my bed and why Kate would have put it there. The only reason would be if she wanted me to think I'd had sex, just as Joaquim suggested. But why on earth would she do that?

'She paid us to spend the night. Emanuel to have sex with her, and me with you, but like I said, you were too drunk.'

I grit my teeth in anger. 'Did she give you a reason why she hired you? Did she say anything at all?'

Joaquim shakes his head. 'No. She just said we were to come back to the apartment with her and a friend – that would be you – and have sex. Emanuel had sex with your friend.'

'How many times?' I ask, wanting to verify his account against what I know.

'Twice,' he says.

I nod, thinking of the two used condoms I found.

'Then we left.'

'What time did you leave?' I ask.

He shrugs, eyes downcast. 'About three I think. I don't remember.'

Konstandin slugs him in the jaw. I let out a startled cry.

125

'Not my face!' Joaquim shouts. 'Fuck!' He cradles his jaw, shoulders hunched.

'What are you doing?' I shout at Konstandin.

'He's lying,' Konstandin responds coolly. He turns back to Joaquim. 'I'm going to break your nose and ruin your pretty face unless you tell the truth.' He raises his fist again and Joaquim flinches. I almost yell at him to stop but then Joaquim holds up his hand to shield himself from the blow and sobs. 'Stop! OK. I'll tell you . . .'

Konstandin half-lowers his fist. I stare at him with my mouth open. How on earth did he know Joaquim was lying? I was about to let him go.

'What are you lying about?' Konstandin presses him.

Joaquim glances nervously at me then at Konstandin before deciding not to risk another hit to the face. 'Emanuel took your friend's bag,' he says to me.

I blink. 'Her handbag? You took Kate's bag?'

'Yes,' he nods. 'No. I mean, Emanuel did.'

I ignore the fact he's trying to protect himself by throwing his friend under the bus. They were obviously in on it together. I think back to what Sebastian the landlord said, about hearing people running down the stairs. That must have been them, running off with Kate's handbag!

'We need to call the police,' I say, turning to Konstandin. There's no argument to be had anymore. They stole Kate's handbag. Joaquim just admitted it. That's a crime. He needs to be arrested.

'No! No police!' Joaquim shouts, raising his arms as though in surrender. 'Please.'

Konstandin gives that one-shouldered, on-the-fence shrug of his, by which I can tell he agrees with Joaquim about involving the police. But it's not their choice. Kate's *my* friend. It's my decision. I pull out my phone. Konstandin lets Joaquim go and steps away, distancing himself from his handiwork, the

126

result of which is blooming across Joaquim's face. His jaw is already turning a deep red colour from the bruise. I realise if I call the police Konstandin will leave to avoid any questions, and a part of me does regret it, but this is now a police matter. I have to involve them.

'Please don't call the police,' Joaquim pleads again.

'Give me the bag back and I won't,' I say. I'm lying. I'm calling the bloody police.

Joaquim glances nervously up at Konstandin, who is standing over him like a grizzly bear, claws extended.

'Do you still have it?' I ask Joaquim.

He nods. 'It's for sale. On eBay. But we still have it.'

'What about all the things that were inside it?' Konstandin asks. 'Her wallet?'

Joaquim shakes his head, eyes lowered. He must have spent all her cash.

'What about her ID and all her cards?'

'We threw them away,' Joaquim mumbles.

'And the phone?' I ask, thinking of the hundreds of calls I've made to it in the last two days. 'What about her phone?'

Joaquim touches his fingertips to the swelling on his jaw, presses gingerly. 'We sold that,' he finally admits.

I stagger backwards a few steps, sucking in air, my hands on my hips, bent over like an old lady climbing stairs. It's suddenly occurred to me that if Kate hasn't had her phone on her, or her wallet or any ID, she can't have gone anywhere. The police thought she'd maybe got on a plane or a train or hired a car, that she'd decided to leave – never mind the fact she left behind all her clothes. I hadn't really thought they were right but I guess I was clinging on to the hope that maybe, just maybe, they were and she was off doing her own thing. But without her wallet, without cash or credit cards, passport, or her phone, where would she go? What could she possibly be doing?

Chapter Sixteen

Twenty minutes later I'm in possession of Kate's Birkin bag. Joaquim called Emanuel and told him to bring it to the park. We waited and did an exchange – Joaquim for the bag. I rummage through it now as we walk back towards Konstandin's car, scratching at the lining, trying to find something I might have missed – a clue, a piece of paper with the entire mystery laid out on it, a phone number perhaps? But this isn't an Agatha Christie novel. The bag is empty.

'Do you believe him?' I ask Konstandin when we're back in the car. 'That he doesn't know where Kate is?'

'Yes,' he says, turning the keys in the ignition. I notice the scrape on his knuckles and wonder what else those hands have done. He doesn't seem to be a stranger to violence and I ask myself again what I am doing driving around with someone who I know almost nothing about except that he's very good at extracting information from people and also at casual violence.

'How did you know he was lying?' I ask, wiping the sweat off my brow. I'm still hot from the running and from the confrontation with Joaquim.

Konstandin turns up the air conditioning and pulls out into

traffic. 'I can tell,' he says. 'When you are around liars and have to make decisions about who to trust – decisions that might lead to your death – you learn how to read people very fast.'

He must be talking about his family and the war.

'What happened to you?' I ask, bluntly and without thinking. 'I'm sorry,' I say quickly. 'It's none of my business.'

'It's OK,' he reassures me, reaching for his pack of cigarettes. He offers me one and I take it. I'm too old to be smoking and I have a baby to think about but I can already feel the nicotine cravings kicking in from the one I smoked earlier. I'll live to regret it I'm sure but right now I think I deserve a free pass. Something terrible has happened to Kate. The thought keeps spinning around my head, like a horse broken out of a stable. I can't seem to catch it or rein it in.

'She's dead,' I say, blurting it out before I have time to catch myself. I cover my mouth with my hand.

Konstandin doesn't say anything or try to argue with me, which only makes my words sink further into me, dragging with them a sense of doom.

He winds the window down and blows smoke out the car before inhaling again, short and sharp like his lungs are demanding he fill them with tobacco smoke, not oxygen. 'We don't know that,' he says, exhaling for a second time.

I bite my lips together. I know Konstandin is only telling me that to reassure me. He thinks she's dead too. I light the cigarette I'm holding and take a deep drag. My hand is trembling slightly. I wind the window down and exhale. 'I need to go to the police. Tell them what we just found out.'

Konstandin nods. 'Yes. After we get the phone I can drop you back at the police station,' Konstandin says.

'Thanks,' I murmur. That woman detective might be there by then. I can speak to her. I'll have to tell them about Joaquim and what we found out about the stolen bag, and I'll need to admit to them too what I've discovered about Kate hiring Joaquim and Emanuel for sex. I wonder if I can avoid telling them about Konstandin? I don't want to get him into trouble. But everything needs to come out now. If they interview Joaquim they'll find out about him anyway.

'I won't tell them your name,' I say. 'I'll just say you're an Uber driver.'

He grunts under his breath and I'm not sure if he's agreeing or disagreeing with me.

'I really appreciate everything,' I say to Konstandin. 'Not just the driving me around.'

He grunts again. He knows I'm talking about his interrogation technique. Yesterday I'd been horrified by the idea of him threatening people but now I'm glad of it. I wouldn't have found out this much without him. And I doubt the police would have either, or not this fast. And I'd also be lying if I said that watching Konstandin punch Joaquim in the face wasn't intensely satisfying.

We drive in silence for a few minutes. I'm not sure how getting Kate's phone from the pawn shop where Joaquim sold it is going to help us locate her, and I wonder if we should go straight to the police or whether I should be working through the list of things to do, like also calling the British Embassy and the English newspaper, but we're almost at the pawn shop so I decide to wait.

Having Kate's phone will be useful when I go back to the police. It'll prove something has happened to her. They won't be able to fob me off so easily if I can show them she doesn't have her phone or her bag or her wallet with her. They'll have to start taking the case more seriously.

As we drive I check my phone. Rob has sent a few messages asking how I am and for news so I text back, telling him I'm OK and will call him later. I miss him and Marlow so much that my throat constricts painfully, trying to suppress the sob when I think of them. My whole body aches to hold my child and feel her soft, pliable limbs against my chest, her sticky hot mouth on my cheek. I want to hold her and I want Rob to hold me and I don't want to be away from them a second longer.

I'll wait until I'm out of the car to call Rob back, because when I talk to him I'm going to have to come clean about the whole thing and I don't want to do that with Konstandin sitting beside me, listening in. It's then that I suddenly realise I should call Kate's mum too. I should have called her already in fact. It's terrible that I haven't. I know she and Kate aren't close but she is her daughter and she needs to know what's happening. I don't have her number, and have only met her a few times, the last time being Kate's wedding, so I'll have to ring Toby to get it.

I scroll through my missed calls for his number then hit dial. He doesn't pick up so I leave a message. 'Toby, it's me, Orla. I really need to talk to you. It's about Kate. She's still missing. And . . . I . . . well call me back. It's important,' I add. 'I need her mum's number.'

After hanging up I check my social media but hesitate about uploading any messages to Facebook or Twitter about Kate still being missing. I should tell her friends and family first what's going on.

I sit with the phone clutched in my hand, my foot tapping, drawing on the last of the cigarette like a prisoner in the final minutes before execution. I feel like I should be doing more, like I should be out on the street, pounding the pavement trying to look for her, calling her name, posting all over social media, getting local news involved. I should be printing up posters and knocking on doors. There's so much I need to do but my brain is fried.

The level of anxiety hasn't eased off now I know for sure that Joaquim didn't touch me, it's only increased. Because another thought has now arisen to take its place. If he didn't drug me, then who did? If that powder in the glass was a drug of some sort, then the only person who could have put it there was Kate.

But what if I'm wrong and I wasn't drugged? What if I was just drunk? I'm back to turning in circles, getting dizzier with each spin. There are so many what ifs and unknowns.

'I was studying to be a doctor when war broke out,' Konstandin says, making me look up in surprise, and also confusion because it's come out of nowhere.

'A doctor?' I ask, stubbing out my cigarette.

'Yes, does that surprise you?' he asks.

'No,' I answer. 'I mean, a little.'

I think about his fist connecting with Joaquim's face. It doesn't seem very doctorly behaviour. Also, he's built like a prize fighter, solid and muscly, with a five-o'clock shadow that's more salt than pepper.

'I never got to take my final exam. But it's what I wanted to be. Came very close. And when the war started and the hospitals were overflowing I worked anyway, to do what I could to help out. There weren't enough actual doctors left you see.'

I nod, not sure what to say. I barely remember the facts about the Kosovo war. I know it was Serbs versus Albanian Kosovars and that horrific war crimes were carried out, mainly against the Kosovars, but that's all.

'Most men from my village had either run away or been killed.'

A wave of sickness washes over me. 'You stayed,' I say.

He nods. 'Yes. My family was there. My parents were too old to leave. My father was bed bound. My mother refused to leave him or her home. And we thought we were safe. It

133

was a small village, a place called Obrinje, and the fighting was miles away.'

'What happened?' I ask quietly.

'I got married.'

I look at him, surprised. He's never mentioned his wife and he doesn't wear a ring.

'She was a doctor,' he says. I note the past tense. 'Her name was Milla.'

I wait for him to continue, not wanting to interrupt his flow. This is the most I've heard him talk about himself since we met and listening to him, however hard it is, is helping me forget for a brief moment about my own problems.

'On our wedding day,' he says, 'we had a feast. The whole village, whoever was left, which wasn't many, came. The Kosovan army had been fighting the Serbian army about ten miles north of us but we wanted to get married, needed to. Milla was pregnant.'

I stop breathing, hanging on to his every word now.

'We thought it was safe. There was a lull in the fighting. But we didn't know that the Kosovan army had killed ten Serbian officers the day before. The Kosovan soldiers fled and came towards Obrinje and the Serbian forces followed them. They wanted revenge. My brother and I rushed everyone into the ravine beneath our house, thinking that they would be safe – that if fighting broke out the women and children at least would not be harmed. My brother and I joined the Kosovan soldiers, trying to defend the house. But the Serbians, they found us, they overran the house, they killed the Kosovan soldiers. They killed my brother. They shot me twice and left me for dead. But I didn't die. I survived and after they were gone I managed to crawl to the ravine.'

He stops. I hold my breath waiting for him to continue.

'I had heard the screams. The gunfire. I already knew what I would find.'

'Oh my God,' I whisper under my breath.

'We thought the women and the children would be safer without the men there to endanger them but they killed everyone. Milla, my parents, my sister, everyone from the village who had come to the wedding. I had five nieces and nephews. All killed too. Thirty-six people in total, and my child too.'

I don't know what to say. How can anyone possibly live through that? It's a wonder he's still here, still breathing, still putting one foot in front of the other, because I don't know how I would if anything ever happened to Rob or to Marlow. I'd want to die. I definitely wouldn't have the courage to continue living. I sit there, feeling shell-shocked, trying to picture it and then trying to push the images out of my head because they're too awful.

I wonder what drove him to tell me – was it because he wanted to let me know that he understands loss? Was he trying to give me a sense of the kind of evil that there is in the world, to ready myself for what might come? Or perhaps was he trying to explain why he's been helping me all this time? Some sense of wanting to help save a person?

'I'm so sorry.' I put my hand on his arm, and let it stay there longer than perhaps I should, feeling a strange sense of connection to him.

He says nothing. After a while he reaches for his cigarettes and lights one and my hand falls away.

He looks at me. 'You remind me of my wife. You smile just like her.'

I wipe a tear before it can fall, understanding now why he told the story.

'She talked a lot too,' he says with a mournful smile.

I smile back.

'You wanted to know why I'm helping you,' he says. 'This is why.'

'Thank you,' I say, my mind still reeling from the story he just told me.

I look at him, seeing him in a whole new light. Konstandin's level coolness, his one-shouldered shrug and nonchalant expression take on a new dimension, as do the scored lines around his eyes that seem now to have been born from pain, not laughter.

'We're here,' Konstandin says. 'Do you want to stay in the car?'

I shake my head, looking out the window at a store in a derelict-looking row of shops. This is not the touristy part of town, but somewhere out towards the airport, where there are more high-rise apartment buildings. The shop has bars on the window and an array of electronic goods and jewellery on display. I can't read the sign but it's universally obvious that it's a pawnshop.

'I should come. I know what her phone looks like,' I say.

Konstandin nods and together we enter the store. There's a man in his early fifties with grey hair and a friendly, watchful smile standing at a counter behind thick bulletproof glass. Konstandin walks over to him. He leans an elbow on the counter and says something to the man in Portuguese and the man answers with a few words accompanied by a shrug, his friendly smile fading.

Konstandin looks at me. 'The man doesn't know what we're talking about but perhaps if you describe the phone it might jolt his memory.'

'It's an iPhone and the case was a pale pink. Two men brought it here yesterday. You gave them five hundred euro for it.'

The man studies me. Was that a flicker of recognition in his eyes?

'It was stolen,' I tell him.

'Nothing stolen here,' he grunts in heavily accented English.

'It's my friend's phone,' I say to the man. 'She's missing. We think she's in serious trouble.' I let the words sink in. 'We just want her phone back. If you let us have it I won't call the police.'

The man scowls at me, indignant at the suggestion he might be fencing a stolen phone, then looks at Konstandin who gives him a pleasant enough smile in return.

'I told you I no have it,' he says.

Damn. What if he's sold it? Or what if Joaquim was lying and they didn't bring it here? I look at Konstandin, not sure what to do next. Perhaps we should give up or let the police handle it. It's just her phone after all. It's not going to give us the answer to where Kate is, but Konstandin has other ideas. He leans forward, so his nose is almost touching the bulletproof divider and says something to the man in Portuguese. He could be asking about the weather from the tone of it but I watch the man's expression.

He inches back away from the glass, fear darkening his expression. It's a fascinating transformation and I wonder yet again what magical, dark powers of persuasion Konstandin has. The man is standing behind bulletproof glass after all. It's not like Konstandin can threaten him with violence.

He mutters something then disappears. Konstandin turns and smiles at me, totally casual in his manner. 'His memory has been jogged.'

'What did you say to him?' I ask but the man is back. And in his hand is Kate's phone. 'That's it!' I cry excitedly. 'That's her phone.'

'I no know it stolen,' the man mumbles, making to slide it through the hatch to me before stopping himself. 'No police, yes? It was mistake.'

I glower at him. There's no way he didn't know this phone was stolen, but I decide that getting the phone back is more important than arguing with him so I nod. He slides the phone through the hatch and I grab for it. It's a connection, however faint, to Kate. I press the home button but the phone's out of juice and won't turn on.

Konstandin and the man speak some more in Portuguese.

'I asked him if he wiped it,' Konstandin says. 'He says no. Not yet.'

'Good,' I say, worrying that it might not matter anyway if we don't have the password to access it.

'Let's go,' Konstandin says, slipping his hand under my elbow and moving me towards the door.

'What did you say to him?' I ask as we walk to the car. 'Before? When you were talking in Portuguese?'

'Nothing much,' Konstandin replies breezily.

'Did it involve the removal of body parts and their injection into small orifices?'

Konstandin smiles and opens the car door for me, but he doesn't answer.

'The police station?' Konstandin asks me once he's sitting behind the wheel.

I nod. 'Yes. Thanks.'

I root in my bag for my cash card, because I want to stop at an ATM on the way to get more cash. I'm going to insist on paying Konstandin for all this driving, but I come across a fifty-euro note. How did that get there? I look at Konstandin. Did he slip it back in my purse when I wasn't looking?

Fine if that's how he wants to play it. I'll just hide it better next time.

'Charge it,' Konstandin says.

'Huh?' I ask.

138

He nods at Kate's phone, which I'm still holding, and then at his charger cable.

I quickly plug the phone in and wait for it to power up. As I do my own phone buzzes in my bag and I pull it out, the familiar flame of hope igniting inside me before quickly fizzling out when I see it isn't Kate – of course it isn't Kate, I've got her bloody phone on my lap – but Toby.

'Hi,' I say, answering.

'Orla,' he replies, quite formally.

'You got my message?' I ask.

'Yes, she's still AWOL then,' he answers, seeming narked. I can picture him rolling his eyes on the other end of the phone.

'It's serious, Toby,' I tell him. 'Her handbag was stolen, and her phone and her wallet. I really think something's happened to her.'

A sigh from Toby. 'She's probably just gone to a spa for the weekend, or out on a bender, or maybe she's fucking some poor bloke who has no idea what hell he's in for later. But maybe, if I'm lucky, she can marry him and take him to the cleaners instead of me.'

'No,' I say, confused. 'She isn't at a spa. We're in Lisbon together. We're on a weekend away.' How does he not remember this? He spoke to her on the phone on Friday night. He was mad about the charges on his credit card. 'She's gone missing,' I tell him, saying it loud and clear in case he hasn't understood it.

'Have you been to the police?' he asks and I notice a slight hesitation in his voice. He's starting to wonder if maybe I'm not acting hysterical and that this might be serious.

'Yes,' I tell him. 'I was calling to get her mum's number. I think someone needs to call her and let her know.'

'Right,' Toby says. 'I can text you it.' Clearly he is dumping that responsibility on me.

'Thanks,' I say.

'Where did you last see her?' Toby asks.

I run a hand through my hair. 'We went out to a bar, after we had dinner—'

'What night was this? Last night?'

'No,' I say. 'Friday night. After you spoke to her—'

'What?' Toby interrupts. 'I didn't speak to her.'

'Yes, you did,' I argue. 'I was there. You rang her about the credit card.'

There's a pause on the end of the line then Toby speaks, his tone icy. 'Orla, I don't know what game Kate's playing but I don't have time for this . . .'

'What game? This isn't a game,' I say, stammering. 'I'm serious . . .'

'I haven't spoken to Kate in over a week,' Toby snaps. 'My solicitor told me not to have any contact with her.'

'But what about the credit card? She told me you had cut it off.'

'What credit card?'

I rub the deepening crease between my eyes, trying to understand what this all means. I remember Kate distinctly telling me that it was Toby on the phone – that he was angry about the spending and had cut off the card. It's one of the few non-patchy memories I have of the evening. She was busy texting in the cab before and I watched her outside the window of the restaurant pacing up and down, waving her arms about. When she came back to the table it looked like she'd been crying and she told me it was Toby. So, if she wasn't talking to him, who was she talking to?

'So, you didn't cancel the card on Friday?' I repeat.

'No! I didn't even know she was still on my cards? Damn it to hell, she's probably fucking spent enough to buy a small island.'

140

'And you didn't speak to her on Friday night, either?' I ask.

'No,' he exclaims impatiently. 'Look, are you sure this isn't some fucking drama-seeking, attention-grabbing plot that she's come up with? It seems like a typical bloody Kate thing to do. Trying to get me to notice, I'm guessing. Probably going for the sympathy vote so I'll take her back.'

I open my mouth to argue with him. As if she'd do all this just to get back at Toby or to muster sympathy. And what does he mean, *take her back*? She dumped him for being unfaithful. She couldn't have cared less about the break-up. At the same time though, Toby isn't wrong about Kate being an attention seeker.

But no! I shake my head. She wouldn't go this far. 'Of course it's not an attention-grabbing plot!' I protest. 'That's ridiculous! She wouldn't do this.'

I hear Toby laugh under his breath – it comes out as more of a snort really.

'What?' I snap back, infuriated at his attitude.

'You don't know her at all, do you?' he sneers.

'Of course, I do,' I exclaim. How dare he? I know her a lot better than he does. They got married after a three-month affair and have only been together a few years. I've known her almost twenty.

'I bet she told you all about it, didn't she?' he continues on. 'Everything I did to her, the shit I put her through, how terribly I treated her. I can just imagine the stories she told you.'

I don't say anything. I can't lie – she did tell me everything he put her through, and it wasn't pleasant.

'Did you ever stop to wonder whether any of it was true?' Toby asks.

'What are you saying?'

'Your friend's a lying bitch. And you fell for it. I feel sorry for you, Orla.'

141

Tears sting my eyes as though I've been slapped. 'How can you—?' I splutter but Toby cuts me off.

'I bet she's just fucking with you,' he says. 'Call me when she shows up. Or better yet, don't bother. I couldn't give two shits whether she's alive or dead. In fact, I hope she is dead, and rotting in a gutter somewhere. At least then she won't get her hands on money she doesn't deserve. And, if she does show up, well, remember that I warned you.'

With that he hangs up. I stare open-mouthed at the phone, wondering if I just imagined the conversation, but my ears are still ringing from his words.

'Everything OK?' Konstandin asks.

I shake my head, unable to answer.

'What did he say? He sounded angry.'

I nod. 'He thinks Kate's faking it.'

Konstandin double-takes at me while driving, not understanding.

'It was her ex-husband, Toby. He said I didn't know her at all. He told me she was a liar, that she'd lied to me about things.'

'What things?' Konstandin asks, frowning.

'I don't know. He didn't say.' What did he mean?

'Do you want to go in still?' Konstandin asks and I look around, confused, before seeing that he's pulled up and parked opposite the police station.

I blink at the low brick building. Shit. My head is all over the place. My heart's beating so fast it's as if I've taken speed. It's anxiety. I recognise the symptoms. My chest is tight and I'm finding it hard to breathe. I need a few moments to pull myself together. What am I going to tell the police? Toby's words keep dinging around my head like bullets, tearing all my previous suppositions to shreds. What if she has done this as an attention-seeking plot?

I'm so tired my brain isn't functioning right. How can I

believe Kate would do something like that? I look down at her phone, charging in my lap. It's got five per cent battery. I press the home button and the screen lights up. It asks me to input a passcode. Damn. Though honestly, what was I expecting?

I look at Konstandin. 'Do you think she is faking it?' I ask, slamming my mouth shut the moment I've asked it, ashamed of myself for voicing doubt. It's Toby's fault.

Konstandin's expression becomes very opaque. He sighs and turns to look out the front window of the car, his hand fumbling as usual for his cigarettes. He doesn't light one, just plays with the box. 'She already deceived you once. She hired those men, one of them to sleep with you. So, if you're asking me if she's capable of lying and faking something, then yes.'

He does have a point.

'Look,' he says. 'I don't know your friend. But I will tell you this: in my experience humans are more capable of deception than we give them credit for. Everyone lies all the time. The question would be why though? Why would she do all this? Why would she want to put you in this position?'

'I don't know.' Why did she lie to me about Toby calling? Who was she talking to outside the restaurant if it wasn't him? Who upset her so much she came back to the table in tears?

'And if the men didn't drug you, who did?' Konstandin asks. I shift uncomfortably. 'The barman?' I ask. 'A stranger? Maybe I wasn't even drugged. Maybe I was really drunk.' I press the heels of my hands over my eyes and stare into a dark void. It had already crossed my mind that it was Kate but hearing Konstandin say it too makes it all too obvious that it was her.

I hear her scream the word 'bitch!'

'You told me you were drugged,' Konstandin says, touching me lightly on the arm so I look up. 'I believe you.'

A sob rises up in my chest unexpectedly. 'You really think

143

Kate might have drugged me?' I ask, removing my hands and blinking away stars.

Konstandin takes a cigarette from the pack. He taps it against the dash before lighting it. 'Maybe,' he says, inhaling.

'But why would she do this?' I ask, my foot hitting the car door as my frustration leaps out of me.

'That's the big question. If you can work that out, maybe you can find out why she is missing and where she is.'

144

Chapter Seventeen

Before I go into the police station I call Rob, but he doesn't pick up so I leave a message, then I summon up the courage and call Kate's mother. It's strange to hear myself explain the situation to her. I can hear my positive reassurances that I'm doing all I can to find her daughter and will keep her updated, and I listen in wonder to how calm and how collected I sound. I don't tell her about the escorts or the drugs of course. All I tell her is that Kate's missing and that I've reported it to the police.

'Do I need to be there?' she asks.

I stammer, unsure what to say. In her shoes, if it were Marlow who was missing, I'd already be on my way to the airport. I wouldn't be asking anyone their opinion. There's not a stone I'd leave unturned to find her either.

'I think it might be a good idea,' I suggest. Partly because I don't want to be here on my own anymore. I need help with this.

'I'm getting my hair done,' she tells me, with a sigh. 'When I get home I suppose I'll look into flights.'

'Right,' I say, bewildered at the lack of emotional response to the news her daughter is missing, before remembering that Kate has always said her mother is a narcissist who only cares about herself.

'I'm about to go and talk to the police,' I say. 'I'll let you know what they say.'

'Is it really that serious?' she asks, finally seeming to realise the severity of what I'm telling her. 'Hasn't she just gone off somewhere? She's done this before you know. She ran away when she was sixteen. Didn't even leave a note, just vanished without a word. I didn't know where she'd gone until she called me a few days later to tell me she was in Ibiza. She had no care for how worried I was.'

A vague memory of Kate telling me this story comes back to me, with a few more hilarious anecdotes thrown in about how she'd stolen money from one of her mum's boyfriend's wallets to pay for her flight. She didn't tell me that she hadn't left a note telling her mum where she'd gone.

'I don't think it's like that,' I say but for the first time I hear that a note of uncertainty has crept into my voice. I was so convinced something terrible had happened to her. Not fifteen minutes ago in the car with Konstandin I blurted out that I thought she was dead. And now here I am, after speaking to Toby and her mum, entertaining the idea that maybe Kate's faking it all. I want to dig my fingers into my skull and yank out all the conflicting thoughts so I can untangle them. Is it true that I don't really know her? Though I claimed to know Kate better than Toby, can I really say that? Do I honestly know her better than her own mother? Better than the man she married and shared a bed with for years?

'I'll let you know if I manage to get a flight,' her mum says, and then she hangs up on me.

I make for the door of the police station. I'll go in and tell the police what I've found out, then I can leave them to investigate and untangle all these threads, because it's clear I can't do this alone anymore.

As I wait for Detective Reza to come out to the waiting room to meet me I upload Kate's photograph to Twitter and ask for anyone in Lisbon to keep an eye out for her.

I hashtag it #Lisbon #BritishWomanMissing #missingperson #help, and then I hesitate. Am I being overly dramatic? But for crying out loud – if I can't be dramatic now when can I be? Maybe someone has seen her? Maybe by some stroke of luck the tweet will go viral and someone will have seen something or know something and can help me solve this . . . whatever *this* is. Is it a kidnapping, an accident, a murder, a hoax?

Detective Reza invites me into her office where the other detective, Nunes, is waiting, perched on the arm of a chair. This time they seem to take my report much more seriously, which is a relief. They listen and Reza makes notes as I explain about Joaquim and Emanuel and how I tracked them down. She seems somewhat annoyed at this, as though I've gone ahead and trodden on their toes, but *what toes*? I want to ask them – they weren't doing anything to track Kate down, so she can hardly blame me.

Nunes interrupts me. 'Are these the men you told Detective Reza about earlier today?' he asks, his accent so thick I struggle a little to understand.

I nod. 'Yes, that's right. We, I mean, *I* managed to find them.' Damn, I wanted to keep Konstandin out of it. I shouldn't have slipped up like that.

'How?' Reza asks. She glances at Nunes.

'I found their social media accounts and arranged a meeting,' I say, skipping over the Konstandin part of it all. 'Joaquim admitted they stole Kate's bag.'

At that Detective Nunes cocks his head. 'He admitted this?' he asks, eyebrows raised.

I nod. 'Yes. He said they stole her bag, her phone and wallet and everything that was inside the bag.' I pick Kate's Birkin bag up off the floor and put it on Reza's desk. 'Here it is.'

She takes it in, then looks up at me, frowning. 'And how do you happen to have it?'

'They gave it to me.'

She frowns. 'Let me get this clear. They stole the bag and then they gave it back?'

I nod. 'Uh-huh.' In my head I picture Konstandin punching Joaquim in the face but I keep quiet. 'They took the money from her wallet and her credit cards but I got the bag. And her phone. They'd sold it to a pawnshop.'

Nunes looks to Reza, frowning. He doesn't recognise the word and she translates it for him.

He looks at me. 'You went to a *case de penhores*?' he asks, surprised.

Reza's fingertips stroke the leather strap of the bag. 'This is a genuine Hermès?'

'Yes,' I say.

'They're expensive aren't they?'

I nod again. 'I think about fifteen thousand pounds. I'm not sure.'

'But these men who you say stole it—'

'They *did* steal it,' I splutter.

Her eyebrow rises almost imperceptibly. Does she not believe me?

'You say these men were escorts – prostitutes – and your friend hired them?'

I nod, starting to get frustrated at having to repeat myself. It's not that hard to understand. 'Yes.'

'How did you find out that they were escorts?' she asks.

I swallow. 'I um, went back to the bar where we met them and the barman there told me.'

'The name of the bar?' Nunes asks.

I turn to him. 'The Blue Speakeasy. It's in Baixa,' I add, naming the nightlife area of the city.

He nods. Between Reza's scepticism and Nunes's scorn I can feel my frustration starting to grow again. 'I've given you their names,' I say, my voice rising. 'You can find them and interview them if you don't believe me. They say they don't know what happened to Kate but maybe they're lying.'

She nods. 'If they exist, we'll find them and bring them in for questioning,' she says.

'What do you mean *if they exist?* Of course they exist! I'm not lying!'

'I didn't mean that,' she says calmly, but what else could she have meant?

'You shouldn't have done all this alone,' Nunes adds. 'It's not good. You should have left it to us.'

I blink at him, astonished. They weren't doing anything!

'I had to do something,' I protest. 'No one was taking it seriously.' I glare at them both, trying to make my point.

'My colleague tried to find these men, based on the information you gave me this morning,' Reza says, nodding at Nunes. 'But he didn't have any luck.'

I bet he tried *really* hard, I think to myself, scouring him with a look.

I turn back to Reza who I think is more amenable to my story, rather than Nunes who seems disbelieving, as well as too lazy to actually do his job. 'Now I've proved something must have happened to her!' I say, almost shouting. 'She can't have got very far without her wallet or her passport or her phone! I said something was wrong but no one believed me.' I shoot another look at Nunes and then hold up the bag. 'This is proof.' *Isn't it?*

Even as I say it though doubt niggles at me, an itch I try to

149

ignore. What if Toby was right and Kate is fucking with us. Is it some type of game? Should I tell the police my concerns – but then, if I do, they might not bother to investigate at all and we'll be back to square one.

I'm keeping so much from them and I sense that they know it. It's making me look suspicious. I'm not a natural liar. I honestly don't know how criminals do it.

'OK,' Reza sighs, making to stand up. 'We will interview the men.'

I nod. Finally. Some progress. I wonder about the promise I made to Joaquim not to involve the cops but dismiss the worry instantly. He deserves to be arrested for what he did. My only concern is that Joaquim will tell them about Konstandin beating him up to get the truth and though they won't be able to identify him they will want to know why I withheld that information. If they do find out about it I'll just tell them he was an Uber driver and that I don't know his name. I won't betray him after all he's done for me.

'What about CCTV?' I ask Reza, thinking about the street outside our apartment. 'Security cameras. Can you check those?'

'Lisbon isn't London,' Nunes answers patronisingly. 'We don't have CCTV cameras everywhere.'

Reza interrupts, shooting him a look that tells him to dial it back. 'We'll ask around the neighbourhood to see if anyone remembers seeing her,' she assures me.

I nod, biting my lip with frustration.

'Please don't leave the country,' Reza says as she opens the door for me to leave. 'Or go anywhere without alerting us first.'

'I don't have any intention of leaving,' I say. 'Not without Kate.'

Chapter Eighteen

Trudging up the stairs to the apartment, I have to suppress the flicker of hope that Kate might be waiting for me; sitting on the sofa legs tucked under her, glass of wine in hand and a crazy tale of adventure to regale me with. Every time my hopes get dashed it's like a drop of water hitting an already sputtering flame so I try not to let them rise, otherwise the hope will soon be completely extinguished.

The thought that something terrible has happened to Kate won't leave my head, and with the rise in my anxiety, the level of doubt that was seeded by Toby falls. Kate would never do this. I simply can't believe it. But I do have so many questions that remain unanswered. Why did she hire escorts and why did she want me to think I'd slept with one of them? And why did Toby make it sound like he was the one who broke up with Kate, not the other way around? He said something about her doing this so he'd take her back, but she never in a million years said anything of the sort to me. She was glad to be rid of him, or so she made it seem.

I try to remember Kate's mood – she seemed happy on Friday night. She told me she loved me. But there was also that unhappy look on her face when we were lying on the bed, earlier in the evening, before we went out. It was brief and I thought I was mistaken but maybe I wasn't. What was going on with her? I have so many questions and so few answers. It's like drowning in quicksand.

It's only one-thirty in the afternoon but it feels much later, probably because I've done so much already today. I'm exhausted and want nothing more than to crawl into bed, burrow under the covers and cry myself to sleep. Actually, I do want something more than that – I want to be heading to the airport with Kate to catch our flight home. I want to be walking up my garden path and opening my front door and seeing Rob and Marlow and falling gratefully into their arms and then onto the sofa in front of the telly with a ready meal from M&S and a bottle of wine, while Marlow sleeps upstairs.

What will I tell Rob? What's he going to do tomorrow with Marlow? He'll have to take her to Denise, the child minder, but she might not be available on such short notice. How will he manage on his own? God, I hadn't thought at all about that. How can I stay here when I have a child at home who needs me? Anger bursts inside me like a geyser – erupting with force before vanishing almost immediately, sucked back down inside the void. I'm too tired to be angry, and far too worried. Nothing matters. Only finding Kate.

When I reach the door to the apartment I pause, my hand freezing halfway to the lock. Someone's inside. I can hear a woman's voice. I shove the key in the lock and throw open the door, hysteria and joy bursting out of me.

'Kate?' I shout, running inside. She doesn't answer. I rush into the living room but she's not there. And neither is she in the kitchen. I pause, wondering if I imagined it. But I swear I heard a voice . . . 'Kate?' I shout again, running into her room.

A woman is on her knees tossing things into the suitcase.

She has brown hair tied in a ponytail and hope blazes for an instant but then she turns around and it fizzles out. It isn't Kate. It's a stranger.

'Who the hell are you?' I shout, my heart pounding. 'And what the hell are you doing?'

The woman who isn't Kate rips earbuds out of her ears and scowls at me. 'I'm packing up your things,' she huffs.

'What?' I shout, crossing towards her and grabbing clothes out of her hands. Those are Kate's things. 'You can't do that!' I yell. 'Stop it. How the hell did you even get in here?'

She stands up, hands on hips. She's about thirty, taller and bigger than me, with muscly forearms and a solid frame, but I'm so angry that I raise my hands and am about to shove her away from Kate's things when she says, 'You were meant to be out of here by twelve o'clock. There are other guests arriving.'

'Oh my God,' I whisper. I step back from the confrontation, dropping my arms to my sides. 'I'd forgotten.'

'I've been calling.'

I spin around at the sound of a man's voice. It's Sebastian. He's standing in the doorway to the bedroom, vibrating with anger. 'You did not answer.'

'I didn't get a call,' I explain.

'I called the number on the booking,' he huffs.

'That's Kate's number. I didn't make the booking. And she's still missing. She doesn't have her phone with her.'

'That is not my problem,' he says. 'We have new guests arriving in two hours and Rita needs to clean and remake the beds.'

'I'm sorry,' I say. 'I forgot we were meant to be leaving today. I've been at the police station filing a missing person's report.'

I cast a glance around Kate's room, half her clothes are still lying on the chair where I piled them yesterday and the other half have been dumped unceremoniously inside her suitcase.

Rita, the cleaner, has moved over to the bin and is picking it up. I watch her nose wrinkle as she spots the used condoms inside.

'I'm sorry about your friend,' Sebastian says, still mealy-mouthed, his nostrils flaring. 'But I need you to vacate the property. I will have to charge you extra for the overstay and inconvenience.'

Is he kidding me? But what can I do? 'Fine,' I say with a weary sigh. 'I'll pack my things. Just give me half an hour and I'll be gone.' I look at Rita. 'And leave Kate's things. I'll pack them.'

Rita shrugs, already moving on to strip the beds, gingerly, as if she suspects they're contaminated.

I hurriedly pack the rest of Kate's clothes and shoes and then rush into the bathroom where I'm surprised to see all her toiletries already zipped into her multiple washbags. What if Rita found Kate's stash of drugs? I gather up the toiletry bags and drop them in the suitcase.

As I zip it up I hear Sebastian talking to Rita in Portuguese and look up to find them both heads bent, studying the carpet. Oh dear. They've discovered the stain. Sebastian is irritated, crouching down to rub at it with his fingers. 'What is this?' he asks tersely, looking at me.

'Um, wine,' I say, hedging. 'I'm sorry.'

He mutters something and before I am made to feel any more like a naughty schoolgirl I rush out of the room. I hurry into my room, half-expecting to see Rita has packed my things too, but luckily she's not made it this far. I drag my bag from inside the wardrobe and start to toss my things inside. Thankfully, I didn't bring much so it doesn't take long. I gather my things from the bathroom, pausing for a moment to catch my breath in front of the mirror. *Don't cry*, I tell myself. *Don't you dare bloody cry.*

But what am I meant to do? I'll have to find a hotel. And what about the cost? And how long will I need to book it for? Reza said not to leave the country. What am I going to do? I pull my phone out and call Rob. He'll know what to do. But the call goes straight to voicemail again. Half-sobbing, I leave a message, asking him to call me back as soon as possible. As I hang up I catch sight of movement in the mirror and let out a startled scream.

Sebastian is standing right behind me, blocking the bathroom door with his lean frame. How long has he been lurking there?

'I'm sorry about your friend,' he says, his eyes skittering from me to the washbag in my hand, to the floor, then back to my face, which is wet with tears. 'And don't worry about the wine stain. Rita says she can get it out.'

I nod and then step towards him hoping he'll move out the way so I can get to my bag and finish packing but he doesn't move. 'I need to finish packing,' I say, holding up my washbag to show him and gesturing at my suitcase behind him.

'I have a spare room. If you would like to stay with me for a night, it's OK.'

'Oh,' I say, surprised by his offer. A moment ago he looked ready to physically throw me out onto the street. Why the change of tune? Then I realise it's probably less about him having a sudden burst of human kindness and more about the extra income he'll earn by renting his spare room to me. I don't much fancy staying with him but it would mean I wouldn't have to deal with the hassle of searching online for a hotel and booking somewhere. And it also means that if Kate does show up I'll be the first to know about it. She doesn't have her phone or her bag so it would make sense that the first thing she'd do would be to come here trying to find me.

'OK,' I say, hesitantly. 'That would be helpful. Thank you.'

'Good, good,' he says, finally moving aside to let me out of the bathroom.

I drop my washbag into my carry-on and zip it up.

'Can I help you carry your bag downstairs?' Sebastian asks, hovering at my shoulder.

'I can manage,' I tell him.

He nods, his gaze darting around the room, his eyes like two flies unable to settle on anything. 'I'll bring your friend's suitcase down.'

'Thanks,' I tell him and watch him scuttle off.

That was weird. My gut feels very iffy about him but I set my misgivings aside. A thought niggles at me: what if *he's* done something to Kate? God, I'm going mad. I can't look at anyone anymore without wondering if they know something or if they're involved somehow in Kate's disappearance. Even the old man in the corner shop downstairs came under suspicion when I bought some water from him ten minutes ago and showed him the picture of Kate. His bored shrug seemed to suggest he knew something and wasn't telling me, or perhaps he just couldn't understand the question. My judgement feels off and that's unsettling. I've always been so good at reading people but now I feel like I can't trust myself or my instincts. Everything's off kilter.

But when I think about Sebastian doing something to Kate it makes me almost laugh. Kate would have socked him one if he'd tried anything. A puff of wind would knock him over he's so slight. He must weigh less than me and Kate's no pushover. I've seen her get physical a few times with men who got too handsy. One time in a club a man groped me and she kneed him in the balls so hard he fell over and couldn't get up for five minutes, and another time when a man grabbed her crotch on a bus in Italy she laid into him with her handbag, swinging it like a baseball bat until he leaped off the bus crying.

There's no scenario I can imagine that would see Sebastian gaining the upper hand over her. At the door to Sebastian's apartment I pause, once again wondering if this is a smart move. What if the weak exterior belies his real personality? What if he's actually a serial killer? What if he's a rapist? What if he's killed Kate?

Sebastian ushers me inside with a nervous smile, though not nearly as nervous as my own, and I don't put up a fight.

His apartment has a similar layout to our apartment upstairs, though the living room is smaller and because there's no roof terrace or French doors to let in the sunlight, it feels darker.

The living room is almost identically furnished with a few more nods to the fact someone lives in it, books and magazines on the coffee table, more art on the walls – movie posters mainly of old movies including one of *The Birds* and another of *Vertigo*.

'You like Hitchcock?' I ask, nodding at the posters on the wall.

'Oh yes,' he says, smiling. He shows me his giant flat screen on the wall of the living room and beneath it an array of DVDs, which I try to feign interest in.

'Here,' he says, 'your room is this way.' He leads me to the second bedroom – identical to the room Kate stayed in upstairs, decorated in similar white tones. It's slightly discombobulating.

'Thank you,' I say, wheeling my bag to the bed. 'Let me know how I should pay you.'

'How long do you need to stay?' he asks.

'The police said I shouldn't leave the country.'

His cocks his head. 'What else did they say?' he asks. 'About your friend?'

'Not much. They're looking into it.'

He frowns, taking that in. 'She hasn't gone home without telling you?'

'She left all her things,' I point out. 'And she didn't have her handbag or passport with her when she went missing.'

'Strange,' he murmurs. 'Is it the two men do you think, who came back with you?'

'I . . .' I break off, staring at him. How did he know it was *two* men? Did I tell him? I don't think I did. He knew there were people besides us in the apartment on Friday night but I don't remember telling him it was two men. Maybe I did though. Or maybe he guessed from having heard their voices. 'The police don't know,' I say, not wanting to give him too much information. 'They're going to interview them.'

'Are they worried something bad has happened to her?' He seems to finally be grasping the seriousness of the situation, judging from the concern on his face, which has been all but absent until now.

My throat tightens and my heart starts to race. 'I don't know.'

Sebastian sees my anxiety and gives me a smile. 'Would you like a cup of tea? You English people like your tea.'

'I'm Irish,' I say, automatically. I'm about to turn him down on the tea but I am so beyond tired I think I need some caffeine to perk me up. 'Yes, thanks. I'll have tea.'

I follow him out to the kitchen. I look around noticing the pristineness of the space. 'What do you do?' I ask, trying to make conversation as he boils the kettle.

'I read textbooks.'

I'm not sure I've understood him correctly so I ask him to repeat it.

'Audiobooks. I record textbooks as digital files. Physics, psychology, science, that kind of thing.'

'Sounds like the perfect thing to put me to sleep,' I say with a laugh, before realising how insulting that sounds. 'I mean, I'm terrible at science. In one ear and out the other.' I'm waffling, trying to make up for my rudeness. What's gotten into me?

He sniffs and looks wounded. 'It is mainly for students who have dyslexia,' he says, pushing his glasses up his nose. 'I work for a couple of publishers but also I have two clients who pay me to record textbooks for their children who are dyslexic.'

'That's . . . great,' I say.

'And I manage all my Airbnb apartments.'

'You have more than one?' I ask.

'Yes, I have five – all over the city. One in Sintra.'

I nod absently. Making small talk is exhausting when your mind keeps drifting to other, more pressing concerns. 'That's nice.'

He makes me a cup of tea and hands it to me before picking up a cloth to wipe down the countertops. He's a clean freak, that's for sure.

I pull out my phone and wave it in the universal symbol of *excuse me, must make a call.* 'My husband,' I explain. 'I should call him and tell him where I am. Don't want him to worry.'

Sebastian nods and I take my cup of tea and head back to my room, pausing slightly in front of a door to what seems like a third bedroom. This is how the apartment differs to ours. Judging by the wall dividing the living room, the room has been custom built.

'That's my recording room,' Sebastian says. He's come up behind me on silent feet.

I notice that the door doesn't have a handle, only a lock, and my stomach folds over on itself, anxiety buzzing through me like a swarm of wasps. I hurry to my bedroom and shut the door behind me. This door doesn't have a lock at all, though at least it has a handle, and I wonder if I'm safe. My paranoia is so extreme that I'm starting to imagine all sorts of wild and crazy things. What if Sebastian's lying about that room being a recording room? What if it's a padded torture cell? What if Kate's locked inside there? *OK, calm the hell down, Orla.*

I have to suppress a giggle, which threatens to turn into a sob as I think about how much Kate would love it if she could hear my thoughts right now. She'd die laughing. I'm perfectly safe, I tell myself firmly. Sebastian isn't a danger. I'm just being silly and overly paranoid. *Better paranoid than dead*, the voice in my head pipes up.

I take a sip of tea and set it down on the side. It tastes funny, which is probably because it's made from Lipton, which for some reason seems to be the only tea you can get when you're abroad. Does anyone else, beside the Irish and the English, not know how to make a decent cuppa?

I perch on the corner of the bed and see that Rob's called and left a message. We keep missing each other. Before I call him back, though, I check my social media. The Twitterverse has retweeted my tweet about Kate thirteen times, which isn't what I'd hoped when I prayed it would go viral. No one has tweeted back to say they remember seeing her either.

I think about adding a Facebook status update about the situation but there isn't much of one. Kate is still missing and what will anyone in England be able to do, other than send thoughts and prayers, which frankly aren't going to be much help? I also don't want to be fielding emails and calls from friends, which could tie up the phone line, in case Kate or the police call.

I'm not even aware of my eyelids drooping or of falling asleep but when I burst awake sometime later it's with the gasp of a drowning woman. I'm sitting bolt upright, heart hammering. The room is dark and for a moment I'm confused as to where I am and think I'm in our Airbnb apartment, but then I remember I'm at Sebastian's in the apartment downstairs. How did I fall asleep? I guess exhaustion finally caught up with me. Groggy, I check my phone only to find that it's died. I root in my bag for the charger and plug it in, anxiously waiting for it to turn on and then, when it finally does, discovering it's gone seven in the evening. I've been asleep for hours and there are several voicemails.

The first is from Kate's mum. 'I'm sorry, I can't manage to book a flight. Can you get Kate to call me? Thanks.'

I have to replay the message to make sure I've heard it correctly. How the hell can I get Kate to call her? She's missing! Kate really wasn't joking when she said her mother redefined the term *batshit crazy*.

There's a voicemail from Detective Reza too. She's calling to tell me they haven't been able to find Joaquim or Emanuel. I gave the police the address from Joaquim's driver's licence. Konstandin had the good sense to make him hand it over so we could take a picture as surety. I wonder if they've done a bunk or gone into hiding. They must have guessed that despite my promises I'd go to the police and are no doubt lying low, but I have to admit it's a disappointment.

Rob has also left a message and I feel bad as I never called him back before falling asleep. I try calling him but it's my turn to miss him. He might be putting Marlow down to sleep. I hope everything's OK with her. Being away from her has pulled into focus just how much I love her. I stare at my screensaver, a picture of Marlow waving a carrot in the air like a flag, until I feel the tears start to build up and I have to put the phone down before I start bawling.

On stiff legs I move to the en-suite bathroom. My clothes feel damp and are sticking to me. I must have sweated in my sleep, probably from nightmares fuelled by my overactive imagination. Like the bedroom, the bathroom doesn't have a lock, and I'm uneasy about it, but I need a shower – I feel rank – so I push my suitcase in front of the bedroom door and lay a rolled-up towel along the floor in front of the bathroom door as a bit of a buffer before stripping naked.

As I wait for the hot water to come through, I try to pummel my thoughts into some kind of order. Kate, what the hell were you up to? Because clear as day, she was up to something and whether or not it's related to her disappearance I don't know, but I also don't think it can be a coincidence. As Konstandin said, figuring out why she might have wanted to drug me and set me up to sleep with, or think I'd slept with, an escort may be the key to all this.

If only I could get into her phone I could find out who it was that called on Friday night. I wonder if I should have given the phone to the police but they didn't ask for it, another thing that makes me wonder about how good they are.

The police probably have ways to crack open phones. But then I recall reading in the paper last year about a spree shooter in the US. The FBI weren't able to access his iPhone and Apple refused to help, citing privacy laws, so perhaps it's a dead end, though surely they could get hold of her phone records and those would contain some information, at least about who she was on the phone to on Friday night.

The shower doesn't do much to wake me up. I'm too exhausted for that, despite the nap I just took. Wrapped in a towel I walk out into the bedroom and find my phone ringing on the bed. Lunging for it I see that it's Konstandin. I answer it. 'Hello?'

'Hi,' he says. 'I was just calling to see if there was any news.'

'No,' I say, feeling cold droplets of water snaking down my spine from my wet hair. 'Nothing. The police tried to find Joaquim and Emanuel but didn't have any luck.'

'They probably left town for a few days to avoid them.'

'That's what I thought,' I muse, chewing on my thumb. 'I didn't tell the police about you, in case you were wondering.'

There's a silence on the end of the phone before he says, 'Thank you. But that's not why I'm calling. Have you eaten?' he asks.

162

I hesitate. 'No,' I admit.

'Do you want to get some food?' he asks.

I am hungry and I don't much fancy staying in the apartment all evening, hiding from Sebastian to avoid conversation about audio textbooks and growing slowly more paranoid about what he's up to in that room *besides* recording audio books. And it would be good to talk through everything with Konstandin. 'Yes, OK,' I finally say.

'I'll pick you up in twenty minutes, how does that sound?'

'Good,' I say, standing up and looking about for my clothes. 'See you then.'

As soon as I hang up I wonder if it's weird to go out to dinner with him. Rob wouldn't like it much. And if I'm honest, I'm not sure of Konstandin's intentions. He's just being a friend I suppose, and I am grateful for everything he's done so far. It would be good to talk everything through with him. I feel so alone over here.

I worry, though, that I'm being too stupid and too trusting. He isn't exactly a law-abiding citizen. The thought occurs to me again that he could be involved in Kate's disappearance. It would explain his interest. But if that were the case, he wouldn't be helping me hunt down clues. In my heightened state of anxiety and exhaustion I can't calibrate properly. I can't figure out who to trust. I can't even trust myself.

Fifteen minutes later I push my improvised barricade suitcase away from the bedroom door and exit the room. Walking quietly through the apartment I cock my ear for any sound of Sebastian but it seems like he's gone out. I don't know what to do about a key – how will I get back in later? – so I call his name. There's no response.

My gaze hovers on the closed door, the one with the lock. Is he in there? From the outside the room looks to be about as big as our third bedroom back home, a tiny box space about six feet by eight, roughly the same size as a prison cell. My previous suspicions about the room come back to me. I tiptoe towards the door and press my ear to it. It might be my imagination but I think I hear a woman's voice on the other side of the door, but then comes silence.

I knock loudly. 'Hello?'

The door opens a crack and Sebastian peeks his head out, looking irritated. He holds the door half-closed and blocks my view with his body. 'Yes?' he asks, tersely.

I crane to look past him, catching sight of a desk against one wall with a computer, and a microphone and a pile of heavy-looking books. The walls are lined with some dark-coloured foam panels. It looks, from what I can see, very much like the kind of office you'd use for recording audio textbooks.

'I was just about to head out to get some food,' I say, forcing a smile. 'If Kate turns up will you make sure she calls me?'

He nods.

'And I wondered if you had a spare key so I don't disturb you later.'

'What time will you be home?' he asks.

I'm taken aback – surely, I can come home whenever I like? I'm a paying guest after all. 'Not late, probably before ten.'

'You don't need a key. I will be home.'

'It might be useful to have a key though,' I say, confused. What does he normally do when he has people to stay?

'I don't have a spare,' he says hurriedly. 'Now I must get back.' He turns back into the room and my eyes track to the monitor, catching sight as I do of movement on it. A black and white movie by the looks of things.

He shuts the door on me and I stand there for a few seconds, staring. Why is he watching a movie in there when he has a whole flat screen in the living room?

Maybe it's porn. But I've never seen black and white porn,

164

though I haven't seen much at all. And I'm assuming he'd want to watch that in the comfort of his bedroom. Though maybe he figured he could watch it at full volume in there, thanks to the soundproofing. I shudder thinking about it. Whatever is going on, he's downright weird. But I can at least put to rest my suspicion that he's holding Kate inside a soundproofed room in his house, torturing her. That's something I suppose. I wish she were here, if only to share my increasing paranoid and crazy ideas about her disappearance with her. She'd find it hilarious.

As I step outside onto the street into the warm night air, I see Konstandin is already outside, waiting for me, leaning against his car smoking a cigarette.

'How long have you been waiting? You should have texted me to say you were here,' I say, walking towards him.

'I got here early,' he says, drawing on his cigarette before tossing it away. He's wearing a beaten-up old leather jacket and he smells of smoke. I am happier to see him than I realised, which is surprising.

'How are you?' he asks as we move towards the car.

I shrug, my cheeks still overheated. 'Not so good,' I admit. 'I've had to move out of—'

'Orla?'

I jerk around at the sound of my name. Oh my God. A man is striding towards me across the street. It's Rob.

Chapter Nineteen

'What on earth are you doing here?' I say, staring in astonishment at my husband.

Rob's gaze moves from me to Konstandin. He frowns, his eyes narrowing, before turning his gaze back to me. Ignoring his look, I throw my arms around his neck and my body reacts like all the air has been sucked out of it at once. I almost go limp, the relief is so great at seeing him. 'I'm so glad you're here,' I stutter before pulling back in alarm. 'Where's Marlow?' I ask, looking around and spotting only a small backpack at Rob's feet but no pushchair or baby.

'She's with Denise.'

'The babysitter?' I say, bewildered. 'Overnight?' We've never left her overnight, not even with her grandparents.

'My parents are away, remember?' Rob says. 'And I couldn't ask your mum to come over from Ireland. It would have taken too long for her to get there and Denise said she could take her for a night or even two if we need.'

'You came,' I interrupt, my eyes watering. I clutch his hand. 'Thank you.' It suddenly feels as if everything might be OK. Rob's here. We'll find Kate together.

I see Rob's smile tighten and his gaze drift back to Konstandin who has stepped away to give us space and is waiting, hands folded in front of him, watching us through lowered eyes.

'This is Konstandin,' I say to Rob, feeling heat rush to my face. 'He's been helping me. He's . . . an Uber driver,' I blurt. Oh, this is awkward.

Konstandin holds out his hand to Rob. 'Konstandin,' he says, introducing himself.

'Rob. Orla's husband,' Rob counters, rather coldly. I wince. Oh dear, he's not happy.

'I figured that,' Konstandin replies with something of a smirk.

Rob shakes his hand and I notice both men's knuckles turn white and they look like they're trying to out-grip each other. 'Konstandin has been the most useful person,' I explain hurriedly to Rob, wondering why I sound so guilty. 'I don't know what I would have done without him. He's been translating and . . . things.' I peter off, knowing that by rambling on I sound guilty of something, even though I've not done anything wrong.

'I see,' says Rob, gesturing towards Konstandin's car. 'And you were just going somewhere?'

I nod. 'Yes.' Shit, should I admit we were going to get dinner together? It seems like something Rob could very easily read into, but I blurt it out anyway like an idiot. 'We were going to get some food actually.'

Rob frowns. 'You couldn't order takeaway?'

I open my mouth to say something but Konstandin gets in first. 'Perhaps I'll go.'

'Mmm,' Rob murmurs.

Konstandin turns to me. 'Let me know if you hear any news.'

I nod, giving him an apologetic look. I grit my teeth as he gets in his car, my face flushing furiously with anger and embarrassment. Once he drives off I turn to Rob and rush into his arms before he can say anything or grill me further.

'I'm so glad you're here,' I say, burrowing into his familiar chest. He hugs me back, dropping a kiss on top of my head. I close my eyes, squeezing them shut. 'Why didn't you let me know you were coming?'

'I was racing to the airport and I tried you but you didn't pick up.' He pulls back. 'Good job I did show up though. Were you really going to go to dinner with him?'

My face flames. 'It's not like that.'

He frowns. 'How is it then? It's a little bit weird to go out to dinner with an Uber driver, don't you think? And he looks a bit dodgy if you ask me.'

'He's not dodgy,' I protest, weakly.

'Is he the guy you told me about? The one who drove you and Kate to the bar?'

I nod. Rob pulls back to stare at me, giving me a look like I'm crazy. 'So how do you know he's not involved in her disappearance? For God's sake, Orla!'

I'm shocked by his tone and glance around. The shopkeeper over the road is staring at us and a couple walking past glance back over their shoulders.

'Look,' I say in a quiet voice. 'I need to tell you something.'

Rob's face darkens and I wonder what he thinks I'm about to say. Judging from his expression he's anticipating an admission of cheating or even murder. I purse my lips, annoyed that he's leaping to conclusions. 'Let's find somewhere to go and talk.'

*

We end up at a restaurant a little way down the street, a cave-like place serving bar food and cheap wine in rattan-covered carafes. It doesn't look particularly nice but it will do. Rob orders a beer and I order a glass of wine, needing something

168

to soothe my nerves and my anxiety. I wait for it to arrive and drink several gulps before setting the glass down.

'So are you going to tell me what's going on?' Rob asks. He's been quiet since we got here and he seems anxious, judging from the way his foot is tapping beneath the table. Rob's a patient guy. It takes a lot to stir him up, but when the fuse is lit he can lose his temper. It's a rare occurrence and usually only involves him yelling, though once, in our twenties, he did punch a wall and break a bone in his hand after we got in a stupid fight. I, on the other hand, am much more volatile. I have huge swings, can go from laughter to tears in the space of five minutes, and lose my temper quite easily, something that's only got worse since I had Marlow. I'm so tired all the time that my patience wears thin.

'I didn't tell you the whole story before,' I begin. 'It was complicated and I didn't want to explain over the phone.'

Rob's frown deepens, a crease forming between his eyes. He runs a hand through his thick dark hair and I think of how Marlow takes after him with her furrowed expression when she doesn't get her way.

'I don't want you to be mad at me,' I say, watching him carefully. 'Because I didn't know.'

'Didn't know what?' he asks, sitting back in his chair as though readying himself to receive bad news from a doctor.

I take another deep breath. 'What I didn't tell you is that the night Kate went missing we brought two men back to the apartment.'

Rob takes a few seconds to absorb that. 'What?' he asks plainly.

'I know, it sounds bad. But it wasn't my decision. Kate invited them.'

'But there were two of them,' Rob hits back, colour flooding his face.

169

'Yes, but I didn't want them to come back with us,' I explain. 'I told Kate not to invite them but she ignored me.'

'Where did you meet them?'

'At a bar,' I admit. 'But, here's the crazy thing: it turns out that Kate hired them.'

'What do you mean she hired them?'

'They were escorts. Kate paid for their services.'

Rob's mouth hinges open. 'Prostitutes?'

I nod. I let him absorb that for a few seconds. 'Before you ask, I don't know why. She didn't tell me. I found out about it after she went missing.'

Rob shuts his eyes, still trying to wrap his head around it. I understand what he's going through, having not so long ago gone through it myself.

'I think I was drugged,' I continue when I think he's had enough time to process. 'I don't know for sure. I was so drunk I passed out. But I think it was more than alcohol. I felt weird. There was this bitter taste in my mouth when I woke up and I couldn't remember anything about the night before, or not much. I blacked out. There's huge pieces of my memory that are missing.'

'Did you go to the hospital?' he asks, real concern crossing his face.

I shake my head.

'Did . . .?' He swallows hard, his jaw tensing. I know what he wants to know. He wants to know if anything happened to me, if I was assaulted.

'No,' I interject fast, setting his mind at rest. 'Nothing happened.'

He reaches across the table and takes my hand and I start to relax. He's taken it very well, considering.

'But Kate slept with one of them,' I continue. 'I found a condom in the bin. Two actually.'

I think about the wrapper I found in my bed. I still have no idea why Kate put it there, except perhaps she wanted to play a practical joke on me when I woke up, so I decide not to mention it to Rob as he'll only suspect the worst.

Rob takes that in quietly, then he looks up at me, frowning. 'But she hired them to sleep with both of you?' he asks.

I nod. 'Yes. I have no idea why though. And there's no way I would ever have . . .'

'I know,' Rob says, squeezing my hand.

'You do?' I say, letting out the breath I've unwittingly been holding. 'I was so worried you wouldn't believe me, that you'd think I was in on it.'

Rob shakes his head, staring off into the middle distance. 'This is so fucked up,' he mutters. 'Why would Kate do that?'

I nod, joining my other hand to his. 'I know. I don't know what she was thinking.'

Rob doesn't speak for a while. He's lost in thought. Finally he turns back to me. 'But you think these two guys might have something to do with her going missing?'

I chew my lip, thinking back to the confrontation with Joaquim – how completely genuine he seemed when he professed his innocence. That look, you couldn't fake the surprise when he heard Kate was missing. 'They said they didn't,' I tell Rob. 'And I think I believe them.'

Rob stares at me, shaking his head in shock, his blue eyes shining with tears. 'I can't believe you didn't tell me any of this. I thought you were over-reacting when you called me. I thought maybe you'd had a fight or Kate had done a Kate and buggered off on a bender somewhere. It was only when you told me you were going to the police that I realised it was serious.'

Tears spring to my own eyes as well. 'I'm sorry,' I say. 'I didn't know what to tell you at first, and then it felt too late to say anything. I wanted to wait until we were face to face, you see.

And I kept hoping that she'd show up and I'd only have to call you to tell you I was on my way home.'

Rob nods. 'You've told the police everything?' he asks.

'Yes. But they haven't been very helpful. Konstandin and I found the guys on our own, the two escorts – we tracked them down and questioned them.' There's no point in going into too much detail about how Konstandin got the truth out of them. 'They admitted they stole Kate's handbag. I got it back. But the police can't seem to find them now so they can't question them.'

I can see Rob struggling to wrap his head around all this new information.

'According to them they left the apartment around three in the morning and didn't see Kate after that,' I carry on. 'I woke up around eleven the next morning and Kate was gone. But she didn't have her phone or her handbag or her wallet.' I look at Rob. 'So where could she possibly have gone to?'

Rob says nothing and I realise I'm holding my breath, waiting for a response that won't come. I was hoping he'd have an answer, or at least an idea, but just like Reza and Nunes when I posed the question to them, he's got nothing.

'I'm so worried,' I mumble.

Rob squeezes my hand again but doesn't say a word. He doesn't try to reassure me or soothe my anxiety. In fact, he looks every bit as worried as me.

Chapter Twenty

'I have to warn you about the man in the apartment.'

Rob pauses mid-step. 'What man?' he asks.

'The landlord,' I whisper. 'Long story. I couldn't stay in the old place as it was rented out tonight so he offered me his spare room. He lives in the apartment below the one we stayed in. And he's a bit odd.'

Rob scowls. 'You said yes to staying with a complete stranger? Orla!'

'I didn't have much choice,' I tell him, annoyed at how patronising he's being. 'And hopefully he won't mind you staying too. He's a bit funny about extra guests.'

Rob's expression morphs from a scowl to befuddlement. We're talking in hushed whispers, just outside the front door when it opens. Sebastian is standing there, looking between Rob and I wonder if he was standing on the other side of the door, watching us through the little spy hole. Creep.

'This is my husband Rob,' I explain, smiling. 'He flew in without telling me, to help me look for Kate.'

Sebastian shakes Rob's hand but he isn't budging from

playing Cerberus at the door so I have to bring it up. 'It's fine if he stays, isn't it?'

Sebastian opens his mouth then shuts it again, obviously put out, but what can he do but let us both in? 'Of course,' he mumbles, stepping aside, and pushing his glasses nervously up his nose. 'I will have to charge you extra. I'm sure you understand.'

Rob and I exchange a look. *See what I mean?* my look says. *God, you're right, what a weirdo,* says Rob's returned glance.

'Sure,' I say, hurrying Rob into the bedroom.

'What a bloody weirdo,' Rob says in a whisper as I shut the door.

'I told you. I thought maybe he was keeping Kate locked in this room he has with soundproofed walls. It's got no door handle.' I giggle.

Rob looks aghast.

'How do you know he isn't?' Rob asks, his eyes widening. He isn't joking. 'Why does he have a soundproofed room?'

'It's a recording studio. And I caught a glimpse. It was empty.'

Rob suddenly reaches out and pulls me into his arms. I wrap my arms around him and squeeze hard. It feels so good, such a relief to be held. The tight knot in my stomach relaxes a little and I can breathe more easily. When you've been with someone as long as Rob and I have been together, sixteen years, it's like having a limb returned to you when you hug them. The only thing that's missing is Marlow between us. I wish Rob could have brought her but I suppose it wouldn't have been practical. I hope she's OK with Denise. I squeeze my eyes shut to stop the tears springing out. I just want to go home so much. When is this nightmare going to be over?

Rob kisses my neck. I love the comforting feeling of his lips and the warmth they infuse through my body, but at the same time it's not the moment for it. I push him gently away and step back.

174

'What's the matter?' he asks, wounded.

'Nothing,' I say. 'I just, I can't right now. I'm so worried.' I start to pace the room. 'I thought tomorrow I'd call the embassy. It's too late now; they'll be shut. And then the English newspapers. What about that friend of yours, the guy you work with whose wife works at the BBC – do you think she might be able to help?'

'Help with what?' Rob asks.

'With getting it on the news,' I answer impatiently. 'We need to get the media involved.'

Rob walks over to the window. 'Right,' he says. 'Yes, sure, I can talk to him tomorrow. See what she says.' He looks out onto the darkened street.

'Someone must have seen something,' I say, rubbing my hands over my face, trying to push away the exhaustion. 'We should make some posters too and put them up around the neighbourhood,' I say.

'Good idea,' Rob murmurs.

I walk up behind him and link my arms around his waist, pressing my forehead to his back and closing my eyes.

'What do you think has happened to her?' Rob finally says under his breath, as though scared to say it too loudly.

'I don't know,' I say.

We stay like that for a few moments. 'Do you think Kate would ever do something like this for a laugh? Or for attention?' I blurt. I hadn't wanted to give the idea serious weight. It seemed somehow disloyal, which is ridiculous given that Kate probably drugged me and tried to get me to sleep with an escort. But I need to bounce the idea off someone and Rob's the only person who knows Kate almost as well as me.

Rob turns to look at me over his shoulder. 'Are you serious?' he asks.

175

I shrug, already feeling bad for having suggested it. 'I don't know. I'm just running through all the scenarios. It's all I've been doing for days. Her mum and Toby both suggested she might be faking it.'

Rob takes a deep breath and lets it out in a rush. 'God, I don't know. Why though?' he asks. 'Fuck,' he says rubbing his face with his hand. 'Maybe.'

'Maybe?' I respond loudly, surprised that he's giving weight to my suggestion. I only raised it because I wanted him to dismiss it out of hand and tell me it was a stupid idea. That way I could put it finally to bed.

'It is Kate we're talking about,' he replies with a shrug. 'When you said she was missing my first thought was that she'd fucked off on her own.'

'But that's different to faking your own disappearance.'

'Yes, but if anyone was going to fake their disappearance it would be Kate.'

'But why?' I ask, repeating his first question. 'It's too far, even for her. She might do it for a joke, but she wouldn't let it go on this long. She'd know how worried I'd be.'

'Did you fight?' Rob asks.

I shake my head. 'No . . . I don't think so. The problem is I don't remember too much about that night. I did wonder if maybe we argued and she went off in a mood. But she'd have to have planned this, leaving her passport and her wallet and things, and that doesn't make sense.' I sink down on the bed, head in my hands.

'Look, why don't you lie down?' Rob asks, resting his hand gently on my shoulder. 'You're exhausted.'

'I can't sleep,' I say. 'I'm too anxious.' It feels as if there's an anthill in my head.

He sits beside me and puts an arm around my shoulders. 'It'll be OK,' he says, kissing my temple. I lean into him and feel the tears start to well once more. As they start to flow the doorbell buzzes. I pull away, wiping my tears, and look at Rob.

It's late – past eleven. Who could be knocking on the door at this time of night? It could be guests I suppose, checking in upstairs or with a query about how to work the hot tub. I wait, listening to Sebastian's footsteps as he heads towards the front door, and then to the sound of him unlocking it. Rob and I both crane to hear the conversation that comes next. It's a woman speaking. At first my hopes rise that it's Kate, but no, the woman is speaking Portuguese. A few moments later, there's a knock on my bedroom door. It opens before we can get to it and Sebastian's face peers in. He looks pale, pushing his glasses up his nose in that nervous habit he has. 'There's someone here to see you,' he says to me.

'Who?' I ask, alarmed.

'The police.'

I look at Rob. What are the police doing here this late at night? It can't be good, that's for sure.

'Orla?' Rob says, jolting me out of my stasis.

He's already on his feet, looking down at me.

I stand up on shaking legs and take a step towards the door, reaching for Rob's hand as I pass, not sure I can do this alone. It's like walking to the gallows. Maybe it isn't bad news, I tell myself; maybe they've found her and have come to tell me she's in hospital.

Detective Reza stands in the doorway with Detective Nunes. Both of their expressions are blank and impossible to read though Nunes's gaze is fixed on me, his eyes burrowing into me as though he wants to dig into my mind.

My insides pull tight, cinching into a knot. The whole world seems to shrink in on me so it's just this narrow hallway and Reza and Nunes standing at the end of it.

'What is it?' I hear myself ask, my voice barely a whisper.

'Can we come in?' Reza asks.

'Please, just tell me,' I say.

Reza pauses. 'We've found a body.'

Chapter Twenty-One

Somehow I find myself sitting on the sofa in Sebastian's surgically neat living room, Rob beside me with his arm around my shoulders, and Sebastian leaning over me with a glass of water, which I can't take because my hand is trembling too hard. He sets it on a coaster on the table in front of me instead.

Reza sits opposite me. Her expression has softened slightly but Nunes stands behind her like a sentry, his gaze lasering me.

'Is it definitely Kate?' Rob asks, his voice breaking.

'We need a formal identification before we can confirm it,' Reza says. 'But, the body matches the description.'

I look up. 'So, you aren't sure then?' I ask. 'It might not be her?' I can hear the desperate hope in my voice, the anxious pleading tone. *Please don't let it be her. Please let it be a mistake. Kate can't possibly be dead.*

Reza bites her lip and hesitates before carrying on. 'We're fairly certain that it is your friend,' she says to me.

'How did she die?' Rob asks, his face mirroring my own shock.

Reza turns to look at him. 'There needs to be an autopsy so we can establish that for certain, but it looks like she drowned.'

I draw in a sharp, stabbing breath as though I'm breathing through cracked ribs. 'Where?' I ask. 'How?'

'In the river.'

'But what was she doing there?'

Reza shakes her head and shrugs. 'The body was pulled from the water near the docks but we don't know where she fell in exactly. We're looking at tide times and trying to establish that.'

I clutch at Rob's hand. I think I'm going to be sick. This can't be happening. 'But it doesn't make sense,' I hear myself say. 'What was she doing by the river? It can't be her. You must be wrong.'

'That's why we're here actually,' Nunes says. 'We need you to come and identify the body.'

'Oh my God,' I whisper, clutching Rob's hand.

Reza makes to stand up.

'You mean, right now?' I ask, dumbfounded.

She nods. 'Yes.'

It takes me a moment to collect myself. 'OK,' I say and stand up. It's like I'm floating all of a sudden above myself, looking down on the room, seeing Rob standing beside me, holding my arm like I'm an invalid, and Sebastian, lurking in the corner like a gargoyle, watching.

Reza steps aside to let Rob and I pass. I hear Rob telling her we'll just be a minute to get our things. He guides me back to the bedroom. There, away from the others, he turns to me and says something, but I'm still floating overhead, and I can't make out what he's saying. With effort, I drop back into my body and tune in.

'Where did you put your bag?' he's asking me. He looks around the room and moves towards Kate's Birkin.

'That's not mine,' I say. 'That's Kate's.' I point at my own bag, lying on the floor by the bed. He picks that up and my coat too.

'Ready?' he asks.

I shake my head. No. I can't do this. There's no way I can identify a body.

Rob walks over to me and takes me by the top of the arms. He looks into my eyes. 'Come on,' he says. 'I'll be there with you. We'll do it together.'

He takes my hand and leads me back out into the hall where Reza and Nunes are waiting. We follow them outside, past Sebastian, and then down the stairs and into the car they came in. It's not a police car but a normal car and Rob and I sit in the back, holding hands, not speaking.

I can't speak. My mind is a dense fog I can't fight my way through. Nothing makes sense. How can Kate be dead? It's not possible. It can't be her. Kate knows how to swim. She can't have drowned. They must have made a mistake. I'll walk in and see a stranger lying on a slab. Someone who looks like her but isn't her.

Before I know it we've stopped and Reza and Nunes are getting out of the car. I look out the window. We're on a nondescript side street, parked in front of a grey building with no visible windows, a bit like a prison. Rob helps me out the car and steers me towards the building's door, which Reza is holding open for us.

Everything passes in a blur as we're led down a corridor and through more doors, the kind you get in hospitals. The only thing I really register is the smell, part bleach and part rust and part something else that I can only identify as decay. My head swims and I think I might faint. Reza tells us she's going to find someone and will be back in a moment. Nunes stays with us and I glance at him, noticing his hand is resting on the gun strapped to his waist. It feels like he's guarding us. I collapse down into a plastic chair.

I try to focus on small details to stop from thinking about

what comes next – the colour of the walls, avocado green; the sign in Portuguese alongside an icon of a camera with a slash through it, and another one telling people not to smoke. *Who would want to take photographs in here?* I wonder. And then I think, *Damn, I need a cigarette.* I can feel the need for it as an itch inside my lungs. I sit on my hands to stop them fidgeting, not wanting Nunes to look at me with any more suspicion.

After what feels an eternity Reza returns, and with her is a middle-aged man in green scrubs and white plastic clogs. He's thin and pale, as though working here has sucked the life out of him. I stand up to greet him.

'This is Doctor Correia,' Reza says. 'He's doing the autopsy.'

He shakes my hand and I feel shocked by the warmth of it, having expected it to feel cold as marble. He smiles kindly at me then pulls a clipboard from under his arm. 'I'm going to show you a photograph,' he says.

'What?' I say.

'You just need to tell us if it is your friend or not.'

'A photograph?' I say, feeling a huge rush of relief that I don't have to see an actual dead body.

He winces. 'I'm afraid there's been some decomposition. We're lucky the water was cold and so it's not as bad as it might have been.'

I place a hand to my mouth to hold back the vomit as black dots dance in front of my eyes.

'Why don't you sit down?' the doctor suggests.

I sink back into the plastic chair.

'Can I make the identification?' Rob asks, heroically stepping up. 'I knew her too.'

'No,' I interject. 'No. I need to do it.' I don't know why I've said it. I don't want to look at any photograph, am terrified of what I might see and never be able to unsee, but I also know

I need to do it. If I don't make the identification, how will I ever believe it, either way?

Before I can allow second thoughts to stop me, I stand up again and reach for the clipboard. Rob stands with me, at my side, arm around me. The doctor hands it over, turning it around so I can see the large photograph tacked to the front. I gasp and hear Rob do the same. The photo shows a woman from the neck up. Her eyes are closed and her skin is grey, tinged slightly green. Her eyes are closed, the eyelids bruised blue, and her lips, bloodless and pale, are slightly parted giving a glimpse of swampy blackness inside the mouth. Her face is puffy and bloated and her hair is bedraggled and wet, sticking in slime-like tendrils to her neck and the side of her face.

'Is it her?' the doctor asks gently.

I stare at the photograph, trying to find something in it that will prove me wrong. Rob squeezes my hand so hard the bones crunch but I don't feel it. I shake my head, trying to blot the hideous image of death away but knowing too that I will see it for the rest of my life every time I close my eyes.

'Orla? Do you recognise this woman?' Reza asks.

I force myself to look away from the photograph. The sob erupts out of me as I sink to the ground. 'Yes. That's her. That's Kate.'

Chapter Twenty-Two

There are voices but it's as if they're on the other side of a metal door – echoey and indistinct, and there are hands, pulling and prodding at me, though I barely notice them. I've retreated into some small, terrifying dark cave inside my head, but even in here the knowledge that Kate is dead roars around me like a hurricane.

That photograph. I will never be able to unsee it. Her face – bloodless as stone, swollen to almost splitting. My brain tries furiously to black it out, erase it from my mind, but it's going nowhere. It has staked a claim. I try to picture her alive instead, cheeks flushed, eyes sparking, a witty retort flying off her tongue, but no matter how hard I try I can't see it. The image of her dead is now superimposed over every memory I have of her.

There's an alarm going off – an odd keening sound, and I wonder for a split second if it's a fire alarm until I realise the sound is coming from me. I clamp my fist to my mouth, trying to block it, but there's no way of stopping it. It's a gut-wrenching, agonising pain that's being dredged from the deepest part of my being. A howl like an animal caught in a gin trap, serrated teeth gnawing through bone. I'm only vaguely aware of Rob pulling me to my feet and wrapping his arms around me.

'It's OK,' he whispers into my ear, his voice filled with shock. 'I've got you.'

I cling to him like he's a life raft. I bury my head against his chest and my howl burrows into him. He absorbs it and when my shoulders start to shake with sobs he pulls me closer, rocking me.

After a few minutes the shock of it starts to ebb. Rob pulls away slightly, pale and still reeling from the shock, and I draw my hands across my face, pressing my palms hard against my eyes. That image of Kate is burned into my retinas. Not even pressing until I see stars makes it vanish.

'Orla, if you could please sign here.'

I turn my head to find the pathologist is there, waiting, still holding the clipboard. I shrink backwards, afraid he's about to show me the photograph again, but when he hands me the clipboard I see he's removed the photo and it's just a form. He offers me a pen. 'It confirms that it's Kate,' he says, indicating where I should sign.

I scrawl my name on the dotted line.

'What happens now?' Rob asks him, and I see that he too has been crying.

'We'll carry out the autopsy and confirm how she died,' the pathologist says. His English is excellent but his accent is so thick it takes me a while to understand. What does he mean that they need to confirm how she died?

'I thought she drowned,' I say.

'Yes, but the body shows signs of trauma to the skull.'

'What?' I ask confused. 'Someone hit her?'

'Or she banged her head as she fell. It's difficult to say. We'll know more after the autopsy. Because of the nature of her death we'll be prioritising it. We should have the results fairly quickly.'

185

I look at Rob who is frowning too. Like me, when we heard Kate had drowned, he must have assumed it was an accident.

'You're saying that maybe it wasn't an accident?' Rob presses.

Reza interrupts. 'We don't know. Let's not make any assumptions.'

'Maybe she kill herself. She could have jumped, then hit her head on something when she was in the water.'

I spin around to see Nunes is speaking. Reza glares a warning at him to shut his mouth.

'It wasn't suicide,' I tell him, outraged at the suggestion. How dare he? I turn back to the doctor. 'She didn't kill herself,' I insist.

'Was she depressed?' he asks. 'Taking any medication?'

I can't believe it. They're not listening to me. 'She didn't kill herself,' I repeat angrily. Kate's been on and off antidepressants for decades but she's never been suicidal.

'We'll do a toxicology report,' the doctor reassures me.

Oh shit, I think in alarm. What about all the other drugs she took that night? Those will all show up on the toxicology report. Another thought strikes me that until now hadn't occurred: it's possible Kate had some kind of adverse reaction to the drugs she took. I've heard stories of people on coke and other drugs thinking they could fly and throwing themselves off roofs and balconies trying to prove it. It's a possibility, and certainly no more out there than the other ones I've come up with so far.

'Let's let the doctor do his post mortem,' Reza says, gently. 'I have officers looking at the cameras all along the riverfront, trying to establish where she fell in the water.'

The doctor shakes our hands, takes his leave and walks off.

'What do we do?' Rob asks Reza. 'How long will it take? How do we arrange for the body to be flown home?'

'The public prosecutor will open an inquiry,' she says.

'Prosecutor? I don't understand,' I stammer.

'It is standard for suspicious deaths.'

'Right,' I answer, nodding and frowning at the same time.

'In Portugal, once the body is released to the family, it must be cremated or buried within seventy-two hours,' Reza explains. 'After the autopsy we can help you arrange this. Or your embassy can.'

How can we be talking about cremations and burials? How is any of this real? It's a nightmare and I need someone to pinch me awake.

'OK,' Rob says, taking charge. He seems as stunned as me but luckily is holding it together better than I am. I'm so grateful that he's here. I don't think I could do any of this alone.

'You should call her family and friends,' Reza says to us, 'and let them know before the media starts to report it. We'll release her name to the public in a few hours' time.'

A shudder racks me. How in God's name will I tell her mum?

'And you need to stay in the country until we've finished the inquiry.' Nunes's eyes flash to me as he says it, and maybe I'm imagining it but there's a hard look in them, as though he suspects me of pushing Kate in the river or something.

'How long will that be?' Rob asks.

'Possibly a day, maybe longer,' he answers. 'We can't say for sure.'

'But we have a baby at home,' I interject. 'We can't stay.'

'You can leave,' Nunes says to Rob. 'She needs to stay.' He jerks her head in my direction and it feels sharp as a nettle sting.

'But why?' Rob protests on my behalf. 'It's not like Orla had anything to do with it.'

Reza interrupts. 'It is just the way we do things here.'

'Fine,' Rob says wearily. He turns to me. 'Let's go. Can we go?' he checks with Reza.

She nods and steps aside to let us by. I'm a few steps past her when I stop and turn back around. 'The men – Joaquim and Emanuel – did you find them yet? Did you speak to them?'

She shakes her head and I let Rob guide me to the exit and outside into the warm night-time air.

We don't speak. I just lean against Rob, folded into him, my fingers clutching his shirt. The howl is still there, trapped in my chest, a typhoon of grief just waiting to be unleashed.

'What do we do?' I finally manage to whisper.

'Let's get a drink,' he answers.

I nod. We start to walk without any sense of direction but it doesn't take long before we find a bar, signalling us with its glowing sign. My gut lurches at the sight of it. It reminds me of the Blue Speakeasy sign. Kate's voice calls suddenly in my head. Her laughter rings around me so loud I think for a moment she's there and I turn to look for her but of course she isn't. She isn't anywhere.

Now we're away from that awful mortuary place I can't help but wonder if it was all a hideous mistake. What if it wasn't her? What if I got it wrong and identified the wrong person, someone who looks like her but isn't her? But Rob agreed. It was her.

As we stumble inside the bar like battle-weary soldiers and collapse at a small table, I catch myself thinking how not even an hour ago Rob and I were discussing whether or not Kate was capable of faking her own disappearance. Now I wish to God she was.

Guilt makes me bury my head in my hands, elbows resting on the tabletop. How could I have believed her capable of such a thing? While I was there contemplating it with Rob, her body was being pulled from the water, already puffy and bloated and . . . I scrunch my eyes shut trying to blot the image from my mind.

I try not to think about her disappearing beneath waves, unconscious, drifting to the bottom of the river. How dark and cold. What a horrible way to die. And there I was, asleep and oblivious to it all as it was happening. Though they didn't say for sure when she fell in, did they?

'How can she be dead?' I ask Rob, lifting my head an inch from the tabletop.

'What do you want to drink?' he asks me in reply. He's already standing, making for the bar, too impatient to wait for the incredibly slow waiter service that seems to be the rule of thumb in Lisbon.

I shake my head. I don't know. He heads for the bar and comes back a minute later with two shot glasses filled to the brim with clear liquid. Without a word we knock the drinks back. It's tequila and it burns the back of my throat before hitting my stomach like liquid flame. I shiver and become aware of how cold I am. The chill of the mortuary has seeped into my bones and numbed my flesh. My teeth start to chatter and Rob gets up and puts his coat around my shoulders. 'It's shock,' he tells me.

As my body goes rigid, tensing against the cold that has wrapped its way around me like tendrils of steel, he heads to the bar and comes back with a Coke. 'Drink this,' he tells me. 'The sugar will help.'

My hand shakes as I pick up the glass and it rattles against my teeth but a few minutes later I can feel the effect of the sugar rush. My body starts to relax, though the cold is still so bone-deep I wonder if I'll ever feel warm again.

Rob has another couple of shot glasses lined up in front of us. I reach for one and empty it into my Coke glass. I feel the sudden, overwhelming urge to get drunk. It might be the

189

only way to obliterate these images from my mind and to deal with the reality of the giant black hole that's opened up in the world in the space that Kate once occupied.

How can she be dead? I feel like I'm never going to stop asking this question because I'm never going to get an answer to it that makes sense.

'What do you think happened?' Rob asks, staring into his drink.

'I don't know.' So many thoughts and conjectures race through my mind. What was she doing by the water? Why did she lie to me about the call she was on earlier that night, and who was she talking to? Why did she hire escorts and why did she want me to believe I'd slept with one? There are so many questions and now I'll never get answers.

'Why was she out by the water?' Rob asks, the same question bothering him.

'Maybe she wanted to go clubbing,' I suggest. 'Or she went for a walk.' I pause. A fragment of memory comes back. The glimmer of water under moonlight. Was I there? Or is this something I'm pulling from my imagination?

'You don't think that policeman was right do you, that she would kill herself?' Rob asks.

'No!' I say loudly. 'There's no way Kate killed herself. She was talking about buying a house, having kids . . . she had all these plans for the future.'

'We should really call her mum,' says Rob, glancing at his watch.

Oh God. I take a huge gulp of my drink, feeling the head-giddiness of the alcohol start to kick in. I pull out my phone and scroll for Kate's mum's number. 'What do I say?' I ask Rob.

'Do you want me to do it?' he asks and I smile at him for the generosity of the offer.

'No,' I say. 'It should be me.'

Before I can think too hard about it I knock back another

shot and hit dial. My stomach knots with apprehension. It's late, so I wonder if she'll pick up but she surprises me by answering on the second ring, her voice thick with sleep.

'Hi,' I say, my own voice coming out as a squeak. 'It's Orla. Sorry to wake you.' *Sorry?* Why am I saying sorry for waking her? What I'm really sorry for is that I'm about to shatter her world. I'm sorry that after this moment she'll probably never sleep another night of peace in her life.

'Is it Kate?' she asks, sounding more alert. I picture her sitting up in bed, maybe reaching to turn on the light. 'Did you find her?'

She knows. I can hear it in her tone, the edge of fear creeping into her voice, that she's trying hard to disguise.

'Yes,' I say, forcing out the words. 'I'm sorry.'

There's a pause on the end of the phone. I hear a ragged intake of breath, the shudder of a heart beating one final time before it knows it must break. 'She's dead, isn't she?' she says.

'Yes,' I say, though it comes out as a sob.

Her voice trembles on the other end of the line. 'What happened?'

'She drowned.'

'What? How? Where?'

'The river. The Tagus. She slipped or fell. We don't know yet. The police are investigating.' I don't mention the other theories – that maybe she was pushed, that she was murdered, that maybe she jumped. I can't say it out loud.

'Was she drunk? On drugs?' her mum asks and there's a new tone in her voice that instantly raises my heckles. It's barely noticeable and maybe I should put it down to shock, but she sounds accusatory, as though this is something Kate has brought on herself, that she's to blame for her own death.

'I . . . I don't know,' I finally stammer. 'They're doing toxicology reports.' As I say it I realise that with so many drugs in her system the police will assume she was off her head. They'll blame her for her own death too, just like her own mother is doing. Even if she was murdered, it will be her fault. That's what happens all the time when women are victims of crimes. They're blamed for their own injuries. Whether it's rape or domestic violence or assault, the inference is always that women bring it on themselves.

'You don't need me over there, do you?' Kate's mum asks in an almost impatient voice.

'Um . . .' I reel, not sure what to say. What mother wouldn't rush to be by their child's side – even if that child was no longer living? The thought of leaving Marlow on a cold mortuary slab in a foreign country, with other people making decisions about her, makes the typhoon of grief and shock in my chest batter at my ribs. I'm so enraged I'm afraid I might start screaming and never stop. 'You don't want to be here?' I manage to ask in as calm a voice as I can manage. Rob squeezes my free hand. He can hear I'm struggling to hold it together.

'Can you handle things?' she answers.

'Sure,' I find myself replying.

'I don't know what to do about a funeral,' she says and though she sounds very matter-of-fact, and devoid of emotion, I wonder if she's just covering up her grief. 'You knew her best, perhaps you can decide.'

'Right,' I stammer. Am I supposed to plan the whole funeral then? Shouldn't it be her mother doing that? Kate doesn't have siblings and her father died when she was thirteen so I guess then I am family, or as close as. And we were like sisters. 'Of course,' I hear myself say. I can do this for her. She'd want me to. I can hear her in my head telling me: *For fuck's sake don't let my mother read the eulogy, and make sure everyone drinks a lot and has a good time. No tears!*

'OK, I'll be in touch when I know more,' I say. 'Bye. I'm so sorry for your loss,' I choke out, but she's already hung up.

I stare at the phone in shock.

Now you know why I drink, I hear Kate say. Her voice is so loud, so real, I almost jump around in my seat to look for her standing behind me. Is this what it will be like from now on? Will she haunt me forever? Will I hear her voice in my head all the time as a ghostly presence, accompanying me through life? I don't think I'll mind too much, to be honest. It's something of a comfort, as though she's still alive. I put the phone down and swallow the new shot of tequila Rob has set in front of me. Kate always used to say she didn't want kids because she was worried she'd turn out like her own mother and now I know why. 'That was weird,' I say, looking at Rob. 'Her mum wants me to plan the funeral.'

'What about Toby?' Rob asks, necking back his own drink. He seems to be hammering them back faster than me. That's already his fifth, I think. 'Can't he do it? They are still married.'

Oh God, Toby. I remember that call we had a few hours ago. He was so damn rude, so cynical about Kate's disappearance. I want to rub it in his face that he was wrong but at the same time, what is there to be gleeful about in being right? All that stuff he said about her wanting him to come back to him, and about her lying to me, seem now like nothing more than bitter remarks from a jilted husband.

'Want me to tell him?' Rob offers again.

I shake my head, pick the phone up and dial Toby's number. He answers immediately. 'Orla,' he says, both impatient and on edge, as if he's been waiting on the call.

'It's Kate,' I tell him without preamble. 'She's dead.'

'What?' Toby whispers into the phone.

'She's dead,' I repeat like an automaton. Maybe the more times I say it the easier it will be to believe.

'What the fuck are you talking about?' Toby asks, angrily.

'They found her—'

'Who found her?' he interrupts.

'The police. She drowned. In the river.'

'Jesus,' Toby mutters. 'Fuck. How?'

'I don't know. The police don't know. They're investigating.' It's too much to explain about the head injury and I don't want to mention that they're wondering if it was a suicide. I'll wait until I know more.

'But, Jesus . . . was she drunk?' he asks. 'She was fucking high, wasn't she?'

I take a deep breath, trying to hold in the rage. Why is everyone looking to blame her? She's dead! Can we not cut her a goddamn break? 'No, not especially,' I say through gritted teeth. 'I don't know what happened.'

'What can I do?' he finally says, snapping into pragmatic mode. 'What's happening to the body?'

Ignoring the jarring way he's described her as *a body*, I let out a heaving sigh of relief. This is what I actually need, someone like Toby who knows how to handle the ugly, writhing messes of life, who knows how to fix things or to find the people to fix things. That's his skill, why he's so successful at his job.

'I have to organise the funeral,' I say.

'Right,' he says.

'I don't even know what she wanted.'

'Cremation,' he says, not missing a beat.

I nod. Of course, he'd know. They were married; they must have talked of these things.

'I'll start letting her friends know,' I say, beginning a mental list in my head of all the things I have to do. 'I've told her mother already.'

'Christ,' Toby says, and I picture him sitting in their old apartment, at the dining table, head in his hand or perhaps standing at the window looking out over the city. 'What a thing to happen.' He pauses. 'What do the police say?'

'They think it was an accident,' I tell him. I don't mention the other possibilities.

'Where were you?' he asks. 'When it happened.'

I'm a little stunned by the question and the slightly accusatory tone buried in his voice. 'I was asleep. I don't know why she went out or why she was down by the river.'

Bitch! Kate's voice bursts in my head.

'OK,' Toby says. 'Are you good to organise things your end?'

'Yes, I think so,' I say, shaking off the confusion. 'Rob's with me.'

'Well, let me know what you need. I'll figure things out this end. The funeral and everything. I mean, we are technically still married. God,' he says again and now I can hear the shock and the bewilderment in his voice as he really starts to process what's happened. 'I just used the present tense,' he says. 'We *were* married. Fuck.'

Past tense. Kate is past tense. She will never again *be*.

'I'll call you when I know more,' I tell Toby quickly, and then hang up.

I finish my drink in two swallows, enjoying the way it makes the world foggy and holds the present at a distance. In this state I can keep Kate alive. I don't have to use the past tense when I think of her.

'Are you OK?' Rob asks. His eyes are bloodshot and his face white as a ghost. I dread to think how I must look.

Bitch!

Kate's voice is so loud I stare at Rob wondering if he has heard it too. But it's just in my head. I can hear her scream the word but I can't see her or where we were when she said it.

'Orla?' Rob says, tapping me on the arm. 'Are you OK?' he asks, worried.

I startle. 'Yeah, I'm fine.'

Bitch! she screams again.

195

Chapter Twenty-Three

Monday

For a blissful moment when I wake the world is full of sunlight and air. I stretch my toes and turn my face towards the window, feeling the sun's rays warm my eyelids. And then the memories return, along with a pounding headache. I open my eyes, for a split second hoping and praying I'll find myself back in England, in my own bed, having dreamed everything, but no such luck. I'm in the spare room of Sebastian's apartment. And Kate is dead. I let the weight of it sink into me. The sunlight evaporates; the air becomes chill. My body is cast in lead.

I must have drunk enough to knock out a bull elephant last night, anything to try to push away the reality of what we were dealing with, and now my mouth is dry and my head feels as fragile and dangerously delicate as a wasp's nest. I remember the tequila bottle on the table and Rob telling me to slow down. I vaguely recall posting something on Facebook about Kate, tears streaming down my face as I typed, and Rob helping me back to the apartment and into bed. I think when we came in that Sebastian said something about how sorry he was.

I remember crying myself to sleep and maybe that's also why I have such a splitting headache now, and my eyes are puffy and dry. That thought conjures the image of Kate dead, her flesh putrid. And the next thing I know I'm stumbling from bed and into the bathroom, throwing open the door and making it to the toilet just in time to throw up the entire contents of my stomach, which is mainly liquid.

Afterwards, shaky and nauseous and still green around the gills, I lean back against the cold tile wall and close my eyes. My shoulders shake but the tears won't come. I'm too exhausted. Where's Rob? I wonder. What time is it? Groggy, I reach for my phone. It's almost midday. There are dozens of missed calls, texts and emails from friends who must have seen the Facebook post about Kate. I can't face them right now. Grappling my way to standing I head out into the hall. The door to the secret room is shut.

I creep into the living room. It's dark – the shutters drawn – but I can hear the muffled sound of someone crying. I spot Rob kneeling in the gloom beside a suitcase.

'What are you doing?' I ask.

He jumps around in fright. 'You're awake,' he says. 'I wanted to let you sleep. How are you feeling?'

I walk closer. 'Awful.' It's only then I notice it's Kate's suitcase.

Rob's got one of Kate's tops in his lap. He notices me glancing at it. 'I don't know what I'm doing,' he says, wiping at his tears. 'I guess I thought maybe I'd find a clue or something if I went through her stuff.'

I kneel beside him. 'Yeah,' I say, 'I did the same when she first went missing.'

Rob's face is red, his lashes wet. I put my arm around him. 'I can't believe she's gone,' he says, shaking his head in disbelief. He shoves the top back on the pile of her clothes, jumbled in her bag. I want to tell him to fold it but it's not like it matters.

'I've booked a flight for this afternoon,' Rob says, rubbing an arm over his face and standing up.

'Oh,' I say, turning to him.

'We can't leave Marlow any longer.'

'Yes, sorry, I know. I just . . .' I stop as my throat squeezes shut. His mention of Marlow has hit me hard. More than anything right now I want to hold my daughter in my arms. 'I wish I could come too,' I sigh, my eyes stinging.

'They said you needed to stay.'

I nod. Yes, they did.

'I've called the embassy already,' Rob says.

'You have?' I ask, surprised.

'Yes, but they can't do much. They gave me a list of English-speaking funeral directors. I called one and I've arranged for them to collect the body once they're done with the autopsy. They said they'd co-ordinate with the authorities. But it should be today or tomorrow. They'll cremate the body. You just have to pick up the ashes.'

The body. There it is again, that word. Not Kate's body, but *the* body.

My phone rings and I pull it out my back pocket. It's Konstandin.

Rob is peering over my shoulder at the phone ringing in my lap. 'Why's *he* calling?' he asks.

I ignore him and stand up to answer the call. 'Hi,' I say into the phone.

'I saw the news,' Konstandin answers. 'It's your friend.'

The news. Of course. Reza warned me they'd release the information to the media. 'Yes,' I say. I head towards the window and open the shutter. Buttery golden sunlight floods into the room and I turn my face to it, hoping it will in some way chase away the darkness inside.

'I'm sorry,' Konstandin says. I can hear the genuine sorrow in his voice. 'Can I do anything to help?'

I take a deep breath. 'No. But thank you.'

'Let me know if that changes,' he tells me. 'I'm here if you need something.'

'Thank you,' I repeat.

'I'm sorry,' he says again.

When I hang up I find Rob is in the bedroom packing his shaving gear into his small backpack. 'Are you leaving right now?' I ask, a pang of anxiety hitting. I don't want to be here alone, dealing with everything all by myself again. I need him. He's my rock.

'Fairly soon,' he says with an apologetic shrug. 'Flight's at three-twenty. I'll make it back by seven to pick up Marlow.'

I nod. God, I wish I could go with him. My bottom lip starts to tremble at the thought of him leaving without me.

The intercom buzzes just then and we both freeze, turning our heads in the direction of the front door. I flash-back vividly to last night, to the police knocking with their horrendous news.

Both Rob and I make a move for the intercom at the same time but are interrupted in the hall by Sebastian exiting his recording room. I didn't realise he was home. He jumps when he sees Rob and I in the hallway, quickly pulling the door to his recording room shut behind him. He grabs for the intercom on the wall as it buzzes for a third time, pressing it to his ear before hitting the button to let whoever it is in.

'It's the police,' he tells us, moving to open the door.

I exchange a worried look with Rob. Why are they back? What more news could there be? Sebastian opens the door to Nunes. I've already taken against him, initially for his lack of engagement with the case when I first came to report Kate missing and then for his pointed suspicion and his comment that Kate might have killed herself, and now I bristle even more at his terse nod when he enters the apartment. There's an arrogance to him and a swagger that doesn't feel deserved, as though he's learned how to be a detective from watching too many Netflix Scandi-noirs.

'The autopsy report has come back,' he says, pulling out his notebook and flipping it open.

'And?' I ask, after he pauses for what feels like dramatic effect.

'There's evidence that your friend fought off an attack.'

'What?' I ask, feeling faint.

He looks down and reads directly from the notebook. 'Her hands and arms show signs of bruising and injuries consistent with a physical fight.'

My head is filled with pins and needles. I think I might fall over.

'She couldn't have sustained the injuries in the water, once she fell in?' I hear Rob ask.

Nunes shakes his head. 'The doctor says no. They occurred prior to drowning.' He looks down at his notebook again. 'Significant scratches on her arms and hands. She fought with someone before she died.'

'But she died by drowning? She wasn't . . . killed . . . and then dumped in the water?' Rob asks.

Nunes nods. 'She drowned.'

I struggle to draw a breath and fight the nausea rising up my throat.

'So someone pushed her in then,' I deduce. 'She fought with someone and they pushed her. Or they hit her and she fell in and . . .' I break off, having to put my hand on Rob's arm to steady myself. 'But who? Who would do that?'

Nunes doesn't have an answer. 'You need to come to the police station,' he says.

I blink rapidly, my heart starting to beat fast and a bead of sweat beginning to trickle down my spine. 'Why?' I manage to ask.

'What's this about?' Rob interrupts, putting his arm around me protectively.

200

'We have questions for your wife. Detective Reza will meet us there.'

'I've answered everything I possibly can already,' I protest. 'I've told you everything I know. If you need to talk to anyone it should be those two men I told you about. Have you found them yet? Are you even looking? They're the ones who saw her last!'

Nunes glances between us. 'Now it's become a murder inquiry, we need to get new statement.'

His expression remains neutral but his eyes tell a different story – there's a suspicious glint to them. Shit. A cold weight settles on my shoulders. Do the police think I had something to do with Kate's dying? They can't. That's ludicrous. Why on earth would I hurt her or want her dead? If only I could remember more about that night.

I look to Rob who gives me a confused, worried shrug, like he doesn't know what to make of it either, but what other choice do I have except to go with them? I don't think I'm being given an option.

'I'll get my things,' I say, and head to the bedroom, past Sebastian who shrinks away from me as I pass, as though I'm contagious.

In the bedroom I run a comb quickly through my hair, change my top, and brush my teeth. I could use a shower, as I still feel grimy and dishevelled from drinking too much. The tequila fumes coming off me could ignite a small blaze. Rob has followed me into the bedroom. I'm worried but try to hide it from him by forcing a smile. It feels silly to give my fears a voice. Of course, they can't be looking at me as a suspect.

'It'll be OK,' Rob tells me, trying to sound reassuring. 'Don't worry. They probably just want to go over your statement and see if they missed anything.'

I nod absently, trying to convince myself he's right, but the cold weight on my shoulders has seeped into my limbs and is weighing me down.

Rob pulls me in for a hug, whispering in my ear that everything will be OK. I clutch at him, pressing my forehead into his broad chest, trying to fight panic. I want to burrow into him and hide. I wish I'd got on a plane already and headed home. I want to see Marlow, but leaving would only have made me look guiltier.

Rob kisses the top of my head. 'It's going to be OK,' he says.

Over Rob's shoulder I notice Kate's Birkin handbag sitting on the floor. Out of the fog of my mind an idea starts to emerge.

'Do you think they'll let me see her?' I ask, pulling away from Rob.

Rob stares at me in bewilderment. 'Kate? You want to see her?'

He looks horrified by the idea and, honestly, I am too, but I nod all the same. 'Yes, before they cremate her.'

Rob shrugs, still looking aghast. 'Maybe. Ask them. But why?'

I shrug. I don't tell Rob what my idea is because I'm not sure if it's a good one or if it will work. It's something that might offer a clue to who killed her though, and it's the only idea I've got. I pick up Kate's bag and root inside it for her phone, sliding it into my own bag.

When we enter the living room I force another smile. 'OK, I'm ready.'

I turn and give Rob a quick, awkward hug, feeling like we're on display. 'Kiss Marlow for me,' I say, fighting back tears.

He nods, though he can't disguise the look of worry on his face, or is it suspicion? 'See you soon,' he says.

Chapter Twenty-Four

I follow Nunes down the stairs to his waiting car. It's a proper police car this time and when he opens the back passenger door to let me in, my face starts to burn. I duck my head to avoid the stares of the shopkeeper over the road and the pedestrians who pause to watch. I look like a criminal being arrested.

'Would it be possible to stop first so I can see the body, before they cremate her?' I ask, once he has started driving.

Nunes glances at me in the rear-view mirror. I meet his stare, pleading silently with him for this one small favour. He frowns, obviously not wanting to deviate from his orders to bring me in for questioning and probably wondering why on earth I'd want to look at the body, given its state.

'Please,' I press. 'I want to say goodbye. She was my best friend.'

He nods, grudgingly, and twenty minutes later we arrive back at the building we visited last night. In daylight it looks no less blank and horrifying. The smell of the place bombards me as soon as we walk through the door, making my eyes water.

An orderly in green scrubs meets us, not the doctor from

last night, and Nunes speaks to him in Portuguese – I assume explaining to him why we're there. He disappears for five minutes before coming back and leading me into a large tiled room with a drain set in the centre of the floor. My stomach heaves at the sight of a metal table and a tray of instruments beside it, lying pristine and shiny, ready to work their dark business on a body. It's so cold I have to wrap my arms around myself.

The orderly offers me something – a Vaseline-like salve that smells of menthol – and demonstrates to swipe it beneath my nose. I do, then the orderly points over my shoulder and I turn and see behind me there's another metal table, this one with a body on it, covered by a stiff, green surgical sheet. When I walked in I hadn't noticed it, my attention drawn immediately to the tools.

Sweat breaks out all over my body and I think for a second that I might faint. I take a deep breath through my mouth, trying to avoid the smell, which is thickly pungent and stomach-heaving, despite the salve doing its best to block it.

The orderly walks to the table and stops beside it. I step towards him, aware of Nunes waiting by the door, giving me space to say goodbye, or perhaps he isn't used to death either and doesn't want to see the body up close.

I'm not here to say goodbye. I don't want to see Kate this way or remember her like this. It's bad enough I saw the photograph, but I do need to see her in the flesh. My hand slides into my bag and grasps her phone.

The orderly peels back the sheet from Kate's face and I gasp, almost gagging. It's Kate but not Kate. It's a sick, horrific version of her, more like a special effects latex mask, something used in a horror film. Struggling to hold it together and to keep my stomach from heaving, I turn to the orderly. 'Could I have a minute alone with her?' I croak.

He steps respectfully away and I glance over my shoulder at Nunes, who appears to be fighting his own wave of nausea, swiping another dollop of the menthol salve beneath his nose and looking anywhere but at the body.

This is my moment. Shaking and fighting back terror I reach for Kate's hand beneath the sheet. I almost let out a cry at how cold and heavy it feels, like frozen rubber. I fumble a little with the phone, almost dropping it before I manage to align her thumb with the home button. I glance down at the screen, glad that my back is to Nunes and the orderly, which is buying me some extra cover.

I don't know if what I'm doing is explicitly wrong, though the fact I'm being so secretive is telling me it probably is. I should hand Kate's phone over to the police as it might contain important evidence, but I don't want to do that before I know what the evidence is. What if there's a clue on the phone that the police won't understand? Or private photos she wouldn't want them to see? If they're looking at me as a suspect it's important I gather as much information as I can before it's too late.

The screen miraculously unlocks. I'm startled, not having fully expected my idea to work. I can't let it lock again so I frantically access the phone settings, hit the display button and change the auto-lock setting to never. Praying it works, I slip the phone carefully into my pocket. I practised on my own phone on the way here and the key is to make sure I don't hit any of the buttons that might switch the screen off. I can only circumvent the fingerprint once and I can't change the passcode as I don't know it.

Nunes clears his throat. I spin around. He's standing with the door open, obviously keen to go.

I look back at Kate. It doesn't look like her and it isn't how I want to remember her, but I can't stop myself from looking. *Oh God, Kate, what happened?*

When we walk out into the hallway I see a sign for a bathroom and point at it. 'I just need to go the loo,' I tell Nunes and dart inside before he can say anything. As soon as I'm locked in a cubicle I pull out Kate's phone, relieved to see it's still unlocked and the screen is still on. This might be my only chance to check the email and texts on it.

First things first, I check her call log. The very last call she received was on Friday at ten fifty-six p.m. That was the call when we were at the restaurant. She said it was from Toby but it's not. The number's saved as *RJ Plumbing*. Why was she taking a call from a plumber at that time of night? I hit dial, because it's the only thing I can think of doing.

It rings and after ten seconds someone picks up. 'Hello?' they ask tremulously.

The breath catches in my throat like barbed wire. I hang up instantly and almost drop the phone into the open toilet, my hands are shaking so hard from shock. What the hell? Leaning against the cubicle door I press the little ID button beside the plumber's name and check the number. Then recheck it. And recheck it again, the blood pounding so loudly in my head I think I might go deaf.

It's Rob's number. It was his voice I recognised just now. But why is it saved as *RJ Plumbing* on Kate's phone and, more importantly, why the hell was she arguing with him on the phone hours before she died?

Chapter Twenty-Five

RJ. Robert John. Rob.

Feeling faint I flip the toilet seat down and collapse onto it, aware that time is rushing by and I don't have long. I scroll to Kate's texts. There are lots of unread ones, a dozen or more from the last three days, mainly me asking her where she is and begging her to call and some from friends, but I ignore them and scroll down to the ones from *RJ Plumbing.* With a gnawing sense of horror I open up the text chain. There are hundreds of texts. Words leap out at me.

Please don't.

I'm begging you don't tell her.

Kate, stop fucking around.

You said you'd leave her. You lied!

Let's talk.

I love you.

The words do what Kate's corpse could not. I fall off the toilet, scrambling to lift the lid in time to dry-heave into the bowl. My stomach aches from retching earlier but I barely notice because the pain inside my chest is so immense I think I might die from it. My heart, already cracked from grief, breaks clean in two. 'Rob,' I whisper to myself, 'how could you?'

The phone jerks alive in my hand and I almost drop it. It's Rob! He's calling me back. Oh God. He must think he's getting a call from a dead woman. Though I told him I had Kate's phone. Maybe he knows it's me. In a panic I hit the button to cut off the call. I'm not ready to talk to him and I don't have the time either.

I force myself to go back and scroll further back through the text chain but there are simply too many to read and I don't have time to go over them in detail, not with the policeman outside waiting for me. I've got a minute or two at most. The messages stretch back over a year. Before Marlow was born. Further. When I was pregnant. Further. Before I got pregnant. Oh my God. They've been having an affair for years, right under my nose. There seems to be a period where they don't talk, of nearly a year. But then a few months ago they start back up again.

I rock back on my heels.

Kate . . . how could you?

You're my best friend. You know I love you.

The bitch! She told me that and the whole time she was lying to me.

Bitch!

I jerk around in the stall. I can hear her voice. But now I'm wondering if in fact, it was me, saying it to her? Deep down, did I know about the affair? Did I learn about it on Friday night? Did I black out not just from the drugs, but because psychologically I was trying to blank out what I'd discovered?

Did Kate tell me on Friday night? Did we fight? Rob was worried I'd find out. Was he begging her not to tell me? Was she planning on it? How does it fit with the rest of the story though, with the escorts and the drugs? If she had told me about it, how would I have reacted? But I already know the answer. *I would have killed her.*

I rack my brain, trying to clear the fog, but I can't figure out what happened. It doesn't seem possible that she told me. My body has gone into such a state of shock that I don't think I could have known before now, even subconsciously.

The door to the bathroom creaks open. 'Orla?' Nunes asks. 'Are you in here?'

I startle. 'Um, yes, I just . . . don't feel very well,' I manage to croak. 'I'll be there in a minute.'

The door bangs shut. *Damn, pull it together.* There's no time to dwell. I swipe at my eyes and then go through the texts, screenshotting as many as I can, dozens of photos that I then email to myself with a shaking hand.

Bitch, I think. *Bastard. No time to dwell on it now.*

I check her emails too but don't find anything from Rob's email address. Perhaps they only used text messaging, thinking it was safer, or perhaps Rob set up a private, dedicated account so I wouldn't find it on his laptop by accident.

The bathroom door opens again. 'Hello?' Nunes calls, impatiently. I hear his footsteps coming closer, then he raps on the door sharply.

'Coming,' I stammer, before shoving the phone into my pocket again and unlocking the cubicle door.

I throw water on my face while Nunes stands behind me watching suspiciously, and I try not to look his way because I know my expression must be a turmoil and I don't want him knowing why, not until I have my head wrapped around this new information. Let him think I'm just recovering from seeing my friend's body and saying goodbye. At least the shock and the tears can pass for grief.

I follow Nunes to the car in a daze. My mind is flitting

to times Rob held me in his arms, told me he loved me, kissed me.

A scream batters against my rib cage, trying to escape. That howl that's been locked inside me since they told me the news about Kate grows in volume. Somehow, I manage to keep it locked inside, but when I get in the car I have to grip the door handle to steady myself.

Rob and Kate were having an affair. I cannot process it.

Toby's comment about Kate lying to me makes total sense now. Was that the real reason why they broke up? Did she lie to me about Toby sleeping with escorts? Did he in fact find out about Rob and their affair? Is that why he wanted a divorce? Why didn't Toby tell me, though, if that's the case? And why did Kate beg me to go on this weekend away with her? Why did she hire those escorts? What was her plan?

I want nothing more than to dig the phone out and read through the texts and look for emails that might explain it, but I can't, not here in the back seat of the car, with that nosy, awful Nunes glancing at me in the rear-view mirror.

Another thing occurs to me then. I remember how I found Rob this morning, bent over Kate's suitcase crying and holding her clothes in his hands. I thought he was just sad, but now I see he was heartbroken. He must have been grieving her even harder than I was. Another blow comes, swift as it is savage. Did he love her? In the text messages I read it was Kate who said she loved him. But did he love her back?

My hand starts to cramp as it squeezes the door handle. The howl trapped in my chest grows louder and bats even harder against my ribs to be let out. I have a police interview to give though. I have to keep everything inside me. Or, should I tell them what I've found out? Show them the texts?

Something hits me then, a thought so huge that it quiets the howling inside, makes everything go still. If I tell the police about Rob and Kate having an affair they'll think for sure that I killed her. It's a motive isn't it? A pretty damn good one too.

If Kate were still alive I might kill her. I certainly want to kill Rob. I want to roar my anger into his face and tear him limb from limb. I want to slap him and punch him and scream at him: *Why? How could you do this? What was wrong with me? Was I not enough? Did you love her more than me? Would you have left us for her?*

Chapter Twenty-Six

Dulled by grief and numb with shock, I sit opposite Reza and Nunes. She seems even more severe today. Her hair is scraped harshly back and she's wearing dark red lipstick that reminds me of dried blood. She's trying to explain to me why they haven't been able to pinpoint where Kate fell into the river, saying something about tide times. All they can do is speculate that it was somewhere near where the cruise liners dock, which is not too far from the apartment in Alfama.

We go through the statement I made two days ago when I first reported Kate missing, and the whole time the knowledge that I'm holding on to about Kate and Rob sits inside me like a caged animal trying to break free. I feel like the lies must be written across my face, and it makes me wonder how the hell Rob deceived me for so long. How could he do it, and so damn easily? I never once suspected a thing. I'm such an idiot.

My mind wanders to all the times he said he was working late or meeting a client for an after-work drink. Was he lying? And what about his new-found obsession with the gym? Was that real? Or was he not actually going to spin classes but meeting her for a quickie? He did get fitter, showing off a newly toned stomach and biceps. Was he doing it all to impress her? He told me that now he was a dad he wanted to be fitter.

You bastard, I think again. After everything we went through to have a baby. Did he even want Marlow? I gave birth to our child for Christ's sake and had stitches in my vagina, not to mention leaking breasts and depression and he was sneaking off to have sex with her . . .

Is it my fault? I didn't want sex after Marlow was born. And maybe he was just not that into me given all of the above. No. I refuse to blame myself. The affair started long before we had Marlow, I remind myself, when our sex life was still good. At least, *I* thought it was good. But the whole time we were having sex, trying for a baby, going through the awful IVF process, he was busy shagging my best friend.

My face heats up with humiliation. Kate asked me about mine and Rob's sex life when we were at dinner, probing into how often we were having it, warning me he might have an affair. She was laughing at me, basically taunting me.

Hate turns every cell in my body incendiary. How could she do this to me? We were sisters. Is that why she stayed away after Marlow was born? Because she couldn't stand seeing Rob's child – the evidence of our marriage? Is that why Rob pushed back when I said I wanted Kate to be her godmother?

'We interviewed Joaquim and Emanuel this morning.'

My head flies up at that. How long have I been sitting here, zoning out?

'You did?' I ask Reza, leaning forward across the desk. 'And?'

'They have alibis. We have checked them. The Uber driver who picked them up from your apartment and took them home. He confirmed they were alone. And their flatmate confirmed their arrival and that they stayed in the apartment until eleven o'clock the next morning.'

213

I try to switch mental gears and focus on this new piece of information, rather than on the affair between Kate and Rob. My suspicions of Joaquim and Emanuel were already mostly quashed after Konstandin and I confronted them, so the news of their alibis doesn't do much, except settle it once and for all. They didn't kill Kate.

'If only we knew why she left the apartment,' Reza muses.

I nod.

'The toxicology report came back,' Nunes says.

I look at him, trying to keep my face blank. I have nothing to feel guilty about. It's not like *I* took any drugs. But they'll probably assume I did and now it's too late to prove otherwise. I should have got myself tested after I woke up and thought I'd been assaulted.

'Your friend had multiple substances in her blood,' Nunes tells me, in a slightly gloating way. 'She tested positive for cocaine, ecstasy and even ketamine.'

I frown at that. Ketamine? The horse tranquilliser?

'And you? Did you take drugs also?'

'I have a baby,' I reply, as though that answers it.

Nunes shrugs. 'So?'

'I didn't take any drugs,' I tell him, angrily.

Nunes flips through some pages in his notebook. 'You told me you had taken drugs.'

'I didn't!' I shoot back. 'I told you I thought I had *been* drugged. There's a huge difference.'

'Did your friend give you drugs without you knowing?' Reza asks, shooting Nunes a look that is telling him to play it more gently.

I bite my lips shut. Yes, I think she did. And now, knowing what I know about her and Rob, I'm fairly certain she did. When Reza mentioned ketamine it did get me thinking. I've never taken it, but I know from reading an article in the paper about date rape that with a high enough dose it can knock a person out and give them memory loss. Is that what happened to me? Did Kate slip Ketamine in my drink? But why?

'Your friend, where did she get the drugs from?' Reza presses.

'She brought them with her,' I admit.

'On the plane?' she asks.

I nod. 'Yes. She had the cocaine in a little silver pillbox in her bag. I saw it. She hid it in her bag.'

'You didn't tell us she had taken drugs when you gave your statement,' Nunes says accusingly.

I look between them, starting to wonder if I should ask for a lawyer. But won't that make me look guilty or like I have something to hide? And I don't even know if this is a proper interview. Aren't I here to help go over my statement? Reza's not exactly the good cop to Nunes's bad, but at least she seems neutral, whereas Nunes seems like he wants to lock me up right now and throw away the key. He totally thinks I killed her.

'We'll need you to give us the drugs so we can test them against what was in her system,' Reza says.

I nod.

'We interviewed your landlord,' Nunes says next.

Sebastian? That news surprises me.

'He says that there was a lot of noise in the apartment on Friday night, early Saturday morning. What sounded like an argument. A loud one.'

'I wouldn't know,' I answer as coolly as I can. 'I wasn't arguing with anyone. I was passed out remember? I'm sure Joaquim and Emanuel can both confirm it. Joaquim is the one who put me to bed.'

Reza nods. 'Yes, he said that. But they also say that you and Kate had an argument earlier in the evening.'

'No, we didn't,' I shoot back.

'Outside the club, you two didn't get into a fight?'

I shake my head. 'No. I mean . . . didn't want them coming back with us. But it wasn't an argument.'

'Kate ignored you though. She brought them back anyway despite you not wanting them to come.'

I press my lips together.

'You must have been angry,' Reza goes on. 'You're a married woman and your friend is inviting strange men back to the apartment for sex. Encouraging you to sleep with one of them too, even though you're married. Strange behaviour isn't it? Why would she do that?'

'I don't know,' I admit, beginning to feel mounting apprehension with where this conversation is going. 'But it wasn't an argument,' I protest. But it was, wasn't it?

'The bouncer at the Blue Speakeasy says he saw you grab her arm. He says you were angry with her.'

'That's not true,' I answer, flustered. The truth is my memory is still patchy and I don't remember very much at all about the night. But I don't remember fighting with her, not exactly.

Bitch! I push the memory away, bury it down deep.

'You said you found her handbag and her phone,' Reza goes on.

I nod. Shit. I'm going to have to hand the phone over. They'll find the text messages between Kate and Rob, all the evidence of the affair. That'll only add fuel to the fire. If I'm not a suspect already, then I most certainly will be if they find out my husband was shagging her. What better motive would there be to kill her? The scorned wife offs the best friend who was sleeping with her husband. The headlines write themselves.

The safest thing to do is wipe the phone clean before I give it to them. It's tampering with evidence though, which is dangerous and possibly very stupid, but what choice do I have?

Fuck. My foot is jangling up and down with nerves. I force myself to stay calm.

'Do you have the phone on you?' Reza asks.

'Huh?' I startle. The phone burns like a glowing coal in my pocket. 'No,' I tell Reza with as straight a face as I can muster. 'It's at the apartment.'

Can she tell I'm lying? I don't think I'm a very convincing liar – not like Rob and Kate, the bastards. It's hard to lie well, I discover as I struggle to hold Reza's gaze and my face starts to heat up like I've got a fever.

'We'll send someone with you to pick it up.'

'OK,' I murmur, wondering when I'll find a moment to delete all the messages and if that will even matter as won't they be able to get her phone records?

'You need to also surrender your passport.' It's Nunes telling me, complete with a smug smile.

'Why? Am I a suspect?' I ask, alarmed.

'We need to make sure you stay here in Portugal until the inquiry is concluded,' is all Nunes will offer by way of reply.

My stomach drops away. That's not really an answer and only goes to confirm that they really think I might have done this – killed my best friend. 'How long is that going to take?' I manage to ask.

Reza shrugs. 'As long as it takes.'

'But I have a baby,' I argue. 'I can't stay here. I need to get home.'

'I'm sorry,' Reza says, implacable as a stone wall. She stands, pushing back her chair. 'My colleague will take you back home.'

Home, I think to myself. It's not home. Home is England. Home is Marlow. And I just want to get back there to her.

Chapter Twenty-Seven

The whole ride back to the apartment I have to force the hysteria and panic down, strangle it before it strangles me. How is this happening? How am I under suspicion? I think of all the lies I've told – about the drugs, about the phone, about Konstandin – I'm hardly a model witness. Maybe it's not too late to admit about the phone – but no, I can't. Not now. If they find out about the affair it will only seal the deal in their eyes that I'm guilty. But they're going to find out. I know they will, eventually.

How can I prove it wasn't me who killed her? Nunes doesn't seem to be interested in finding out the real story or looking for the real killer. And I don't think Reza is on the fence about it either, despite her more inscrutable face. They both think it's me so why bother looking elsewhere? But I'm not going down for this. I refuse to.

What if they arrest me though? What if I get sent to jail? What about Marlow? Oh my God ... Marlow. I start to shake so hard my teeth chatter. What if I go to jail? I don't even know how things work over here in a foreign country. My breathing becomes shallow and ragged, my lungs not able to draw in enough oxygen. My head is full of pins and needles.

Stop it, I silently shout at myself. *Focus, goddamn it! Getting hysterical isn't going to help. If you're going to get out of this you need to figure it out for yourself. Make a list. Take control. Don't let your anxiety overwhelm you. Not now.* Deep breath. And another.

What really happened to Kate? That's what I need to find out. And fast.

My hand itches to reach into the bag and wipe Kate's phone before I have to hand it over. I don't know how I'll stall the policeman at the apartment long enough. I need to do it now; it's my only chance. Then, as soon as I'm alone, I need to call Rob and have it out with him. No, I think to myself. Scratch that. I need to call Toby first and find out from him what he knows before I confront Rob. I need to arm myself with whatever facts I can dig up.

I glance at Nunes. I made sure to sit diagonally away from him when I got in the back, to make it harder for him to spy on me in the rear-view mirror. Now, trying to be as inconspicuous as possible, I pull out Kate's phone. He won't know whose phone it is, I tell myself. I just need to be bold and act like it's mine.

The screen still hasn't locked, thank goodness, so I quickly scroll to Kate's call list. There are dozens of calls from Rob. Anger flares as I count them. The shithead. How long the two of them lied to me. But there's no time for anger right now. I notice the little red icon over the voicemail. There are two voicemails Kate never listened to that were left on Friday night. I press play on the first one, which was sent while we were at dinner, and press the phone to my ear.

'Kate, it's me.' Rob's voice jolts me. 'Listen,' he says, 'I hope you were joking. Please don't tell her. You promised.' And now his voice breaks a little and he sobs, pathetically. 'Please, call me back.' He hangs up.

I swallow drily, whatever's left of my heart breaking into

pieces. I remember Kate frantically texting in the back of the Uber. That must have been to Rob. Then, at dinner, ignoring a call and letting it go to voicemail. That was Rob too.

I remember as well how she finally took the call and how I watched her pacing outside, having an argument with someone. It was Rob she was on the phone with. He was terrified Kate was going to tell me about the affair and he was calling to beg her not to. Had she really been planning on it or had she threatened it in the heat of the moment? Maybe he'd broken up with her. On the plane she'd seemed subdued and at the apartment before we went out she did seem like she'd been crying – but was it guilt making her emotional? Or was she building up the nerve to tell me? Is that what Friday night was about? One last wild night together before she told me and our friendship was blown to smithereens?

Holding back tears I press the next message. It's Rob again, an earlier message, from Friday morning. 'Kate, call me back, please. I know you're at the airport with Orla but I just want to make sure you're not going to tell her or anything stupid. Call me when you land. Please. Let's talk. Call me back. I'm sorry.'

Sorry? Sorry! I'll give him fucking sorry. How dare he apologise to her?! What about me?

There's another saved message from Rob, left about four months ago. I stab the button to listen to it, sadness turning to rage. I want to throw the phone out the window, scream and cry and let this beast of a howl out of its cage, but in the back seat of the police car I can't do anything except keep a demurely blank face, which is something of a struggle.

'Kate, I'm sorry about the other day,' Rob says. 'It was a mistake. OK, not a mistake – sorry, wrong word.' What's he talking about? What mistake? 'I know I said it was over. But I mean it this time. We can't do that again. I'm sorry.'

I take that in, trying to understand its meaning. Obviously they must have broken up when I got pregnant and then I presume they met up and had sex again when Marlow was a few months old – that must be the mistake he regrets. I wonder, though, if things continued on after that? It seems like they must have.

My stomach cinches tight and I grit my teeth so hard my jaw hurts. Hate is a black liquid pulsing through my veins, soaking into every fibre and cell of my being, drowning out everything else. I could kill both of them right now – strangle them, crush them, pummel them to death with my bare hands – that's how angry I am. And it feels way better than being sad. When I think of Kate lying dead in the mortuary I feel glad.

'We're here,' Nunes says, interrupting my very violent imaginings.

I look out the window to see we're outside the apartment already. There are other voicemails from Rob that Kate hasn't deleted and I want to listen to them but now I don't have time. Nunes is getting out the car and I need to wipe the phone before I hand it over. Damn. This might be my only chance to do it. Quickly, I scroll to settings, then to reset. A dialogue box pops up to ask if I'm sure. Nunes opens the door. I hit yes. The screen turns blank and I slip the phone into my pocket.

I stumble from the car, following Nunes in a daze, floating somewhere outside of my body, my brain busy, struggling to process all this new information while also trying to manage simple things like getting me to walk straight and not collapse right there on the ground and start screaming.

Sebastian opens the door to his apartment, his gaze hungry and curious as we step inside. I can see he's dying to know what's happening and I almost lash out at him as I pass,

221

remembering how he gave Reza a statement and told her he heard arguing in the apartment on Friday night. It's his fault they're looking at me as a suspect. He's responsible for hammering a nail into my coffin.

'Where's the phone?' Nunes asks, when we reach the bedroom.

I walk towards Kate's Birkin bag lying on the bed, slipping my hand into my pocket. I'll need to make it look like I'm pulling the phone out of her bag. I keep my back to Nunes and slide my hand inside the bag, turning around and pulling it out, hoping I managed to fake it convincingly.

Nunes takes the phone with a frown and slips it into an evidence bag. 'And your passport,' he says.

I take a deep breath, trying to hold myself steady. Handing it over feels like giving an executioner the rope to hang me with. I'll be stuck here now, at their whim. I think of Marlow and when I'll see her again. Nunes pries the passport out of my hand.

'You need to stay here. If you move we need your new address.'

'You've got my passport; it's not like I can leave the country,' I tell him.

Nunes nods at that, no smile. Once he leaves I collapse down onto the bed. Shit. Shit. Shit. I bury my head in a pillow and let out the rage that's been building, stuffing the pillow into my mouth to mute the scream.

'Are you OK?'

I lift my head to see Sebastian standing in the doorway.

'Would you like a cup of tea?' he asks.

I nod, just to make him leave. Once he's gone I roll off the bed and crawl towards Kate's suitcase, which Sebastian must have wheeled into the room earlier. I remember seeing something in there. At the time it didn't register – not properly. In a fury I toss everything out of the bag, piece by damn piece, until I find her bag of underwear. All those bits of black lace and dental floss thongs. Did she wear them for Rob? Did it turn him on? Probably more than my granny pants.

I yank out the bra I'm looking for. I remember noticing it the other day but not putting the pieces together at the time, but now I look closely I see it's the exact same one Rob got me for Valentine's Day from Agent Provocateur. Only this one is red. Nude for his wife, red for his lover. There are even the crotchless knickers to go with it. I bet Kate found a lot more use for them than I ever did.

I rip both apart, shredding the thin lace. If it's possible I might very well vomit with rage. Staggering to my feet I start to pace. I'm so angry; angry with Kate for her betrayal; angry with Kate for being dead; angry with Kate for not being able to answer any of the questions I have churning around my head. No. I tell myself, as I pace back and forth, hot tears falling down my face, I'm not going to give in to upset and anger. I need to stay focused. The walls are closing in and I need to fight back before it's too late. There's no time to dwell on the betrayal.

If Kate brought me here to Lisbon for a reason I need to know why.

It was me who suggested the trip, though, the weekend away — or was it her? No, she was the one who brought it up and I went along with it. Rob didn't seem too keen now I look back, wondering if it was too soon to leave Marlow, but he couldn't protest too much or it would have looked suspicious.

I search through my bag for my phone and dial Toby.

'You knew,' I say as soon as he answers. 'You knew about the affair.'

He takes a deep breath in. 'Yes,' he answers.

I sink down onto the bed. 'How long have you known for?' I ask.

'How did you find out?' he replies.

'Her phone. There were messages.'

'I tried to warn you.'

'Why didn't you just tell me?' I ask, thinking of his obscure comments about Kate being a liar and that I shouldn't trust her.

He sighs. 'I didn't feel like it was my place to. She ruined our marriage. I didn't want her ruining yours too.'

'How long was it going on for – do you know?'

'A couple of years I think, on and off. I could never get a straight answer.'

'Is that why you're getting the divorce? Or was she lying about you cheating on her?'

'No,' he sighs. 'I cheated too. I'll admit it. But only after I found out about her and Rob. It felt justified.'

I nod to myself. 'How did it start? Do you know?'

Toby snorts under his breath and my irritation cranks up. I already feel like enough of an idiot without him making me feel even more ignorant. 'She's been in love with Rob for years. I knew it when I married her but I stupidly convinced myself she was over him.'

My throat closes so tight I can't breathe. Years? 'What do you mean?' I stammer. What on earth is he talking about?

'Didn't she introduce you to Rob?' Toby asks. 'They were old friends.'

'Yes,' I say, but I didn't know that Kate ever had feelings for Rob. She never once told me about them, or ever acted like she liked him in that way. I always thought she considered him a bit dull or, at least, far too normal for her tastes. And why didn't she tell me she liked him before Rob and I got together if that was the case? I felt like an idiot before but

224

now I feel like the world's biggest fool that I never knew my best friend was in love with my husband.

'She hated you for nabbing him,' Toby says. 'I think she thought she was in with a shot, then you two got together.'

She thought she and Rob were in with a shot? The idea would have seemed preposterous to me a few hours ago. Kate always dates alpha men, rich arseholes in the main if I'm honest. And Rob isn't an arsehole or rich. Actually, scratch that, he's a huge arsehole. How could I have been so blind for so long? If I missed the fact my best friend was in love with my husband for over a decade, what else have I missed? I feel as if our entire friendship, as well as my marriage, has been a sham.

'I know she tried to be happy for you,' Toby says. 'She wasn't a horrible person.'

I scoff at that. Not a horrible person? Wrong. She wins the damn prize for shittiest person who ever lived. Even though she's dead I don't care that I'm thinking it. It's true.

'She told me once that you and Rob were probably better suited anyway, but I don't know, maybe she was just telling me that to make me feel better.'

I make a grunting sound because words are failing me.

'I think the affair started a couple of years ago,' Toby tells me. 'Around Christmas time. I remember her acting odd. We were meant to be going away to the Bahamas, and she was acting out, being a bitch, waxing hot and cold. I confronted her at the time, suspected something was up, not with Rob, but that she was having an affair with some guy at work, and she fobbed me off, told me I was being stupid.'

Two years ago, at Christmas. I think back. We were in the depths of IVF and I was depressed at all the failures, blaming myself. Rob and I were arguing a lot. We'd even briefly talked about splitting up. Rob had pulled away, been distant, but I blamed myself for that too. Did he turn to Kate for comfort?

Did I push him into it? Or was he distant because he'd already embarked on an affair?

'I had her followed. That's how I found out. Private detective guy. He took photos. That's how I discovered it was Rob. They were meeting during lunch breaks, occasionally in the evenings, at a hotel in Covent Garden.'

I take a long, deep breath, trying to wrangle the fury racing through me.

'When I confronted her about it, she tried to deny it of course, until I showed her the photos. She begged me not to tell you. I told her I wouldn't. Not for her, but because I didn't want to do that to you. You'd just found out you were pregnant. I knew what that meant to you. And Kate told me it was over between them. Promised me it was.'

'Did you confront Rob?'

'Yeah.'

That shocks me. 'What did he say?' I ask.

'He cried.' Toby snorts again. 'Told me it was a big mistake, the biggest of his life. He told me some sob story about how you were pushing him away, tried to make out that it was Kate who'd made the moves on him and he was powerless to resist. And you know what? I can believe it. That's Kate isn't it? I mean, that *was* Kate. If she wanted something she went after it. I think we can probably congratulate her for keeping her hands off him for so long. She did try. In the end though, she couldn't help herself.'

He's right. That is Kate. I can picture it. She probably thought she deserved Rob as a reward for keeping her hands off him for as long as she did.

'Rob begged me not to tell you. I said I wouldn't so long as he never fucking saw my wife again. But to be honest, I knew Kate and I were over by that point.'

'He only stayed with me because of Marlow. Because I was

pregnant.' It's a sudden realisation, like a crack of lightning illuminating the truth. When I found out I was pregnant, when those two blue lines appeared on the test, I was shaking with joy and amazement and incredulity, and I staggered out of the bathroom to show Rob, holding the test like it was a winning lottery ticket. I remember he was stunned into silence by it. He couldn't talk for five straight minutes. He just kept staring at the plastic stick. I thought at the time he was as overwhelmed as I was that our dream was finally coming true, but it wasn't that. I see it now. He was coming to terms with the fact that now he couldn't leave me. Those two blue lines were prison bars.

After the second attempt at IVF was unsuccessful, Rob worked so hard to convince me not to try for a third time. He pushed and pushed me to give up the dream of a child. We argued, even slept in separate beds for a time. He was in the middle of the affair then. Was he making plans with Kate to leave me? When I pressed ahead with the IVF he was angry, but I thought it was because we were having to spend out of our own pocket for it and because he was tired of the strain it was putting us under.

I was so stupid not to see the truth. He must have been hoping and praying it wouldn't work so he'd be able to leave me, perhaps he could even blame the infertility and my depression, and then it did work and I got pregnant and all his plans fell apart. He couldn't leave me after that, not when I was pregnant with his child.

I try to imagine what went through his mind. He would likely have been tormented. I know Rob enough to understand that deep down he isn't a terrible man. This thing he's done, this betrayal is terrible, and I will never forgive him for it, but I also know he isn't a monster. He has some heart. He broke up with her.

They obviously stayed apart for a while, according to the text messages, but then, for some reason, they got back together again. Maybe they ran into each other. Maybe it was at Marlow's christening. Maybe the sexual chemistry was too much or he was repulsed enough by me and my post-pregnancy body that he flew into her slender open arms like a magnet, repelled by one and drawn to another.

And now I come to think about it, didn't I wonder where Rob was after the church service? He disappeared for ten minutes, told me he was taking a phone call. And Kate was there in her role of glamorous godmother, looking fabulous in five-inch high heels and a skin-tight dress more suited to a strip club than a christening. Didn't she say she had to go and reapply her lipstick for the photos? And when she came back didn't I notice that it seemed like she'd forgotten to reapply it?

'If it makes you feel any better,' Toby says, 'I don't think Kate ever meant to hurt you.'

'Bit damn late for that,' I answer.

'Well, she's dead,' he says, as though that erases what she did, as though she's paid for her crimes by drowning. A sudden thought hits me like a punch to the chest. What if . . . Toby killed her? Or arranged for her to be killed? He did just admit to hiring a private detective. What if he hired someone to kill her? I wouldn't put it past him. She was after his money after all.

No, I'm being crazy – what an absurd thought! But then again, I'm also being accused, and the fact is there are two jilted spouses in this situation, not just me, and if they are going to use the affair as a motive then Toby is as much a suspect as me, maybe even more so given how much money Kate was trying to take him for.

But how will I find out if he's involved? I need a lawyer, or a detective of my own, but I don't work in those circles. I don't have those connections or contacts. Where would I even find one, especially over here? I don't speak the language.

'You should know that the police think someone killed her,' I tell Toby.

Toby goes silent on the end of the phone. 'What?' he finally splutters.

I listen hard to his reaction. Does he sound nervous? Innocent? Or is that a hint of fear in his voice? Is it the voice of a guilty man? 'They say she had injuries consistent with a fight. They're considering it a murder.'

'Holy shit,' Toby whispers. 'That's . . . but who?'

'I don't know,' I say. 'I need to go,' I tell him.

'Will you let me know what happens with the police?' he interjects.

'Yes. And, Toby,' I add, 'Rob's already arranged for the cremation. I think they're doing it later today. But can you handle the rest? I'm not sure I'll be able to.'

The thought of having to arrange a funeral ceremony or celebration of life for Kate is too much to contemplate. I'd hardly be the best person to lead the eulogies. Perhaps we should ask Rob.

'Of course,' Toby says quietly. 'Listen, Orla, I'm sorry you had to find out. Especially now.'

'Yes,' I answer. 'Me too.'

Chapter Twenty-Eight

'Rob,' I say, in as even a tone as I can muster over voicemail. 'Call me back.'

I check the time. It's four-twenty. He's already on the plane. He must be wondering if it was me who called him from Kate's phone. If so he's probably panicking at what I might have found out. I open the bedroom door and startle Sebastian who is standing there with a cup of tea in his hand. How long has he been lurking there? Was he listening to my conversation with Toby? He hands me the cup of tea, his eyes darting around the room, refusing to settle on my face. I see him notice the pile of Kate's clothes strewn around and the ripped-up bra and knickers.

'Thank you,' I tell him, moving to block his way into the room, and his view. I don't need him snooping any more than he already has.

'Is everything OK?' he asks. 'Can I do anything? Did they tell you what happened to your friend?'

I shake my head, wondering if his kindness has an ulterior motive, namely a desire to gather gossip. 'No.'

He frowns at that. 'The police were asking questions. It seemed like they thought your friend's death was suspicious.'

'They're investigating, that's all. They don't know what happened.' Nosy bugger.

He leaves the room and I pace, wringing my hands, trying to get my thoughts in order. I try to name all I'm feeling – a technique my therapist taught me when I'm feeling overwhelmed with anxiety. I count humiliation, grief, pain, confusion, fear and panic. It's too much to feel, too much to deal with, all piled on top of each other. How can I hold all this inside without going mad?

I look at the teacup on the side. I don't need tea. I need a proper drink. Something strong, to settle my nerves and help clear my head, or maybe the opposite, erase everything, at least temporarily. My first thought is to call Konstandin. I need someone I can talk to about all this. Before I can think it through I pick up my phone and dial his number. He answers instantly.

'Hi, is everything OK?' he asks. 'Do you need a ride somewhere?'

'Yes,' I say.

Half an hour later he picks me up. I leave the apartment without a word to Sebastian who is locked inside his recording room. Konstandin is outside the apartment, waiting by his car. He opens the door to let me in then hops in the driver's side. 'Where are we going?' he asks as he starts the engine.

'I need a drink,' I say, staring straight ahead.

Konstandin pauses to look at me but says nothing and starts driving. He drives for ten minutes before he pulls down a narrow, cobbled street with colourful buildings on either side, and he parks. We get out the car and I follow him to a tall wooden door. There's no sign or anything that it's a bar, and in fact it looks more like these are houses. There are washing lines spread overhead, white sheets flapping. When Konstandin pulls out a key and unlocks the door I look at him askance. 'Where are we?' I ask.

'My place,' he answers.

He leads me into a cool, tiled foyer. There's a communal stairwell and two doors leading off it. He gestures at one of the doors and walks towards it, unlocking it. For a brief moment I have to swallow down nerves. Am I walking into a stupid situation? What if Konstandin should be on my list of suspects?

I look at him as he steps aside to let me into the apartment. I've seen him punch a man. I've seen him threaten others. I know what he's capable of. It's not a stretch too far to wonder if he could have killed Kate. But my gut keeps telling me it's not him.

I walk into the apartment.

Konstandin shuts the door behind us. I hear him lock it. I'm inside his apartment and no one knows where I am. I shouldn't be here.

I turn around. Konstandin is standing blocking the door, watching me watching him. His expression, with its dark hooded eyes, gives nothing away.

'What would you like?' Konstandin asks. 'I have whisky, brandy, beer.'

'Whisky,' I answer.

'Ice?'

I nod. 'Yes please.'

I follow him into a small kitchen. The apartment seems to be just the living room we entered, this kitchen and then two other doors off the living room, which I'm guessing are a bedroom and a bathroom. It looks like he lives alone. *Orla*, a voice in my head says, *what are you doing?*

I watch him take the ice tray from the freezer. He cracks several cubes into a glass and pours the whisky over the top, then hands it to me before making himself the same. He holds up his glass up to mine.

'*Gëzuar*,' he says.

'*Sláinte*,' I reply.

We watch each other over the rims of our glasses as we drink.

Konstandin gestures back out to the living room and moves a pile of laundry from the sofa so I can sit. He pulls up a hard-backed chair and sits opposite me. I drop my gaze to the whisky in my hand and then knock it back in one big swallow, closing my eyes as it burns a trail down my throat. It does nothing to extinguish whatever storm is brewing inside me. The rage and sadness are still doing battle to see which will emerge triumphant.

'Kate was murdered,' I say, choking out the words. 'The police say there was evidence of a struggle.' I look up at Konstandin. He's leaning with his elbows resting on his knees, glass held loosely his hands. 'She was having an affair with my husband,' I tell him. 'The police don't know. I just found out about it.'

Konstandin's expression doesn't alter. He doesn't move or say anything for about five seconds but then he stands up and goes into the kitchen. He returns with the whisky bottle – a fine Scotch I note – and fills my glass again, almost to the brim. I take another large swallow. This time the liquid fire does seem to rub the sharp edges off the pain.

'How did you find out?' he asks.

'There were messages on her phone. I've had to hand it over to the police, but I wiped it clean first. Deleted everything.' I chew my lip, wondering if it was the right thing to do. Too late now, though.

Konstandin doesn't say anything and I find myself wishing he would, watching him for his reaction. I want to know whether he thinks I did something stupid. I want his opinion. In truth I want his help – that's really why I called him.

'I don't know what to do,' I say and now the tears come,

sliding down my face in an endless stream. 'The police think I did it. If they find out about the affair they'll think it was a motive.' I wipe at the tears rolling down my face and dripping off my chin.

'It is.'

I look up in alarm at Konstandin. What's he saying? 'You can't think I did it!' I shout, lurching to my feet. 'I didn't! You saw me the day after she disappeared. You know I didn't do it . . . I couldn't . . .'

Konstandin is on his feet too. 'That's not what I meant,' he reassures me. 'I meant that perhaps there were other people who were hurt by the affair, who might also have been angry, who also had it as a motive.'

Relief washes over me. He's confirmed my own suspicions. 'Yes! Toby, Kate's ex-husband! He admitted to me that he knew about the affair. And he was furious about the divorce and Kate trying to take his money.' I start to pace up and down the small living room. Could it really be Toby? Is he capable of this? Did he follow us to Lisbon or have someone follow us? He's the kind of person who'd hire someone to do his dirty work.

'I was actually thinking of your husband,' Konstandin says, interrupting my chain of thought.

'What?' I turn and stare at Konstandin in shock.

'What was he doing in Lisbon?' He shrugs.

'I asked him to come here,' I exclaim. 'It wasn't Rob. He was home on Friday night. He was taking care of Marlow.'

'Are you sure?'

I shake my head at him, bewildered. 'Yes . . . yes! She's a baby. She can't exactly take care of herself.' I called him on the Saturday once I woke up and found Kate was missing. He was home then. He was about to take Marlow to the park.

'How did your husband feel about his mistress going on holiday with his wife?' Konstandin asks.

I reach for my whisky glass and take another swig. It helps burn off the last of my tears. 'He was worried. I listened to the messages he left on Kate's phone. He thought she was going to tell me about the affair. He begged her not to.'

Konstandin says nothing. He doesn't have to. He's right. That's a motive right there. 'Shit,' I say, clamping my hands around my head. 'I deleted the messages. I erased everything on her phone. I didn't want the police to find out.' I pull my own phone out of my back pocket. 'But I took screenshots of the texts they sent and emailed them to myself. There were hundreds of them.'

I open up my email and click on the first of them. The earlier ones are all full of aubergine emojis and times and meeting places. As I keep scrolling I notice the increase in heart emojis and more mundane things about work and life. Kate tells him often that she misses him. Every message that I read twists the knife another savage turn. I shove the phone at Konstandin. 'I can't do this.'

He takes the phone and starts reading as I pace behind him, eyes scrunched shut.

'Tell me the gist,' I say.

'It looks like he broke up with her.'

'Why? Was it because I was pregnant?'

'Yes,' Konstandin says. 'He says he's sorry but he can't walk away now, not with a baby on the way.'

I finish the rest of my whisky and reach for the bottle.

'She's not happy,' Konstandin continues. 'She tries to convince him to stay with her, tells him they can make it work. That she loves him.'

'Does he ever say it back?' I ask, through gritted teeth, watching Konstandin's face as he reads through the texts.

He glances up at me and nods. 'But he says he loves you too.'

'Well, that's OK then, isn't it?' I remark, pouring myself

another hefty measure of whisky. 'Shame we aren't Mormons. We could have been sister wives.'

'You might want to slow down,' Konstandin remarks as I bring the glass to my lips.

I glare at him.

'You need to keep a straight head,' he tells me evenly.

He's right; I know. Grudgingly, I set the glass down.

'It makes sense,' Konstandin says, pulling a cigarette packet out of his back pocket. He offers one to me and I take it and let him light it for me. I inhale deeply, letting the head-spinning effect calm me.

'What makes sense?' I ask.

'The reason Kate hired the escorts.'

'What do you mean?'

'She hired them to sleep with you so she had something to show your husband. If she could prove to him that you had been unfaithful then maybe he would finally leave you and be with her.'

It's like he's slapped me. The truth is suddenly, brilliantly and harshly, illuminated. 'If I slept with someone then it wouldn't just be *him* who cheated! He'd have an excuse to divorce me. He wouldn't be the bad guy. He could blame *me*!'

'Kate thought he only needed a nudge and then he'd be free.'

'And she could make her move. They could be together.' I drop down onto the sofa, the whisky and the cigarette smoke combining with the knowledge of Kate's betrayal, making me feel suddenly sick as a dog.

Konstandin glances over the texts again. 'It looks like they didn't speak or see each other for almost a year but then they met up again about four months ago.'

'At Marlow's christening,' I say, doing the maths. I was right.

'Afterwards Kate sends a lot of texts pleading with him to

speak to her. He ignores them all but for . . .' Konstandin abruptly stops reading.

'What?' I ask.

'Nothing,' he says. 'You don't need to hear it.'

'What?' I ask, grabbing for the phone. Konstandin keeps a tight grip on it, pulling it away from me but I tear it from his hand.

'Orla . . .' he pleads, reaching for it back, but I dance out of his way.

Rob: *I love you, Kate, and one day maybe we can be together but right now I need to be here, with Marlow. I can't walk out on them.*

Kate: *We could be a family. You, me and Marlow.*

Rob: *I wish, but I can't.*

The howl that's been trapped inside me for days finally bursts free. All the grief and worry and anger erupting out of me. I fall to my knees, hurling the phone across the room. The world collapses in on me. He wanted to be with her. He wanted to be a family with her, to replace me with Kate. He only stayed out of a sense of duty. And all that talk from Kate about a house in the suburbs with a garden, about starting a family. She didn't need to start one, she was planning on stealing mine! Becoming stepmother to my child! And then probably having a baby with Rob.

And maybe Rob killed her because she threatened to tell me before he was ready.

I want to tear a hole in the ground with my bare hands and curl up in it, pull the earth down on top of me and stay there, buried in darkness. I want the pain to stop, the noise in my head to stop, the questions racing around my brain to stop. And then suddenly darkness does fall but it's just Konstandin, kneeling in front of me, wrapping his arms around me. He holds me, stroking my back, and I collapse against him, sobbing so hard I soak his shirt.

I don't know how long the pain consumes me for, how long I cry for. It feels like an eternity, but at some point I become aware I'm hiccupping, not sobbing, and that the sound of Konstandin's murmurs in my ear in a language I don't understand are louder than my crying. After I stop crying Konstandin disentangles himself and stands up.

'Let me make you a cup of tea. Or coffee?'

'Coffee,' I mumble, my head throbbing. 'Thank you,' I say.

He nods, then walks into the kitchen and after a few seconds I follow him in.

He heats water in an espresso maker as I stand watching. 'The police say Joaquim and Emanuel have alibis. It wasn't them.'

He nods. 'You should check where Rob was on Friday night. And Toby.'

'It could have been a stranger,' I say. I don't want to believe it could be Rob.

'Most murder victims know their murderers.'

And I don't want to dig further into that memory I have. I'm afraid to unearth it from the darkness. The moonlight on water. A woman screaming *bitch!*

Konstandin pours the coffee into a little espresso cup. 'I must ask you something,' he says, handing the cup to me. 'You've never wondered if it was me? If I had anything to do with Kate's death?'

I open my mouth to deny his question, but what's the point of lying? 'Yes,' I tell him. 'I've considered everyone. Every person we met that night, down to the old man who owns the shop opposite the apartment. I've gone mad with wondering.'

'But do you honestly think I might have anything to do with it?'

I look him in the eye. He gives me his same even gaze as always. The truth is I've seen him threaten and beat up a man. I know he's capable of violence but still I shake my head. 'No,' I say.

He nods, a smile brushing the edge of his mouth. 'You're too trusting,' he says.

'Have you ever killed anyone?' I ask, the words flying out my mouth before I can stop them.

'If I had, I wouldn't tell you,' he answers deadpan, casting a sideways look my way as he pours sugar into his coffee.

Chapter Twenty-Nine

Konstandin tells me he has to take care of some business and drops me back at the apartment. 'Be careful,' he says as I get out the car. 'And if anything happens, call me.'

If anything happens. What does he mean? If the police arrest me I suppose.

Once I'm back in my bedroom I get to work. I quickly locate the number of Toby's office and call the central switchboard. I ask to be put through to Toby's assistant, hoping that they're still in the office working late, and thank God, they are.

'Hi,' I say, trying to hide the tremor in my voice. 'It's Aisling in accounts.'

'Aisling?' the assistant interrupts, obviously confused.

'I'm new,' I say hastily. 'I'm just calling about the charges on the company credit card.'

'What company credit card?'

'Toby's card,' I bluster. 'Can you confirm where he was Friday night so I can make sure I'm signing off the right things . . . items.' I cringe inwardly at how terrible I am at lying. The assistant sighs loudly. I close my eyes. I should have thought harder before I made the call, come up with a better-sounding story.

'He was with clients that night,' I hear her say, a mouse clicking in the background. She must be going over his diary on the computer.

'Great,' I say. 'And after?'

'I don't know. It just says dinner and drinks with ADC Media.'

'Do you know where?' I ask.

'Why do you need to know?' she queries.

'Um, I just need to match the receipt to what's on the sheet.'

'Soho House in Shoreditch,' she answers.

'Fabulous,' I say. 'Thanks.' I hang up, adrenalin buzzing. He was in London that night.

It doesn't take Toby completely out of the running. He's not a man to get his own hands dirty. I can fully believe he might be the sort of person to hire someone to 'solve' his problems. Or am I being a fantasist? Do people really do that sort of thing in real life? Hire hitmen? Still, I don't have time to dwell so I move on.

The next call is far harder to make and the adrenalin firing through my body seems to ratchet up so I'm shaking when I place the phone to my ear.

'Hello?'

'Hi, Denise,' I say, picturing the child minder on the other end of the phone, probably balancing a baby on one hip.

'It's me, Orla.'

'Hi, Orla! Rob just picked up Marlow a couple of minutes ago.'

I check the time. That's about right. He would have landed about six and gone straight to Denise's from Heathrow. He hasn't called me back though, which is odd, unless he's panicked about the message I left him and the call from Kate's phone.

'Are you still in Lisbon?' she asks. 'I heard about your friend. I'm so sorry. What an awful thing to happen. What's going on now?'

'Um, well, I need to stay here and deal with a few things,' I say, deciding not to mention the fact I might be under suspicion for murder and the police are holding my passport.

'You know I'll do anything I can to help. I'm happy to have Marlow again overnight. She was a love. So easy.'

'Thank you,' I say, a pain twisting up my throat at the sound of Marlow's name. 'Did you have Marlow on Friday too?'

'Yes,' Denise says, 'Actually now you mention it, Rob forgot to pay me for Friday night.'

'Oh,' I manage to croak, my heart skipping beats. 'I'll see to it he pays you the extra he owes.'

'Thank you,' she says. I hear a child scream in the background.

'Did Rob say where he went Friday night?' I ask just before she hangs up, keeping my tone light. 'Why he needed you to look after Marlow?'

'He said he was out for a night with the boys. Taking advantage of you being gone.' The screaming in the background gets louder. 'I better go. I'm sorry again for what's happened.'

She rings off and I stand there holding the phone, staring at it in disbelief. Where was Rob Friday night? Was he really out with the boys? It's a possibility I suppose. He did mention a few weeks ago that he was missing seeing his friends. I encouraged him to have a boys' night out. Maybe he decided to take advantage while I was gone. But why didn't he tell me about it? I guess when I spoke to him on Saturday the conversation was all about Kate going missing. He wouldn't have brought it up necessarily. Remembering something else, I check my messages from him. He sent me a photo of Marlow on Friday night – of her eating spaghetti covered in sauce like an Oompa-Loompa. The bastard. It was a deliberate deception, to

242

make me think he was with her. The photo is an old one from a couple of weeks ago. I know because in the background is a vase of flowers, ones that Rob bought me for Mother's Day that I threw away before I left for Lisbon because they'd wilted.

Frantically, I do the calculation. It's possible Rob could have flown over to Lisbon Friday and back to London Saturday morning, and then I suppose he could have come back again on Sunday when I called and asked him to. It's only a two-and-a-half-hour flight. If that was a drive we wouldn't think it was any time at all, the distance from London to Birmingham. But if he did fly over then there would be records of it. He wouldn't have been so stupid to put the flights on the joint credit card. He's hidden his affair for years, paying for hotel rooms, without me finding out. He's clearly an expert at duplicity and leading a double life; it's not a stretch to think he could pull something like this off.

If he was on a boys' night out I can easily confirm it.

I call Tom, his best friend.

'Hey, Orla,' he answers. I can hear a football game going on in the background on the television. 'What's up?'

'Hi, Tom,' I say, wondering if he's heard about Kate. He might not have seen my post on Facebook and if he hasn't spoken to Rob then there's a chance he hasn't heard yet. I don't know if the UK press has picked up the story.

'Were you out with Rob on Friday night?'

He doesn't say anything and I can practically hear his brain whirring over the top of the footie commentary. I realise too late that I've blundered into the conversation. What if Tom knows about Kate and Rob and the affair? He might think I'm calling to sniff around. He might be panicking about whether he's meant to provide Rob with an alibi.

'Er . . .' he stammers. In the background a massive cheer goes up and the commentator's voice rises an octave.

'Tom,' I interrupt coolly. 'I know about the affair. I know about Rob and Kate.'

He draws a breath but says nothing, confirming that he knew. The bastard. I wonder if I'm the only one who didn't. I feel like such a damn fool.

'Orla . . .' Tom starts but I cut him off again. I don't want to hear his apology or his excuses. And I most definitely don't want to hear the note of pity in his voice.

'Just tell me if he was with you on Friday night; that's all I want to know. You aren't betraying him. He's the one who's betrayed me. I'm owed the truth on this. You know I am.'

He pauses for a brief second, weighing his loyalty to Rob over his debt of guilt to me. 'No, he wasn't with me.'

'There was no boys' night out?'

'No, there was. A few of the lads, we met up down the pub. Rob was meant to come but . . . he didn't make it.'

My heart gives a little stutter. 'Do you know why?'

'No,' Tom answers, then a little contrite, adds: 'I didn't ask.' Which means he thought he was seeing Kate.

'Thanks,' I say and hang up before he can say anything else. He'll probably dive right onto a call with Rob, to warn him, so I pre-empt him by dialling Rob immediately.

The line's busy. Shit. I shouldn't have given Tom a heads up. Not that it probably matters. What matters is finding out where Rob was on Friday night.

I'm jangling with nerves, my stomach writhing like it's filled with live eels. What if Rob was here? It seems more and more likely. What if he followed me and Kate to Lisbon, panicked about what Kate might say or do? What if he lured her outside the apartment that night after he saw us bring home Joaquim and Emanuel? Or he could have emailed her and arranged to meet her. Maybe when she had that phone call with him outside the restaurant he was telling her to meet him later, arranging

244

a rendezvous time and place. But why then would she have slept with Emanuel? That's not the behaviour of a woman dying to leap into the arms of her lover. It's the action of a woman scorned who's on the rebound.

I try to picture Rob and Kate fighting. Rob's never been physical with me so it's hard to picture. I can see Kate maybe slapping him, screaming at him, begging him to leave me. But maybe with her he's a different person. I would never have expected he would cheat on me, so how well do I really know him? And, if he thought she might destroy his life by telling me, would he have had enough incentive to hurt her or even silence her? I'm succumbing to the idea that it must have been Rob. It's all adding up.

Of course it could have been an accident. Maybe she went for him and he restrained her and accidentally pushed her. She could have fallen and hit her head. Did he see she was unconscious or think she was dead and roll her into the water to hide his crime?

The problem is I don't want to believe it was Rob. And at the end of the day, this is all wild conjecture – my imagination trying to fill gaps. I need to know!

Think, Orla, *think*, I tell myself. If he did fly over here to Lisbon on Friday night how can I confirm it? It comes to me in a flash. He wouldn't be able to resist the points. Rob is religious about collecting air miles. It's part of his economising, tightwad, accountant nature. He would have bought a flight on his credit card and added the miles to his Avios account and I have access to the Avios account as it's a joint one. He wanted to make sure we both capitalised on the points. Last year it paid for a return flight to the Canaries where we went for a winter break.

I log into my Avios account, struggling to remember the password. It loads slowly and the tension makes me want to scream. The whisky from earlier has worn off and now I feel exhausted, my nerves spent. I'm clinging on by my fingernails to the very edge of sanity. When the page loads it takes me a few seconds to navigate to the statement and there I see the evidence I don't want to see.

Three return flights to Lisbon in total. My own flight on Friday afternoon, plus another flight to Lisbon at six thirty-five p.m. the same day with a return at six the next morning. A third flight on Sunday is the one Rob took back here when I begged him to come over. Goddamn it. My legs give way and I sink to the floor, not even making it to the bed. He was here. He was in Lisbon the night Kate died . . . was murdered. What do I do with this information?

I try his number again. It goes straight to voicemail. He's probably on the phone to Tom who's warning him I'm on the warpath. I send a text, debating what to write. In the end I type: I KNOW. Then press send.

He doesn't respond. And when I call again five minutes later it rings and rings and he doesn't pick up. What's going on? He must be avoiding me, the coward. He's probably freaking out that I know the truth, trying to figure out how much I know and how, and what lies he might be able to get away with now Kate's not around to contradict them. I like to imagine his panic. I hope he's experiencing one hundredth of the anguish that I'm going through, but still, I need him to pick up.

I spend five minutes trying to figure out my next move and finally I type out a text. I KNOW WHERE YOU WERE FRIDAY NIGHT. CALL ME BACK OR I WILL TELL THE POLICE.

Chapter Thirty

After I hit send, I wait, sitting cross-legged on the floor, holding the phone, barely breathing. Seconds later the phone jerks alive in my hand. It's Rob.

'You bastard,' I say, answering.

'What are you talking about?' he asks.

He's decided to opt for innocence. I draw a breath that feels like fire, then let it roar out of me. 'Don't you dare try and lie to me again! Don't you dare deny it. I know! I've read all the texts. I've seen the messages you sent to her. I know everything!'

There's a pause that's so long and so dark that it feels as if I've plummeted into a void. A yawning abyss is opening up between us. I can feel it.

Finally, I hear him take a breath. 'I'm sorry,' he whispers, his voice cracking.

'No! You don't get to be sorry!' I yell. I've started crying and angrily I swipe at my tears and take a deep breath. I'm not going to act the hysterical jilted wife. I must stay in control. I don't want the details of the affair. Not right now. I don't want to hear his excuses or apologies. I only need to know one thing. 'Just tell me,' I say through gritted teeth. 'Did you kill her?'

I hold my breath, willing the answer to be no, but even if he says no, how will I believe him given the lies he's told me? How can I trust a word out of his mouth?

'Orla,' Rob says, shock or maybe panic making his breathing hike. 'What the hell are you talking about?! What are the police saying? I thought it was an accident?'

'No. They say there was evidence of a struggle. She fought with someone before she died . . .'

'It wasn't me!' Rob interjects.

'Why were you here? Why were you in Lisbon on Friday?!' I ask, my voice a cold hiss, barely above a whisper. I don't want Sebastian hearing me.

Rob doesn't answer.

'Rob?' I probe, wondering if he's hung up. Terror grips my insides. It has to be him. It makes sense.

A huge sob echoes down the line. The sound of it leaves me cold. 'I needed to stop her,' Rob cries.

A chill runs up my body. 'Stop her from doing what?'

'From telling you,' he splutters through his tears.

My jaw drops open in astonishment. The world tilts under my feet. Oh my God. He did it. He just admitted it to me.

'You can't think it was me though . . . I didn't do anything!' Rob carries on. 'I didn't kill her. I swear to you. I didn't even see her! She wouldn't meet me.'

I'm only tentatively relieved because I don't know if he's telling me the truth. Of course he'd deny it. 'How do I know you're telling the truth?' I ask. 'I can't trust you.'

'I'm sorry,' he whispers again.

'You're only sorry that I found out,' I spit, new waves of anger washing over me. I know if we were face to face I'd find it almost impossible not to pummel him with my fists.

'I didn't want to hurt you,' he says. 'I'd called it off. We were over with, me and Kate. Things were good between you and me.' He sniffs. 'And then I found out you were going away with her for the weekend and I got worried. You know Kate . . . she liked to play games. She was angry about . . .' He breaks off.

'I know why she was angry,' I tell him, my voice an iron rod. 'I've read all your texts. I listened to the messages.'

I can almost hear his panic scratching at his throat as he takes that in.

'Keep going,' I order him.

'She was angry and I thought maybe because she was so angry she'd tell you about . . .' He breaks off.

'The affair,' I finish for him.

'I panicked,' Rob says. 'It was stupid. I don't know what I was thinking. But I couldn't stay at home waiting to get a call from you asking me if it was true. I figured I'd fly here and try to talk to Kate, convince her not to say anything to you. And if I couldn't talk to her or convince her, I could at least be there to talk to you if she did tell you.'

I shake my head. He must have been out of his mind with panic to leave Marlow with the babysitter and fly out here. 'But you didn't speak to her? You didn't see her?'

'No,' he says. 'I . . . she promised me she wasn't going to say anything. I think . . .' He breaks off again.

'What?' I press.

'I think it was a power game for her. She wanted to know that I'd come running. Her way of asserting control. She was playing with me. She wanted my attention.' He says it through gritted teeth, the anger in his voice obvious.

'And that made you mad,' I say.

'No! I mean, yes,' he says, flustered, 'but I didn't hurt her. How could you even think that?'

'Are you kidding me?' I snort. 'How could I think that? I don't know what to think. You've been lying to me for years!

You were sleeping with my best friend. You don't even want to be with me.'

'That's not true!' he protests.

'You only stayed because of Marlow.'

'No!'

'Stop bloody lying to me, Rob!' I shout before quickly lowering my voice. 'I've read the texts.' My fists are clenched and my nails dig bloody half-moons into my palms as I remember. 'She wanted to start a family with you. You wanted it too.'

Rob falls silent.

'Look,' I say, closing my eyes and taking a deep breath. 'I can't do this now.'

'I'm sorry,' he whispers.

'Don't,' I mutter.

He falls silent. The tension crackles down the line.

'Orla,' he finally says. 'I didn't kill Kate. I swear to God.'

I say nothing. His word means nothing.

'It was probably those men, the escorts you told me about. Have the police interviewed them yet?'

'It wasn't them,' I tell him wearily. 'You know, she hired them because she wanted me to sleep with one of them and when I didn't she tried to fake it so I'd think I had. She did it on purpose, Rob, and when I didn't want to sleep with him she drugged me so in the morning I wouldn't remember and then she could tell you I'd been unfaithful.'

'What? Why would she do that?' Rob asks.

'So you'd have a reason to leave me.'

He breathes in sharply. 'My God,' he whispers under his breath. 'That's crazy.'

'Yes. Guess what though, Rob?'

'What?' he asks.

'I'm the one leaving you.'

'No, Orla, please, come on . . .' he begs.

'Stop talking,' I tell him, trying to hold back the sob that's building in my chest. 'I don't want to hear another word.'

'What about the police?' he asks, ignoring me. 'You aren't going to tell them are you? About me being there?'

I snort. 'Why shouldn't I? They think I have something to do with her murder. They're looking at me as a suspect.'

'Shit,' he says loudly. 'For real?'

'They haven't charged me but, yes, I can tell they think I had something to do with it. You were here; you saw how suspicious they were. And now, once they find out about the affair they'll think I have a motive, won't they? So thanks, thanks a lot!' I add, sarcastically.

'Oh my God, Orla. What are you going to do?'

I shake my head. Suddenly I'm on my own in this. There's no offer to fly out and set the record straight, no sense that he's the one who's helped put me in this situation.

'If the police find out about the affair then we're both screwed,' he says. 'If they find out I was over there we could both end up arrested. I mean, they might think we planned it together, or that we all had a falling-out about it and one thing led to another and . . .' He tails off.

I mull that over in my mind. Would the police think that? Or would I be in the clear? Would they turn to Rob as the prime suspect? And won't they find out he was in Lisbon eventually?

'What would happen to Marlow?' Rob asks, interrupting my thoughts.

Oh God. He may as well have reached through the phone and grabbed me by the throat. I know what he's doing. He's using our child as a pawn. If Rob's arrested or questioned, what would happen to her? Rob's parents aren't often around to help out. They're in Ecuador at the moment on a month-long trip, and my mum is in Ireland, taking care of my dad who has Parkinson's. It's not like they'll be able to have her, and we can't foist her on Denise. Marlow needs one of her parents there. But why shouldn't it be me? I'm the innocent party here. But I can't get home without my passport. I could yell at the injustice of it. It should be Rob here in my place, coming under suspicion and having to surrender his passport. I'm the one who should be home with our daughter.

'Just say nothing for now, OK?' Rob urges. 'Maybe the police will find who really did it.' He's willing me to get on board with his plan. There's a pleading desperation in his voice. But what's in it for me? Other than the fact I don't want to tell them about the affair in case it gives them ammunition against me.

I suppose though, if I hold on to the information I can use it down the line if and when I need to.

'OK,' I tell him, reluctant to feel like I'm offering him anything, 'for now I won't say anything.' He lets out the breath he's holding. 'But, Rob,' I add, 'I'm not promising anything.'

'OK,' he answers. 'I understand. I'm sorry. I'm so sorry.'

I close my eyes as I hang up and let the words bounce off me, meaningless as sleet blowing against a cold pane of glass.

Chapter Thirty-One

The door buzzer goes and my heart makes a valiant effort to smash its way out of my chest. My nerve endings are raw and exposed. Since the call with Rob about half an hour ago I've been anxiously pacing the room, trying to write down a to-do list, but I'm too distracted, too panicked to write anything, to process much more than the fact my husband was having an affair with my best friend and may have killed her.

I feel like an innocent prisoner on death row, who knows the seconds are ticking by but can't figure out how to stay the executioner's hand. I've tried to discount the two people with motives besides me – Toby and Rob – and failed. And there's still the very real possibility that it was an accident or Kate was killed by a stranger. In which case, I'll never find out what happened.

I wait, holding my breath, until the knock on my bedroom door comes. It's Sebastian telling me that it's the police again. His gaze slides across my face and over the room. I can't tell what's going on in his mind, only that he seems to be in a perverse way enjoying the drama I'm providing. I'm a form of reality TV I suppose, or a Hitchcockian thriller playing out in front of him in real time.

I walk to the front door to meet Nunes.

'What is it? Did you find out who killed Kate?' I ask.

'We have some more questions,' he answers, a master in holding back. 'You must come to station.'

I sigh loudly. 'Again? I've already been in for an interview a few hours ago. What other questions are there?' I may be presenting a calm exterior but inside I'm freaking out. Are they going to arrest me?

He looks like he wants to just order me into the car without further ado but my belligerence stops him. 'We want to ask you some questions about your friend.'

'Kate?' I ask, confused.

'No, the Uber driver. Konstandin Zeqiri.'

'Konstandin?' That pulls me up short. How the hell do they know about Konstandin? Was it Joaquim? Did he tell them about the man who beat him up? But how would they have been able to identify Konstandin? Joaquim didn't know his name.

'Can you come with me?' Nunes repeats, indicating the front door.

I turn to see Sebastian hovering in the living room, listening in.

'OK,' I say. 'Fine, let me get my bag.'

I dart back into my room, questions racing through my mind as I pull on a sweater. How do they know about Konstandin? Why do they need to ask questions about him? What was it he said when I asked him if he'd killed anyone? *If he had, he wouldn't tell me.*

Oh my God. What if I've been wrong about him this whole time?

Gathering my handbag, I hurry back to meet Nunes, who is waiting for me in the hallway.

Chapter Thirty-Two

Despite the fact it's almost nine in the evening, the police station seems busier than normal. People are bustling around and when I walk through with Nunes at my side, I notice a lot of the police officers stop to watch me. My skin prickles under their gaze. I've done a walk of shame before, when I was at university, but this feels like that times ten. Everyone is looking at me like I'm guilty.

In the background of the reception area the news is playing on a TV, and I recognise Reza on screen. I can't understand what she's saying but she's giving a press conference to a room of journalists and Kate's photo sits in the bottom corner of the screen. I skid to a stop, shocked. I haven't been on social media, haven't been aware that the news has picked up the story.

Reza is in her office, surrounded by coffee cups, and looking stressed. She doesn't smile or offer me anything to drink, she just jerks her head towards a chair, indicating I sit.

I look around as I do. Nunes stays planted in the doorway, as though worried I might try to bolt. My pulse leaps, my heart rate doubling. Sweat trickles down my spine and prickles beneath my arms.

'How do you know Konstandin Zeqiri?' Reza asks with no preamble.

'Um . . . he drives an Uber.'

'That's how you know him?'

'Yes, he took Kate and I to the bar we went to on Friday night. Is something . . .?'

Reza leans forward across the desk. 'But you've seen him since then?' she interrupts.

I swallow. No point denying anything. 'Yes.'

'Why?'

'He's an Uber driver,' I say. 'He's been driving me around.'

'You have receipts for that?'

I open my mouth, then shut it. Damn. I left fifty euro in the glove compartment of his car but I didn't get a receipt for it. 'No,' I say.

'Do you normally go to Uber driver's houses?' Reza asks with a curious smile.

I draw a breath. 'How do you know that?' I ask. 'Are you following me?'

'Why were you there?' Nunes asks, ignoring my question. There's a pointed look on his face, a snide smile accompanying it. I get his inference and it makes me mad.

'It's not like that,' I say.

'Why did you go to his house then?' He's stepped away from his sentry post at the door and taken a seat beside Reza.

'I . . . we . . . we're just friends,' I stammer.

Nunes pulls a sceptical face. 'Friends? You met three days ago.'

'He's been helping me,' I stammer, 'translating and bringing me here to file a missing person's report. He was helping me look for Kate. That's all. Is he a suspect?' I ask, wringing my hands. 'Do you think he killed Kate?'

Reza leans back in her chair, pressing her fingertips together. 'What did he tell you about himself?'

I shake my head, trying to understand. 'Not very much. I know he's from Kosovo, that he came here in the war as a refugee.'

Nunes snorts. 'I thought you were friends. Don't friends know things about each other?'

I glance at Reza and notice the flash of irritation on her face. She's annoyed that Nunes is interfering with her questioning of me. She's the one in charge, not him.

'Did he tell you what he does for a job?' Reza asks.

'He told me he was studying to be a doctor. Now he drives an Uber.'

'His other job.'

I shake my head slowly. 'No.'

She leans forwards, her eyes lighting up, clearly happy at her little victory of knowledge. 'He works for the Albanian mafia.'

I wonder for a moment if she's having me on or joking. 'What do you mean?'

'Konstandin Zeqiri is a well-known associate of the Albanian criminal organisation,' Nunes says. 'The mafia.'

'Mafia?' I repeat dumbly. All I can think of is *The Sopranos* and *Goodfellas* and Marlon Brando in *The Godfather*.

'Yes. The Albanians have a big presence here in Portugal – illegal guns, drugs, trafficking.'

I start to laugh but then stop, thinking of how Konstandin extracted the information I needed from the barman and the bouncer and Joaquim. Oh. No wonder he was so good at it. He's a pro. I'm stunned into silence. *But he seemed so nice*, I want to protest. Apart from the threat of violence. And the *actual* violence. And the time he jokingly suggested he might have killed someone. Oh good Lord, what if that wasn't a joke?

Orla, you really are an idiot. Here you are, running around town with a known criminal. I'm clearly the most dupable person on the planet. My instincts are terrible. It also helps explain the deferential reaction of that man in the Turkish restaurant, and why he kept turning down my offers to pay him for driving me around. Perhaps driving an Uber is just his cover story. It's not how he makes his money.

'Was it him?' I ask, my voice quavering. 'Did he kill Kate? Is that what you think happened?'

Reza shakes her head. 'We don't know. But he does have a background that puts him on the suspect list.'

'OK,' I say, mind leaping ahead and trying to sort through all the knowledge I have. That previous idea I had about Toby hiring someone to kill Kate has re-awoken. Konstandin could easily be that person, if what the police are telling me about him is true.

'Why do you think he's so interested in you and in helping you?' Reza asks. 'Did you not think it was strange?'

'A little,' I stammer. 'I mean, but he said he wanted to help because . . .' How do I explain? Telling them that I remind him of his dead wife, isn't going to help. Even to my ears now it seems weird.

Reza waits for me to finish my sentence.

'I don't know,' I admit finally with a shrug. 'Have you checked his alibi?' I ask. 'He was working the night Kate vanished. It would be easy enough to find out where he was when she died. The app would have tracked all his journeys.'

Reza's mouth purses. 'We're looking into it.'

I nod, but my brain is spinning at a million miles a minute, trying to test the theories against what I know and what I remember. Could Konstandin really be involved in this? On the one hand it would mean that Rob isn't guilty but on the other it means I've been hanging out with Kate's killer without realising it.

'Your landlord say that Konstandin caused an argument between you and your husband,' Nunes says.

That pulls me up. How did Sebastian know about that? It was on the street outside the apartment. The only way he could know that is if he was spying on us from a window.

'No, not really,' I hedge. 'It wasn't an argument.'

'He said you had big fight,' Nunes says.

Alarm bells start to sound. 'No, that's not true,' I answer as evenly as I can, given my heart is undergoing a series of miniature attacks. Goddamn Sebastian. What if he was listening at the door when I was talking to Toby and Rob, confronting them over the affair? How much do the police know, I wonder? I have to force my fingers to stop worrying at the skin around my nails. I don't want to give away my nervousness. It might be read as guilt.

Should I tell them the whole truth now — about the affair and about Rob being in Lisbon on Friday night? If they do already know, they could be bluffing to see if I'll admit it. Won't I look more guilty if I don't speak up? Crap. I don't know what to do. I don't want to give them any more reason to suspect me, especially if they don't already know.

'Was your husband upset you went away for the weekend?' Nunes asks.

'No,' I answer, shaking my head. 'Of course not. Kate and I always went away. It was a regular thing. We must have gone on over a dozen trips over the years. We've been to Seville and Valencia and Marrakech . . .'

'Don't forget Paris,' Nunes scoffs.

'But this time your husband wasn't so happy about you going away with Kate,' says Reza, wresting the conversation back from Nunes who I can see she's getting annoyed with. Her lips keep pursing angrily in his direction.

'He was fine,' I argue, unsure why we're going down this road.

'Even though he was having an affair with her?' Nunes cuts in.

I draw in a breath. Oh dear. They know. How did they find

out? It must have been Sebastian. He must have overheard me on the phone.

Reza glances sharply at Nunes. Was he not supposed to have given it away that they know? Did he just make a rookie blunder?

'You knew about it,' Nunes says, a triumphant gleam in his eye.

I should have admitted it straight up. They've caught me out. I don't answer. I'm too scared and don't want to say anything that might land me in even more trouble or incriminate me in some way.

'You found out your best friend and husband were having an affair but you still decided to come on a weekend away with her?' Reza asks, mildly.

'No,' I splutter. 'I didn't know. I just found out. After she died.'

'How? When exactly?' Reza presses.

'Her phone,' I respond in a panic. 'The messages on her phone. I found them.'

Reza cocks her head. 'Her phone was wiped clean. There was nothing on it.'

I gulp. I look so damn guilty, but what else is there to do but admit it and explain why I did it?

'Yes,' I blurt out. 'I did that. I wiped the phone, deleted everything on it. I was worried if you found out about the affair you'd think I did it, that I killed her. And I didn't. I didn't do anything! I wouldn't!' I'm gripping the edge of the desk, leaning forwards, trying to impress on them the truth but they don't seem interested.

'You knew about the affair, you came away with Kate on purpose. You planned to get rid of her while you were here. You wanted to make it look like an accident.'

'What?! No!' I shout back at Nunes who is now leaning

over the table, hands pressed to its surface. Adrenalin pumps into my veins so hard I think I might pass out. 'That's absurd,' I shout. 'It wasn't me. I swear to God, I didn't know until this morning about the affair.'

Nunes leans in so his face is pressed to mine. 'I don't yet know how you found Konstandin, but we'll find out. You needed someone to do the job for you so you hired him to kill Kate.'

'What are you talking about?' I whisper, completely blindsided by the accusation. 'That's ridiculous. It's not true!'

Nunes ignores me. 'You went around to his house today to pay him. Or maybe he was blackmailing you for more money.'

I shake my head, not sure I can be understanding properly. Maybe something's being lost in translation. 'What are you on about? I didn't hire him for anything!' I protest, but I can hear how weak I sound, how pathetic. I'm on the verge of tears.

'You paid him to kill your friend,' Nunes says, spitting the words at me.

'No! I didn't!' I cry again, tears welling at the frustration of not being understood or listened to.

'You didn't want your husband to leave you for her,' Reza says, more quietly. 'You had to do it. Get her out of the picture.'

I shake my head at her, mute, realising that she too believes this nonsense and nothing I say is going to convince them of my innocence. But then I remember that I'm not the only suspect.

'What about her husband?' I shoot back. 'What about Toby? Or Rob? He was here on Friday night. He flew to Lisbon. You need to investigate them if you're going to investigate me. They had just as much motive.'

I know I'm throwing them under the bus. But there's no way I'm going down for something I didn't do. 'You said you had a list of suspects,' I say to them. 'They should be top of that list. Not me!'

Reza looks surprised by the knowledge that Rob was here

on Friday night in Lisbon. She glances at Nunes, then gives him an order in Portuguese and he leaves the room, probably to look into the truth of what I've said. Sorry, Rob, I think to myself. But not sorry really. When it comes down to it I'll do anything I have to do to get back to Marlow, whatever it takes. My loyalty is to her, not Rob. He can go to hell for all I care.

'I want a lawyer,' I hear myself say.

'Why?' Reza responds, shaking her head as though confused.

'Aren't you arresting me?'

She studies me and I wait, holding my breath.

'Not yet,' she answers, tersely. She sounds annoyed about it, as though she brought me here to try to wrangle a confession. That must mean they don't have enough to charge me. That's something I suppose.

I exhale, trying not to show my relief, but in truth I'm shaking all over. 'So I can leave?' I ask, praying she says yes.

Clearly very annoyed, she nods. 'For now.'

I stand up, expecting her to tell me to sit back down, or to slap cuffs on me, but she doesn't. I'm able to exit her office and as soon as I'm out of it I hurry towards the front desk, head down, aware I'm being looked at by all the police officers there, that speculation and gossip are swirling around me. They all think I did it.

Weak-legged I stumble outside into the humid night, reaching a hand to steady myself against the wall. I need to sit down. The inky sky tilts around me; sounds are muffled; time is speeding up then slowing down. I put my head between my legs and force a few deep breaths, trying to get control over my anxiety.

Finally, I lift my head and take in my surroundings. I'm outside. I'm free.

For the moment at least.

Chapter Thirty-Three

As the Uber drives me back to the apartment, I check Konstandin's Uber profile. He has a rating of 4.8 and hundreds of reviews.

All those things he told me about himself, the story about how he came to flee his country and be in Lisbon, were they true? Was he hired by Toby? Is he involved in Kate's murder? If he is, why haven't they arrested him? I test the theory out in my mind but it comes up blank. Not because I'm discounting him – I'm learning not to do that anymore about anyone, not since the people I trusted the most turned out to be the ones hiding the biggest secrets – but because something else is niggling at me, something Nunes said. I can't quite pinpoint it, I can just feel it, like when you forget something on your shopping list and you try to remember what, but it's swimming just out of reach. My mental fog is dense and a lot of things are getting lost in it.

I stare out the window of the car, my brain dully noticing the sights. We're passing the big castle on the hill. Kate and I were meant to do a tour of it as part of the e-bike trip. I try to avoid looking right, towards the glittering blue water.

That's it! The thing I've been trying to grasp at emerges from the fog. *Paris*. Nunes mentioned Paris. He knew Kate and I had been there. But how? I never told him or Reza about that trip. I rack my memory to double-check but I'm certain that I didn't. There's no way the police could know about it. The trip was years ago, almost twenty years ago in fact, before even Facebook was around to document it on. Nunes was probably still in nappies.

But I do remember talking about it to Kate when we were lying on the bed in the apartment, before we went out for dinner. We listed off all the places we'd been together. She had that look on her face – a sad look as if she'd been crying. She probably had. I'll never know for sure what about, but perhaps she was thinking of Rob, or perhaps she was thinking ahead to the escorts she'd booked and having a moment of introspective guilt at what she was about to do to our friendship. She must have known that causing a rupture in my marriage and then moving in on my husband would definitely destroy our friendship. Did she care at all? Was she pretending to be friends with me all this time, just to stay close to Rob?

But I'm getting distracted. The point is how did Nunes know about Paris? Is it the same way I think they found out about the affair? Through Sebastian's spying and informing? But no, Sebastian lives downstairs from the apartment I stayed in with Kate. How would he have heard the conversation? We were in the bedroom. The only way Sebastian could have overheard that conversation was if he had been in the room with us. My skin prickles with goose bumps, the hair on the back of my neck standing on end.

I think about how he's always lurking, skulking around in the background, eager to hoover up gossip. I think about that room he always locks himself into and am overcome with queasiness.

I scroll on my phone to the Airbnb app on my phone and quickly tap in the details of the apartment and Sebastian's name. His profile comes up and I click on it. The apartment is listed underneath, along with the other four he mentioned to me. The bedroom in his own apartment isn't listed though. He told me he rented it out, so that's weird. Why would he lie, unless he doesn't usually rent it but he wanted me to stay close by? It would explain the lack of lock on the bedroom and bathroom doors, but why would he want me to stay with him? Unless of course he wanted to keep an eye on me, and the investigation.

I click on the listing for the apartment Kate and I stayed in, and scroll down to read the reviews. There are almost eight hundred and they're all five stars for cleanliness, location and amenities, but I notice a couple of people have given him one-star ratings. They're both women and they both comment on feeling uncomfortable. One mentions the 'creepy owner with his annoying rules' and the other 'a lack of privacy and an anal owner spying on my every move.'

Spying.

The chill intensifies and I lean forward and ask the Uber driver to turn the air conditioning down as I've started to shiver uncontrollably. What if he's done more than just spy?

A minute later we pull up outside the apartment and I get out the car, glancing up at the building with its whitewashed walls. Is Sebastian up there now, looking down on me?

What about that room of his? I wonder, as I climb the steps to the front door. And what about his strange behaviour, not wanting to let me see inside that room? I need to find a way to get into it. I feel sure it'll hold answers.

I knock on the front door – still having no key – and Sebastian opens it. He asks me straightaway how things are and what the police wanted. He's anxious, I bet, that the police haven't given him away to me for his spying, so I smile politely

265

and respond to his friendliness in kind, faking it as much as I can so he doesn't get suspicious that I know he's a slimy, spying liar. I'm vague with details about what the police wanted, saying it was just to run through some details about Kate's history. He seems to buy it.

After turning down a cup of tea with him I make my excuses and head to my bedroom, passing the recording room and eyeing the sleek door without a handle, only a keyhole. Where is the key? He must have it on him.

In my bedroom a feeling of claustrophobia presses in on me. All I want to do is grab my things and leave. I'm desperate to get the hell out of here. But I need to get into that room.

I had Sebastian on my suspect list at the very start and for some reason dropped him – because I thought he was too weak and too pathetic to have been able to overpower Kate – but thinking on it now, he *was* angry about the noise and the extra guests. It's possible he went upstairs to complain when I was passed out, and he got in a fight with Kate about it. I can totally see Kate telling him where to go if he made a complaint. She wouldn't have liked it. And she wouldn't have held back from telling him so.

'Hello?'

I startle. Sebastian is standing in the doorway to my room. I try not to look frightened but can't help the quick glance around as I search for something to defend myself with.

'I'm going out,' Sebastian tells me.

'OK,' I say, my heart pounding. 'Could you leave a key?'

'You're going out again?' he questions.

'I might do,' I answer, wondering why he cares so much.

'It's only that I don't have another set,' he explains, essentially confirming the fact that he doesn't rent this room out ever. He holds up his key ring as he says it, which contains a cluster of a dozen keys.

'Right,' I say. How do I get those keys away from him? 'Well maybe I could order food in. Can you recommend anywhere that does delivery?' I ask.

He nods, eager to help. 'Of course, here.' He gestures for me to follow him into the kitchen. I do, keeping my eyes on the keys as he sets them down on the side. He opens a drawer and pulls out a pile of delivery menus.

'Some are in Portuguese,' he says. 'Do you know what you want?'

I shake my head. 'No, what's good?' I ask, my focus on the keys.

'There's pizza, Thai, tacos.'

'Pizza,' I mumble.

He hands me the menu. 'If you choose I can order for you.'

'Thanks,' I say taking the menu. I watch Sebastian reach for the keys and drop them into his leather backpack. Shit.

'A small Hawaiian is fine,' I tell him, handing him back the menu.

He smiles and takes out his phone to place the order, turning away for a moment to do it. It's my chance. Without stopping to think about it I reach into his bag and grasp hold of the keys, gripping them tight to stop them clinking together, and pull them quickly out.

Sebastian turns, his eyes flashing to his bag and then to me. Did he see?

'And some garlic bread,' I tell him, smiling widely.

He must be able to see the sweat on my brow and the pulse jumping like live bait in my throat but he says nothing, just adds to the order and then hangs up. 'It will be here in twenty-five minutes,' he tells me.

'Wonderful,' I say. 'Thanks.'

I am holding the keys still in my fist, hidden behind my back. I need to get out of here without him noticing they're gone and that I have them, but his gaze is already falling to my odd stance and he's frowning. He must have seen.

I stretch my other arm high in the air and pretend to be stretching and I give a big yawn. 'I hope I'm not asleep by then. It's been such a hard day. And then there's the funeral to plan.'

'Oh yes.' He grabs his bag. *Please don't check inside*, I pray. 'I better go,' he says.

I watch him head for the door, wondering where he's heading to at this time of night. It's almost ten already. Once he's gone I hurry to the window in the living room and peer down until I see him exit onto the street, then I race to the little locked room and rapidly flick through the keys trying to find the one that fits. I try four before I hit on the right one and the little click tells me I'm in.

The room's as I saw from my quick glimpse the other day. The walls are covered in soundproofing material. There's a desk with a computer monitor on it, as well as what looks like recording equipment. A pile of textbooks sits beside the computer and on the monitor I can see an audio file is open. It's some kind of recording program.

I'm about to turn away when my attention is caught by a second monitor on the desk. If all Sebastian does is record textbooks in here, why does he need so many monitors? I reach over and turn it on.

The screen is divided into four equal rectangles. It looks like the screens you see on police shows when they are checking CCTV footage. Each rectangle is a still image of a room.

My heart leaps into the stratosphere. I recognise the room in the top left corner. It's the room I slept in, in the apartment upstairs. I recognise the tiles on the wall. My eyes fly to the next rectangle. It's Kate's old room. The rectangle below is a shot of the living area and kitchen from above – the camera must be hidden in the light fitting. And the final rectangle shows a feed from the bathroom. The en-suite bathroom that connects to the master bedroom. I was right all along – Sebastian has been spying on me.

My heart stops at the realisation he watched me shower and go to the loo. He watched me strip naked and sleep too. He must have watched Kate having sex.

A movement catches the corner of my eye. I scan the monitor and jump back in fright when I see the shower curtain in the bathroom video yank back. A woman steps out naked, reaching for a towel. It's live! I'm watching the woman in the apartment upstairs as she gets out the shower and starts to towel off.

Horrified I look away, feeling like a voyeur, but my whole body is suffused with rage. I feel dirty, covered in grime.

Sebastian locks himself in this room and pervs on people in their most intimate moments; as they shower, undress, sleep. He spied on Kate and me, as he must have spied on countless others. Another thought occurs: did he see anything the night she went missing? Was he watching? He knew how many people we brought home. He must have watched on the video feed. So what else does he know?

I press the keyboard's space bar, wondering if I there's a way to navigate to a homepage. It doesn't take long before I discover sixteen more live feeds, a total of four cameras installed at each of his five apartments. Every feed is much the same. I watch people sleeping, eating, watching movies, and am shocked when I land on one screen and see two people having sex. The camera must be installed right above the bed.

I notice a pair of headphones on the desk in front of me and reach for them. The audio comes through loud and clear; groans and moan and gasps. It's the couple having sex. I rip the headphones off, pressing a hand to my mouth in shock.

That's how Sebastian knew so much. He's not just watching, he's listening too. Where has he hidden the mics?

I click on the one final camera image, recognising instantly my handbag on the bed and my suitcase by the door. He's even been spying on me in his own apartment! What a sick pervert. I back away from the screen in disgust. Is that all he does, I wonder, watch and listen? Does he get off on it? Does he sit in here, masturbating as he watches?

Thoroughly creeped out and more than a little horrified, I move to the door. I need to get out of here. I need to report this to the police. They need to bring Sebastian in and question him. He must know what happened to Kate on Friday night. He's even a suspect himself.

What if Kate found out about the cameras? What if she came down here to confront Sebastian and they got in a fight? It's a theory, like all my other theories, backed up with zero evidence. But if Kate had discovered Sebastian's fetish he'd be terrified she'd expose him. He could go to jail for this. Would he have been terrified enough to kill her, to stop her talking?

The buzzer to the front door jolts me. It sounds like someone angrily leaning on it with all their weight. I hurry to pick up the intercom. 'Yes?' I ask.

'It's me. I left my keys.'

Shit. It's Sebastian. I hit the entry button, my heart pounding, then glance at the door to the locked room. It's ajar. Shit. I run back and shut it, scrambling to find the right key to lock it with. As I hear the front door start to open I race to the kitchen and set the keys down on the counter.

Sebastian enters the room, his eyes darting to the keys and to my hand, not inches away from them. Did he see? My disgust at him has altered, metamorphosed into unease and even fear. I want to get the hell out of here and fast.

Sebastian snatches the keys up. He turns around – his

eyes narrowed with suspicion. 'I swear I put them in my bag,' he says.

My smile is so fake he must see through it. 'Weird,' I manage to mumble. 'Maybe they fell out.'

Before he can press me any more I turn and walk away, hurrying back to my room. My spine stiffens as I think about the camera watching me from above. I sit on the bed, trying not to look around for the hidden lens and microphone. I'll wait until he leaves again before I grab my things and flee.

I can hear him moving around in the apartment. Shit. What if he's guessed I've been in the recording room? Did I leave the screen on? I tiptoe to the door. What's he doing? I thought he was leaving. Hearing silence, I step out into the hallway. I didn't hear the door bang shut. Is he still in the apartment?

'Forget something?'

I spin around. Sebastian is right behind me, holding my phone. Oh God. The world skids to a jarring stop. I left it inside the room. My eyes fly to Sebastian's face. He knows I know. For a split second I'm frozen in terror – and then I run.

Chapter Thirty-Four

Sebastian chases me. I scream and sprint for the door as his hand grazes my shoulder, trying to tug me backwards. 'Get off!' I yell.

My leg hits the corner of the table in the hallway and I trip. Sebastian is on me, pulling me away from the front door, darting in front of it to block my way.

'Get out of my way!' I scream at him.

He stands with his arms outstretched across the door, as though he's a zookeeper trying to herd an escaped animal.

'What were you doing in my room?' he asks. 'You broke in. You were trespassing.'

'Trespassing?!' I yell, my blood boiling. 'You're spying on people without their knowledge! You're a sick pervert!'

Sebastian's face scrunches up in rage. 'I am not!'

'Yes, you are! I've seen the evidence. You're spying on people. You've got cameras everywhere, in all the apartments. You're disgusting! I'm going to the police.' I move to get past him. I'm not staying in this apartment a second longer. I'll fight my way out if I have to. 'Get away from the door!' I shout as I push him out of the way.

He pushes me back, his arms flailing as he fights me. I scream and we tussle for a bit as I try to barge past him and out the door and he tries to stop me. My elbow smashes him in the face. Blood spurts. The next thing I know he's on the ground at my feet, hugging my ankles, looking up at me through tear-stained eyes and sobbing.

'Please,' he begs, his anger transmuted into pleading. 'Don't tell the police.'

I stare down at him in horrified confusion. He's no longer in any way frightening. He's pathetic. I try to kick him away, to free myself from his limpet grip, but he won't let go and I almost topple over. 'Please,' he sobs again. 'I wasn't spying.'

'What are the cameras for then?!' I shout.

'I'm just ensuring that guests respect the property.'

'What?' I snort. 'Get off me!' Frustrated, I try to kick him off again but he's attached to me like a slimy, suckered sea creature, tentacles winding around my legs.

'Sometimes people were inviting extra guests and not telling me,' he snivels, 'or having parties and making lots of noise. And parties are against the rules. I've made it very clear. But people don't care about the rules. And the neighbours complain. I'm running a business.' He says all this in a long stream, tears rolling down his face, his arms still embracing my legs.

'So you installed cameras to make sure they were behaving?' I ask, sceptically.

He nods.

'In the bathrooms? Did you want to monitor in case they didn't flush?'

He looks down at the ground, and his shoulders heave.

'You're just a pervert,' I hiss. 'You like watching people have sex.'

'No!' he says, but he can't look me in the face and I know I'm right.

I finally wrestle my feet free from his grip and step away from him.

'Please don't tell anyone,' he sobs, looking up at me from the floor where he's still collapsed. 'Not the police. They'll arrest me.'

'Good,' I say, stepping even further away from him. 'You should go to jail for this! I hope they lock you up and throw away the key.'

He looks at me in alarm, eyes wide as saucers, shaking his head. 'I can't go to jail!'

His whining and pleading only fills me with even more disgust. He's repulsive, lying on the ground trying to defend himself. How on earth was I afraid of him? He's a pathetic worm. 'You spied on me and Kate.'

He falls silent.

I step towards him. 'You watched us, didn't you?! You know what happened on Friday night.'

I can see by the way he swallows and looks guiltily away that I'm right. I crouch down beside him, no longer wanting to put distance between us but wanting instead to shake him by the shoulders and make him talk. 'What happened? Did you see what happened?' I ask, the note of desperation now in my own voice.

He glances up at me, cowering.

'What did you see?!' I say, shaking him by the collar. 'Tell me what you saw!'

I can see him weighing up whether or not to tell me so I twist his collar hard. He lets out a choking gasp. 'Tell me what you know or I'll rip your liver out of your body through your arsehole and make you eat it!'

The words are out of my mouth before I even have time to think about what I'm saying. And my fist is raised, hovering an inch above his head. He shrinks from me in terror and I feel an answering thrill of satisfaction, a sudden understanding of what it is to have power over someone.

'OK,' he cries, holding his hands up to shield his face. 'I'll tell you. Don't hit me!'

Wowed and a little afraid of the power I've just wielded, I let him go. He scrambles back away from me in fear. 'Please don't tell the police,' he begs again.

'Did you kill her?' I ask.

He looks at me aghast, his eyes wide as saucers. 'No! I swear. I didn't do anything!'

How many times have I heard that from how many men?

'Why should I believe you?'

'Why would I hurt her?' he sobs.

'I don't know! But why would you spy on people?'

'I didn't hurt her,' he simpers. 'I promise. But I did see something.'

He's completely crazy if he thinks I'm letting him get away with this but I've got the power here and hold all the cards. 'OK,' I say. 'Let's do a deal. Do you keep recordings?' I ask.

He nods. 'For twenty-four hours. Then they get automatically erased.'

My spirits sink. He won't have the recording from Friday night then.

'But I saved Friday's,' he adds, seeing my disappointment.

'You did?' I ask, unable to keep the excitement from my voice.

He nods but there's a calculating look in his eyes that makes me suspicious and puts me on edge.

'I'll show it to you, if you promise you won't tell the police.'

I narrow my eyes at him. The slimy little bastard. He's trying to blackmail me. Of course he'd try to leverage something like this for his own benefit.

He pulls his phone out of his back pocket and waves it in my face. 'Swear it or I'll delete the recording.'

'Fine,' I hiss. 'I swear. Now show me the footage.'

275

Chapter Thirty-Five

'I'm not a pervert,' Sebastian simpers. 'And I didn't kill your friend.'

I glance sideways at him. 'We clearly have different definitions of the word,' I tell him, my skin still crawling at the thought he's seen me naked.

We're in his soundproofed room, the door propped open with a textbook, as I couldn't stand the idea of being in too close confines with him. There's still a chance he did something to Kate. I'm not taking his word for anything. He's a liar as well as a pervert.

Nervous, I glance at the door. He could lock me in here and no one would hear me scream, which is why I propped open the door and am standing closest to it.

I watch him bend over the keyboard and tap away, and finally up pops the footage from Friday night into Saturday morning. He fast-forwards through it and then stops. The time stamp in the corner of the screen reads 2.12 a.m.

It's a feed from the living room in the apartment upstairs. There's stillness for a few seconds, then movement blots the screen. It's Kate. I inhale sharply, painfully, the sight of her

276

unleashing a million arrows of anger, sorrow and grief, but also joy.

For the last few days all I've seen whenever I think of her is her grey, bloated face and blue lips. And yet, here she is, as I wanted to remember her, animated and alive, bursting with energy as she strides through the shot. Emanuel follows her, sauntering into the apartment, looking around as he goes. He takes off his jacket and flings it onto one of the sofas in the living room as Kate dances into the kitchen. She's like a firework, I think to myself, shining so brightly and with such effervescence. How did I not appreciate it while she was alive? No wonder Rob was in her thrall. I watch as she fills a glass with water from the tap.

'This, you should see,' Sebastian tells me, freezing the shot and then zooming in.

'What?' I ask, unsure what he's showing me. It's all blurry.

He fast-forwards frame by frame and then hits play again. 'Did you see that?' he asks as Kate picks up the glass of water and turns away.

I shake my head. 'No, play it again.'

Sebastian rewinds the footage and plays it one more time, on slow. I draw breath as I watch Kate pull the little pillbox from her pocket and dump the contents into the glass.

'She put something in the water,' Sebastian says, pointing at the screen.

I had already surmised it was Kate who drugged me, but seeing her actually do it, drop the powder in the glass and swirl it around with a light motion of the wrist, makes me realise how hard I've been praying that it wasn't her. It's so hard to watch, one more betrayal on top of the affair she was having with my husband.

I watch her carry the glass out into the living room. She must have drugged me in the bar too when she gave me the gin and tonic instead of water, perhaps trying to disguise the taste of whatever she was plying me with, which I'm guessing was ketamine. She must have been trying to make me pliant so I'd go along with her little plan to sleep with Joaquim. After I refused, she probably decided to take things further. If she drugged me with enough ketamine she knew I'd pass out and then she could move to plan B – framing me instead, so I'd wake up and not know the truth. The bitch. How could she think up a plan like that, let alone execute it? I'm her best friend. *Was* her best friend. Or was I? I don't know and now I'll never be able to ask her.

'Show me the camera in the bedroom,' I tell Sebastian, but he's already switching camera feeds. Now we're in my room. And there I am. It's sudden and shocking and strange to watch myself on screen – almost like an out-of-body experience. It feels like I'm watching a stranger. Joaquim is helping me towards the bathroom, holding me up, his arm around my waist as I stumble blindly.

Sebastian switches cameras again, this time to the one in the bathroom. The camera must be hidden in the light fitting over the mirror. I cringe at how awful I look, how drunk and out of it, my make-up smeared all over my face. I wince as I fall to the ground with a thunk and hurl into the toilet as Joaquim hovers behind me, looking disgusted and a little awkward. He does kneel behind me, however, and pull my hair out of the way as I flop against the toilet seat.

Sebastian glances in my direction but I ignore him, my attention on the monitor.

Kate appears then, holding the glass of water. She hands it to Joaquim who helps me sit up and props me against the loo. I sip from the glass at his urging. I don't remember this part. I was already out of it, and yet Kate was still plying me with more drugs. She could have killed me with an overdose. Did she not stop to think about that?

'You OK?' Kate asks, bending down and patting me on the back. 'Why don't you get to bed?'

Hearing her voice is like feeling a whip lash against broken skin. I flinch and want to cover my ears. She sounds like she's in the room, right behind me.

'Joaquim, put her to bed,' she orders, her expression taking on a hardness as she turns to him.

Joaquim has to pull me to my feet as I'm slumped on the ground, almost unconscious. As Kate waltzes out of the bathroom Joaquim picks me up and carries me out, back into the bedroom. Sebastian switches feeds and we watch as Joaquim lowers me into the bed.

He takes off my shoes, slides the covers over me, then pauses, hovering over me for a few seconds. 'Do you want me to take off your clothes?' he asks.

I hold my breath, watching my eyes close and my body sink into the mattress.

Joaquim leaves the room, turning off the light and I let out the breath I was holding.

Sebastian switches back to the living room camera, eager now to show me the rest of the night. Kate's put on some music and it's blaring loudly. I can't hear what she's saying over the top of it but I watch her dancing with Emanuel, flinging her arms around his neck, gyrating against him. His hands rove over her body. Joaquim pours himself a drink and sits down on the sofa. He pulls out his phone, ignoring them.

'Fast-forward,' I tell Sebastian. 'Did you record them having sex?'

He flushes guiltily. 'Skip over it,' I say. I don't want to watch it. 'Go to the part where they leave.'

He does, fingers flying over the buttons. We must miss the hot tub and the sex. We jump all the way to 3.05 a.m. I watch Joaquim and Emanuel leave the apartment. They seem rushed as they head out the door, but they aren't running, only hurrying as if the taxi is outside waiting, carrying their jackets and, of course, Kate's bag.

'When does Kate leave?' I ask.

'Wait,' Sebastian says to me tersely.

The seconds tick by on the counter and nothing happens. Forty-three seconds go by and then, just as I'm about to tell Sebastian to fast-forward . . . boom, Kate comes rushing past, heading towards the front door. She's wearing a loose T-shirt dress and sandals. We hear the door slam.

'Where's she going?' I murmur to myself.

Sebastian leans over the keyboard and types something in. The image shifts to the camera in Kate's room. He rewinds the footage about ten minutes. Emanuel's pulling on his clothes. Kate's lying face down, naked, sprawled on the bed. I pull a face, grateful not to have watched the five minutes previous. They've just had sex; that much is obvious. Kate rolls over and gets up and I try to ignore the fact I'm watching my naked best friend. She picks up the used condom from the bedside table and drops it in the trash. Then I see her pause. She leans over the bin and picks up the torn foil condom wrapper. I can practically see the idea forming in her brain as she does it.

I watch her pull on the dress and then walk out the room, still holding the condom wrapper.

'She puts it in your bed,' Sebastian says, switching to the camera in my room. Kate and Emanuel enter. I'm fast asleep, head turned to the side, limbs splayed like a starfish. Kate stands over me for a second and I hear my pulse thrumming loudly in my ears as I watch her watching me.

She slides the wrapper into the bed beneath the covers.

'What's that for?' Emanuel asks her.

'None of your business,' she answers, laughing.

How could she laugh? Who is this person? I never really knew her, I think to myself.

'I'm going to take a shower,' she says, walking to the door, 'be gone by the time I'm done.'

Emanuel watches her go, shaking his head at her retreating back.

Sebastian switches the camera back to Kate's room. We watch her enter and cross into the bathroom, stripping as she goes.

'I don't want to see,' I tell him.

'You'll want to see this,' he answers. 'Wait until you see what they did while she was in the shower.'

'I know. They stole her bag,' I tell him, furious that he was sitting on all this information when the police could have used it, while I was out there running around, desperately trying to find out what had happened to her.

Sebastian seems annoyed that I already know and stays silent as the scene plays out on the monitor. We watch Emanuel sneak into the room when Kate's in the shower. He picks up her bag and then he's out of the room, quick as lightning.

The camera switches to the one in the living room, which I'm guessing is hidden on the mantelpiece. Emanuel's grabbing Joaquim, who's still sitting on the sofa, watching something on his phone. He says something to him and the two of them grab their jackets and make for the door.

Sebastian switches back to Kate's room. 'Look,' he says.

The bathroom door opens and Kate walks out, wearing only a towel. She stops, pausing and looking around, aware that something's out of place in the room. She twigs it's her bag. She scours the room for it, then screams: 'Son of a bitch!'

The breath flies out of my chest. Oh my God! That's it! That's the memory. I must have heard her scream. I was passed out in my room but the word 'bitch!' must have penetrated through the dark of my unconsciousness. It's why I couldn't ever see her, only hear her. I draw in a huge breath, relief flooding through me. This whole time I've been harbouring a deep-seated fear that maybe . . . no. I shake the idea off. It was so absurd and yet for a time . . . I actually thought I might have done something to Kate.

'Are you watching?' Sebastian snaps.

I turn my attention back to the screen. There's Kate, darting out of the bedroom and into the hallway. Within seconds she's back, grabbing her dress from the bedroom floor, accidentally knocking over a glass of wine in the process, ignoring the spill as she tosses sheets and pillows aside, looking for something, maybe her phone, before she gives up and slides on some sandals. She's out the door in seconds, pulling the dress on as she goes.

'She chased after them,' I say, feeling a sudden urge to sit down. It's so damn obvious, how did I not see it? Of course, Kate ran after them. She didn't leave the apartment to buy drugs or to go clubbing or to meet Rob or because Konstandin had lured her there on Toby's orders, or for any other mysterious reason. She ran after Joaquim and Emanuel because they stole her fifteen-thousand-pound Birkin bag and she wanted it back.

Sebastian freeze-frames the screen on Kate dashing out the door at 3.06 a.m.

'You knew!' I say, furiously rounding on him. 'You bloody knew and you didn't say a word! You arsehole!'

He opens his mouth as though to argue with me but I cut him off. 'I spent days walking around wondering why she'd left, where she was . . . You could have told me. You could have told the police, but you were more interested in saving yourself.'

Sebastian scowls at me, cheeks turning pink. He doesn't like being confronted with the ugly truth. He turns suddenly and hits a button on the screen.

'What are you doing?' I say as a dialog box pops up.

He hits delete.

'No!' I say, but it's too late. The screen goes blank.

He quickly navigates to another box and taps out a few more commands.

'Stop it!' I say grabbing for his arm.

He shakes me off, intent on deleting any evidence. 'You promised you wouldn't go to the police,' he cries. 'You were lying. I know you're going to tell them.'

I take hold of his arm again and drag him away from the computer. He yelps and turns to me. Too late I see he's holding one of the textbooks from the desk in his free hand. He smashes it into my face. I reel backwards, letting out a cry, smashing into the far wall, my cheekbone blazing. Then he turns back to the monitor and presses delete on the new dialog box that has appeared on screen.

'You won't have any proof,' he says to me.

'You can't remove all the cameras,' I answer, a hand flying to my cheek, which is throbbing painfully.

Sebastian crosses to the door. 'I don't want to have to do this,' he says to me, 'but you're giving me no option.'

My blood runs cold. What is he talking about? Before I can stop him he moves to shut the door in my face. He's going to lock me in here!

'I'll only keep you in here until I remove the cameras. Then I'll let you go.'

I dart forward and shove him hard in the chest, kicking the door back at the same time and wedging my foot into the gap so he can't slam it on me. There's no way I'm letting him lock me in here. We tussle, me clawing at him and him slapping at me and pushing me off him. I grab him by the shoulders and knee him in the crotch and he bends over double, groaning. I take the advantage and leap past him, racing out of the room and making straight for the front door.

Halfway there a hand grabs my shoulder and yanks me back.

I stumble and Sebastian tugs my arm, trying to pull me away from the front door. I spin around, bringing my elbow up. It smacks into his face with a satisfying crunch and he lets go of me, staggering backwards, blood pouring from his nose. His feet slip and he goes down, his head smacking with a loud crack off the edge of the table.

I don't stop to see if he's OK. I keep running, throwing myself at the door, fumbling with the lock before leaping down the stairs three at a time until I reach the bottom, the foyer, and burst out of the front door onto the street, gasping and shaking.

A hand closes around my arm. I let out a scream and shove at the person in a panic, before realising it's not Sebastian. It's Konstandin.

Chapter Thirty-Six

'What is it? What's happening?' Konstandin asks, hands gripping my shoulders.

'It's him. Sebastian,' I splutter, looking over my shoulder in fear, half-expecting to see him racing out the door behind me.

'What about him?' Konstandin asks, following my gaze.

'He's been spying on us. He has all these cameras . . . I tried to get away . . .'

'Did he do this?' Konstandin growls, nodding at my cheekbone. I touch my fingertips to it and wince. I'd forgotten about the blow from the textbook.

I nod. 'Yes. He wasn't going to let me go . . .'

'Is he still inside?' Konstandin asks, cutting me off.

I nod again, adrenalin pumping through me in torrents, my blood still pounding loudly in my head. Konstandin moves to the door. I want to stop him but it's too late, he's already inside, rushing up the stairs. I glance up the street. I just want to run away, get the hell out of here, go to the police and tell them before Sebastian can remove the cameras from the apartments and do away with all the evidence, but I realise my phone and wallet and everything are still in the apartment and if I'm going to go back inside to get them I'd rather do it with Konstandin at my side.

I chase after him and catch up with him at the door to the apartment, which is wide open. Konstandin steps warily inside and I follow, unable to see past him. He walks a few steps and crouches down and that's when I see Sebastian is lying on the ground in the hallway, face down.

Konstandin presses his fingers to Sebastian's neck, feeling for a pulse. I cover my mouth with both hands and let out a choking gasp. Oh my God. He's dead. I've killed him. But it was an accident.

Konstandin rolls Sebastian gently over and I fully expect to see his eyes, staring glassily up at me, or for blood to be leaking out the corner of his mouth, but instead I hear a groan and see his lips move. He's alive! Thank God. But shit, his face is covered in blood and his nose looks like it might be broken. That must have been from when I clocked him in the face with my elbow.

'Oh God, this is bad,' I say, biting my nails as I stare down at Sebastian's supine body. Even though he's lying unconscious and his face is blood-splattered and bruised, it's hard to summon any sympathy.

'He's breathing,' Konstandin says. 'He'll have concussion but I don't think anything is broken, other than his nose.' He says it with a scowl, as though he wishes there was more damage.

'He was chasing me,' I explain again, anxiety welling up. 'He tried to lock me in his room.' I wring my hands and am aware of my voice rising in pitch so I sound on the verge of hysteria. 'I ran. He came after me. He grabbed my arm. I pushed him off . . . he must have fallen.'

'He hit his head,' says Konstandin pointing to the edge of the table.

There's blood on the edge of it. My stomach heaves at the sight.

'We should call an ambulance,' I mumble.

'The paramedics will want to know what happened,' he says. 'The police will probably come.'

He's right. And now Sebastian has deleted all the tapes I don't have evidence. The police already think I hired Konstandin to kill Kate. God knows what they'll make of this little scene. They'll leap to conclusions. They'll think Konstandin and I tried to kill Sebastian to shut him up or something. They might even think I was the one who deleted the videos.

Sebastian groans at our feet. I still need to call an ambulance.

'You should go,' I tell Konstandin, pulling out my phone to dial 112. 'It's best they don't find you here.'

Konstandin nods, absently, then turns to me, his eyes sharp. 'What did you mean, he was spying?' he asks.

I point at the room down the hallway, the door still hanging open. 'I got into Sebastian's secret room,' I tell him. 'I was suspicious. He was acting funny. He knew things he couldn't have known unless he'd been listening in to conversations. He's the one who told the police about you by the way, and about Rob and Kate having the affair. He's been spying on me this whole time.'

Konstandin glowers but I can see he's still confused.

'He's got all these video feeds,' I explain. 'Hidden cameras in the bedrooms and the bathrooms of all his apartments. They're everywhere! I saw all the footage of the night Kate disappeared. He had it all on tape.'

Konstandin's eyes go wide. 'Show me,' he orders.

I shake my head. 'I can't. He deleted everything. He knew I was going to go to the police. He didn't want to get arrested. He was trying to stop me from leaving . . .' I tail off, glancing down at Sebastian.

Konstandin rubs his jaw, thinking. 'What was on the video? Did you see anything?'

'Yes,' I say, nodding. 'Kate ran after Joaquim and Emanuel. She was trying to get her bag back.'

Konstandin takes that in, shaking his head in frustration at the obviousness of it. I want to nod and tell him I felt the same way when I saw it. I could have kicked myself. It was staring us in the face – the reason she left the apartment – and we never figured it out.

'It was less than a minute,' I find myself blurting out. 'Forty seconds between them leaving and her following them. I saw it all.'

'But she didn't catch up with them outside?' Konstandin asks.

I shrug. 'There are no cameras outside so I don't know, but the police said that Joaquim and Emanuel got a taxi back to their place. The driver was an alibi for them.'

Konstandin nods. 'OK, so what if Kate ran outside after them and saw them getting into the Uber?'

'She would have tried to follow,' I say, imagining Kate running after them. She wouldn't have quit and come back inside. That's not Kate.

'She could have got a taxi,' Konstandin says.

I nod. That makes sense.

'Taxis pass by all the time on this road. Say she managed to jump in one and chase after them . . .'

I look at Konstandin. He's right. There are dozens of licensed taxis in the neighbourhood. I've seen them crawling along, trying to pick up tourists who've had enough of the hills. 'Yes,' I say, nodding. 'It's possible. But how would we find out?' My excitement vanishes. 'It would be like looking for a needle in a haystack.'

'Let's go,' he says, already moving for the door.

I don't move. I stare down at Sebastian, still passed out on the ground at my feet, blood bubbling on his lip every time he breathes in.

'Call an ambulance on the way,' Konstandin says, though I can tell he thinks we shouldn't bother.

'Maybe I should stay. I could explain it all to the police. Tell them what I saw on the tapes?'

Konstandin glowers at me. 'Why not put handcuffs on and sit and wait for them to come and arrest you?' he asks, opening the door and gesturing for me to follow.

I hesitate. 'Won't that look bad though?' I ask. 'If I run?'

Konstandin exhales loudly. 'They already think you killed one person . . .'

'They think we both did,' I shoot back. 'They think I hired you to kill Kate for me.'

We exchange a look. He nods ruefully. 'I know. They brought me in for questioning.' He gestures again at the door. 'Let's go. We need to find out what happened to Kate. The police don't seem to care about the truth so we have to find it ourselves. It's our only chance at clearing our names.'

As we dash out the door I dial 112, the number for the emergency services, and give them the address, worrying my Irish accent is hard for the operator to understand.

Halfway down the stairs I realise I should have taken evidence with me; one of the hidden cameras perhaps, but what use would a disconnected spy camera be? I worry though. What if Sebastian wakes up and hurries to dismantle the evidence of his crimes before I have a chance to tell the police or the police can search his apartments? If he does it will be his word against mine. And my word doesn't count for much.

I pause, mid-step. 'Hang on!' I yell to Konstandin and I turn around and race back upstairs, past the door to Sebastian's apartment and up to the top floor, to the apartment where I stayed with Kate. I hammer on the door with my fists and someone quickly rushes to open up. It's a bewildered-looking man in his late sixties, wearing pyjamas. 'Yes?' he asks in a strong German or maybe Dutch accent. 'Can I help you?'

A woman, around the same age, appears behind him, in her dressing gown, looking anxious.

'The bathroom and the bedrooms. There are spy cameras hidden in the lights and behind the mirror I think.'

'What?' the man asks, frowning. He doesn't understand but I look at the woman behind him and see, from the shocked expression on her face, that she has. She grips the man's arm and says something to him in flustered German. He turns to look at me, confused as to who I am and why I'm turning up on his doorstep at night to deliver the message.

'I stayed here,' I explain. 'My friend and I. The landlord spied on us. He has cameras everywhere. Call the police.'

Before they can ask anything else I turn and rush back down the stairs, ignoring them when they shout questions after me. Konstandin is waiting at the bottom of the stairs, frowning at me, clearly wondering what the hell I was doing. I shrug at him. 'I'll explain later.'

He pushes the door open with his shoulder and holds it for me. I walk out onto the street and slap bang into a pizza delivery boy, holding a pizza. My pizza, I realise. He's pushing the buzzer to Sebastian's apartment. I keep my head down but notice he glances at Konstandin and I as we head for his car. Shit. He's a witness now.

Chapter Thirty-Seven

It's only when I'm in the car with Konstandin that I stop for a moment and gather my senses. In the midst of all the drama I'd forgotten what the police told me earlier – about who Konstandin is and who he works for.

'What were you doing here?' I ask as Konstandin starts the car, my fingers moving to the door handle.

'Looking for you,' he answers, pulling out into traffic.

'Why?' I ask.

'Because the police paid me a visit after you left this afternoon. They wanted to know my whereabouts the night Kate went missing.'

I take a deep breath and press my lips together.

'I gave them the names of all the people who I drove that night. I was working all night until the morning. I have alibis.'

I let out the breath I'm holding. 'That's great,' I say, feeling a huge wash of relief, though trying not to show it.

He shakes his head, still grim-faced. 'I don't know if the alibis will be enough. They don't know what time she died. I was home alone the next day.'

I don't say anything.

'They told you, didn't they?' he asks. 'About who I work for?'

I give a tiny shrug in answer.

'It was difficult to get away,' he says, frowning hard. 'Everyone was trying to flee Kosovo but I didn't have papers or money. And if you were a man and you weren't fighting it was difficult to escape. People asked questions.'

He looks at me and I nod for him to go on.

'I could have stayed. Perhaps I should have but I was tired of the killing, of all the death. And it wasn't safe. I knew a man. I'd helped save his brother's life when he was brought in to the hospital where I worked. I gave him blood from my own arm because the hospital had none left. And I knew this man, the brother, was powerful, rich. Before the war he'd been a criminal. Everyone knew who he was. Here, they would call him mafia. But to me he was a ticket out of that place. Out of hell.'

I nod to show him I understand. And who am I to judge, anyway?

'I went to him,' he says, his voice quiet, like the tide rushing out over gravel stones. 'He remembered me and what I'd done for his brother. His name was Goran. He gave me the money and the means to get to Europe. He helped me get to Lisbon. He had contacts here.' He stops and takes a breath. 'I didn't have any money. I didn't speak the language. I couldn't find work. It was difficult. I didn't want to beg so after three months of trying to find work and sleeping in the park and down by the river I went to Goran's friends who lived here and I asked them for work. It was the only thing I could think of if I wanted to stay alive and not starve to death. A man must work.' He pauses, shaking his head as though he regrets the choice he made. 'They took me on as a driver.'

He glances at me, and I see a nervousness in his eyes, as though he's afraid I'm judging him. I nod for him to continue, wanting to hear the rest of the story.

'I told them I wouldn't do anything illegal for them,' he continues, speaking faster now. 'I didn't want to jeopardise my asylum claim. But these people, it's true, they are not, how do you say? Squeaky clean?'

I nod. I guess that's one word to describe the mafia.

'I drove for them at first,' he explains. 'Then they discovered I had trained to be a doctor. So that's what I became for them.'

I frown, not understanding.

'They would come to me when they needed help to fix things. When they could not have the police asking questions.'

Oh. The penny drops. He must mean beatings or gunshots or stab wounds: injuries that would arouse suspicion and maybe police interest.

'I did not want to keep working for them, but there are not many choices for a man like me and the more helpful I was to them the harder it was to get out. And then, if I'm honest, it felt good to be using my medical training for something. And to be able to help people.'

'So you're not a hitman, then?' I ask, laughing despite myself.

He pulls a face, not sure if I'm joking with him, but then laughs. 'No. Is that what you thought?'

It's my turn to shrug. 'They told me you had criminal associates. I assumed . . .' I break off. I can't trust any of my assumptions these days.

Konstandin shakes his head ruefully. 'Is it the stubble? Does it make me look criminal? Do I need to shave?'

I smile. 'No, I think it's the fact you make threatening people look like the easiest thing in the world.'

He gives a half smile but then his expression turns serious. 'I never killed anyone. Not even for revenge,' he tells me. 'I had the chance. It was offered to me. Revenge on the neighbour who led the soldiers to my house. Goran brought him to me as a gift for saving his brother. Killing him wasn't going to bring my family or Milla back though. Whatever was left of my life, I wanted to live it well. So instead I asked him to help me escape from Kosovo.'

'Do you still work for them?' I ask.

'Sometimes. But most of the time I drive an Uber. But the police, they do not know this. It is why they suspect me,' Konstandin says. 'And why it's so important we find the truth about Kate. I don't think the police care about the truth, you see. They just want to be able to say they have caught someone and put them in jail.'

I nod. He's right. That's been my feeling for a while now. Reza and Nunes weren't interested in finding Kate and now they're not interested in finding who killed her. They just want to tick it off their to-do list and look like they did their jobs.

Konstandin pulls down a dark street and parks. I glance out the window. 'Where are we?' I ask.

'The taxi company.'

'What taxi company?' I ask.

'There are only two big taxi companies in Lisbon. This is the biggest. We start here.' He gets out the car and I follow after him. The office is in a side street close to the railway station and even though it's later in the evening there are still lots of people milling around. I'm nervous and check my reflection in the window of the car, seeing my cheek is swollen with a purple line across it from the book that Sebastian hit me with. There's nothing I can do about it so I dart after Konstandin who is already walking towards the taxi office.

Inside there's a man sitting behind a desk reading a newspaper. I can't follow the conversation that Konstandin has with him but whatever Konstandin says works. I don't think he threatened him, as the man smiles at me, then looks at his computer screen and starts fiddling with the mouse as though looking something

294

up. After a minute he glances over at Konstandin and says something to him.

Konstandin nods, grateful, and I make out the word 'obrigado' several times. *Thank you.* Then he takes me by the elbow and leads me a few steps away from the desk to a row of plastic chairs by the window.

'I told him that you lost a valuable ring inside a taxi last week,' he says in a murmur. 'It belonged to your dead mother and you are desperate to get it back. I gave him the address of the apartment you stayed in. They record all the rides their drivers make. Each time they pick up a passenger the driver has to call in with the address. He found a driver who picked up at the corner of Paraiso just after three in the morning on Saturday. That's just around the corner from your place.'

I stare at Konstandin in amazement. 'You think it might have been Kate that he picked up?'

Konstandin shrugs. 'The driver's coming here now. We can ask him.'

I drop down into one of the plastic chairs, exhaustion overwhelming me. Konstandin sits down beside me. Ten minutes pass before the door pings and a man enters. He has a beer gut hanging over his belt and a shirt, undone to the chest, revealing a religious medallion lying in a nest of grey chest hair. He seems defensive from the moment he walks in, barrelling over to us, scowling, chest thrust forwards. No doubt he thinks he's been summoned by someone accusing him of stealing jewellery.

Immediately he starts talking to Konstandin, waving his arms about and shouting. I assume he's denying everything and it takes a while for Konstandin to find a break in the stream of anger and cut in. I can't follow any of the conversation, but after a few seconds Konstandin turns to me. 'Show him a picture of Kate,' he says.

I pull out my phone and scroll to my camera roll and pull

up the first photo of her I find – the one of us that we took at the airport, both of us grinning in anticipation of the upcoming trip. The taxi driver looks at the photo and then at me and finally at Konstandin. His anger has faded. His shoulders slump. 'Is girl on news,' he says in broken English.

I nod, standing up straighter, my hopes rising even though I try to keep a lid on them. 'Yes, do you recognise her? Did you pick her up on Friday night?'

The man has started fumbling with the medallion around his neck, rubbing it between his thumb and forefinger. He looks like the textbook definition of the word *shifty*. 'You know something,' I say. 'Did you pick her up?' My hopes rise and I try to keep a lid on them.

The man glances at me, then quickly away. Definitely shifty.

Konstandin takes a small step towards him, getting into his space and the man steps back in alarm but I'm right there, blocking his exit. There's no way we're letting this man get away without telling us what he knows; even if it's something tiny that leads nowhere, we need to know it.

'Did you pick her up or not?' I demand. 'Answer us or I'm calling the police right now.'

The driver glances over Konstandin's shoulder at the man behind the desk who is on the phone but keeping one curious eye fixed on us. The taxi driver shakes his head at me. 'No. It wasn't me,' he says in broken English. 'I did not drive taxi that night.'

'That man over there told us you picked someone up from outside my apartment at just gone three in the morning . . .'

The taxi driver darts a furtive glance at the man on the phone – possibly his boss. 'My cousin drive,' he whispers.

I don't understand and look to Konstandin in confusion.

'He's not allowed to lend his taxi to anyone else,' he explains to me. 'It's against the rules.'

'Don't tell! Please,' the driver says. 'I lose my licence.'

'Where's your cousin?' Konstandin asks him.

The man bites his lip and looks away, obviously torn.

'Please,' I say, pulling on his sleeve. 'You don't know how important this is.'

'He not do it,' the man says, hissing at me under his breath. 'He not bad. He has a wife, children. He not hurt anyone.'

'We just want to know if he picked her up and if so, where he took her, that's all.'

'We won't involve the police,' Konstandin reassures him.

The man looks between us, still weighing it up. 'OK,' he nods finally. 'We go see him.'

Chapter Thirty-Eight

Thirty minutes later, it's almost midnight and we're on the outskirts of the city, somewhere near the airport where high-rise apartment blocks sprout thick as bushes. We park in a car park beside one particularly run-down one, and the taxi driver who led us here in his taxi, gets out of his car and walks over to ours. Konstandin winds down the window.

'My cousin come,' the taxi driver tells us, then pulls out a cigarette packet. He offers one to Konstandin who takes one, then to me. I take one too, to settle my nerves.

The three of us stand outside the car, smoking. Konstandin chats in Portuguese to the taxi driver and I pray silently that this man who is meeting us – his cousin – is the man who picked up Kate on Saturday morning and that he can tell us where he took her and give us another clue to what happened. What if he did something to her though? He isn't going to tell us that.

The taxi driver keeps checking his phone and finally his cousin skulks out of the building, pulling a beanie hat on low, and shoving his hands in his pockets. He looks suspicious, darting dark glances between Konstandin and I as the taxi driver introduces us. We don't shake hands. He seems to take some convincing from his cousin to talk to us, but finally he nods.

Konstandin takes over the questioning. He shows him Kate's photograph on my phone and the man nods. They seem to be speaking a third language, not Portuguese. Maybe Arabic or Turkish?

'He picked her up!' I say.

Konstandin confirms it. 'Yes. He picked her up.'

'Where did he take her?'

The man starts to wave his arms about, talking rapidly. 'What's he saying?' I ask, impatiently.

Konstandin finishes the conversation and turns to me. 'He says she told him to follow another vehicle. An Uber.'

I nod. 'The one with Joaquim and Emanuel in.'

'She told him that the men in the Uber had stolen her handbag.'

The cousin starts gesticulating angrily. 'What?' I ask, tugging on Konstandin's arm.

'Money!' the man says to me. 'You give. Me. Owe.' His English is broken and I look at Konstandin.

'She didn't pay him.'

I shake my head in disbelief. 'She had her bag stolen! That's why she couldn't pay him.' I rummage in my bag and pull out my wallet but before I can open it Konstandin is already handing over a couple of ten-euro notes from his own wallet.

'Did he follow Emanuel and Joaquim back to their apartment?' I ask, on tenterhooks.

Konstandin asks the question and even I understand the answer.

The cousin shakes his head and then says a few more words.

Konstandin looks at me. 'He says he lost them. They hit a red light, and then got caught in a one-way system.'

I frown. 'So where did he take her after that?'

Konstandin pauses before answering. 'The police station.'

Chapter Thirty-Nine

'If he dropped Kate at the police station then . . .' I break off. 'I don't understand,' I say to Konstandin.

We're pacing a few steps away from the taxi driver and his cousin, who both look concerned and seem to be having some kind of whispered argument between themselves. They're both worried about being drawn into it, I suppose, and I can't blame them. I'm a whirlpool dragging everyone who comes close to me towards an unfortunate end.

'The cousin is an illegal,' Konstandin says, drawing heavily on another cigarette. This whole affair has got him chain-smoking, or perhaps he's always smoked this much. My own hands itch to take the cigarette from his mouth and steal a drag. 'It's why they didn't go to the police when they saw the news about Kate. He shouldn't have been driving the taxi.'

'It doesn't matter,' I say, frustrated. 'I just want to know what happened to Kate.'

'He says she went inside the police station.'

I stare at Konstandin in shock. 'Really? He saw that? He actually saw her walk inside the building?'

He nods. 'He remembers because he was nervous about taking her to the police station. He stopped down the street but remembers looking in his mirror as she walked inside.'

I glance at the taxi driver. He's on his phone now, talking to someone, and the cousin is watching us, chewing on his thumbnail.

'Which police station?' I ask Konstandin.

'The one in the centre of town. The same one where I took you to report her missing. It's the main one for tourist crimes. That's why he took Kate there. He knew they spoke English and that they'd be open at that time in the morning.'

I start to pace up and down, trying to puzzle my way through the mystery. 'But if she went inside she would have filed a report, wouldn't she?'

Konstandin nods, frowning. He's on the same page as me. 'Yes.'

'So, how come the police never mentioned it?'

He shakes his head. 'I don't know. It's strange.'

It is. I walk a few paces then stop. 'Unless the person who took the report never made the link between Kate and the missing person's report I made a day later.'

'But her name would have been on both,' Konstandin says.

We pause, musing on it. Konstandin's right. It is strange, though feasible I suppose. But I've got a funny buzzing feeling in my gut, like we've finally found a thread. It feels like we should tug on it, but we need to be careful, in case the thread snaps before we can pull whatever's on the end of it out into the light.

'We need to find out who was working that night. Who was on duty at the police station,' I say. 'Whoever took her statement might remember where she went next.'

Konstandin nods.

A sudden shriek fills the air. I turn around, startled to see a

301

police car in the distance, heading our way, its sirens blaring and its lights flashing.

'Shit,' I murmur, wondering for a second if they're there for us because how on earth could they have found us? Unless they were following us! My first instinct is to run and I glance around frantically for a way out. The taxi driver's cousin has disappeared. And the taxi driver is jumping in his car, gunning the engine. Did he call the police? Why? I think of the pizza delivery guy we ran into outside Sebastian's apartment. Did he deliver the pizza and find Sebastian? Has it been on the news? Perhaps they've put out an alert and someone spotted us.

I look at Konstandin. He's watching the police car too, and I see a flicker of panic cross his face. He hesitates just a second before he turns to me. 'I'm sorry,' he says, then before I can ask what for, he takes off, sprinting not for his car but towards a dark alley that runs down the side of the apartment building.

I stare after him astonished. I want to shout after him. *What the hell?!* But I'm frozen, a hare caught in headlights, or rather a hare with my neck caught in a snare. For a brief second, I think about following him but I know I won't get far and if I run it will only be worse for me. So I force myself to stand there, my gut twisting into knots and my heart racing as the blue and red lights get nearer and the screaming wail gets louder, until the police car eventually swerves in front of me to a stop.

The doors fly open. Two policemen in uniform jump out and run towards me, yelling at me in Portuguese. Terrified, I raise my hands in the air. They rush me, hauling my arms behind my back and snapping on a pair of handcuffs, shouting something in a language I can't understand.

The metal tears my skin and I gasp in pain but they don't care. They hustle me into the back of the police car and I start to hyperventilate, the world distorting like a hall of mirrors as I look out the window, at the alley down which Konstandin

302

vanished, the buildings seeming to grow giant, closing out the sky. Another patrol car arrives and the officers leap out of that car and race off in pursuit of Konstandin, though he's had a head start.

By the time we arrive back at the police station some twenty minutes later, I'm so dazed that I can barely focus on what's happening to me. I am led places and forced into chairs and given pieces of paper to sign. I should ask for a lawyer but I can't seem to speak. It feels as though I'm underwater. Everything – every word and every face – is blurry and distorted. I'm sinking further and further to the bottom, drowning, just like Kate, I think to myself.

I'm searched and my belongings are taken away from me. A bored-looking woman behind a desk asks me to hand over the laces from my shoes and I bend down to unthread them but I take so long, my fingers so rubbery and useless, that Nunes – who has appeared, along with Reza, probably both to enjoy this moment of triumph – interrupts and tells them it's fine, to leave me be. Eventually I find myself sitting in a room with a mirror along one wall, and a table with two chairs on either side. Reza sits down opposite me with a large manila folder. Nunes stands in his usual sentry position in front of the door.

'Are you arresting me?' I ask. I don't know what the policeman who cuffed me and brought me here said, as it was in Portuguese, but I'm assuming they were arresting me.

'Yes,' Reza says. 'You've been charged with murder.'

'I didn't do it,' I say, then stop myself from saying anything more.

'What's that bruise on your face from?' Reza asks.

My hands instinctively move to touch my cheek. I shake my head. I can't tell her.

'Why did you try to kill him?' she asks.

'What?' I ask.

303

'Who?' she repeats, snorting with derision at my playing dumb. 'Sebastian. Your landlord. We found him an hour ago. We were there to arrest you for one murder and what do we find? You're leaving quite a trail. Any other murders we should know about?'

'He's dead?' I stammer in horror. We shouldn't have left him.

Reza holds my gaze. 'No. You're lucky. He was found in time. We know it was you who called the ambulance. We have the recording. So there's no point in denying it. You had a motive. You were angry with him for telling us about you and Konstandin. Maybe he knew more. You wanted to silence him.'

'No! It was an accident,' I splutter. 'I can explain . . .'

'So, you're admitting you caused the injuries?' she asks, leaning forwards, eyes flashing with triumph.

'No! He fell!' Oh God. I'm putting my foot in it.

She leans back in the chair, eyes resting on me, carefully appraising, and I bite my lips shut to stop myself from saying anything else incriminating.

'We have Kate's Facebook messages and phone records,' she says after a while. 'We subpoenaed them. They confirm the affair with your husband, so we have a motive. We also have witnesses who saw you two fighting.'

'Outside the bar?' I blurt. 'That's not true! We weren't fighting.'

'We know you are friends with a man with criminal connections,' she continues, reading off the evidence they have against me as though it's incontrovertible. 'Who was also there tonight at the scene of the crime. We have a witness.'

The damn pizza boy.

'There's a warrant out for Konstandin Zeqiri's arrest.'

'But it wasn't him! He had nothing to do with it.'

She ignores me. 'It's lucky a witness recognised you both after seeing you on the news and called it in to the police.'

Yes, I think to myself, very lucky. She must be talking about the taxi driver. The police must have rushed to Sebastian's, summoned by the paramedics, and then issued an alert on the news for people to be on the look-out for us. The taxi driver must have called the police on us. Perhaps he thought it better that we got arrested than his cousin did.

'With all the evidence we have, you're looking at twenty to twenty-five years for Kate's murder,' Reza informs me. 'And an additional ten for the attempted murder of your landlord.'

Oh dear God. I stare down at my hands. They're trembling in my lap.

'How old is your daughter?'

I can't breathe. Marlow. I can't go to jail. She needs me. My foot starts tapping out a staccato rhythm as my anxiety grows, crawling up my body like big, fat spiders. I take a deep, gulping breath and then another, trying not to think about Marlow and the fact I might never see her again. Twenty-five years, longer even! I'll be an old woman. She'll be grown.

'Look,' I protest, desperately scrambling for something to stave off the panic, to stay Reza's hand. 'Sebastian was spying on us. Speak to the people in the upstairs apartment I stayed in with Kate. Sebastian had cameras hidden everywhere. I found them. He recorded me and Kate. There was footage of her, videos of her leaving the apartment! He was trying to stop me from getting away, from telling you about it!'

Reza glowers at me but I can see I've said something that's caught her interest. I try to reel her in, keep her listening. 'It's true. I swear. You just have to go and look in his apartments. You'll find the cameras. You'll see I'm telling the truth! Maybe he even recorded the fight we had.'

'We'd need a warrant to search his apartments. And no judge is going to give me one based on the crazy accusations of someone under arrest for one murder and one attempted murder.'

'Please!' I say. 'Please. You have to believe me! There were some German tourists staying in the apartment we stayed in. Go and speak to them!'

She keeps staring at me, and I can't tell what she's thinking, but finally she stands up and walks over to the door. 'I'll be back,' she says and walks out, leaving me with Nunes, a tall, dark presence in the corner of the room. He walks over and sits down, clearly taking advantage of the boss being away to try to crack the case.

'You're going to prison for this,' he says, leaning over me menacingly. 'So you may as well confess.'

'But I didn't do it,' I protest angrily.

'Confess and you'll do ten years, maybe fifteen. A sympathetic judge. People will understand. She was your friend. She betray you. Give us Konstandin and maybe we can strike a plea deal. You'll get out in time to see your daughter grow up.'

'She came here!' I shout. 'Kate came here and made a report!' I can't believe I've waited until now to remember this.

'What?' Nunes asks, frowning at me.

'The night she died,' I say, eager to share now I think it might help derail the train that's rushing towards me. 'She came here to file a report about her stolen bag.'

'How do you know this?' he asks. 'Why did you not mention it before?'

'I only just found out.' I swallow. 'It's why I was with Konstandin tonight. We tracked down the taxi driver who brought her here.'

'We would know if she came here,' he retorts, sarcastically.

'Why don't you check?' I urge, sitting forwards, feeling the sting of the handcuffs rubbing my raw wrists. 'Konstandin and I were trying to find evidence to clear our names, that's all.'

He stares at me, unmoving. I meet his stare, pleading with him silently. Why isn't he going and checking? 'Fine,' I huff.

'I'll tell Detective Reza when she gets back. At least one of you is doing your job.'

I say it to rile him as I know he's hungry to make the case. If I can poke him, and make him look like he's missing an opportunity, he'll probably jump to it. But he doesn't move. Instead a look of panic crosses his face. It's brief. He covers it quickly, but not quickly enough. My heart bursts like a bomb in my chest.

Oh God. Everything slips into place.

I lift my eyes from the tabletop and stare at him. It was Nunes. He was on duty that night. I can tell just from the look on his face. He took Kate's statement. I don't need confirmation because it's written in his eyes. Guilt.

And now I remember something else, something that bobs up to the surface of my memory. At that first meeting, when I gave him the details of Kate's disappearance he said something about her being recently divorced. At the time I was too tired and emotional to notice but I never told him that. So how did he know? Unless Kate told him.

'It was you!' I say. 'You took her statement.'

He glances quickly over his shoulder at the door. There it is again, that panic flitting across his face. Shit. It hits me then that I'm alone in here with him. Where's Reza? I tug at my wrists but I'm cuffed to the chair. Another bomb goes off in my chest.

'Why didn't you tell anyone?' I ask. 'When I reported her missing? Why did you not say anything?'

The whole time he's been pretending to search for her, and he knew all along that she'd been to the police station to report her bag missing. It doesn't make sense. Why did he not say anything? The realisation sinks in. There's only one reason he wouldn't have said anything. 'Oh my God,' I whisper, staring at him in shock as the pieces slot into place. 'It was you!' I cry. 'You killed her!'

He shakes his head. 'No!' he hisses, his eyes leaping furtively to the door.

'Yes,' I say, because guilt is written all over his face. 'It was you.'

'No! Stop it!' He leaps to his feet, his head whipping to the door again before he turns back to me, speaking in a hushed shout. 'Be quiet! You don't know what you're saying!'

'What happened?' I ask. 'Tell me what happened!' I need to know.

He looks like he might lunge across the table at me. I shrink back away from him but I've got nowhere to go because I'm cuffed to the chair. 'Be quiet!' he spits furiously.

I obey, staring at him in frozen disbelief. This is the man who killed Kate. 'They're going to find out,' I tell him. 'You may as well come clean. Tell me what happened. Admit it.'

His face reddens, his mouth twisting into a grimace. He runs a hand through his dark hair in a panic. 'It was a mistake, that's all.'

His admission hits me like a slap. 'What was a mistake?' I stammer.

He blinks at me as though shocked to have said it out loud.

'Nothing,' he says. 'Nothing! I didn't hurt her. I swear!'

'Then what did you mean? What was a mistake?' I push, my voice rising, hoping that someone outside the room might hear. Where the hell is Reza?

'Shhhh!' Nunes says, trying to get me to hush.

I look up at the ceilings. There aren't any cameras installed. When I look back at Nunes, sweating profusely and agitated, he reminds me of a wounded animal caught in a trap. With chilling horror, I realise the danger I'm in. I need to keep him calm until Reza returns.

'Tell me what you meant,' I say quietly. 'What mistake?'

'Offering to drive her home,' Nunes says.

He drove her home! He's admitted it!

'And then what happened?' I press. How did he end up killing her? I need to know. 'I'm sure it was an accident,' I say gently, hoping he'll open up to me if he thinks I'm on his side.

His brow furrows and he seems lost in thought, probably replaying the events in his head.

'I'm sure you didn't mean to kill her,' I say, though I feel no such certainty.

His eyes jerk to me, flashing with fury. 'I didn't kill her! Stop saying that!' He leans over the table, his face inches from my own. The fury emanating off him is so immense that my insides quiver with fear. He looks like he's about to hit me. Is that how he looked at Kate? What if he tries to hurt me?!

I open my mouth and scream at the top of my lungs. 'Help!'

But before I can even get the first syllable out his hand slams into my throat like a guillotine blade. The force of the blow sends me flying sideways but because the chair is screwed to the ground and I'm attached to the chair I go nowhere, only jerk violently, my head snapping back with force. I try to suck in air but my windpipe has been crushed and it's like trying to breathe through a flattened straw.

My vision darkens and I can hear a horrible gasping, choking sound that I realise is coming from me. Over the top of it I can hear Nunes saying something. It sounds like he's pleading, begging or maybe even crying.

He's beside me, or rather behind me. I can't see. My eyes are filled with tears and the room is getting darker. I want to fill my lungs and scream but it's impossible. I struggle against the cuffs, the pain in my chest expanding. With what little breath is left in my lungs I try to shout but it comes out as a grunting groan. A hand slams over my mouth. His hand. It's hot and he presses down hard over my mouth and nose.

'Be quiet!' he urges. 'Please, be quiet!' He sounds hysterical and angry at the same time. A million lights burst in my field of vision. A firework display goes off inside my head, the lights fading quickly to embers.

The darkness descends like a velvet cowl, wrapping me completely in its warmth and softness. Marlow, I think to myself, as tears spring from my eyes.

I won't get to see her grow up.

Chapter Forty

Tuesday

'Orla. Orla, can you hear me?'

Someone is calling me from far away, but I'm buried in darkness so complete I can't figure out which direction it's coming from. But then I feel a pair of warm, strong hands, pulling me forwards, leading me out of the dark and back into the light.

'Orla!'

It's a new voice. A voice I recognise – gruff but smooth as water rushing over gravel. I open my eyes. It's Konstandin. He's leaning over me. It takes me a few seconds to remember what happened and then I panic and glance around but I don't recognise the room I'm in. It's not the police cell. It looks like a hospital room. What am I doing here? Am I still under arrest?

'It's OK. You're OK,' Konstandin reassures me, squeezing my hand. 'You're at the hospital.'

My eyes widen in panic. Konstandin shouldn't be here! What if the police see him?

He smiles at me. 'They arrested Nunes,' he says.

Nunes. Now I remember what happened. Oh God. He killed Kate. But why? I have a million questions that need answers. I look at Konstandin, hoping he can read all the questions in my eyes because I can't speak them out loud, my throat is too sore and when I try to speak I can only manage a croak.

'I used my contacts,' Konstandin says. 'My associates. They know people in the police. They had them look into it. They found out Nunes was on duty that night. I raised the alarm.'

I give a weak smile of thanks.

'I'm sorry I ran off,' Konstandin says. 'I thought that it was better that I stayed free and kept trying to find out what happened.'

I nod. The words don't come; my throat is so tightly closed. My hand goes to my neck, which feels swollen and sore.

Konstandin scowls as he sees me wince. 'He hit you hard,' he says to me. 'It's going to take some time for the bruising to go down.'

I close my eyes, the memory of the assault bursting into bloom against the back of my eyelids. Nunes's hand smothering my mouth. The desperate terror I felt at not being able to breathe. The realisation I was going to die and never see Marlow again. Who saved me?

'A detective, Reza is her name, she came back into the room, just in time. You were lucky. He almost killed you.'

Tears flow down my cheeks. Does that mean Konstandin and I are both in the clear? And Rob too? What about Sebastian, I wonder? Will they let me off for that? Or am I still in trouble? I wonder if they found the cameras in his apartment, if Reza now believes me about him spying. I have to assume she does, and that I'm not going to be charged with anything, as I'm not handcuffed to the bed and Konstandin is sitting here beside me, also a free man.

But it doesn't explain why he killed Kate. I frown at Konstandin and he intuits the question and shrugs. 'He won't say. He's refusing to talk. And he lawyered up immediately.

But my contacts dug into him. They say Nunes had a previous corruption charge against him dropped. He allegedly forced two prostitutes to give him oral sex in exchange for being let off a solicitation charge. Internal affairs investigated but the women wouldn't testify. They were probably afraid to. So in the end they had to let Nunes return to work. He's admitted he offered to give Kate a ride home after he took her report about the theft of her bag. But he only admitted it after they confronted him with evidence. Until then he was denying it.'

'How do they know he was lying?' I ask.

'A traffic camera caught his car on camera, close to the docks on the night Kate died. They have an image of Nunes driving the car and Kate in the passenger seat.'

My vision swims and even though I'm lying down I feel faint.

'His shift was ending when she came in to report her bag stolen, and so he offered her a ride home. She said yes because she didn't have the cash for a taxi. He says he drove her to the dockside, near to your apartment. It's quiet at night. And he admits that he propositioned her . . .' Konstandin tails off.

I can fill in the gaps on my own. Nunes made a pass at Kate. He suggested she repay his favour with one of her own.

'When Kate realised what he wanted she got out the car,' I say, picturing it in vivid detail. 'He followed her and they got in a fight.'

Konstandin nods. 'That's what the police believe.'

I close my eyes and keep on imagining it: Nunes making the request. Kate threatening to report him and getting out of the car. Nunes seeing his career hanging in the balance. If she reports him, maybe this time he *will* be prosecuted, so he chases after her. He catches up to her and lunges for her. She hits him. He raises his hand and hits her back, the same way he hit me, across the throat. She stumbles, arms windmilling. Her head smashes into the dockside and then she disappears under the surface of the water.

I open my eyes.

'Under interrogation Nunes admitted they got in a fight and that Kate stormed off,' Konstandin says. 'He claims that he didn't kill her though.'

'But he said he made a mistake. He admitted it to me!'

'He says he meant the mistake was propositioning her.'

My mouth gapes open. 'What?'

Konstandin gives a one-shouldered shrug. 'He says he doesn't know how she ended up in the water or how she drowned, or even how she hit her head. He says that he left her and drove off.'

I stare at Konstandin for a long time, trying to picture it, struggling to revise the images in my head of how it all played out. How did Kate fall in the water then? Was it an accident after all?

'Nunes is lying,' Konstandin says. 'He's facing a murder charge. He knows that if he has any chance with a jury he has to seed doubt. And there's no way of confirming he killed her or if it was even deliberate. For all we know it might have been manslaughter.'

'So he'll get away with it?' I ask, starting to tremble all over.

Konstandin shakes his head. 'Even if he does he'll still go to jail for trying to kill you.'

I nod, though I'm barely concentrating anymore. For a moment, it felt as though the truth was lit up bright as the sun, but now a shadow has passed in front of it and everything is murky once more, shrouded in mystery. We don't know what happened. And we probably never will.

I glance at the window. It's still dark outside and when I turn my head a fraction I see a clock on the wall in the corridor outside. Konstandin turns his head to see where I'm looking. 'It's four in the morning,' he says.

I reach my hand across the starched sheet and Konstandin slips his rough, warm palm into mine. I squeeze and he squeezes back.

We stay like that for I don't know how long, until I fall asleep at least, and I think even while I sleep, because when I wake up hours later and the sun is streaming into the room, he's still there, and he's still holding my hand.

Chapter Forty-One

Two Weeks Later

I choose a bright purple scarf because I don't want to wear black and, even though it's hot and not scarf weather, I need something to hide the gruesome yellowy-green bruise on my throat. I've been told by the doctor the bruise will fade, just as the hoarseness in my throat did. Not enough to give a eulogy though. At least, that's the excuse I gave Kate's mother when she asked if I would.

I sit on a wooden bench outside the venue where the memorial is being held, with Marlow asleep in the pushchair beside me. Toby chose an old Huguenot church in Spitalfields that's been converted into an event space, but I'm not going in.

There are hundreds of people inside; Kate knew lots of them no doubt, but I'm guessing most are here for the gossip; acquaintances or strangers, who just want to get close to the drama, have some of her fame rub off on them. This is Kate's send-off and I don't want to detract from it. I know that if I step foot inside I'll become the main attraction.

The story hasn't fully died away yet. It was headline news and I'm still getting interview requests from daytime TV chat shows and the lower-level tabloids. I've decided not to respond to any in the hope the interest will die away. It's too raw. And one day Marlow will be old enough to read.

As I gently rock the pushchair with one hand, I pull out my phone and see that Konstandin has sent me a new text. He is getting a lot of information from his insider connections on the Lisbon police force. He keeps me up to date on everything.

Reza, despite the fact she was working side by side with a murderer, and that she never did her job properly, has been awarded some kind of honour, a medal, for saving my life.

Sebastian has been charged with kidnapping and assault. I thought kidnapping was a little over the top at first but Reza explained that's the charge that fits. He did try, after all, to lock me inside his apartment and stop me leaving. Having watched the movie *Room*, we all know how that could have ended.

He's also been charged with withholding evidence, for not telling the police what he knew about Kate's movements on the night she went missing. It could have saved us all so much time. Though ultimately the outcome wouldn't have changed. She would still be dead.

He has, of course, been booted off Airbnb because they have rules about things like hidden cameras and pervert landlords. I'm not too sure he's worried about that though, given the amount of jail time he's facing. I'm finding it hard to locate any sympathy for either him or for Nunes. At least Sebastian is pleading guilty, hoping to throw himself on the mercy of the judge, which means I don't have to go to court and testify about what happened, at least in that case.

However, Nunes is another story. He's pleading innocent to both my attempted murder and to murdering Kate, even though they offered to reduce the charge to manslaughter with regards to her, and so it's going to trial.

I suppose he is staring down the barrel of life in prison and I know that cops don't get cut much slack on the inside. But still, it's a little hard to understand how he hopes to plead innocent over my attempted murder, given he was a hair's breadth away from killing me when they pulled him off me in the interview room. He claims that he panicked and that he was just trying to stop me shouting. He didn't mean to hurt me, he says. I wonder if he said the same thing after he killed Kate. I've had time to think about it and I can't get the look in his eyes when he attacked me out of my mind. Having seen him lose his temper with me, having almost been killed by him myself, I don't believe his claim of innocence over Kate's death. I know he killed her.

When it comes to the court case, I'll be called as a witness and I will do my best to make sure he pays for what he's done. When I take the stand I can testify to how indifferent Nunes was when I reported Kate missing, how he tried to push me off the scent and when that didn't work how he tried to turn me into the suspect. His past history and the marks on his police record mean he'll have a hard time convincing a jury that he's innocent. At least, that's what Konstandin says.

I open the text from Konstandin. He's sent a link to a video. It's from his associates' friends in the Lisbon police force. They have finally managed to track down some security footage from the dock.

'It confirms Nunes killed Kate,' Konstandin writes.

I gasp. That's it then. They have all the evidence they need to convict him. He may even be forced to change his plea to guilty. It means that Nunes will be in prison for so long that I don't need to worry about him getting out after a few years and trying to find me.

I read the rest of the text. Konstandin says that they only found the footage today; apparently it took a while to locate because there was confusion over who owned the camera and which security company managed it. It hasn't yet been released to the public, he adds.

My hand shakes as I press play on the video. I don't know if I want to watch. But I force myself to, if only so the mystery can finally be resolved and the remaining gaps in the story be filled in.

For several seconds after I hit play, I wonder if the video is still loading as it's all fuzzy. But as I peer closer, I start to see shapes forming in the gloom. I was expecting something HD and sharp, something that would give me incontrovertible evidence, but this looks like someone has recorded the static off their TV.

But then what appear to be two shadowy figures show up on screen. It's black and white and hard to make them out and they're far from the camera, probably at a distance of fifty-odd feet, but if you peer closely enough it's possible to see them through the gloom. I recognise Kate funnily enough from the way she's standing, so full of attitude. I've seen her strike that pose a hundred times before, one hand on her hip, chin jutting up.

Nunes has his back mostly to camera. I shudder at the sight, my throat throbbing, the bruise coming to life, as I watch him move towards Kate. She's gesticulating wildly but the movements are jerky and indistinct. It's like watching people through a blizzard. And then it happens, so fast I blink and almost miss it. He lashes out, grabbing her arm. She tries to fight him off, and he punches her in the face. Kate stumbles backwards and falls, smashing her head into what looks like a concrete bollard.

I stare in horror. Kate's still moving. She lifts her hand. Nunes bends down and crouches in front of her. It looks like he's going to help her up. He even seems to press his hand to her head, like he's giving her a benediction.

My eyes remain glued to the screen, my nose almost pressed

319

to it as I struggle to both make out what is happening and also to watch and bear witness to the awfulness of Kate's last moments. She looks like she's trying to crawl away from him and I can almost feel her terror rising off the screen, gripping me. I want to reach in and do something, stop him from hurting her any further. I want to hit pause on the video as though that will change the outcome, but instead I just watch in utter, useless, paralysed horror.

After a few seconds Nunes stands up but he doesn't walk away. He seems to be considering what to do. And then he decides. He crouches down again and starts heaving Kate towards the dock, his hands beneath her shoulders, dragging her across the ground before finally rolling her into the water. Once he's done it, thrown her in like a bag of trash, he stands there on the edge of the dockside, just watching. Was he waiting to see if she would sink or swim? Was he watching her drown? Did she try to pull herself out? Did she rise above the surface? Did she fight to stay alive?

After another minute of standing there, appearing like some dark phantom on the video, he turns and vanishes into the pixelated wilderness, and there's nothing but blank fuzziness filling the screen, as though someone has pressed a pause button on the world.

I stare at my phone too stunned to move or even to breathe. At least now I know what happened. At least I will no longer have to stop my imagination from furnishing the details. Now I'll just have to live with this much worse reality instead. I sit there for a long while, trying to banish the images, trying to avoid thinking about those last few moments of Kate's life. I hate her for what she did to me but I wouldn't wish that on anyone. Finally, Marlow's sleepy mumbles stir me into checking the time. God, I'm late.

I get up from my bench and get going, heading for Liverpool

Street, deciding to walk south down Bishopsgate towards the river, retracing old steps as I go.

Kate and I used to walk this way on our way home from clubbing. One of the unexpected sorrows about what's happened is that almost all of my best memories of my twenties and thirties are now ruined. I wonder if I'll ever be able to salvage anything from the wreckage, or if I'll ever be able to think of Kate without feeling such a mix of feelings: betrayal and loss, love and hate, anger and sadness. And yet, still, fondness.

On London Bridge I stop and, ignoring the streams of pedestrians and thundering buses, I stare down into the churning brown sewage-coloured water. I think of Kate. Of course I do. I will always think of Kate whenever I see water.

'I hope you're at peace,' I whisper under my breath.

Just as I turn to leave a yellow butterfly lands on my purple scarf. I watch it spread its translucent gold wings, flutter them a few times, and then take off, twisting in the wind like an autumn leaf falling from a tree.

'Goodbye, Kate,' I whisper, imagining it's her come to say a final farewell.

As I watch it disappear I feel a strange lightening, as though the vice of grief that's been gripping me around the rib cage has been loosened a notch. Perhaps that's how it will happen, a gradual loosening until finally I can breathe freely again.

Chapter Forty-Two

'Hey.'

I turn around. It's Rob, walking along the bridge towards me. He crouches down to kiss Marlow's cheek and stroke her flyaway brown curls. She's fast asleep still, clutching her blankie in her fist.

'I'm sorry I'm late,' Rob says as he straightens up. He looks sheepish and overly eager to please, as he has done ever since I found out about him and Kate. 'How are you?' he asks, nodding to the scarf hiding my bruises.

'I'm fine,' I say, deciding not to mention the video of Kate's death, not now at least. 'How are you?' I ask.

He swallows, as though there's a hard, spiky lump caught in his throat. His eyes glint with tears. 'You know . . .' he says, forcing a wobbly smile.

My mum thinks I should take Rob back. I laughed when she suggested it. I asked him to leave as soon as I got back and he did, moving into his parents' place. I think he's holding out hope that I'll change my mind but I'm going ahead with the divorce. I've already met with a lawyer, one recommended to me by Toby.

Perhaps one day I'll be able to forgive Rob, but even if I do I'll never be able to trust him again. From now on, it's Marlow and me, and even though my life feels ruptured, as though I've had my internal organs rearranged and now some are missing, it also feels like I've survived the worst, so I know I'll survive this too. I'm determined to move on and, aware of how life can be short, I'm also trying to follow Konstandin's advice and live it well.

'Well, I better be going,' I say, looking down at Marlow. I've agreed to let him have her overnight, until we work out a more formal custody arrangement with the lawyers. But now my heart breaks at the idea of handing her over. I was so desperate to get back to her, so happy to hold her in my arms again, that I vowed I'd never let her go out of my sight ever again. And here I am handing her over. It's just to her father, I remind myself. And I'm not going out of the country. I doubt I ever will again.

I hand Rob a bag filled with snacks, and some clothes and nappies, as well as some extra toys because I don't think he has much at his parents' house. I stop myself from giving him a list of the things she can and can't eat. One of the things to come out of all this is that I've learned to let go of the little things.

'I'm sorry,' Rob mumbles, staring down at his feet as he takes the bag from me.

He's said sorry a thousand times but I don't know what to do with his apologies. Well, I do know what I want to do with them: I want to take them and shove them up his arse but unfortunately I can't, so instead I ignore him.

I bend down to kiss my daughter again on the top of her sleeping head, breathing in deeply; an addict getting a hit.

'I'll see you tomorrow,' I say to Rob. 'Bring her back safe.'

He lifts his hand and I think he's going to wave but he isn't. He's just running his hand through his hair, which is getting windswept. He's still wearing his wedding ring I note, though I took mine off the day I came back to London, my engagement ring too, and they've been sitting in a drawer ever since. I wish he'd take his off. It feels like a reproach, or like some sad harbinger of hope he's still clinging to.

'Bye,' I say turning away so he doesn't see me tearing up over leaving Marlow and think I'm upset about breaking up with him or having second thoughts.

I walk along. I've no idea where I'm going; maybe I'll walk all the way from London Bridge to Waterloo, along the river, letting the breeze blow away the cobwebs. It's nice to have no plans, just to be outside in the fresh air, relishing the freedom I came so close to losing and which will soon be curtailed when I go back to work.

A part of me dreads the idea of returning to my job and leaving Marlow with the child minder, but a bigger part of me is excited about getting back into the swing of things. Though I'm not looking forward to having to say goodbye to her every day, there will be the excitement of getting to see her every evening, after a long day at work.

Oh my God. I freeze mid-step. A tourist bumps into me from behind and mutters something in Japanese. I ignore them, as well as the crowds of people having to break around me as I stand there like a rock in the middle of a surging river.

I wrestle my phone from my pocket and frantically click on my texts, clicking on the video from Konstandin.

I hit play, zooming in close.

This time watching I don't stare at Kate, gesturing wildly and almost hypnotically. I don't watch the fight. I pause it before I see Kate get hit.

I focus in on the man in the video, his arm outstretched, a split second away from coiling his hand into a fist. I zoom in closer. He's mainly in shadow and for almost the entire duration of the footage, which runs to just over two minutes, there's only a view of his back. It's too dark and too fuzzy to really make anything out in detail.

I can see why anyone would think it's Nunes. Who else could it be, after all? I mean, Nunes admitted he propositioned Kate and that they got into a fight. The traffic camera placed him at the docks with Kate. His denial of murder seemed like the desperate act of a guilty man trying to avoid prison time. But it wasn't him who killed her.

I hit play and the video moves forward. The killer crouches down by Kate. Oh God. I flash back to just a moment ago: Rob bending down to say hello to Marlow. His legs splayed in the exact same pose, rocking back on his heels in front of the pushchair. He even touched the top of Marlow's head, stroked her hair, in that familiar way he does. He does the same to Kate now on the video, gives her what looks like a benediction, before he drags her to the dockside and rolls her still conscious, into the water.

They're the same height. The same build. They even have the same dark hair, just long enough that they both have to run their hands through it when it gets windswept.

I stare at the figure of the man disappearing into the murk.

Oh God.

Rob.

Were you waiting at the apartment when Kate got back? Did she suggest you walk and talk somewhere private? Did she lead you back to the docks, to the place she'd just been with Nunes? When you got there did you beg her again not to tell me about the affair? Did she ask you to leave me? Did she bring up the idea of a house in the suburbs with you and her playing happy families with Marlow?

My hand flies to my mouth. Oh my God! Marlow!

I turn around, desperately scouring the crowd, my heart in

Acknowledgements

Thanks, as ever, go to the following people;

Nichola, for being the kind of best friend all women should be so lucky to have. Thanks for coming to Lisbon with me, and for all the other weekends away. I love you.

John and Alula, for bringing such sunshine and love to my life.

My wonderful, smart and super-savvy agent Amanda, and to Phoebe Morgan at Avon for her stellar editing skills.

The team at Avon, including Helena, Caroline, Andrew, Ellie, Sanjana, Sabah and Bethany, who have been instrumental in getting this book out into the world.